The Iron Woman

Margaret Deland

"*This was the iniquity ... fulness of bread, and abundance of idleness....*" —EZEKIEL, xvi., 49

TO MY

PATIENT, RUTHLESS, INSPIRING CRITIC LORIN DELAND

August 12, 1911

Chapter 1

"Climb up in this tree, and play house!" Elizabeth Ferguson commanded. She herself had climbed to the lowest branch of an apple-tree in the Maitland orchard, and sat there, swinging her white-stockinged legs so recklessly that the three children whom she had summoned to her side, backed away for safety. "If you don't," she said, looking down at them, "I'm afraid, perhaps, maybe, I'll get mad."

Her foreboding was tempered by a giggle and by the deepening dimple in her cheek, but all the same she sighed with a sort of impersonal regret at the prospect of any unpleasantness. "It would be too bad if I got mad, wouldn't it?" she said thoughtfully. The others looked at one another in consternation. They knew so well what it meant to have Elizabeth "mad," that Nannie Maitland, the oldest of the little group, said at once, helplessly, "Well."

Nannie was always helpless with Elizabeth, just as she was helpless with her half-brother, Blair, though she was ten and Elizabeth and Blair were only eight; but how could a little girl like Nannie be anything but helpless before a brother whom she adored, and a wonderful being like Elizabeth?—Elizabeth! who always knew exactly what she wanted to do, and who instantly "got mad," if you wouldn't say you'd do it, too; got mad, and then repented, and hugged you and kissed you, and actually cried (or got mad again), if you refused to accept as a sign of your forgiveness her new slate-pencil, decorated with strips of red-and-white paper just like a little barber's pole! No wonder Nannie, timid and good-natured, was helpless before such a sweet, furious little creature! Blair had more backbone than his sister, but even he felt Elizabeth's heel upon his neck. David Richie, a silent, candid, very stubborn small boy, was, after a momentary struggle, as meek as the rest of them. Now, when she commanded them all to climb, it was David who demurred, because, he said, he spoke first for Indians tomahawking you in the back parlor.

"Very well!" said the despot; "play your old Indians! I'll never speak to any of you again as long as I live!"

"I've got on my new pants," David objected.

"Take 'em off!" said Elizabeth. And there is no knowing what might have happened if the decorous Nannie had not come to the rescue.

"That's not proper to do out-of-doors; and Miss White says not to say 'pants.'"

Elizabeth looked thoughtful. "Maybe it isn't proper," she admitted; "but David, honest, I took a hate to being tommy-hocked the last time we played it; so please, *dear* David! If you'll play house in the tree, I'll give you a piece of my taffy." She took a little sticky package out of her pocket and licked her lips to indicate its contents; —David yielded, shinning up the trunk of the tree, indifferent to the trousers, which had been on his mind ever since he had put them on his legs.

Blair followed him, but Nannie squatted on the ground content to merely look at the courageous three.

"Come on up," said Elizabeth. Nannie shook her little blond head. At which the others burst into a shrill chorus: "'Fraid-cat! 'fraid-cat! 'fraid-cat!" Nannie smiled placidly; it never occurred to her to deny such an obviously truthful title. "Blair," she said, continuing a conversation interrupted by Elizabeth's determination to climb, "Blair, *why* do you say things that make Mamma mad? What's the sense? If it makes her mad for you to say things are ugly, why do you?"

"'Cause," Blair said briefly. Even at eight Blair disliked both explanations and decisions, and his slave and half-sister rarely pressed for either. With the exception of his mother, whose absorption in business had never given her time to get acquainted with him, most of the people about Blair were his slaves. Elizabeth's governess, Miss White—called by Elizabeth, for reasons of her own, "Cherry-pie"—had completely surrendered to his brown eyes; the men in the Maitland Works toadied to him; David Richie blustered, perhaps, but always gave in to him; in his own home, Harris, who was a cross between a butler and a maid-of-all-work, adored him to the point of letting him make candy on the kitchen stove—probably the greatest expression of affection possible to the kitchen; in fact, little Elizabeth Ferguson was the only person in his world who did not knuckle down to this pleasant and lovable child. But then, Elizabeth never knuckled down to anybody! Certainly not to kind old Cherry-pie, whose timid upper lip quivered like a rabbit's when she was obliged to repeat to her darling some new rule of Robert Ferguson's for his niece's upbringing; nor did she knuckle down to her uncle;—she even declared she was not at all afraid of him! This was almost unbelievable to the others, who scattered like robins if they heard his step. And she had greater courage than this; she had, in fact, audacity! for she said she was willing—this the others told each other in awed tones—she said she had "just as lieves" walk right up and speak to Mrs. Maitland herself, and ask her for twenty cents so she could treat the whole crowd to ice-cream! That is, she would just as lieves, *if she should happen to want to*. Now, as she sat in the apple-tree swinging her legs and sharing her taffy, it occurred to her to mention, apropos of nothing, her opinion of Mrs. Maitland's looks:

"I like Blair's mother best; but David's mother is prettier than Blair's mother."

"It isn't polite to brag on mothers," said David, surveying his new trousers complacently, "but I know what I think."

Blair, jouncing up and down on his branch, agreed with unoffended candor. "'Course she's prettier. Anybody is. Mother's ugly."

"It isn't right to say things like that out of the family," Nannie observed.

"This *is* the family. You're going to marry David, and I'm going to marry Elizabeth. And I'm going to be awfully rich; and I'll give all you children a lot of money. Jimmy Sullivan—he's a friend of mine; I got acquainted with him yesterday, and he's the biggest puddler in our Works. Jimmie said, 'You're the only son,' he said, 'you'll get it all.' 'Course I told him I'd give him some," said Blair.

At this moment Elizabeth was moved to catch David round the neck, and give him a loud kiss on his left ear. David sighed. "You may kiss me," he said patiently; "but I'd rather you'd tell me when you want to. You knocked off my cap."

"Say, David," Nannie said, flinging his cap up to him, "Blair can stand on his head and count five. You can't."

At this David's usual admiration for Blair suffered an eclipse; he grew very red, then exploded: "I—I—I've had mumps, and I have two warts, and Blair hasn't. And I have a real dining-room at my house, and Blair hasn't!"

Nannie flew to the rescue: "You haven't got a real mother. You are only an adopted."

"Well, what are you?" David said, angrily; "you're nothing but a Step."

"I haven't got any kind of a mother," Elizabeth said, with complacent melancholy.

"Stop fighting," Blair commanded amiably; "David is right; we have a pigsty of a dining-room at our house." He paused to bend over and touch with an ecstatic finger a flake of lichen covering with its serpent green the damp, black bark in the crotch of the old tree.

"Isn't that pretty?" he said.

"You ought not to say things about our house," Nannie reproved him. As
Blair used to say when he grew up, "Nannie was born proper."

"Why not?" said Blair. "They know everything is ugly at our house. They've got real dining-rooms at their houses; they don't have old desks round, the way we do."

It was in the late sixties that these children played in the apple-tree and arranged their conjugal future; at that time the Maitland house was indeed, as poor little Blair said, "ugly." Twenty years before, its gardens and meadows had stretched over to the river; but the estate had long ago come down in size and gone up in dollars. Now, there was scarcely an acre of sooty green left, and it was pressed upon by the yards of the Maitland Works, and almost islanded by railroad tracks. Grading had left the stately and dilapidated old house somewhat above the level of a street noisy with incessant teaming, and generally fetlock-deep in black mud. The house stood a little back from the badly paved sidewalk; its meager dooryard was inclosed by an iron fence—a row of black and rusted spears, spotted under their tines with innumerable gray cocoons. (Blair and David made constant and furtive attempts to lift these spears, socketed in crumbling lead in the granite base, for of course there could be nothing better for fighting Indians than a real iron spear.) The orchard behind the house had been cut in two by a spur track, which brought jolting gondola cars piled with red ore down to the furnace. The half dozen apple-trees that were left stretched gaunt arms over sour, grassless earth; they put out faint flakes of blossoms in the early spring, and then a fleeting show of greenness, which in a fortnight shriveled and blackened out of all semblance of foliage. But all the same the children found it a delightful place to play, although Blair sometimes said sullenly that it was "ugly." Blair hated ugly things, and, poor child! he was assailed by ugliness on every side. The queer, disorderly dining-room, in which for reasons of her own Mrs. Maitland transacted so much of her business that it had become for all practical purposes an office of her Works, was perhaps the "ugliest" thing in the world to the little boy.

"Why don't we have a real dining-room?" he said once; "why do we have to eat in a office?"

"We'll eat in the kitchen, if I find it convenient," his mother told him, looking at him over her newspaper, which was propped against a silver coffee-urn that had found a clear space on a breakfast table cluttered with papers and ledgers.

"They have a bunch of flowers on the table up at David's house," the little boy complained; "I don't see why we can't."

"I don't eat flowers," Mrs. Maitland said grimly.

"I don't eat papers," Blair said, under his breath; and his mother looked at him helplessly. How is one to reply to a child of eight who makes remarks of this kind? Mrs. Maitland did not know; it was one of the many things she did not know in relation to her son; for at that time she loved him with her mind rather than her body, so she had none of those soft intuitions and persuasions of the flesh which instruct most mothers. In her perplexity she expressed the sarcastic anger one might vent upon an equal under the same circumstances:

"You'd eat nothing at all, young man, let me tell you, if it wasn't for the 'papers,' as you call 'em, in this house!" But it was no wonder that Blair called it ugly—the house, the orchard, the Works— even his mother, in her rusty black alpaca dress, sitting at her desk in the big, dingy dining-room, driving her body and soul, and the bodies and souls of her workmen—all for the sake of the little, shrinking boy, who wanted a bunch of flowers on the table. Poor mother! Poor son! And poor little proper, perplexed half-sister, looking on, and trying to make peace. Nannie's perplexities had begun very far back. Of course she was too young when her father married his second wife to puzzle over that; but if she did not, other people did. Why a mild, vague young widower who painted pictures nobody bought, and was as unpractical as a man could be whose partnership in an iron-works was a matter of inheritance—why such a man wanted to marry Miss Sarah Blair was beyond anybody's wisdom. It is conceivable, indeed, that he did not want to.

There were rumors that after the death of Nannie's mother, Herbert Maitland had been inclined to look for consolation to a certain Miss Molly Wharton (she that afterward married another widower, Henry Knight); and everybody thought Miss Molly was willing to smile upon him. Be that as it may, he suddenly found himself the husband of his late partner's daughter, a woman eight years older than he, and at least four inches taller; a silent, plain woman, of devastating common sense, who contradicted all those femininities and soft lovelinesses so characteristic, not only of his first wife but of pretty Molly Wharton also.

John Blair, the father of the second Mrs. Maitland, an uneducated, extremely intelligent man, had risen from puddling to partnership in the Maitland Works. There had been no social relations between Mr. Maitland, Sr., and this new member of the firm, but the older man had a very intimate respect, and even admiration for John Blair. When he came to die he confided his son's interests to his partner with absolute confidence that they would be safe. "Herbert has no gumption, John," he said; "he wants to be an 'artist.' You've got to look after him." "I will, Mr. Maitland, I will," said John Blair, snuffling and blowing his nose on a big red pocket-handkerchief. He did look after him. He put Herbert's affairs ahead of his own, and he made it clear to his daughter, who in business matters was, curiously enough, his right-hand man, that "Maitland's boy" was always, as he expressed it, "to have the inside track."

"I ain't bothering about you, Sally; I'll leave you enough. And if I didn't, you could scratch gravel for yourself. But Maitland's boy ain't our kind. He must be taken care of."

When John Blair died, perhaps a sort of faithfulness to his wishes made his Sally "take care" of Herbert Maitland by marrying him. "His child certainly does need a mother," she thought;—"an intelligent mother, not a goose." By and by she told Herbert of his child's need; or at any rate helped him to infer it. And somehow, before he knew it, he married her. By inheritance they owned the Works between them; so really their marriage was, as the bride expressed it, "a very sensible arrangement"; and any sensible arrangement appealed to John Blair's daughter. But after a breathless six months of partnership—in business if in nothing else—Herbert Maitland, leaving behind him his little two-year-old Nannie, and an unborn boy of whose approaching advent he was ignorant, got out of the world as expeditiously as consumption could take him. Indeed, his wife had so jostled him and deafened him and dazed him that there was nothing for him to do but die—so that there might be room for her expanding energy. Yet she loved him; nobody who saw her in those first silent, agonized months could doubt that she loved him. Her pain expressed itself, not in moans or tears or physical prostration, but in work. Work, which had been an interest, became a refuge. Under like circumstances some people take to religion and some to drink; as Mrs. Maitland's religion had never been more than church-going and contributions to foreign missions, it was, of course, no help under the strain of grief; and as her temperament did not dictate the other means of consolation, she turned to work. She worked herself numb; very likely she had hours when she did not feel her loss. But she did not feel anything else. Not even her baby's little clinging hands, or his milky lips at her breast. She did her duty by him; she hired a reliable woman to take charge of him, and she was careful to appear at regular hours to nurse him. She ordered toys for him, and as she shared the naive conviction of her day that church-going and religion were synonymous, she began, when he was four years old, to take him to church. In her shiny, shabby black silk, which had been her Sunday costume ever since it had been purchased as part of her curiously limited trousseau she sat in a front pew, between the two children, and felt that she was doing her duty to both of them. A sense of duty without maternal instinct is not, perhaps, as baleful a thing as maternal instinct without a sense of duty, but it is sterile; and in the first few years of her bereavement, the big, suffering woman seemed to have nothing but duty to offer to her child. Nannie's puzzles began then. "Why don't Mamma hug my baby brother?" she used to ask the nurse, who had no explanation to offer. The baby brother was ready enough to hug Nannie, and his eager, wet little kisses on her rosy cheeks sealed her to his service while he was still in petticoats. Blair was three years old before, under the long atrophy of grief, Sarah Maitland's maternal instinct began to stir. When it did, she was chilled by the boy's shrinking from her as if from a stranger; she was chilled, too, by another sort of repulsion, which with the hideous candor of childhood he made no effort to conceal. One of his first expressions of opinion had been contained in the single word "uggy," accompanied by a finger pointed at his mother. Whenever she sneezed—and she was one of those people who cannot, or do not, moderate a sneeze—Blair had a nervous paroxysm. He would jump at the unexpected sound, then burst into furious tears. When she tried to draw his head down upon her scratchy black alpaca breast, he would say violently, "No, no! No, no!" at which she would push him roughly from her knee, and fall into hurt silence. Once, when he was five years old, she came in to dinner hot from a morning in the Works, her moist forehead grimy with dust, and bent over to kiss him; at which the little boy wrinkled up his nose and turned his face aside.

"What's the matter?" his mother said; and called sharply to the nurse: "I won't have any highfalutin' business in this boy! Get it out of him." Then resolutely she took Blair's little chin in her hand — a big, beautiful, powerful hand, with broken and blackened nails — and turning his wincing face up, rubbed her cheek roughly against his. "Get over your airs!" she said, and sat down and ate her dinner without another word to Blair or any one else. But the next day, as if to purchase the kiss he would not give, she told him he was to have an "allowance." The word had no meaning to the little fellow, until she showed him two bright new dollars and said he could buy candy with them; then his brown eyes smiled, and he held up his lips to her. It was at that moment that money began to mean something to him. He bought the candy, which he divided with Nannie, and he bought also a present for his mother, — a bottle of cologne, with a tiny calendar tied around its neck by a red ribbon. "The ribbon is pretty," he explained shyly. She was so pleased that she instantly gave him another dollar, and then put the long green bottle on her painted pine bureau, between two of his photographs.

In the days when the four children played in the orchard, and had lessons with Miss White, in the school-room in Mr. Ferguson's garret, and were "treated" by Blair to candy or pink ice-cream — even in those days Mercer was showing signs of what it was ultimately to become: the apotheosis of materialism and vulgarity. Iron was entering into its soul. It thought extremely well of itself; when a new mill was built, or a new furnace blown in, it thought still better of itself. It prided itself upon its growth; in fact, its complacency, its ugliness and its size kept pace with one another.

"Look at our output," Sarah Maitland used to brag to her general manager, Mr. Robert Ferguson; "and look at our churches!

We have more churches for our size than any town west of the Alleghanies."

"We need more jails than any town, east or west," Mr. Ferguson retorted, grimly.

Mrs. Maitland avoided the deduction. Her face was full of pride. "You just wait! We'll be the most important city in this country yet, because we will hold the commerce of the world right here in our mills!" She put out her great open palm, and slowly closed the strong, beautiful fingers into a gripping fist. "The commerce of the world, right *here*!" she said, thrusting the clenched hand, that quivered a little, almost into his face.

Robert Ferguson snorted. He was a melancholy man, with thin, bitterly sensitive lips, and kind eyes that were curiously magnified by gold-rimmed eyeglasses, which he had a way of knocking off with disconcerting suddenness. He did not, he declared, trust anybody. "What's the use?" he said; "you only get your face slapped!" For his part, he believed the Eleventh Commandment was, "Blessed is he that expecteth nothing, because he'll get it."

"Read your Bible!" Mrs. Maitland retorted; "then you'll know enough to call it a Beatitude, not a Commandment."

Mr. Ferguson snorted again. "Bible? It's all I can do to get time to read my paper. I'm worked to death," he reproached her. But in spite of being worked to death he always found time on summer evenings to weed the garden in his back yard, or on winter mornings to feed a flock of Mercer's sooty pigeons; and he had been known to walk all over town to find a particular remedy for a sick child of one of his molders. To be sure he alleged, when Mrs. Maitland accused him of kindness, that, as far as the child was concerned, he was a fool for his pains, because human critters ("I'm one of 'em myself,") were a bad lot and it would be a good thing if they all died young!

"Oh, you have a fine bark, friend Ferguson," she said, "but

when it comes to a bite, I guess most folks get a kiss from you."

"Kiss?" said Robert Ferguson, horrified; "not much!"

They were very good friends, these two, each growling at, disapproving of, and completely trusting the other. Mrs. Maitland's chief disapproval of her superintendent—for her reproaches about his bark were really expressions of admiration—her serious disapproval was based on the fact that, when the season permitted, he broke the Sabbath by grubbing in his garden, instead of going to church. A grape-arbor ran the length of this garden, and in August the Isabellas, filmed with soot, had a flavor, Robert Ferguson thought, finer than could be found in any of the vineyards lying in the hot sunshine on the banks of the river, far out of reach of Mercer's smoke. There was a flagstone path around the arbor, and then borders of perennials against brick walls thick with ivy or hidden by trellised peach-trees. All summer long bees came to murmur among the flowers, and every breeze that blew over them carried some sweetness to the hot and tired streets outside. It was a spot of perfume and peace, and it was no wonder that the hard-working, sad-eyed man liked to spend his Sundays in it. But "remembering the Sabbath" was his employer's strong point. Mrs. Maitland kept the Fourth Commandment with passion. Her Sundays, dividing each six days of extraordinary activity, were arid stretches of the unspeakable dullness of idleness. When Blair grew up he used to look back at those Sundays and shudder. There was church and Sunday-school in the morning, then a cold dinner, for cold roast beef was Mrs. Maitland's symbol of Sabbatical holiness. Then an endless, vacant afternoon, spent always indoors. Certain small, pious books were permitted the two children —*Little Henry and His Bearer, The Ministering Children*, and like moral food; but no games, no walks, no playing in the orchard. Silence and weary idleness and Little Henry's holy arrogances. Though the day must have been as dreary to Mrs. Maitland as it was to her son and daughter, she never winced. She sat in the parlor, dressed in black silk, and read *The Presbyterian* and the Bible. She never allowed herself to look at her desk in the dining-room, or even at her knitting, which on week-days when she had no work to do was a great resource; she looked at the clock a good deal, and sometimes she sighed, then applied herself to *The Presbyterian*. She went to bed at half-past seven as against eleven or twelve on other nights, first reading, with extraordinary rapidity, her "Chapter." Mrs. Maitland had a "system" by which she was able to read the Bible through once a year. She frequently recommended it to her superintendent; to her way of thinking such reading was accounted to her as righteousness.

Refreshed by a somnolent Sunday, she would rush furiously into business on Monday morning, and Mr. Robert Ferguson, who never went to church, followed in her wake, doing her bidding with grim and admiring thoroughness. If not "worked to death," he was, at any rate, absorbed in her affairs. Even when he went home at night, and, on summer evenings, fell to grubbing in his narrow back yard, where his niece "helped" him by pushing a little wheelbarrow over the mossy flagstones,—even then he did not dismiss Mrs. Maitland's business from his mind. He was scrupulous to say, as he picked up the weeds scattered from the wheelbarrow, "Have you been a good little girl to-day, Elizabeth?" but all the while, in his own thoughts he was going over matters at the Works. On Sundays he managed to get far enough away from business to interrogate Miss White about his niece:

"I hope Elizabeth is behaving herself, Miss White?"

"Oh yes; she is a dear, good child."

"Well, you never can tell about children,—or anybody else. Keep a sharp eye on her, Miss White. And be careful, please, about vanity. I thought I saw her looking in the mirror in the hall this morning. Please discourage any signs of vanity."

"She hasn't a particle of vanity!" Miss White said warmly.

But in spite of such assurances, Mr. Ferguson was always falling into bleakly apprehensive thoughts of his little girl, obstinately denying his pride in her, and allowing himself only the meager hope that she would "turn out fairly decently." Vanity was his especial concern, and he was more than once afraid he had discovered it: Elizabeth was not allowed to go to dancing-school—dancing and vanity were somehow related in her uncle's mind; so the vital, vivid little creature expressed the rhythm that was in her by dancing without instruction, keeping time with loud, elemental cadences of her own composing, not always melodious, but always in time. Sometimes she danced thus in the school-room; sometimes in Mrs. Todd's "ice-cream parlor" at the farther end of Mercer's old wooden bridge; once—and this was one of the occasions when Mr. Ferguson thought he had detected the vice he dreaded—once she danced in his very own library! Up and down she went, back and forth, before a long mirror that stood between the windows. She had put a daffodowndilly behind each ear, and twisted a dandelion chain around her neck. She looked, as she came and went, smiling and dimpling at herself in the shadowy depths of the mirror, like a flower —a flower in the wind!—bending and turning and swaying, and singing as she danced: "Oh, isn't it joyful—joyful—joyful!"

It was then that her uncle came upon her; for just a moment he stood still in involuntary delight, then remembered his theories; there was certainly vanity in her primitive adornment! He knocked his glasses off with a fierce gesture, and did his duty by barking at her,—as Mrs. Maitland would have expressed it. He told her in an angry voice that she must go to bed for the rest of the day! at least, if she ever did it again, she must go to bed for the rest of the day.

Another time he felt even surer of the feminine failing: Elizabeth said, in his presence, that she wished she had some rings like those of a certain Mrs. Richie, who had lately come to live next door; at which Mr. Ferguson barked at Miss White, barked so harshly that Elizabeth flew at him like a little enraged cat. "Stop scolding Cherry-pie! You hurt her feelings; you are a wicked man!" she screamed, and beating him with her right hand, she fastened her small, sharp teeth into her left arm just above the wrist—then screamed again with self-inflicted pain. But when Miss White, dismayed at such a loss of self-control, apologized for her, Mr. Ferguson shrugged his shoulders.

"I don't mind temper," he said; "I used to have a temper myself; but I will *not* have her vain! Better put some plaster on her arm. Elizabeth, you must not call Miss White by that ridiculous name."

The remark about Mrs. Richie's rings really disturbed him; it made him deplore to himself the advent as a neighbor of a foolish woman. "She'll put ideas into Elizabeth's head," he told himself. In regard to the rings, he had not needed Elizabeth to instruct him. He had noticed them himself, and they had convinced him that this Mrs. Richie, who at first sight seemed a shy, sad woman with no nonsense about her, was really no exception to her sex. "Vain and lazy, like the rest of them," he said cynically. Having passed the age when he cared to sport with Amaryllis, he did not, he said, like women. When he was quite a young man, he had added, "except Mrs. Maitland." Which remark, being repeated to Molly Wharton, had moved that young lady to retort that the reason that Sarah Maitland was the only woman he liked, was that Sarah Maitland was not a woman! "The only feminine thing about her is her petticoats," said Miss Wharton, daintily. For which *mot*, Robert Ferguson never forgave her. He certainly did not expect to like this new-comer in Mercer, this Mrs. Richie, but he had gone to see her. He had been obliged to, because she wished to rent a house he owned next door to the one in which he lived. So, being her landlord, he had to see her, if for nothing else, to discourage requests for inside repairs. He saw her, and promised to put up a little glass house at the end of the back parlor for a plant-room. "If she'd asked me for a 'conservatory,'" he said to himself, "I wouldn't have considered it for a moment; but just a few sashes—I suppose I might as well give in on that? Besides, if she likes flowers, there must be something to her." All the same, he was conscious of having given in, and to a woman who wore rings; so he was quite gruff with Mrs. Richie's little boy, whom he found listening to an harangue from Elizabeth. The two children had scraped acquaintance through the iron fence that separated the piazzas of the two houses. "I," Elizabeth had announced, "have a mosquito-bite on my leg; I'll show it to you," she said, generously; and when the bite on her little thigh was displayed, she tried to think of other personal matters. "My mother's dead. And my father's dead."

"So's mine," David matched her, proudly. "I'm an adopted child."

"I have a pair of red shoes with white buttons," she said. David, unable to think of any possession of his own to cap either bite or boots, was smitten into gloomy silence.

In spite of the landlord's disapproval of his tenant's rings, the acquaintance of the two families grew. Mr. Ferguson had to see Mrs. Richie again about those "sashes," or what not. His calls were always on business—but though he talked of greenhouses, and she talked of knocking out an extra window in the nursery so that her little boy could have more sunshine, they slipped after a while into personalities: Mrs. Richie had no immediate family; her—her husband had died nearly three years before. Since then she had been living in St. Louis. She had come now to Mercer because she wanted to be nearer to a friend, an old clergyman, who lived in a place called Old Chester.

"I think it's about twenty miles up the river," she said. "That's where I found David. I—I had lost a little boy, and David had lost his mother, so we belonged together. It doesn't make any difference to us, that he isn't my own, does it, David?"

"Yes'm," said David,

"David! Why won't you *ever* say what is expected of you? We don't know anybody in Mercer," she went on, with a shy, melancholy smile, "except Elizabeth." And at her kind look the little girl, who had tagged along behind her uncle, snuggled up to the maternal presence, and rubbed her cheek against the white hand which had the pretty rings on it. "I am so glad to have somebody for David to play with," Mrs. Richie said, looking down at the little nestling thing, who at that moment stopped nestling, and dropping down on toes and finger-tips, loped up—on very long hind-legs, to the confusion of her elders, who endeavored not to see her peculiar attitude—and, putting a paw into David's pocket, abstracted a marble. There was an instant explosion, in which David, after securing his property through violent exertions, sought, as a matter of pure justice, to pull the bear's hair. But when Mrs. Richie interfered, separating the combatants with horrified apologies for her young man's conduct, Elizabeth's squeals stopped abruptly. She stood panting, her eyes still watering with David's tug at her hair; the dimple in her right cheek began to lengthen into a hard line.

"You are very naughty, David," said Mrs. Richie, sternly; "you must beg
Elizabeth's pardon at once!" At which Elizabeth burst out:

"Stop! Don't scold him. It was my fault. I did it—taking his marble.
I'll—I'll bite my arm if you scold David!"

"Elizabeth!" protested her uncle; "I'm ashamed of you!"

But Elizabeth was indifferent to his shame; she was hugging

David frantically. "I hate, I hate, I *hate* your mother—if she does have rings!" Her face was so convulsed with rage that Mrs. Richie actually recoiled before it; Elizabeth, still clamoring, saw that involuntary start of horror. Instantly she was calm; but she shrank away almost out of the room. It seemed as if at that moment some veil, cold and impenetrable, fell between the gentle woman and the fierce, pathetic child—a veil that was not to be lifted until, in some mysterious way, life should make them change places.

The two elders looked at each other, Robert Ferguson with meager amusement; Mrs. Richie still grave at the remembrance of that furious little face. "What did she mean about 'biting her arm'?" she asked, after Elizabeth had been sent home, the bewildered David being told to accompany her to the door.

"I believe she bites herself when she gets angry," Elizabeth's uncle said; "Miss White said she had quite a sore place on her arm last winter, because she bit it so often. It's of no consequence," he added, knocking his glasses off fiercely. Again Mrs. Richie looked shocked. "She is my brother's child," he said, briefly; "he died some years ago. He left her to me." And Mrs. Richie knew instinctively that the bequest had not been welcome. "Miss White looks after her," he said, putting his glasses on again, carefully, with both hands; "she calls her her 'Lamb,' though a more unlamblike person than Elizabeth I never met. She has a little school for her and the two Maitland youngsters in the top of my house. Miss White is otherwise known as Cherry-pie. Elizabeth, I am informed, loves cherry-pie; also, she loves Miss White: ergo!" he ended, with his snort of a laugh. Then he had a sudden thought: "Why don't you let David come to Miss White for lessons? I've no doubt she could look after another pupil."

"I'd be delighted to," Mrs. Richie said, gratefully. So, through the good offices of Mr. Ferguson, the arrangement was made. Mr. Ferguson did not approve of Mrs. Richie's rings, but he had no objection to helping her about David.

And that was how it happened that these four little lives were thrown together—four threads that were to be woven into the great fabric of Life.

Chapter 2

On the other side of the street, opposite the Maitland house, was a huddle of wooden tenements. Some of them were built on piles, and seemed to stand on stilts, holding their draggled skirts out of the mud of their untidy yards: some sagged on rotting sills, leaning shoulder to shoulder as if to prop one another up. From each front door a shaky flight of steps ran down to the unpaved sidewalk, where pigs and children and hens, and the daily tramp of feet to and from the Maitland Works, had beaten the earth into a hard, black surface — or a soft, black surface, when it rained. These little huddling houses called themselves Maitland's Shantytown, and they looked up at the Big House, standing in melancholy isolation behind its fence of iron spears, with the pride that is common to us all when we find ourselves in the company of our betters. Back of the little houses was a strip of waste land, used for a dump; and beyond it, bristling against the sky, the long line of Mercer's stacks and chimneys.

In spite of such surroundings, the Big House, even as late as the early seventies, was impressive. It was square, with four great chimneys, and long windows that ran from floor to ceiling. Its stately entrance and its two curving flights of steps were of white marble, and so were the lintels of the windows; but the stone was so stained and darkened with smoky years of rains and river fogs, that its only beauty lay in the noble lines that grime and time had not been able to destroy. A gnarled and twisted old wistaria roped the doorway, and, crawling almost to the roof, looped along the eaves, in May it broke into a froth of exquisite purple and faint green, and for a week the garland of blossoms, murmurous with bees, lay clean and lovely against the narrow, old bricks which had once been painted yellow. Outside, the house had a distinction which no superficial dilapidation could mar; but inside distinction was almost lost in the commonplace, if not in actual ugliness. The double parlors on the right of the wide hall had been furnished in the complete vulgarity of the sixties; on the left was the library, which had long ago been taken by Mrs. Maitland as a bedroom, for the practical reason that it opened into the dining-room, so her desk was easily accessible at any time of night, should her passion for toil seize her after working-hours were over. The walls of this room were still covered with books, that no one ever read. Mrs. Maitland had no time to waste on reading; "I *live*," she used to say; "I don't read about living!" Except the imprisoned books, the only interesting things in the room were some *cartes-de-visite* of Blair, which stood in a dusty row on the bureau, one of them propped against her son's first present to her— the unopened bottle of Johann Maria Farina. When Blair was a man, that bottle still stood there, the kid cap over the cork split and yellow, the ribbons of the little calendar hanging from its green neck, faded to streaky white.

The office dining-room, about which Blair had begun to be impertinent when he was eight years old, was of noble proportions and in its day must have had great dignity; but in Blair's childhood its day was over. Above the dingy white wainscoting the landscape paper his grandfather had brought from France in the thirties had faded into a blur of blues and buffs. The floor was uncarpeted save for a Persian rug, whose colors had long since dulled to an even grime. At one end of the room was Mrs. Maitland's desk; at the other, filing cases, and two smaller desks where clerks worked at ledgers or drafting. The four French windows were uncurtained, and the inside shutters folded back, so that the silent clerks might have the benefit of every ray of daylight filtering wanly through Mercer's murky air. A long table stood in the middle of the room; generally it was covered with blue-prints, or the usual impedimenta of an office. But it was not an office table; it was of mahogany, scratched and dim to be sure, but matching the ancient claw-footed sideboard whose top was littered with letter files, silver teapots and sugar-bowls, and stacks of newspapers. Three times a day one end of this table was cleared, and the early breakfast, or the noon dinner, or the rather heavy supper eaten rapidly and for the most part in silence. Mrs. Maitland was silent because she was absorbed in thought; Nannie and Blair were silent because they were afraid to talk. But the two children gave a touch of humanness to the ruthless room, which, indeed, poor little Blair had some excuse for calling a "pigsty."

"When I'm big," Blair announced one afternoon after school, "I'll have a bunch of flowers on the table, like your mother does; you see if I don't! I like your mother, David."

"*I* don't; *very* much," Elizabeth volunteered. "She looks out of her eyes at me when I get mad."

"I don't like to live at my house," Blair said, sighing.

"Why don't you run away?" demanded Elizabeth; "I'm going to some day when I get time."

"Where would you run to?" David said, practically. David was always disconcertingly practical.

But Elizabeth would not be pinned down to details. "I will decide that when I get started."

"I believe," Blair meditated, "I will run away."

"I'll tell you what let's do," Elizabeth said, and paused to pick up her right ankle and hop an ecstatic yard or two on one foot; "I tell you what let's do: let's all run away, *and get married!*"

The other three stared at her dumfounded. Elizabeth, whirling about on her toes, dropped down on all—fours to turn a somersault of joy; when she was on her feet she said, "Oh, *let's* get married!" But it took Blair, who always found it difficult to make up his mind, a few moments to accept the project.

They had planned to devote that afternoon to playing bury-you-alive under the yellow sofa in Mrs. Richie's parlor, but this idea of Elizabeth's made it necessary to hide in the "cave"—a shadowy spot behind the palmtub in the greenhouse—for reflection. Once settled there, jostling one another like young pigeons, it was David who, as usual, made the practical objections:

"We haven't any money."

"I suppose we could get all the money we want out of my mother's cash-box," Blair admitted, wavering.

"That's stealing," Elizabeth said.

"You can't steal from your mother," Nannie defended her brother.

"I'll marry you, Elizabeth," Blair said, with sudden enthusiastic decision.

But David demurred: "I think *I'd* like Elizabeth. I'm not sure I want to marry Nannie."

"You said Nannie's hair was the longest, only yesterday!" Blair said, angrily.

"But I like Elizabeth's color of hair. Nannie, do you think I'd like you to marry best, or Elizabeth?"

"I don't believe the color of hair makes any difference in being married," Nannie said, kindly. "And anyway, you'll have to marry me, David, 'cause Blair can't. He's my brother."

"He's only your half-brother," David pointed out.

"You can have Nannie," said Blair, "or you can stay out of the play."

"Well, I'll marry Nannie," David said, sadly; and Blair proceeded to elaborate the scheme. It was very simple: the money in Mrs. Maitland's cash-box would pay their fare to—"Oh, anywhere," Blair said, then hesitated: "The only thing is, how'll we get it?"

"I'll get it for you," Nannie said, shuddering.

"Wouldn't you be scared?" Blair asked doubtfully. Everybody knew poor
Nannie was a 'fraid-cat.

"Little people," somebody called from the parlor, "what are you chattering about?"

The children looked at one another in a panic, but Blair called back courageously, "Oh, nothing."

"Perhaps," said Mrs. Richie, smiling at Mr. Robert Ferguson, who had dropped in to find Elizabeth—"perhaps you didn't know that my conservatory was a Pirates' Cave?"

There was a sort of hesitant intimacy now between these two people, but it had never got so far as friendship. Mrs. Richie's retreating shyness was courteous, but never cordial; Robert Ferguson's somber egotism was kind, but never generous. Yet, owing no doubt to their two children, and to the fact that Mr. Ferguson was continually bringing things over from his garden borders, to transplant into hers—it improves the property, he told her briefly— owing to the children and the flowers, the landlord and the tenant saw each other rather frequently. On this especial afternoon, though Mr. Ferguson had found Elizabeth, he still lingered, perhaps to tell the story of some extraordinary thing Mrs. Maitland had done that day at the Works. "She's been the only man in the family since old John died," he ended; "and, judging from Blair, I guess she'll continue to be."

"She is wonderful!" Mrs. Richie agreed; "but she's lovable, too, which is more important."

"I should as soon say a locomotive was lovable," he said; "not that that's against her. Quite the contrary."

The pretty woman on the yellow damask sofa by the fireside flushed with offense. The fact was, this dry, dogmatic man, old at thirty-six, lean, and in a time of beards clean-shaven, with gray hair that stood fiercely up from a deeply furrowed brow, and kind, unhappy eyes blinking behind the magnifying lenses of his gold-rimmed glasses, this really friendly neighbor, was always offending her—though he was rather nice about inside repairs. "Why do I endure him?" Mrs. Richie said to herself sometimes. Perhaps it was because, in spite of his manners, and his sneer that the world was a mighty mean place to live in, and his joyless way of doing his duty to his little niece, he certainly did see how good and sweet her David was. She reminded herself of this to check her offense at his snub about Mrs. Maitland; and all the while the good, sweet David was plotting behind the green tub of the palm-tree in the conservatory. But when Mr. Ferguson called to Elizabeth to come home with him, and then bent over and fussed about the buttons on her jacket, and said, anxiously, "Are you warm enough, Pussy?" Mrs. Richie said to herself: "He *is* good! It's only his manners that are bad."

Robert Ferguson went out into the brown November dusk with his little girl clinging to his hand, for so he understood his duty to his niece; and on their own doorstep Elizabeth asked a question:

"Uncle, if you get married, do you have to stay married?"

He looked down at her with a start. "*What?*" he said.

"If you don't like being married, do you have to stay?"

"Don't ask foolish questions!" he said; "of course you have to."

Elizabeth sighed. As for her uncle, he was disturbed to the point of irritation. He dropped her hand with a gesture almost of disgust, and the lines in his forehead deepened into painful folds. After supper he called Elizabeth's governess into the library, and shut the door.

"Miss White," he said, knocking his glasses off, "Elizabeth is getting to be a big girl; will you kindly make a point of teaching her —things?"

"I will do so immejetly, sir," said Miss White. "What things?"

"Why," said Robert Ferguson, helplessly, "why—general morals." He put his glasses on carefully, with both hands. "Elizabeth asked me a very improper question; she asked me about divorce, and —"

"*Divorce*!" exclaimed Miss White, astounded; "I have been at my post for eight years, sir, and I am positive that that word has never been used in Elizabeth's presence!"

He did not explain. "Teach her," he said, harshly, "that a woman has got to behave herself."

Blair having once decided upon it, clung to his purpose of running away, with a persistency which was his mother's large determination in little; but the double elopement was delayed for two days because of the difficulty of securing the necessary funds. The dining-room, where Mrs. Maitland "kept all her money," was rarely entirely deserted. In those brief intervals when the two clerks were not on hand, Harris seemed to be possessed of a clean devil, and spent an unusual amount of time "redding up"; or when Harris was in the kitchen, and Blair, dragging the reluctant Nannie, had peered into the room, he had been confronted by his mother. She never saw him—sometimes she was writing; sometimes talking to a foreman; sometimes knitting, for when Sarah Maitland had nothing else to do, she made baby socks for the missionary barrel; once when Blair came to the door, she was walking up and down knitting rapidly, thinking out some project; her ball of zephyr had fallen on the floor, and dragging along behind her, unwinding and unwinding, had involved her hurrying tramp in a grimy, pink tangle.

Each time Blair had looked into the room it was policed by this absorbed presence. "We'll *never* get married!" he said in despair. The delay had a disastrous effect upon romance, for David, with the melancholy candor of a reasoning temperament, was continually saying that he doubted the desirability of Nannie as a wife; and Elizabeth was just as hesitant about Blair.

"Suppose I took a hate to you for a husband? Uncle Robert says if you don't like being married, you can't stop."

"You won't want to stop. Married people don't have to go to school!"

Elizabeth sighed. "But I don't know but what maybe I'd like David for a husband?"

"He doesn't have but ten cents a week allowance, and I have a dollar,"
Blair reminded her.

"Well, I don't believe I like being married, anyway," she fretted; "I like going out to the toll-house for ice-cream better."

Her uncertainty made Blair still more impatient to finance his journey; and that day, just after dinner, he and Nannie stood quaking at the dining-room door. "I-I-I'll do it," Blair gasped, with trembling valor. He was very little, and his eyes were dilating with fright. "I'll do it," he said, chattering. Nannie rushed into the breach; Nannie never pretended to be anything but a 'fraid-cat except in things that concerned Blair; she said now, boldly:

"I'm the oldest, so I ought to."

She crept across the floor, stopping at every step to listen breathlessly; nothing stirred, except her own little shadow crouching at her heels.

"Grab in the top drawer," Blair hissed after her; and she put a shrinking hand into the japanned box, and "grabbed" all the bills she could hold; then, not waiting to close the drawer, she fled back to Blair. Up-stairs in her room, they counted the money.

"We can travel all round the world!" Blair whispered, thrilled at the amount of their loot. But at the last moment there was a defection—Elizabeth backed out. "I'd rather go out to the toll-house for ice-cream," she said; "ice-cream at Mrs. Todd's is nicer than being married. David, don't you go, either. Let Blair and Nannie go. You stay with me."

But David was not to be moved. "I like traveling; I've traveled a good deal all my life; and I want to go round the world with Blair."

Elizabeth gave him a black look. "You like Blair better 'an me," she said, the tears hot in her amber eyes. A minute later she slipped away to hide under the bed in her own room, peering out from under a lifted valance for a hoped-for pursuer. But no one came; the other three were so excited that her absence was hardly noticed.

How they started, the adventurous ones, late that afternoon— later, in fact, than they planned, because Blair insisted upon running back to give Harris a parting gift of a dollar; "'Cause, poor Harris! *he* can't go traveling"—how they waited in the big, barn-like, foggy station for what Blair called the "next train," how they boarded it for "any place"—all seemed very funny when they were old enough to look back upon it. It even seemed funny, a day or two afterward, to their alarmed elders. But at the time it was not amusing to anybody. David was gloomy at being obliged to marry Nannie; "I pretty near wish I'd stayed with Elizabeth," he said, crossly. Nannie was frightened, because, she declared, "Mamma'll be mad;—now I tell you, Blair, she'll be mad!" And Blair was sulky because he had no wife. Yet, in spite of these varying emotions, pushed by Blair's resolution, they really did venture forth to "travel all around the world!"

As for the grown people's feelings about the elopement, they ran the gamut from panic to amusement.... At a little after five o'clock, Miss White heard sobbing in Elizabeth's room, and going in, found the little girl blacking her boots and crying furiously. "Elizabeth! my lamb! What is the matter?"

"I have a great many sorrows," said Elizabeth, with a hiccup of despair.

"But what *are* you doing?"

"I am blacking my red shoes," Elizabeth wailed; and so she was, the blacking-sponge on its shaky wire dripping all over the carpet. "My beautiful red shoes; I am blacking them; and now they are spoiled forever."

"But why do you want to spoil them?" gasped Miss White, struggling to take the blacking-bottle away from her. "Elizabeth, tell me immejetly! What has happened?"

"I didn't go on the journey," said Elizabeth; "and David wouldn't stay at home with me; he liked Blair and Nannie better 'an me. He hurt my feelings; so pretty soon right away I got mad—mad —mad—to think he wouldn't stay with me. I always get mad if my feelings are hurt, and David Richie is always hurting 'em. I despise him for making me mad! I despise him for treating me so—*hideous*! And so I took a hate to my shoes." The ensuing explanation sent Miss White, breathless, to tell Mrs. Richie; but Mrs. Richie was not at home.

When David did not appear that afternoon after school, Mrs. Richie was disturbed. By three o'clock she was uneasy; but it was nearly five before the quiver of apprehension grew into positive fright; then she put on her things and walked down to the Maitland house.

"Is David here?" she demanded when Harris answered her ring; "please go up-stairs and look, Harris; they may be playing in the nursery. I am worried."

Harris shuffled off, and Mrs. Richie, following him to the foot of the stairs, stood there gripping the newel-post.

"They ain't here," Harris announced from the top landing.

Mrs. Richie sank down on the lowest step.

"Harris!" some one called peremptorily, and she turned to see

Robert
Ferguson coming out of the dining-room: "Oh, you're here, Mrs. Richie?
I suppose you are on David's track. I thought Harris might have some
clue. I came down to tell Mrs. Maitland all we could wring from Elizabeth."

Before she could ask what he meant, Blair's mother joined them. "I haven't a doubt they are playing in the orchard," she said.

"No, they're not," her superintendent contradicted; "Elizabeth says they were going to 'travel'; but that's all we could get out of her."

"'Travel'! Oh, what does she mean?" Mrs. Richie said; "I'm so frightened!"

"What's the use of being frightened?" Mrs. Maitland asked, curiously; "it won't bring them back if they are lost, will it?"

Robert Ferguson knocked his glasses off fiercely. "They couldn't be lost in Mercer," he reassured David's mother.

"Well, whether they've run away or not, come into my room and talk about it like a sensible woman," said Mrs. Maitland; "what's the use of sitting on the stairs? Women have such a way of sitting on stairs when things go wrong! Suppose they are lost. What harm's done? They'll turn up. Come!" Mrs. Richie came. Everybody "came" or went, or stood still, when Mrs. Maitland said the word! And though not commanded, Mr. Ferguson came too.

In the dining-room Mrs. Maitland took no part in the perplexed discussion that followed. At her desk, in her revolving chair, she had instinctively taken up her pen; there was a perceptible instant in which she got her mind off her own affairs and put it on this matter of the children. Then she laid the pen down, and turned around to face the other two; but idleness irritated her, and she reached for a ball of pink worsted skewered by bone needles. She asked no questions and made no comments, but knitting rapidly, listened, until apparently her patience came to an end; then with a grunt she whirled round to her desk and again picked up her pen. But as she did so she paused, pen in air; threw it down, and pounding the flat of her hand on her desk, laughed loudly:

"I know! I know!" And revolving back again in leisurely relief to face them, she said, with open amusement: "When I came home this afternoon, I found this drawer half open and the bills in my cash-box disturbed. They've"—her voice was suddenly drowned in the rumble of a train on the spur track; the house shook slightly, and a gust of black smoke was vomited against the windows; —"they've helped themselves and gone off to enjoy it! We'll get on their trail at the railroad station. That's what Elizabeth meant by 'traveling.'"

Mrs. Richie turned terrified eyes toward Mr. Ferguson.

"Why, of course!" he said, "the monkeys!"

But Mrs. Richie seemed more frightened than ever. "The railroad!—*Oh*—"

"Nonsense," said Mrs. Maitland; "they're all right. The ticket-agent will remember them. Mr. Ferguson, telegraph to their destination, wherever it is, and have them shipped back. No police help at this end yet, if you please."

Robert Ferguson nodded. "Of course everything is all right," he said. "I'll let you know the minute I find traces of them, Mrs. Richie." When he reached the door, he came back. "Now don't you worry; I could thrash those boys for bothering you!" At which she tried to smile, but there was a quiver in her chin.

"Harris!" Mrs. Maitland broke in, "supper! Mrs. Richie, you are going to have something to eat."

"Oh, I can't—"

"What? You are not saying *can't?* 'Can't' is a 'bad word,' you know." She got up—a big, heavy woman, in a gray bag of a dress that only reached to the top of her boots—and stood with her hands on her hips; her gray hair was twisted into a small, tight knot at the back of her head, and her face looked like iron that had once been molten and had cooled into roughened immobility. It was not an unamiable face; as she stood there looking down at Mrs. Richie she even smiled the half-amused smile one might bestow on a puppy, and she put a kindly hand on the other mother's shoulder. "Don't be so scared, woman! They'll be found."

"You don't think anything could have happened to him?" Mrs. Richie said, trembling; "you don't think he could have been run over, or—or anything?" She clutched at the big hand and clung to it.

"No," Mrs. Maitland said, dryly; "I don't think anything has happened to him."

Mrs. Richie had the grace to blush. "Of course I meant Blair and

Nannie, too," she murmured.

"You never thought of 'em!" Mrs. Maitland said, chuckling; "now you must have some supper."

They were in the midst of it when a note came from Mr. Ferguson to say that he was on the track of the runaways. He had sent a despatch that would insure their being returned by the next train, and he was himself going half-way up the road to meet them. Then a postscript: "Tell Mrs. Richie not to worry."

"Doesn't seem much disturbed about my worry," said Mrs. Maitland, jocosely significant; then with loud cheerfulness she tried to rally her guest: "It's all right; what did I tell you? Where's my knitting? Come; I'll go over to the parlor with you; we'll sit there."

Mrs. Maitland's parlor was not calculated to cheer a panic-stricken mother. It was a vast room, rather chilly on this foggy

November evening, and smelling of soot. On its remote ceiling was a design in delicate relief of garlands and wreaths, which the dingy years had not been able to rob of its austere beauty. Two veined black-marble columns supported an arch that divided the desert of the large room into two smaller rooms, each of which had the center-table of the period, its bleak white-marble top covered with elaborately gilded books that no one ever opened. Each room had, too, a great cut-glass chandelier, swathed in brown paper-muslin and looking like a gigantic withered pear. Each had its fireplace, with a mantelpiece of funereal marble to match the pillars. Mrs. Maitland had refurnished this parlor when she came to the old house as a bride; she banished to the lumber-room, or even to the auctioneer's stand, the heavy, stately mahogany of the early part of the century, and purchased according to the fashion of the day, glittering rosewood, carved and gilded and as costly as could be found. Between the windows at each end of the long room were mirrors in enormous gilt frames; the windows themselves, topped with cornices and heavy lambrequins, were hung with crimson brocade; a grand piano, very bare and shining, sprawled sidewise between the black columns of the arch, and on the wall opposite the fireplaces were four large landscapes in oil, of exactly the same size. "Herbert likes pictures," the bride said to herself when she purchased them. "That goose Molly Wharton wouldn't have been able to buy 'em for him!" The only pleasant thing in the meaningless room was Nannie's drawing-board, which displayed the little girl's painstaking and surprisingly exact copy in lead-pencil, of some chromo—"Evangeline" perhaps, or some popular sentimentality of the sixties. In the ten years which had elapsed since Mrs. Maitland had plunged into her debauch of furnishing—her one extravagance!—of course the parlors had softened; the enormous roses of the carpets had faded, the glitter of varnish had dimmed; but the change was not sufficient to blur in Mrs.

Maitland's eyes, all the costly and ugly glory of the room. She cast a complacent glance about her as she motioned her nervous and preoccupied guest to a chair. "How do you like Mercer?" she said, beginning to knit rapidly.

"Oh, very well; it is a little—smoky," Mrs. Richie said, glancing at the clock.

Mrs. Maitland grunted. "Mercer would be in a bad way without its smoke. You ought to learn to like it, as I do! I like the smell of it, I like the taste of it, I like the feel of it!"

"Really?" Mrs. Richie murmured; she was watching the clock.

"That smoke, let me tell you Mrs. Richie is the pillar of cloud, to this country! (If you read your Bible, you'll know what that means.) I think of it whenever I look at my stacks."

Mrs. Maitland's resentment at her guest's mild criticism was obvious; but Mrs. Richie did not notice it. "I think I'll go down to the station and meet the children," she said, rising.

"I'm afraid you are a very foolish woman," Sarah Maitland said;—and Mrs. Richie sat down. "Mr. Ferguson will bring 'em here. Anyway, this clock is half an hour slow. They'll be here before you could get to the station." She chuckled, slyly. Her sense of humor was entirely rudimentary, and never got beyond the practical joke. "I've been watching you look at that clock," she said; then she looked at it herself and frowned. She was wasting a good deal of time over this business of the children. But in spite of herself, glancing at the graceful figure sitting in tense waiting at the fireside, she smiled. "You are a pretty creature," she said; and Mrs. Richie started and blushed like a girl. "If Robert Ferguson had any sense!" she went on, and paused to pick up a dropped stitch. "Queer fellow, isn't he?" Mrs. Richie had nothing to say. "Something went wrong with him when he was young, just after he left college. Some kind of a crash. Woman scrape, I suppose. Have you ever noticed that women make all the trouble in the world? Well, he never got over it. He told me once that Life wouldn't play but one trick on him. 'We're always going to sit down on a chair—and Life pulls it from under us,' he said. 'It won't do that to me twice.' He's not given to being confidential, but that put me on the track. And now he's got Elizabeth on his hands."

"She's a dear little thing," Mrs. Richie said, smiling; "though I confess she always fights shy of me; she doesn't like me, I'm afraid."

Mrs. Maitland lifted an eyebrow. "She's a corked-up volcano. Robert
Ferguson ought to get married, and give her an aunt to look after her."
She glanced at Mrs. Richie again, with appraising eyes; "pity he hasn't
more sense."

"I think I hear a carriage," Mrs. Richie said, coldly. Then she forgot Mrs. Maitland, and stood waiting and trembling. A minute later Mr. Ferguson ushered the three sleepy, whimpering children into the room, and Mrs. Richie caught her grimy, crying little boy in her arms and cried with him. "Oh, David, oh, David—my darling! How could you frighten mother so!"

She was on her knees before him, and while her tears and kisses fell on his tousled thatch of yellow hair, he burrowed his dirty little face among the laces around her white throat and bawled louder than ever. Mrs. Maitland, her back to the fireplace, her hands on her hips, stood looking on; she was very much interested. Blair, hungry and sleepy and evidently frightened, was nuzzling up against Mrs. Richie, catching at her hand and trying to hide behind her skirts; he looked furtively at his mother, but he would not meet her eye.

"Blair," she said, "go to bed."

"Nannie and me want some supper," said Blair in a whisper.

"You won't get any. Boys that go traveling at supper-time can get their own suppers or go hungry."

"It's my fault, Mamma," Nannie panted.

"No, it ain't!" Blair said quickly, emerging from behind Mrs. Richie; "it was me made her do it."

"Well, clear out, clear out! Go to bed, both of you," Mrs. Maitland said. But when the two children had scuttled out of the room she struck her knee with her fist and laughed immoderately.

The next morning, when the two children skulked palely into the dining-room, they were still frightened. Mrs. Maitland, however, did not notice them. She was absorbed in trying in the murky light to read the morning paper, propped against the silver urn in front of her.

"Sit down," she said; "I don't like children who are late for breakfast. Bless, O Lord, we beseech Thee, these things to our use, and us to Thy service and glory. Amen!—Harris! Light the gas."

Mercer's daylight was always more or less wan; but in the autumn the yellow fogs seemed to press the low-hanging smoke down into the great bowl of the hills at the bottom of which the town lay, and the wanness scarcely lightened, even at high noon. On such days the gas in the dining-room—or office, if one prefers to call it so—flared from breakfast until dinner time. It flared now on two scared little faces. Once Blair lifted questioning eyebrows at Harris, and managed when the man brought his plate of porridge to whisper, "mad?" At which the sympathetic Harris rolled his eyes speechlessly, and the two children grew perceptibly paler. But when, abruptly, Mrs. Maitland crumpled her newspaper together and threw it on the floor, her absorbed face showed no displeasure. The fact was, she had forgotten the affair of the night before; it was the children's obvious alarm which reminded her that the business of scolding and punishing must be attended to. She got up from the table and stood behind them, with her back to the fire; she began to nibble the upper joint of her forefinger, wondering just how to begin. This silent inspection of their shoulders made the little creatures quiver. Nannie crumbled her bread into a heap, and Blair carried an empty spoon to his mouth with automatic regularity; Harris, in the pantry, in a paroxysm of sympathy, stretched his lean neck to the crack of the half-open door.

"Children!"

"Yes, ma'am," Nannie quavered.

"Turn round."

They turned. Nannie began to cry. Blair twisted a button on his coat with a grip that made his fingers white.

"Come into my room."

The children gasped with dismay. Mrs. Maitland's bedroom was a nightmare of a place to them both. It was generally dark, for the lower halves of the inside shutters were apt to be closed; but, worse than that, the glimmering glass doors of the bookcases that lined the walls held a suggestion of mystery that was curiously terrifying. Whenever they entered the room, the brother and sister always kept a frightened eye on those doors. This dull winter morning, when they came quaking along behind their mother into this grim place, it was still in the squalor of morning confusion. Later, Harris would open the shutters and tidy things up; he would dust the painted pine bureau and Blair's photographs and the slender green bottle of German cologne on which the red ribbons of the calendar were beginning to fade; now everything was dark and bleak and covered with dust. Mrs. Maitland sat down; the culprits stood hand in hand in front of her.

"Blair, don't you know it's wrong to take what doesn't belong to you?"

"I took it," said the 'fraid-cat, faintly; she moved in front of her brother as though to protect him.

"Blair told you to," his mother said.

"Yes," Blair blurted out, "it was me told her to."

"People that take things that don't belong to them go to hell," Mrs.
 Maitland said; "haven't you learned that in Sunday-school?"

Silence.

"You ought to be punished very severely, Blair—and Nannie, too. But I am very busy this morning, so I shall only say"—she hesitated; what on earth should she say! "that—that you shall lose your allowance for this week, both of you."

One of them muttered, "Yes'm."

Mrs. Maitland looked as uncomfortable as they did. She wondered what to do next. How much simpler a furnace was than a child! "Well," she said, "that's all—at present"; it had suddenly occurred to her that apprehension was a good thing; "*at present*," she repeated darkly; "and Blair, remember; thieves go to hell." She watched them with perplexed eyes as they hurried out of the room; just as they reached the door she called: "Blair!"

The child stopped short in his tracks and quivered.

"Come here." He came, slowly, his very feet showing his reluctance. "Blair," she said—in her effort to speak gently her voice grated; she put out her hand as if to draw him to her, but the child shivered and moved aside. Mrs. Maitland looked at him dumbly; then bent toward him, and her hands, hanging between her knees, opened and closed, and even half stretched out as if in inarticulate entreaty. Nannie, in the doorway, sobbing under her breath, watched with frightened, uncomprehending eyes. "My son," Sarah Maitland said, with as much mildness as her loud voice could express, "what did you mean to do when you ran away?" She smiled, but he would not meet her eyes. "Tell me, my boy, why did you run away?"

Blair tried to speak, cleared his throat, and blurted out four husky words: "Don't like it here."

"Don't like what? Your home?"

Blair nodded.

"Why not?" she asked, astonished.

"Ugly," Blair said, faintly.

"Ugly! What is ugly?"

Blair, without looking up, made a little, swift gesture with his hand. "This," he said; then suddenly he lifted his head, gave her a sidewise, shrinking look, and dropped his eyes. The color flew into Mrs. Maitland's face; with an ejaculation of anger, she got on her feet. "You are a very foolish and very bad little boy," she said; "you don't know what you are talking about. I had meant to increase your allowance, but now I won't do it. Listen to me; it is no matter whether a house, or a—a person, is what you call 'ugly.' What matters is whether they are useful. Everything in the world ought to be useful—like our Works. If I ever hear you saying you don't like a thing because it's ugly, I shall—I shall not give you any money at all. Money!" she burst out, suddenly fluent, "money isn't *pretty*! Dirty scraps of paper, bits of silver that look like lead—perhaps you call money 'ugly,' too?"

Her vehemence was a sort of self-defense; it was a subtle confession that she felt in this little repelling personality the challenge of an equal; but Blair only gaped at her in childish confusion; and instantly his mother was herself again. "Clear out, now; and be a good boy." When she was alone, she sat at her desk in the dining-room for several minutes without taking up her pen. Her face burned from the slap of the child's words; but below the scorch of anger and mortification her heart was bruised. He did not like her to put her arm about him! She drew a long breath and began to read her letters; but all the while she was thinking of that scene in the parlor the night before: Blair crouching against Mrs. Richie, clinging to her white hand;—voluntarily Sarah Maitland looked at her own hand; "I suppose," she said to herself, "he thinks hers is 'pretty'! Where does he get such notions? I wonder what kind of a woman she is, anyway; she never says anything about her husband."

Chapter 3

There came a day when Miss White's little school in the garret was broken up. Mr. Ferguson declared that David and Blair needed a boot instead of a petticoat to teach them their Latin—and a few other things, too! He had found Mrs. Richie in tears because, under the big hawthorn in her own back yard, David had blacked Blair's eye, and had himself achieved a bloody nose. Mrs. Richie was for putting on her things to go and apologize to Mrs. Maitland, and was hardly restrained by her landlord's snort of laughter.

"Next time I hope he'll give him two black eyes, and Blair will loosen one of his front teeth!" said Mr. Ferguson.

David's mother was speechless with horror.

"That's the worst of trusting a boy to a good woman," he barked, knocking off his glasses angrily; "but I'll do what I can to thwart you! I'll make sure there isn't any young-eyed cherubin business about David. He has got to go to boarding-school, and learn something besides his prayers. If somebody doesn't rescue him from apron-strings, he'll be a 'very, very good young man'—and then may the Lord have mercy on his soul!"

"I didn't know anybody could be too good," Mrs. Richie ventured.

"A woman can't be too good, but a man oughtn't to be," her landlord instructed her.

David's mother was too bewildered by such sentiments to protest—although, indeed, Mr. Ferguson need not have been quite so concerned about David's "goodness." This freckled, clear-eyed youngster, with straight yellow hair and good red cheeks, was just an honest, growly boy, who dropped his clothes about on the floor of his room, and whined over his lessons, and blustered largely when out of his mother's hearing; furthermore, he had already experienced his first stogie—with a consequent pallor about the gills that scared Mrs. Richie nearly to death. But Robert Ferguson's jeering reference to apron-strings resulted in his being sent to boarding school. Blair went with him, "rescued" from the goodwoman regime of Cherry-pie's instruction by Mr. Ferguson's advice to Mrs. Maitland; "although," Robert Ferguson admitted, candidly, "he doesn't need it as poor David does; his mother wouldn't know how to make a Miss Nancy of him, even if she wanted to!" Then, with a sardonic guess at Mrs. Richie's unspoken thought, he added that Mrs. Maitland would not dream of going to live in the town where her son was at school. "She has sense enough to know that Blair, or any other boy worth his salt, would hate his mother if she tagged on behind," said Mr. Ferguson; "of course you would never think of doing such a thing, either," he ended, ironically.

"Of course not," said Mrs. Richie, faintly. So it was that, assisted by her landlord, David's mother thrust her one chicken out into the world unprotected by her hovering wing. About the time Miss White lost her two masculine pupils, the girls began to go to a day-school in Mercer, Cherry-pie's entire deposition as a teacher being brought about because, poor lady! she fumbled badly when it came to a critical moment with Elizabeth. It all grew out of one of the child's innumerable squabbles with David—she got along fairly peaceably with Blair. She and Nannie had been comparing pigtails, and David had asserted that Elizabeth's hair was "the nicest"; which so gratified her that she first hugged him violently, and then invited him to take her out rowing.

"I'll pay for the boat!" she said, and pirouetted around the room, keeping time with:

"'Oh, that will be joyful, joyful, joyful!
Oh, that will be—'

"Uncle gave me a dollar yesterday," she interrupted herself, breathlessly.

To this David, patiently straightening his collar after that ecstatic embrace, objected; but his magnanimity was lessened by his explanation that he wasn't going to have any *girl* pay for him! This ruffled Elizabeth's pride for a moment; however, she was not averse to saving her dollar, so everything was arranged. David was to row her to Willis's, a country tavern two miles down the river, where, as all middle-aged Mercer will remember, the best jumbles in the world could be purchased at the agreeable price of two for a cent. Elizabeth, who was still congratulating herself on having "nicer hair than Nannie," and who loved the river (and the jumbles), was as punctual as a clock in arriving at the covered bridge where at the toll-house wharf they were to meet and embark. She had even been so forehanded as to bargain with Mrs. Todd for the hire of the skiff, in which she immediately seated herself, the tiller-ropes in her hands, all ready for David to take the oars. "And I've waited, and waited, and waited!" she told herself angrily, as she sat there in the faintly rocking skiff. And after an hour of waiting, what should she see but David Richie racing on the bridge with Blair Maitland! He had just simply forgotten his engagement! (Elizabeth was so nearly a young lady that she said "engagement.")

"I'll never forgive him," she said, and the dimple hardened in her cheek. Sitting in the boat, she looked up at the two boys, David in advance, a young, lithe figure, in cotton small-clothes and jersey, leaping in great, beautiful strides, on and on and on, his face glowing, his eyes like stars; then, alas, he gave a downward glance and there was Elizabeth, waiting fiercely in the skiff! His "engagement" came back to him; there was just one astonished, faltering instant; and in it, of course, Blair shot ahead! It must be confessed that in his rage at being beaten David promptly forgot Elizabeth again, for though she waited still a little longer for him and his apology, no David appeared, he and Blair being occupied in wrangling over their race. She went home in a slowly gathering passion. *David had forgotten her!* "He likes Blair better than me; he'd rather race with another boy than go out in a boat with me; and I said I'd pay for it—and I've only got one dollar in the whole world!" At that stab of self-pity a tear ran down the side of her nose (and she was still a whole block away from home!); when it reached her lip, she was obliged to put her tongue out furtively and lick it away. But repression made the outbreak, when it came, doubly furious. She burst in upon Miss White, her dry eyes blazing with rage.

"He made me wait; he didn't come; I hate him. I'll never speak to him again. He hurt my feelings. He is a beast."

"Elizabeth! You mustn't use such unladylike words! When I was a young lady I never even heard such words. Oh, my lamb, if you don't control your temper, something dreadful will happen to you some day!"

"I hope something dreadful will happen to him some day," said Elizabeth. And with that came the tears—a torrential rain, through which the lightning played and the thunder crashed. Miss White in real terror, left her, to get some smelling-salts, and the instant she was alone Elizabeth ran across the room and stood before her mirror; then she took a pair of scissors in her shaking hand and hacked off lock after lock, strand after strand, of her shining hair. When it was done, she looked at the russet stubble that was left with triumphant rage. "There, now! I guess he won't think my hair is nicer than Nannie's any more. I *hate* him!" she said, and laughed out loud, her vivid face wet and quivering.

Miss White, hurrying in, heard the laugh, and stood transfixed: "Elizabeth!" The poor, ugly, shorn head, the pile of gleaming hair on the bureau, the wicked, tear-stained, laughing face brought the poor lady's heart into her throat. "Elizabeth!" she faltered again; and Elizabeth ran and flung her arms about her neck.

"David forgot all about me," she sobbed. "He is always hurting my feelings! And I can't *bear* to have my feelings hurt. Oh, Cherry-pie, kiss me! Kiss me!"

That was the end of the outburst; the ensuing penitence was unbridled and temporary. The next morning she waylaid David to offer him some candy, which he took with serene unconsciousness of any bad behavior on his part.

"Awfully sorry I forgot about Willis's," he said casually; and took a hearty handful of candy.

Elizabeth, looking into the nearly empty box, winced; then said, bravely, "Take some more." He took a good deal more.

"David, I—I'm sorry I cut my hair."

"Why, I didn't notice," David said, wrinkling up his freckled nose and glancing at her with some interest. "It looks awfully, doesn't it?"

"David, don't tell your mother, will you? She looks so sort of horrified when I've been provoked. It almost makes me mad again," Elizabeth said, candidly.

"Materna thinks it's dreadful in you."

"Do you mind about my hair?" Elizabeth asked.

David laughed uproariously. "Why on earth should *I* mind? If I were a girl, you bet I'd keep my hair cut."

"Do you forgive me?" she said, in a whisper; "if you don't forgive me,
I shall die."

"Forgive you?" said David, astonished, his mouth full of candy; "why, it's nothing to me if you cut off your hair. Only I shouldn't think you'd want to look so like 'Sam Hill.' But I tell you what, Elizabeth; you're too thin-skinned. What's the use of getting mad over every little thing?"

"It wasn't so very little, to be forgotten."

"Well, yes; I suppose you were disappointed, but—"

Elizabeth's color began to rise. "Oh, I wasn't so terribly disappointed. You needn't flatter yourself. I simply don't like to be insulted."

"Ah, now, Elizabeth," he coaxed, "there you go again!"

"No, I don't. I'm *not* angry. Only—you went with Blair; you didn't want—" she choked, and flew back into the house, deaf to his clumsy and troubled explanations.

In Miss White's room, Elizabeth announced her intention of entering a convent, and it was then that Cherry-pie fumbled: she took the convent seriously! The next morning she broke the awful news to Elizabeth's uncle. It was before breakfast, and Mr. Ferguson —who had not time to read his Bible for pressure of business—had gone out into the grape-arbor in his narrow garden to feed the pigeons. There was a crowd of them about his feet, their rimpling, iridescent necks and soft gray bosoms pushing and jostling against one another, and their pink feet actually touching his boots. When Miss White burst out at him, the pigeons rose in startled flight, and Mr. Ferguson frowned.

"And she says," Miss White ended, almost in tears—"she says she is going to enter a convent immejetly!"

"My dear Miss White," said Elizabeth's uncle, grimly, "there's no such luck."

Miss White positively reeled. Then he explained, and Cherry-pie came nearer to her employer in those ten minutes than in the ten years in which she had looked after his niece. "I don't care about Elizabeth's temper; she'll get over that. And I don't care a continental about her hair or her religion; she can wear a wig or be a Mohammedan if it keeps her straight. She has a bad inheritance, Miss

White; I would be only too pleased to know that she was shut up in a convent, safe and sound. But this whim isn't worth talking about."

Miss White retired, nibbling with horror, and that night Robert
Ferguson went in to tell his neighbor his worries.

"What *am* I to do with her?" he groaned. "She cut off her hair?" Mrs.
Richie repeated, astounded; "but why? How perfectly irrational!"

"Don't say 'how irrational'; say 'how Elizabeth.'"

"I wish she would try to control her temper," Mrs. Richie said, anxiously.

But Mr. Ferguson was not troubled about that. "She's vain; that's what worries me. She cried all afternoon about her hair."

"She needs a stronger hand than kind Miss White's," Mrs. Richie said; "why not send her to school?" And the harassed uncle sighed with relief at the idea, which was put into immediate execution.

With growing hair and the wholesome companionship of other girls, of course the ascetic impulse died a natural death; but the temper did not die. It only hid itself under that sense of propriety which is responsible for so much of our good behavior. When it did break loose, the child suffered afterward from the consciousness of having made a fool of herself—which is a wholesome consciousness so far as it goes—but it did not go very far with Elizabeth; she never suffered in any deeper way. She took her temper for granted; she was not complacent about it; she did not credit it to "temperament," she was merely matter of fact; she said she "couldn't help it." "I don't want to get mad," she used to say to Nannie; "and of course I never mean any of the horrid things I say. I'd like to be good, like you; but I can't help being wicked." Between those dark moments of being "wicked" she was a joyous, unself-conscious girl of generous loves, which she expressed as primitively as she did her angers; indeed, in the expression of affection Elizabeth had the exquisite and sometimes embarrassing innocence of a child who has been brought up by a sad old bachelor and a timid old maid. As for her angers, they were followed by irrational efforts to "make up" with any one she felt she had wronged. She spent her little pocket-money in buying presents for her maleficiaries, she invented punishments for herself; and generally she confessed her sin with humiliating fullness. Once she confessed to her uncle, thereby greatly embarrassing him:

"Uncle, I want you to know I am a great sinner; probably the chief of sinners," she said, breathing hard. She had come into his library after supper, and was standing with a hand on the back of his chair; her eyes were bright with unshed tears.

"Good gracious!" said Robert Ferguson, looking at her blankly over his glasses, "what on earth have you been doing now?"

"I got mad, and I chopped up the feather in Cherry-pie's new bonnet, and I told her she was a hideous, monstrous old donkey-hag."

"Elizabeth!"

"I did."

"Have you apologized?"

"Yes," said Elizabeth; "but what's the good of 'pologizing? *I said it.* 'Course I 'pologized; and I kissed her muddy rubbers when she wasn't looking; and I gave her all my money for a new feather" — she stopped, and sighed deeply; "and here is the money you gave me to go to the theater. So now I haven't any money at all, in the world."

Poor Robert Ferguson, with a despairing jerk at the black ribbon of his glasses, leaned back in his chair, helpless with perplexity. Why on earth did she give him back his money? He could not follow her mental processes. He said as much to Mrs. Richie the next time he went to see her. He went to see her quite often in those days. For the convenience of David and Elizabeth, a doorway had been cut in the brick wall between the two gardens, and Mr. Ferguson used it frequently. In their five or six years of living next door to each other the acquaintance of these two neighbors had deepened into a sort of tentative intimacy, which they never quite thought of as friendship, but which permitted many confidences about their two children.

And when they talked about their children, they spoke, of course, of the other two, for one could not think of David without remembering Blair, or talk of Elizabeth without contrasting her with Nannie. Nannie had none of that caroling vitality which made the younger girl an acute anxiety and a perpetual delight. She was like a little plant growing in the shade—a gently good child, who never gave anybody any trouble; she continued to be a 'fraid-cat, and looked under the bed every night for a burglar. With Blair at boarding-school her life was very solitary, for of course there was no intimacy between her and her stepmother. Mrs. Maitland was invariably kind to her, and astonishingly patient with the rather dull little mind—one of those minds that are like softly tangled skeins of single zephyr; if you try to unwind the mild, elusive thoughts, they only knot tightly upon themselves, and the result is a half-frightened and very obstinate silence. But Mrs. Maitland never tried to unwind Nannie's thoughts; she used to look at her sometimes in kindly amusement, as one might look at a kitten or a canary; and sometimes she said to Robert Ferguson that Nannie was like her own mother; —"but Blair has brains!" she would say, complacently. School did not give the girl the usual intense friendships, and except for Elizabeth, she had no companions; her one interest was Blair, and her only occupation out of school hours was her drawing—which was nothing more than endless, meaningless copying. It was Nannie's essential child-likeness that kept her elders, and indeed David and Blair too, from understanding that she and Elizabeth were no longer little girls. Perhaps the boys first realized Elizabeth's age when they simultaneously discovered that she was pretty....

Elizabeth's long braids had been always attractive to the masculine eye; they had suggested jokes about pigtails, and much of that peculiar humor so pleasing to the young male; but the summer that she "put up her hair," the puppies, so to speak, got their eyes open. When the boys saw those soft plaits, no longer hanging within easy reach of a rude and teasing hand, but folded around her head behind her little ears; when they saw the small curls breaking over and through the brown braids that were flecked with gilt, and the stray locks, like feathers of spun silk, clustering in the nape of her neck; when David and Blair saw these things—it was about the time their voices were showing amazing and ludicrous register—something below the artless brutalities of the boys' sense of humor was touched. They took abruptly their first perilous step out of boyhood. Of course they did not know it.... The significant moment came one afternoon when they all went out to the toll-house for ice-cream. There was a little delay at the gate, while the boys wrangled as to who should stand treat. "I'll pull straws with you," said Blair; Blair's pleasant, indolent mind found the appeal to chance the easiest way to settle things, but he was always good-natured when, as now, the verdict was against him. "Come on," he commanded, gayly, "I'll shell out!" Mrs. Todd, who had begun to dispense pink and brown ice-cream, for them when they were very little children, winked and nodded as they all came in together, and made a jocose remark about "handsome couples"; then she trundled off to get the ice-cream, leaving them in the saloon. This "saloon" was an ell of the toll-house; it opened on a little garden, from which a flight of rickety steps led down to a float where half a dozen skiffs were tied up, waiting to be hired. In warm weather, when the garden was blazing with fragrant color, Mrs. Todd would permit favored patrons to put their small tables out among the marigolds and zinnias and sit and eat and talk. The saloon itself had Nottingham-lace window-curtains, and crewel texts enjoining remembrance of the Creator, and calling upon Him to "bless our home." The tables, with marble tops translucent from years of spilled ice cream, had each a worsted mat, on which was a glass vase full of blue paper roses; on the ceiling there was a wonderful star of scalloped blue tissue-paper—ostensibly to allure flies, but hanging there winter and summer, year in and year out. Between the windows that looked out on the river stood a piano, draped with a festooning scarf of bandanna handkerchiefs. These things seemed to Blair, at this stage of his esthetic development, very satisfying, and part of his pleasure in "treating" came from his surroundings; he used to look about him enviously, thinking of the terrible dining-room at home; and on sunny days he used to look, with even keener pleasure, at the reflected ripple of light, striking up from the river below, and moving endlessly across the fly-specked ceiling. Watching the play of moving light, he would put his tin spoon into his tumbler of ice-cream and taste the snowy mixture with a slow prolongation of pleasure, while the two girls chattered like sparrows, and David listened, saying very little and always ready to let Elizabeth finish his ice-cream after she had devoured her own.

It was on one of these occasions that Blair, watching that long ripple on the ceiling, suddenly saw the sunshine sparkle on Elizabeth's hair, and his spoon paused midway to his lips. "Oh, say, isn't Elizabeth's hair nice?" he said.

David turned and looked at it. "I've seen lots of girls with hair like that," he said; but he sighed, and scratched his left ankle with his right foot. Blair, smiling to himself, put out a hesitating finger and touched a shimmering curl; upon which Elizabeth ducked and laughed, and dancing over to the old tin pan of a piano pounded out

"Shoo Fly" with one finger. Blair, watching the lovely color in her cheek, said in honest delight: "When your face gets red like that, you are awfully good-looking, Elizabeth."

"Good-looking"; that was a new idea to the four friends. Nannie gaped; Elizabeth giggled; David "got red" on his own account, and muttered under his breath, "Tell that to the marines!" But into Blair's face had come, suddenly, a new expression; his eyes smiled vaguely; he came sidling over to Elizabeth and stood beside her, sighing deeply: "Elizabeth, you are an awful nice girl."

Elizabeth shrieked with laughter. "Listen to Blair—he's spoony!"

Instantly Blair was angry; "spooniness" vanished in a flash; he did not speak for fully five minutes. Just as they started home, however, he came out of his glumness to remember Miss White. "I'm going to take Cherry-pie some ice-cream," he said; and all the way back he was so absorbed in trying—unsuccessfully—to keep the pallid pink contents of the mussy paper box from dripping on his clothes that he was able to forget Elizabeth's rudeness. But childhood, for all four of them, ended that afternoon.

When vacation was over, and they were back in the harness again, both boys forgot that first tremulous clutch at the garments of life; in fact, like all wholesome boys of fifteen or sixteen, they thought "girls" a bore. It was not until the next long vacation that the old, happy, squabbling relationship began to be tinged with a new consciousness. It was the elemental instinct, the everlasting human impulse. The boys, hobbledehoys, both of them, grew shy and turned red at unexpected moments. The girls developed a certain condescension of manner, which was very confusing and irritating to the boys. Elizabeth, as unaware of herself as the bud that has not opened to the bee, sighed a good deal, and repeated poetry to any one who would listen to her. She said boys were awfully rough, and their boots had a disagreeable smell, "I shall never get married," said Elizabeth; "I hate boys." Nannie did not hate anybody, but she thought she would rather be a missionary than marry;—"though I'm afraid I'd be afraid of the savages," she confessed, timorously.

David and Blair were confidential to each other about girls in general, and Elizabeth in particular; they said she was terribly stand-offish. "Oh, well, she's a girl," said David; "what can you expect?"

"She's darned good-looking," Blair blurted out. And David said, with some annoyance, "What's that amount to?" He said that, for his part, he didn't mean to fool around after girls. "But I'm older than you, Blair; you'll feel that way when you get to be my age; it's only when a man is very young that he bothers with 'em."

"That's so," said Blair, gloomily. "Well, I never expect to marry." Blair was very gloomy just then; he had come home from school the embodiment of discontent. He was old enough now to suffer agonies of mortification because of his mother's occupation. "The idea of a lady running an Iron Works!" he said to David, who tried rather half-heartedly to comfort him; David was complacently sure that *his* mother wouldn't run an Iron Works! "I hate the whole caboodle," Blair said, angrily. It was his old shrinking from "ugliness." And everything at home was ugly;—the great old house in the midst of Maitland's Shantytown; the darkness and grime of it; the smell of soot in the halls; Harris's slatternly ways; his mother's big, beautiful, dirty fingers. "When she sneezes," Blair said, grinding his teeth, "I could—swear! She takes the roof off." He grew hot with shame when Mrs. Richie, whom he admired profoundly, came to take supper with his mother at the office table with its odds and ends of china. (As the old Canton dinner service had broken and fire-cracked, Harris had replenished the shelves of the china-closet according to his own taste limited by Mrs. Maitland's economic orders.) Blair found everything hideous, or vulgar, or uncomfortable, and he said so to Nannie with a violence that betrayed real suffering. For it is suffering when the young creature finds itself ashamed of father or mother. Instinctively the child is proud of the parent, and if youth is wounded in its tenderest point, its sense of conventionality —for nothing is as conventional as adolescence—that natural instinct is headed off, and of course there is suffering. Mrs. Maitland, living in her mixture of squalor and dignity, had no time to consider such abstractions. As for there being anything unwomanly in her occupation, such an idea never entered her head. To Sarah Maitland, no work which it was a woman's duty to do could be unwomanly; she was incapable of consciously aping masculinity, but to earn her living and heap up a fortune for her son, was, to her way of thinking, just the plain common sense of duty. But more than that, the heart in her bosom would have proved her sex to her; how she loved to knit the pink socks for dimpled little feet! how she winced when her son seemed to shrink from her; how jealous she was still of that goose Molly,—who had been another man's wife for as many years as Herbert Maitland had been in his grave. But Blair saw none of these things that might have told him that his mother was a very woman. Instead, his conventionality was insulted at every turn; his love of beauty was outraged. As a result a wall was slowly built between the mother and son, a wall whose foundations had been laid when the little boy had pointed his finger at her and said "uggy."

Mrs. Maitland was, of course, perfectly unconscious of her son's hot misery; she was so happy at having him at home again that she could not see that he was unhappy at being at home. She was pathetically eager to please him. Her theory—if in her absorbed life she could be said to have a theory—was that Blair should have everything he wanted, so that he should the sooner be a man. Money, she thought, would give him everything. She herself wanted nothing money could give, except food and shelter; the only use she had for money was to make more money; but she realized that other people, especially young men, like the things it would buy. Twice during that particular vacation, for no cause except to gratify herself, she gave her son a wickedly large check; and once, when Nannie told her that he wanted to pay for some painting lessons, though she demurred just for a moment, she paid the bill so that his own spending-money should not be diminished.

"What on earth does a man who is going to run an Iron Works want with painting lessons?" she said to the entreating sister. But even while she made her grumbling protest, she wrote a check.

As for Blair, he took the money, as he took everything else that she gave him of opportunity and happiness, and said, "Thank you, mother; you are awfully good"; but he shut his eyes when he kissed her. He was blind to the love, the yearning, the outstretched hands of motherhood,—not because he was cruel, or hard, or mean; but because he was young, and delighted in beauty.

Of course his wretchedness lessened after a fortnight or so— habit does much to reconcile us to unpleasantness; besides that, his painting was an interest, and his voice began to be a delight to him; he used to sing a good deal, making Nannie play his accompaniments, and sometimes his mother, working in the dining-room, would pause a moment, with lifted head, and listen and half smile—then fall to work again furiously.

But the real solace to his misery and irritation came to him—a boy still in years—in the sudden realization of *Elizabeth!*

Chapter 4

"I am going to have a party," Blair told Nannie; "I've invited David and Elizabeth, and four fellows; and you can ask four girls."

Nannie quaked. "Do you mean to have them come to supper?"

"You can call it 'supper'; I call it dinner."

"I'm afraid Mamma won't like it; it will disturb the table."

"I'm not going to have it in that hole of a dining-room; I'm going to have it in the parlor. Harris says he can manage perfectly well. We'll hang a curtain across the arch and have the table in the back parlor."

"But Harris can't wait on us in there, and on Mamma in the dining-room," Nannie objected.

"We shall have our dinner at seven, after Harris has given mother her supper on that beautiful table of hers."

"But—" said Nannie.

"You tell her about it," Blair coaxed; "she'll take anything from you."

Nannie yielded. Instructed by Blair, she hinted his purpose to Mrs.
Maitland, who to her surprise consented amiably enough.

"I've no objections. And the back parlor is a very sensible arrangement. It would be a nuisance to have you in here; I don't like to have things moved. Now clear out! Clear out! I must go to work." A week later she issued her orders: "Mr. Ferguson, I'll be obliged if you'll come to supper to-morrow night. Blair has some kind of a bee in his bonnet about having a party. Of course it's nonsense, but I suppose that's to be expected at his age."

Robert Ferguson demurred. "The boy doesn't want me; he

has asked a dozen young people."

Mrs. Maitland lifted one eyebrow. "I didn't hear about the dozen young people; I thought it was only two or three besides David and Elizabeth; however, I don't mind. I'll go the whole hog. He can have a dozen, if he wants to. As for his not wanting you, what has that got to do with it? I want you. It's my house, and my table; and I'll ask who I please. I've asked Mrs. Richie," she ended, and gave him a quick look.

"Well," her superintendent said, indifferently, "I'll come; but it's hard on Blair." When he went home that night, he summoned Miss White. "I hope you have arranged to have Elizabeth look properly for Blair's party? Don't let her be vain about it, but have her look right." And on the night of the great occasion, just before they started for Mrs. Maitland's, he called his niece into his library, and knocking off his glasses, looked her over with grudging eyes: "Don't get your head turned, Elizabeth. Remember, it isn't fine feathers that make fine birds," he said; and never knew that he was proud of her!

Elizabeth, bubbling with laughter, holding her skirt out in small, white-gloved hands, made three dancing steps, dipped him a great courtesy, then ran to him, and before he knew it, caught him round the neck and kissed him. "You dear, darling, *precious* uncle!" she said.

Mr. Ferguson, breathless, put his hand up to his cheek, as if the unwonted touch had left some soft, fresh warmth behind it.

Elizabeth did not wait to see the pleased and startled gesture she gathered up her fluffy tarlatan skirt, dashed out into the garden, through the green gate in the wall, and bursting into the house next door, stood in the hall and called up-stairs: "David! Come! Hurry! Quick!" She was stamping her foot with excitement.

David, who had had a perspiring and angry quarter of an hour with his first white tie, came out of his room and looked over the banisters, both hands at his throat. "Hello! What on earth is the matter?"

"David—see!" she said, and stood, quivering and radiant, all her whiteness billowing about her.

"See what?" David said, patiently.

"A long dress!"

"A *what*?" said David; then looking down at her, turning and twisting and preening herself in the dark hall like some shining white bird, he burst into a shout of laughter.

Elizabeth's face reddened. "I don't see anything to laugh at."

"You look like a little girl dressed up!"

"Little girl? I don't see much 'little girl' about it; I'm nearly sixteen." She gathered her skirt over her arm again, and retreated with angry dignity.

As for David, he went back to try a new tie; but his eyes were dreamy.

"George! she's a daisy," he said to himself.

When, the day before, Mrs. Richie had told her son that she had been invited to Blair's party, he was delighted. David had learned several things at school besides his prayers, some of which caused Mrs. Richie, like most mothers of boys, to give much time to her prayers. But as a result, perhaps of prayers as well as of education, and in spite of Mr. Ferguson's misgivings as to the wisdom of trusting a boy to a "good woman," he was turning out an honest young cub, of few words, defective sense of humor, and rather clumsy manners. But under his speechlessness and awkwardness, David was sufficiently sophisticated to be immensely proud of his pretty mother; only a laborious sense of propriety and the shyness of his sex and years kept him from, as he expressed it, "blowing about her." He blew now, however, a little, when she said she was going to the party: "Blair'll be awfully set up to have you come. You know he's terribly mashed on you. He thinks you are about the best thing going. Materna, now you dress up awfully, won't you? I want you to take the shine out of everybody else. I'm going to wear my dress suit," he encouraged her. "Why, say!" he interrupted himself, "that's funny— Blair didn't tell me he had asked you."

"Mrs. Maitland asked me."

"Mrs. Maitland!" David said, aghast; "Materna, you don't suppose *she's* coming, do you?"

"I'm sure I hope so, considering she invited me."

"Great Casar's ghost!" said David, thoughtfully; and added, under his breath, "I'm betting on his not expecting her. Poor Blair!"

Blair had need of sympathy. His plan for a "dinner" had encountered difficulties, and he had had moments of racking indecision; but when, on the toss of a penny, 'heads' declared for carrying the thing through, he held to his purpose with a perseverance that was amusingly like his mother's large and unshakable obstinacies. He had endless talks with Harris as to food; and with painstaking regard for artistic effect and as far as he understood it, for convention, he worked out every detail of service and arrangement. His first effort was to make the room beautiful; so the crimson curtains were drawn across the windows, and the cut-glass chandeliers in both rooms emerged glittering from their brown paper-muslin bags. The table was rather overloaded with large pieces of silver which Blair had found in the big silver-chest in the garret; among them was a huge center ornament, called in those days an epergne—an extraordinary arrangement of prickly silver leaves and red glass cups which were supposed to be flowers. It was black with disuse, and Blair made Harris work over it until the poor fellow protested that he had rubbed the skin off his thumb—but the pointed leaves of the great silver thistle sparkled like diamonds. Blair was charmingly considerate of old Harris so long as it required no sacrifice on his own part, but he did not relinquish a single piece of silver because of that thumb. With his large allowance, it was easy to put flowers everywhere—the most expensive that the season afforded. When he ordered them, he bought at the same time a great bunch of orchids for Miss White. "I can't invite her," he decided, reluctantly; "but her feelings won't be hurt if I send her some flowers." As for the menu, he charged the things he wanted to his mother's meager account at the grocery-store. When he produced his list of delicacies, things unknown on that office-dining-room table, the amazed grocer said to himself, "Well, *at last* I guess that trade is going to amount to something! Why, damn it," he confided to his bookkeeper afterward, "I been sendin' things up to that there house for seventeen years, and the whole bill ain't amounted to shucks. That woman could buy and sell me twenty times over. Twenty times? A hundred times! And I give you my word she eats like a day-laborer. Listen to this"—and he rattled off Blair's order. "She'll fall down dead when she sees them things; she don't even know how to spell 'em!"

Blair had never seen a table properly appointed for a dinner-party; but Harris had recollections of more elaborate and elegant days, a recollection, indeed, of one occasion when he had waited at a policemen's ball; and he laid down the law so dogmatically that Blair assented to every suggestion. The result was a humorous compound of Harris's standards and Blair's aspirations; but the boy, coming in to look at the table before the arrival of his guests, was perfectly satisfied.

"It's fine, Harris, isn't it?" he said. "Now, light up all the burners on both chandeliers. Harris, give a rub to that thistle leaf, will you? It's sort of dull." Harris looked at his swollen thumb. "Aw', now, Mr. Blair," he began. "Did you hear what I said?" Blair said, icily—and the leaf was polished! Blair looked at it critically, then laughed and tossed the old man a dollar. "There's some sticking-plaster for you. And Harris, look here: those things—the finger-bowls; don't go and get mixed up on 'em, will you? They come last." Harris put his thumb in his mouth; "I never seen dishes like that," he mumbled doubtfully; "the police didn't have 'em."

"It's the fashion," Blair explained; "Mrs. Richie has them, and I've seen them at swell hotels. Most people don't eat in an office," he ended, with a curl of his handsome lip.

It was while he was fussing about, whistling or singing, altering the angle of a spoon here or the position of a wine-glass there, that his mother came in. She had put on her Sunday black silk, and she had even added a lace collar and a shell cameo pin; she was knitting busily, the ball of pink worsted tucked under one arm. There was a sort of grim amusement, tempered by patience, in her face. To have supper at seven o'clock, and call it "dinner"; to load the table with more food than anybody could eat, and much of it stuff that didn't give the stomach any honest work to do—"like that truck," she said, pointing an amused knitting-needle at the olives—was nonsense. But Blair was young; he would get over his foolishness when he got into business. Meantime, let him be foolish! "I suppose he thinks he's the grand high cockalorum!" she told herself, chuckling. Aloud she said, with rough jocosity:

"What in the world is the good of all those flowers? A supper table is a place for food, not fiddle-faddle!"

Blair reddened sharply. "There are people," he began, in that voice of restrained irritation which is veiled by sarcastic politeness —"there are people, my dear mother, who think of something else than filling their stomachs." Mrs. Maitland's eye had left the dinner table, and was raking her son from head to foot. He was very handsome, this sixteen-year-old boy, standing tall and graceful in his new clothes, which, indeed, he wore easily, in spite of his excitement at their newness.

"Well!" she said, sweeping him with a glance. Her face glowed; "I wish his father could have lived to see him," she thought; she put out her hand and touched his shoulder. "Turn round here till I look at you! Well, well! I suppose you're enjoying those togs you've got on?" Her voice was suddenly raucous with pride; if she had known how, she would have kissed him. Instead she said, with loud cheerfulness: "Well, my son, which is the head of the table? Where am I to sit?"

"*Mother!*" Blair said. He turned quite white. He went over to the improvised serving-table, and picked up a fork with a trembling hand; put it down again, and turned to look at her. Yes; she was all dressed up! He groaned under his breath. The tears actually stood in his eyes. "I thought," he said, and stopped to clear his voice, "I didn't know—"

"What's the matter with you?" Mrs. Maitland asked, looking at him over her spectacles.

"I didn't suppose you would be willing to come," Blair said, miserably.

"Oh, I don't mind," she said, kindly; "I'll stick it out for an hour."

Blair ground his teeth. Harris, pulling on a very large pair of white cotton gloves—thus did he live up to the standards of the policemen's ball—came shuffling across the hall, and his aghast expression when he caught sight of Mrs. Maitland was a faint consolation to the despairing boy.

"Here! Harris! have you got places enough?" Mrs. Maitland said. "Blair, have you counted noses? Mrs. Richie's coming, and Mr. Ferguson."

"Mrs. Richie!" In spite of his despair, Blair had an elated moment. He was devoted to David's mother, and there was some consolation in the fact that she would see that he knew how to do things decently! Then his anger burst out. "I didn't ask Mrs. Richie," he said, his voice trembling.

"What time is supper?" his mother interrupted, "I'm getting hungry!" She took her place at the head of the table, sitting a little sidewise, with one foot round the leg of her chair; she looked about impatiently, striking the table softly with her open hand—a hand always beautiful, and to-night clean. "What nonsense to have it so late!"

"It isn't supper," Blair said; "it's dinner; and—" But at that moment the door-bell saved the situation. Harris, stumbling with agitation, had retreated to his pantry, so Mrs. Maitland motioned to Blair. "Run and open the door for your friends," she said, kindly.

Blair did not "run," but he went; and if he could have killed those first-comers with a glance, he would have done so. As for Mrs. Maitland, still glowing with this new experience of taking part in her son's pleasure, she tramped into the front room to say how do you do and shake hands with two very shy young men, who were plainly awed by her presence. As the others came in, it was she who received them, standing on the hearth-rug, her back to the empty fireplace which Blair had filled with roses, all ready to welcome the timid youngsters, who in reply to her loud greetings stammered the commonplaces of the occasion.

"How are you, Elizabeth? What! a long dress? Well, well, you *are* getting to be a big girl! How are you, David? And so you have a swallowtail, too? Glad to see you, Mrs. Richie. Who's this? Harry Knight? Well, Harry, you are quite a big boy. I knew your stepmother when she was Molly Wharton, and not half your age."

Harry, who had a sense of humor, was able to laugh, but David was red with wrath, and Elizabeth tossed her head. As for Blair, he grew paler and paler.

Yet the dreadful dinner went off fairly smoothly. Mrs. Maitland sat down before anybody else. "Come, good people, come!" she said, and began her rapid "Bless, O Lord," while the rest of the company were still drawing up their chairs. "Amen, soup, Mrs. Richie?" she said, heartily. The ladling out of the soup was an outlet for her energy; and as Harris's ideals put all the dishes on the table at once, she was kept busy carving or helping, or, with the hospitable insistence of her generation, urging her guests to eat. Blair sat at the other end of the table in black silence. Once he looked at Mrs. Richie with an agonized gratitude in his beautiful eyes, like the gratitude of a hurt puppy lapping a friendly and helping hand; for Mrs. Richie, with the gentlest tact, tried to help him by ignoring him and talking to the young people about her. Elizabeth, too, endeavored to do her part by assuming (with furtive glances at David) a languid, young-lady-like manner, which would have made Blair chuckle at any less terrible moment. Even Mr. Ferguson, although still a little dazed by that encounter with his niece, came to the rescue—for the situation was, of course, patent—and talked to Mrs. Maitland; which, poor Blair thought, "at least shut her up"!

Mrs. Maitland was, of course perfectly unconscious that any one could wish to shut her up; she did not feel anything unusual in the atmosphere, and she was astonishingly patient with all the stuff and nonsense. Once she did strike the call-bell, which she had bidden Harris to bring from the office table, and say, loudly: "Make haste, Harris! Make haste! What is all this delay?" The delay was Harris's agitated endeavor to refresh his memory about "them basins."

"Is it *now*?" he whispered to Blair, furtively rubbing his thumb on the shiny seam of his trousers. Blair, looking a little sick, whispered back:

"Oh, throw 'em out of the window."

"Aw', now, Mr. Blair," poor Harris protested, "I clean forgot;

is it with these here tomatoes, or with the dessert?"

"Go to the devil!" Blair said, under his breath. And the finger-bowls appeared with the salad.

"What's this nonsense?" Mrs. Maitland demanded; then, realizing Blair's effort, she picked up a finger-bowl and looked at it, cocking an amused eyebrow. "Well, Blair," she said, with loud good nature, "we are putting on airs!"

Blair pretended not to hear. For the whole of that appalling experience he had nothing to say—even to Elizabeth, sitting beside him in the new white dress, the spun silk of her brown hair shimmering in the amazing glitter of the great cut-glass chandelier. The other young people, glancing with alarmed eyes now at Blair, and now at his mother, followed their host's example of silence. Mrs. Maitland, however, did her duty as she saw it; she asked condescending questions as to "how you children amuse yourselves," and she made her crude jokes at everybody's expense, with side remarks to Robert Ferguson about their families: "That Knight boy is Molly Wharton's stepson; he looks like his father. Old Knight is an elder in The First Church; he hands round the hat for other people to put their money in—never gives anything himself. I always call his wife 'goose Molly.' ... Is that young Clayton, Tom Clayton's son? He looks as if he had some gumption; Tom was always Mr. Doestick's friend. ... I suppose you know that that West boy's grandmother wasn't sure who his grandfather was? ... Mrs. Richie's a pretty woman, Friend Ferguson; where are your eyes!" ...

When it was over, that terrible thirty minutes—for Mrs. Maitland drove
Harris at full speed through all Blair's elaborations—it was Mrs.
Richie who came to the rescue.

"Mrs. Maitland," she said, "sha'n't you and I and Mr. Ferguson go and talk in your room, and leave the young people to amuse themselves?" And Mrs. Maitland's quick agreement showed how relieved she was to get through with all the "nonsense."

When their elders had left them, the "young people" drew a long breath and looked at one another. Nannie, almost in tears, tried to make some whispered explanation to Blair, but he turned his back on her. David, with a carefully blase air, said, "Bully dinner, old man." Blair gave him a look, and David subsided. When the guests began a chatter of relief, Blair still stood apart in burning silence. He wished he need never see or speak to any of them again. He hated them all; he hated—But he did not finish this, even in his thoughts.

When the others had recovered their spirits, and Nannie had begun to play on the piano, and somebody had suggested that they should all sing—"And then let's dance!" cried Elizabeth—Blair disappeared. Out in the hall, standing with clenched hands in the dim light, he said to himself he wished they would all clear out! "I am sick of the whole darned business; I wish they'd clear out!"

It was there that Elizabeth found him. She had forgotten her displeasure at David, and was wildly happy; but she had missed Blair, and had come, in a dancing whirl of excitement, to find him. "What are you doing? Come right back to the parlor!"

Blair, turning, saw the smooth cheek, pink as the curve of a shell, the soft hair's bronze sheen, the amber darkness of the happy eyes. "Oh, Elizabeth!" he said, and actually sobbed.

"Blair! What *is* the matter?"

"It was disgusting, the whole thing."

"What was disgusting?"

"That awful dinner—"

"Awful? You are perfectly crazy! It was lovely! What are you talking about?" In her dismayed defense of her first social function, she put her hands on his arm and shook it. "Why! It is the first dinner I ever went to in all my life; and look: six-button gloves! What do you think of that? Uncle told Cherry-pie I could have whatever was proper, and I got these lovely gloves. They are awfully fashionable!" She pulled one glove up, not only to get its utmost length, but also to cover that scar which her fierce little teeth had made so long ago. "Oh, Blair, it really was a perfectly *beautiful*dinner," she said, earnestly.

She was so close to him that it seemed as if the color on her cheek burned against his, and he could smell the rose in her brown hair. "Oh, Elizabeth," he said, panting, "you are an angel!"

"It was simply lovely!" she declared. In her excitement she did not notice that new word. Blair trembled; he could not speak. "Come right straight back!" Elizabeth said; "please! Everybody will have a perfectly splendid time, if you'll just come back. We want you to sing. Please!" The long, sweet corners of her eyes implored him.

"Elizabeth," Blair whispered, "I—I love you."

Elizabeth caught her breath; then the exquisite color streamed over her face. "Oh!" she said faintly, and swerved away from him. Blair came a step nearer. They were both silent. Elizabeth put her hand over her lips, and stared at him with half-frightened eyes. Then Blair:

"Do you care, a little, Elizabeth?"

"We must go back to the parlor," she said, breathing quickly.

"Elizabeth, *do* you?"

"Oh—Blair!"

"Please, Elizabeth," Blair said; and putting his arms round her very gently, he kissed her cheek.

Elizabeth looked at him speechlessly; then, with a lovely movement, came nestling against him. A minute later they drew apart; the girl's face was quivering with light and mystery, the young man's face was amazed. Then amazement changed to triumph, and triumph to power, and power to something else, something that made

Elizabeth shrink and utter a little cry. In an instant he caught her violently to him and kissed her—kissed the scar on her upraised, fending arm, then her neck, her eyes, her mouth, holding her so that she cried out and struggled; and as he let her go, she burst out crying. "Oh—oh—*oh*—" she said; and darting from him, ran up-stairs, stumbling on the unaccustomed length of her skirt and catching at the banisters to keep from falling. But at the head of the stairs she paused; the tears had burned off in flashing excitement. She hesitated; it seemed as if she would turn and come back to him. But when he made a motion to bound up after her, she smiled and fled, and he heard the door of Nannie's room bang and the key turn in the lock.

Blair Maitland stood looking after her; in that one hot instant boyishness had been swept out of his face.

Chapter 5

"They have all suddenly grown up!" Mrs. Richie said, disconsolately. She had left the "party" early, without waiting for her carriage, because Mrs. Maitland's impatient glances at her desk had been an unmistakable dismissal.

"I will walk home with you," Robert Ferguson said.

"Aren't you going to wait for Elizabeth?"

"David will bring her home."

"He'll be only too glad of the chance; how pretty she was to-night! You must have been very proud of her."

"Not in the least. Beauty isn't a thing to be proud of. Quite the contrary."

Mrs. Richie laughed: "You are hopeless, Mr. Ferguson! What is a girl for, if not to be sweet and pretty and charming? And Elizabeth is all three."

"I would rather have her good."

"But prettiness doesn't interfere with goodness! And Elizabeth is a dear, good child."

"I hope she is," he said

"You *know* she is," she declared.

"Well, she has her good points," he admitted; and put his hand up to his lean cheek as if he still felt the flower-like touch of Elizabeth's lips.

"But they have all grown up," Mrs. Richie said. "Mr. Ferguson, David wants to smoke! What shall I do?"

"Good heavens! hasn't he smoked by this time?" said Robert Ferguson, horrified. "You'll ruin that boy yet!"

"Oh, when he was a little boy, there was one awful day, when — " Mrs. Richie shuddered at the remembrance; "but now he wants to really smoke, you know."

"He's seventeen," Mr. Ferguson said, severely. "I should think you might cut the apron-strings by this time."

"You seem very anxious about apron-strings for David," she retorted with some spirit. "I notice you never show any anxiety about Blair."

At which her landlord laughed loudly: "I should say not! He's been brought up by a man—practically." Then he added with some generosity, "But I'm not sure that an apron-string or two might not have been a good thing for Blair."

Mrs. Richie accepted the amend good-naturedly. "My tall David is very nice, even if he does want to smoke. But I've lost my boy."

"He'll be a boy," Robert Ferguson said, "until he makes an ass of himself by falling in love. Then, in one minute, he'll turn into a man. I—" he paused, and laughed: "I was twenty, just out of college, when I made an ass of myself over a girl who was as vain as a peacock. Well, she was beautiful; I admit that."

"You were very young," Mrs. Richie said gravely; the emotion behind his careless words was obvious. They walked along in silence for several minutes. Then he said, contemptuously:

"She threw me over. Good riddance, of course."

"If she was capable of treating you badly, of course it was well to have her do so—in time," she agreed; "but I suppose those things cut deep with a boy," she added gently. She had a maternal instinct to put out a comforting hand, and say "never mind." Poor man! because, when he was twenty a girl had jilted him, he was still, at over forty, defending a sensitive heart by an armor of surliness. "Won't you come in?" she said, when they reached her door; she smiled at him, with her pleasant leaf-brown eyes,—eyes which were less sad, he thought, than when she first came to Mercer. ("Getting over her husband's death, I suppose," he said to himself. "Well, she has looked mournful longer than most widows!")

He followed her into the house silently, and, sitting down on her little sofa, took a cigar out of his pocket. He began to bite off the end absently, then remembered to say, "May I smoke?"

The room was cool and full of the fragrance of white lilies. Mr. Ferguson had planted a whole row of lilies against the southern wall of Mrs. Richie's garden. "Such things are attractive to tenants; I find it improves my property," he had explained to her, when she found him grubbing, unasked, in her back yard. He looked now, approvingly at the jug of lilies that had replaced the grate in the fireplace; but Mrs. Richie looked at the clock. She was tired, and sometimes her good neighbor stayed very late.

"Poor Blair!" she said. "I'm afraid his dinner was rather a disappointment. What charming manners he has," she added, meditatively; "I think it is very remarkable, considering—"

Mr. Ferguson knocked off his glasses. "Mrs. Maitland's manners may not be as—as fine-ladyish as some people's, I grant you," he said, "but I can tell you, she has more brains in her little finger than—"

"Than I have in my whole body?" Mrs. Richie interrupted gaily; "I know just what you were going to say."

"No, I wasn't," he defended himself; but he laughed and stopped barking.

"It is what you thought," she said; "but let me tell you, I admire Mrs.
Maitland just as much as you do."

"No, you don't, because you can't," he said crossly; but he smiled. He could not help forgiving Mrs. Richie, even when she did not seem to appreciate Mrs. Maitland—the one subject on which the two neighbors fell out. But after the smile he sighed, and apparently forgot Mrs. Maitland. He scratched a match, held it absently until it scorched his fingers; blew it out, and tossed it into the lilies; Mrs. Richie winced, but Mr. Ferguson did not notice her; he leaned forward, his hands between his knees, the unlighted cigar in his fingers: "Yes; she threw me over."

For a wild moment Mrs. Richie thought he meant Mrs. Maitland; then she remembered. "It was very hard for you," she said vaguely.

"And Elizabeth's mother," he went on, "my brother Arthur's wife, left him. He never got over the despair of it. He—killed himself."

Mrs. Richie's vagueness was all gone. "Mr. Ferguson!"

"She was bad—all through."

"Oh, *no*!" Helena Richie said faintly.

"She left him, for another man. Just as the girl I believed in left me. I would have doubted my God, Mrs. Richie, before I could have doubted that girl. And when she jilted me, I suppose I did doubt Him for a while. At any rate, I doubted everybody else. I do still, more or less."

Mrs. Richie was silent.

"We two brothers—the same thing happened to both of us! It was worse for him than for me; I escaped, as you might say, and I learned a valuable lesson; I have never built on anybody. Life doesn't play the same trick on me twice. But Arthur was different. He was of softer stuff. You'd have liked my brother Arthur. Yes; he was too good to her—that was the trouble. If he had beaten her once or twice, I don't believe she would have behaved as she did. Imagine leaving a good husband, a devoted husband—"

"What I can't imagine," Helena Richie said, in a low voice, "is leaving a living child. *That* seems to me impossible."

"The man married her after Arthur—died," he went on; "I

guess she paid the piper in her life with him! I hope she did. Oh, well; she's dead now; I mustn't talk about her. But Elizabeth has her blood in her; and she is pretty, just as she was. She looks like her, sometimes. There—now you know. Now you understand why I worry so about her. I used to wish she would die before she grew up. I tried to do my duty to her, but I hoped she would die. Yet she seems to be a good little thing. Yes, I'm pretty sure she is a good little thing. To-night, before we went to the dinner, she—she behaved very prettily. But if I saw her mother in her, I would—God knows what I would do! But except for this fussing about clothes, she seems all right. You know she wanted a locket once? But you think that is only natural to a girl? Not a vanity that I need to be anxious about? Her mother was vain—a shallow, selfish theatrical creature!" He looked at her with worried eyes. "I am dreadfully anxious, sometimes," he said simply.

"There's nothing to be anxious about," she said, in a smothered voice, "nothing at all."

"Of course I'm fond of her," he confessed, "but I am never sure of her."

"You ought to be sure of her," Mrs. Richie said; "her little vanities—why, it is just natural for a girl to want pretty dresses! But to think—Poor little Elizabeth!" She hid her face in her hands; "and poor bad mother," she said, in a whisper.

"Don't pity *her*! She was not the one to pity. It was Arthur who—" He left the sentence unfinished; his face quivered.

"Oh," she cried, "you are all wrong. She is the one to pity, I don't care how selfish and shallow she was! As for your brother, he just died. What was dying, compared to living? Oh, you don't understand. Poor bad women! You might at least be sorry for them. How can you be so hard?"

"I suppose I am hard," he said, half wonderingly, but very

meekly; "when a good woman can pity Dora—that was her name; who am I to judge her? I'll try not to be so hard," he promised.

He had risen. Mrs. Richie tried to speak, but stopped and caught her breath at the bang of the front door.

"It's David!" she said, in a terrified voice. Her face was very pale, so pale that David, coming abruptly into the room, stood still in his tracks, aghast.

"Why, Materna! What's up? Mother, something is the matter!"

"It's my fault, David," Robert Ferguson said, abashed. "I was telling your mother a—a sad story. Mrs. Richie, I didn't realize it would pain you. Your mother is a very kind woman, David; she's been sympathizing with other people's troubles."

David, looking at him resentfully, came and stood beside her, with an aggressively protecting manner. "I don't see why she need bother about other people's troubles. Say, Materna, I—I wouldn't feel badly. Mr. Ferguson, I—you—" he blustered; he was very much perturbed.

The fact was David was not in an amiable humor; Elizabeth had been very queer all the way home. "High and mighty!" David said to himself; treating him as if he were a little boy, and she a young lady! "And I'm seventeen—the idea of her putting on such airs!" And now here was her uncle making his mother low-spirited. "Materna, I wouldn't bother," he comforted her.

Mrs. Richie put a soothing hand on his arm. "Never mind," she said; she was still pale, "Yes, it was a sad story. But I thank you for telling me, Mr. Ferguson."

He tried awkwardly to apologize for having distressed her, and then took himself off. When he opened his own door, even before he closed it again, he called out, "Miss White!"

"Yes, sir?" said the little governess, peering rabbit-like from the parlor.

"Miss White, I've been thinking; I'm going to buy Elizabeth a piece of jewelry; a locket, I think. You can tell her so. Mrs. Richie says she's quite sure she isn't really vain in wanting such things."

"I have been at my post, sir, since Elizabeth was three years old," Miss White said with spirit, "and I have frequently told you that she was not vain. I'll go and tell her what you say, immejetly!"

But when Cherry-pie went to carry the great news she found Elizabeth's door locked.

"What? Uncle is going to give me a locket?" Elizabeth called out in answer to her knock. "Oh, joy! Splendid!"

"Let me in, and I'll tell you what he said," Miss White called back.

"No! I can't!" cried the joyous young voice. "I'm busy!"

She was busy; she was holding a lamp above her head, and looking at herself in the mirror over the mantelpiece. Her hair was down, tumbling in a shining mass over her shoulders, her eyes were like stars, her cheeks rose-red. She was turning her white neck from side to side, throwing her head backward, looking at herself through half-shut eyes; her mouth was scarlet. "Blair is in love with me!" she said to herself. She felt his last kiss still on her mouth; she felt it until it seemed as if her lip bled.

"David Richie needn't talk about 'little girls' any more. *I'm engaged!*" She put the lamp down on the mantelpiece, shook her mane of hair back over her bare shoulders, and then, her hands on her hips, her short petticoat ruffling about her knees, she began to dance. "Somebody is in love with me!

"'Oh, isn't it joyful, joyful, joyful—'"

Chapter 6

When the company had gone,—"I thought they never *would* go!" Nannie said—she rushed at her brother. "Blair!"

The boy flung up his head proudly. "She told you, did she?"

"You're engaged!" cried Nannie, ecstatically.

Blair started. "Why!" he said. "So I am! I never thought of it." And when he got his breath, the radiant darkness of his eyes sparkled into laughter. "Yes, *I'm engaged!*" He put his hands into his pockets and strutted the length of the room; a minute later he stopped beside the piano and struck a triumphant chord; then he sat down and began to play uproariously, singing to a crashing accompaniment:

"'... lived a miner, a forty-niner, With his daughter Clementine! Oh my darling, oh my *darling*—'"

—the riotous, beautiful voice rang on, the sound overflowing through the long rooms, across the hall, even into the dining-room. Harris, wiping dishes in the pantry, stopped, tea-towel in hand, and listened; Sarah Maitland, at her desk, lifted her head, and the pen slipped from her fingers. Blair, spinning around on the piano-stool, caught his sister about her waist in a hug that made her squeak. Then they both shrieked with laughter.

"But Blair!" Nannie said, getting her breath; "shall you tell Mamma to-night?"

Blair's face dropped. "I guess I won't tell anybody yet," he faltered; "oh, that awful dinner!"

As the mortification of an hour ago surged back upon him, he added to the fear of telling his mother a resentment that would retaliate by secrecy. "I won't tell her at all," he decided; "and don't you, either."

"I!" said Nannie. "Well, I should think not. Gracious!"

But though Blair did not tell his mother, he could not keep the great news to himself; he saw David the next afternoon, and overflowed.

David took it with a gasp of silence, as if he had been suddenly hit below the belt; then in a low voice he said, "You—*kissed* her. Did she kiss you?"

Blair nodded. He held his head high, balancing it a little from side to side; his lips were thrust out, his eyes shone. He was standing with his feet well apart, his hands deep in his pockets; he laughed, reddening to his forehead, but he was not embarrassed. For once David's old look of silent, friendly admiration did not answer him; instead there was half-bewildered dismay. David wanted to protest that it wasn't—well, it wasn't *fair*. He did not say it; and in not saying it he ceased to be a boy.

"I suppose it was when you and she went off after dinner? You needn't have been so darned quiet about it! What's the good of being so—mum about everything? Why didn't you come back and tell? You're not ashamed of it, are you?"

"A man doesn't tell a thing like that," Blair said scornfully.

"Well!" David snorted, "I suppose some time you'll be married?"

Blair nodded again. "Right off."

"Huh!" said David; "your mother won't let you. You are only sixteen.
Don't be an ass."

"I'll be seventeen next May."

"Seventeen! What's seventeen? I'm pretty near eighteen, and I haven't thought of being married;—at least to anybody in particular."

"You couldn't," Blair said coldly; "you haven't got the cash."

David chewed this bitter fact in silence; then he said, "I

thought you and Elizabeth were kind of off at dinner. You didn't talk to each other at all. I thought you were both huffy; and instead of that—" David paused.

"That damned dinner!" Blair said, dropping his love-affair for his grievance. Blair's toga virilis, assumed in that hot moment in the hall, was profanity of sorts. "David, I'm going to clear out. I can't stand this sort of thing. I'll go and live at a hotel till I go to college; I'll—"

"Thought you were going to get married?" David interrupted him viciously.

Blair looked at him, and suddenly understood,—David was jealous! "Gorry!" he said blankly. He was honestly dismayed. "Look here," he began, "I didn't know that *you*—"

"I don't know what you're talking about," David broke in contemptuously; "if you think *I* care, one way or the other, you're mistaken. It's nothing to me. 'By"; and he turned on his heel.

It was a hot July afternoon; the sun-baked street along which they had been walking was deep with black dust and full of the clamor of traffic. Four big gray Flemish horses, straining against their breastplates, were hauling a dray loaded with clattering iron rods; the sound, familiar enough to any Mercer boy, seemed to David at that moment intolerable. "I'll get out of this cursed noise," he said to himself, and turned down a narrow street toward the river. It occurred to him that he would go over the covered bridge, and maybe stop and get a tumbler of ice-cream at Mrs. Todd's. Then he would strike out into the country and take a walk; he had nothing else to do. This vacation business wasn't all it was cracked up to be; a man had better fun at school; he was sick of Mercer, anyhow.

He had reached Mrs. Todd's saloon by that time, and through the white palings of the fence he had glimpses of happy couples sitting at marble-topped tables among the marigolds and coreopsis, taking slow, delicious spoonfuls of ice-cream, and gazing at each other with languishing eyes. David felt a qualm of disgust; for the first time in his life he had no desire for ice-cream. A boy like Blair might find it pleasant to eat ice-cream with a lot of fellows and girls out in the garden of a toll-house, with people looking in through the palings; but he had outgrown such things. The idea of Blair, at his age, talking about being in love! Blair didn't know what *love* meant. And as for Elizabeth, how could she fall in love with Blair? He was two months younger than she, to begin with. "No woman ought to marry a man younger than she is," David said; he himself, he reflected, was much older than Elizabeth. That was how it ought to be. The girl should always be younger than the fellow. And anyway, Blair wasn't the kind of man for a girl like Elizabeth to marry. "He wouldn't understand her. Elizabeth goes off at half-cock sometimes, and Blair wouldn't know how to handle her. I understand her, perfectly. Besides that, he's too selfish. A woman ought not to marry a selfish man," said David. However, it made no difference to him whom she married. If Elizabeth liked that sort of thing, if she found Blair—who was only a baby anyhow—the kind of man she could love, why then he was disappointed in Elizabeth. That was all. He was not jealous, or anything like that; he was just disappointed; he was sorry that Elizabeth was that kind of girl. "Very, very sorry," David said to himself; and his eyes stung…. (Ah, well; one may smile; but the pangs are real enough to the calf! The trouble with us is we have forgotten our own pangs, so we doubt his.) … Yes, David was sorry; but the whole darned business was nothing to him, because, unlike Blair, he was not a boy, and he could not waste time over women; he had his future to think of. In fact, he felt that to make the most of himself he must never marry.

Then suddenly these bitter forecastings ceased. He had come upon some boys who were throwing stones at the dust-grimed windows of an unused foundry shed. Along the roof of the big, gaunt building, dilapidated and deserted, was a vast line of lights that had long been a target for every boy who could pick up a pebble. Glass lay in splinters on the slope of sheet-iron below the sashes, and one could look in through yawning holes at silent, shadowy spaces that had once roared with light from swinging ladles and flowing cupolas; but there were a few whole panes left yet. At the sound of crashing glass, David, being a human boy, stopped and looked on, at first with his hands in his pockets; then he picked up a stone himself. A minute later he was yelling and smashing with the rest of them; but when he had broken a couple of lights, curiously enough, desire failed; he felt a sudden distaste for breaking windows,—and for everything else! It was a sort of spiritual nausea, and life was black and bitter on his tongue. He was conscious of an actual sinking below his breast-bone. "I'm probably coming down with brain fever," he told himself; and he had a happy moment of thinking how wretched everybody would be when he died. Elizabeth would be *very* wretched! David felt a wave of comfort, and on the impulse of expected death, he turned toward home again…. However, if he should by any chance recover, marriage was not for him. It occurred to him that this would be a bitter surprise to Elizabeth, whose engagement would of course be broken as soon as she heard of his illness; and again he felt happier. No, he would never marry. He would give his life to his profession— it had long ago been decided that David was to be a doctor. But it would be a lonely life. He looked ahead and saw himself a great physician—no common doctor, like that old Doctor King who came sometimes to see his mother; but a great man, dying nobly in some awful epidemic. When Elizabeth heard of his magnificent courage, she'd feel pretty badly. Rather different from Blair. How much finer than to be merely looking forward to a lot of money that somebody else had made! But perhaps that was why Elizabeth liked Blair;

because he was going to have money? And yet, how could she compare Blair with,—well, *any* fellow who meant to work his own way? Here David touched bottom abruptly. "How can a fellow take money he hasn't earned?" he said to himself. David's feeling about independence was unusual in a boy of his years, and it was not altogether admirable; it was, in fact, one of those qualities that is a virtue, unless it becomes a vice.

When he was half-way across the bridge, he stopped to look down at the slow, turbid river rolling below him. He stood there a long time, leaning on the hand-rail. On the dun surface a sheen of oil gathered, and spread, and gathered again. He could hear the wash of the current, and in the railing under his hand he felt the old wooden structure thrill and quiver in the constant surge of water against the pier below him. The sun, a blood-red disk, was slipping into the deepening haze, and on either side of the river the city was darkening into dusk. All along the shore lights were pricking out of the twilight and sending wavering shafts down into the water. The coiling smoke from furnace chimneys lay level and almost motionless in the still air; sometimes it was shot with sparks, or showed, on its bellying black curves, red gleams from hidden fires below.

David, staring at the river with absent, angry eyes, stopped his miserable thoughts to watch a steamboat coming down the current. Its smoke-stacks were folded back for passing under the bridge, and its great paddlewheel scarcely moved except to get steerageway. It was pushing a dozen rafts, all lashed together into a spreading sheet. The smell of the fresh planks pierced the acrid odor of soot that was settling down with the night mists. On one of the rafts was a shanty of newly sawed pine boards; it had no windows, but it was evidently a home, for a stove-pipe came through its roof, and there was a woman sitting in its little doorway, nursing her baby. David, looking down, saw the downy head, and a little crumpled fist lying on the white, bare breast. The woman, looking up as they floated below him, caught his eye, and drew her blue cotton dress across her bosom. David suddenly put his hand over his lips to hide their quiver. The abrupt tears were on his cheeks. "Oh—*Elizabeth*!" he said. The revolt, the anger, the jealousy, were all gone. He sobbed under his breath. He had forgotten that he had said it made no difference to him,—"not the slightest difference." It did make a difference! All the difference in the world.... "Oh, Elizabeth!"... The barges had slid farther and farther under the bridge; the woman and the child were out of sight; the steamboat with its folded smoke-stacks slid after them, leaving a wake of rocking, yellow foam; the water splashed loudly against the piers. It was nearly dark there on the footpath, and quite deserted. David put his head down on his arms on the railing and stood motionless for a long moment.

When he reached home, he found his mother in the twilight, in the little garden behind the house. David, standing behind her, said carelessly, "I have some news for you, Materna."

"Yes?" she said, absorbed in pinching back her lemon verbena.

"Blair is—is spoony over Elizabeth. Here, I'll snip that thing for you."

Mrs. Richie faced him in amazement. "What! Why, but they are both children, and—" she stopped, and looked at him. "Oh—*David!*" she said.

And the boy, forgetting the spying windows of the opposite houses, dropped his head on her shoulder. "Materna—Materna," he said, in a stifled voice.

Chapter 7

Nobody except David took the childish love-affair very seriously, not even the principals—especially not Elizabeth... .

David did not see her for a day or two, except out of the corner of his eye when, during the new and still secret rite of shaving —for David was willing to shed his blood to prove that he was a man —he looked out of his bedroom window and saw her down in the garden helping her uncle feed his pigeons. He did not want to see her. He was younger than his years, this honest-eyed, inexpressive fellow of seventeen, but for all his youth he was hard hit. He grew abruptly older that first week; he didn't sleep well; he even looked a little pale under his freckles, and his mother worried over his appetite. When she asked him what was the matter, he said, listlessly, "Nothing." They were very intimate friends these two, but that moment on the bridge marked the beginning of the period—known to all mothers of sons—of the boy's temporary retreat into himself... . When a day or two later David saw Elizabeth, or rather when she, picking a bunch of heliotrope in her garden, saw him through the open door in the wall, and called to him to come "right over! as fast as your legs can carry you!"—he was, she thought, "very queer." He came in answer to the summons, but he had nothing to say. She, however, was bubbling over with talk. She took his hand, and, running with him into the arbor, pulled him down on the seat beside her.

"David! Where on earth have you been all this time? David, *have you heard?*"

"I suppose you mean—about you and Blair?" he said. He did not look at her, but he watched a pencil of sunshine, piercing the leaves overhead, faintly gilding the bunches of green grapes that had a film of soot on their greenness, and then creeping down to rest on the heliotrope in her lap.

"Yes!" said Elizabeth. "Isn't it the most exciting thing you ever heard? David, I want to show you something." She peered out through the leaves to make sure that they were unobserved. "It's a terrific secret!" she said, her eyes dancing. Her fingers were at her throat, fumbling with the fastening of her dress, which caught, and had to be pulled open with a jerk; then she drew half-way from her young bosom a ring hanging on a black silk thread. She bent forward a little, so that he might see it. "I keep it down in there so Cherry-pie won't know," she whispered. "*Look!*"

David looked—and looked away.

Elizabeth, with a blissful sigh, dropped the ring back again into the warm whiteness of that secret place. "Isn't it perfectly lovely? It's my engagement ring! I'm so excited!"

David was silent.

"Why, David Richie! You don't care a bit!"

"Why, yes, I do," he said. He took a grape from a bunch beside him, rubbed the soot off on his trousers, and ate it; then blinked wryly. "Gorry, that's sour."

"You—don't—like—my engagement!" Elizabeth declared slowly. Reproachful tears stood in her eyes; she fastened her dress with indignant fingers. "I think you are perfectly horrid not to be sympathetic. It's very important to a girl to get engaged and have a ring."

"It's very pretty," David managed to say.

"Pretty? I should say it was pretty! It cost fifty dollars! Blair said so. David, what on earth is the matter! Don't you like me being engaged?"

"Oh, it's all right," he evaded. He shut his eyes, which were still watering from that sour grape, but even with closed eyes he saw again that soft place where Blair's ring hung, warm and secret; the pain below his own breast-bone was very bad for a minute, and the hot fragrance of the heliotrope seemed overpowering. He swallowed hard, then looked at one of Mr. Ferguson's pigeons, walking almost into the arbor. The pigeon stopped, hesitated, cocked a ruby eye on the two humans on the wooden seat, and fluttered back into the sunny garden.

"Why, you *mind*!" Elizabeth said, aghast.

"Oh, it's nothing to me," David managed to say; "course, I don't care. Only I didn't know you liked Blair so much; so it was a—a surprise," he said miserably.

Elizabeth's consternation was beyond words. There was a perceptible moment before she could find anything to say. "Why, I never dreamed you'd mind! David, truly, I like you best of any boy I know;—only, of course now, being engaged to Blair, I have to like him best?"

"Yes that's so," David admitted.

"Truly, I like you dreadfully, David. If I'd supposed you'd mind—But, oh, David, it's so interesting to be engaged. I really can't stop. I'd have to give him back my ring!" she said in an agonized voice. She pressed her hand against her breast, and poor David's eyes followed the ardent gesture.

"It's all right," he said with a gulp.

Elizabeth was ready to cry; she dropped her head on his shoulder and began to bemoan herself. "Why on earth didn't you *say* something? How could I know? How stupid you are, David! If I'd known you minded, I'd just as lief have been engaged to—" Elizabeth stopped short. She sat up very straight, and put her hand to the neck of her dress to make sure it was fastened. At that moment a new sense was born in her; for the first time since they had known each other, her straightforward eyes—the sexless eyes of a child—faltered, and refused to meet David's. "I think maybe Cherry-pie wants me now," she said shyly, and slipped away, leaving David mournfully eating green grapes in the arbor. This was the last time that Elizabeth, uninvited, put her head on a boy's shoulder.

A week later she confided to Miss White the great fact of her engagement; but she was not so excited about it by that time. For one thing, she had received her uncle's present of a locket, so the ring was not her only piece of jewelry; and besides that, since her talk with David, being "engaged" had seemed less interesting. However, Miss White felt it her duty to drop a hint of what had happened to Mr. Ferguson: had it struck him that perhaps Blair Maitland was—was thinking about Elizabeth?

"Thinking what about her?" Mr. Ferguson said, lifting his head from his papers with a fretted look.

"Why," said Miss White, "as I am always at my post, sir, I have opportunities for observing; in fact, I shouldn't wonder if they were—attached." Cherry-pie would have felt that a more definite word was indelicate. "Of course I don't exactly *know* it," said Miss White, faithful to Elizabeth's confidence, "but I recall that when I was a young lady, young gentlemen did become attached—to other young ladies."

"Love-making? At her age? I won't have it!" said Robert Ferguson. The old, apprehensive look darkened in his face; his feeling for the child was so strangely shadowed by his fear that "Life would play another trick on him," and Elizabeth would disappoint him some way, that he could not take Cherry-pie's information with any appreciation of its humor. "Send her to me," he said.

"Mr. Ferguson," poor old Miss White ventured, "if I might suggest, it would be well to be very kind, because—"

"Kind?" said Robert Ferguson, astonished; he gave an angry thrust at the black ribbon of his glasses that brought them tumbling from his nose. "Was I unkind? I will see her in the library after supper."

Miss White nibbled at him speechlessly. "If he is severe with her, I don't know what she *won't* do," she said to herself.

But Mr. Ferguson did not mean to be severe. When Elizabeth presented herself in his library, the interview began calmly enough. Her uncle was brief and to the point, but he was not unkind. She and Blair were too young to be engaged,—"Don't think of it again," he commanded.

Elizabeth looked tearful, but she did not resent his dictum;— David's lack of sympathy had been very dampening to romance. It was just at the end that the gunpowder flared.

"Now, remember, I don't want you to be foolish Elizabeth."

"I don't think being in love is foolish, Uncle."

"Love! What do you know about love? You are nothing but a silly little girl."

"I don't think I'm very little; and Blair is in love with me."

"Blair is as young and as foolish as you are. Even if you were older, I wouldn't allow it. He is selfish and irresponsible, and—"

"I think," interrupted Elizabeth, "that you are very mean to abuse Blair behind his back. It isn't fair." Her uncle was perfectly dumfounded; then he went into harsh reproof. Elizabeth grew whiter and whiter and the dimple in her cheek lengthened into a long, hairline. "I wish I didn't live with you. I wish my mother were alive. *She* would be good to me!"

"Your mother?" said Robert Ferguson; his involuntary grunt of cynical amusement touched the child like a whip. Her fury was appalling. She screamed at him that she hated him! She loved her mother! She was going to marry Blair the minute she was grown up! Then she whirled out of the room, almost knocking over poor old Miss White, whose "post" had been anxiously near the key-hole.

Up-stairs, her rage scared her governess nearly to death: "My lamb! You'll get overheated, and take cold. When I was a young lady, it was thought unrefined to speak so—emphatically. And your dear uncle didn't mean to be severe; he—"

'"Dear uncle'?" said Elizabeth, "dear devil! He hurt my feelings. He made fun of my mother!" As she spoke, she leaped at a photograph of Robert Ferguson which stood on her bureau, and, doubling her hand, struck the thin glass with all her force. It splintered, and the blood spurted from her cut knuckles on to her uncle's face.

Miss White began to cry. "Oh, my dear, my dear, try to control yourself, or you'll do something dreadful some day!" Cherry-pie's efforts to check Elizabeth's temper were like the protesting twitterings of a sparrow in a thunder-storm. When she reproved her now, the furious little creature, wincing and trying to check the bleeding with her handkerchief, did not even take the trouble to reply. Later, of course, the inevitable moment of penitence came; but it was not because she had lost her temper; loss of temper was always a trifling matter to Elizabeth; it was because she had been disrespectful to her uncle's picture. That night, when all the household was in bed, she slipped down-stairs, candle in hand, to the library. On the mantelpiece was a photograph of herself; she took it out of the frame, tore it into little bits, stamped on it, grinding her heel down on her own young face; then she took off the locket Mr. Ferguson had given her,—a most simple affair of pearls and turquoise; kissed it with passion, and looked about her: where should it be offered up? The ashes in the fireplace? No; the house-maid would find it there. Then she had an inspiration—the deep well of her uncle's battered old inkstand! Oh, to blacken the pearls, to stain the heavenly blue of the turquoise! It was almost too frightful. But it was right. She had hurt his feelings by saying she wished she didn't have to live with him, and she had insulted his dear, dear, *dear* picture! So, with a tearful hiccup, she dropped the locket into the ink-pot that stood between the feet of a spattered bronze Socrates, and watched it sink into a black and terrible grave. "I'm glad not to have it," she said, and felt that she had squared matters with her conscience.

As for Robert Ferguson, he did not notice that the photograph had disappeared, nor did he plunge his pen deep enough to find a pearl, nor understand the significance of the bound-up hand, but the old worry about her came back again. Her mother had defended her own wicked love-affair, with all the violence of a selfish woman; and in his panic of apprehension, poor little Elizabeth's defense of Blair seemed to be of the same nature. He was so worried over it that he was moved to do a very unwise thing. He would, he said to himself, put Mrs. Maitland on her guard about this nonsense between the two children.

The next morning when he went into her office at the Works, he found the place humming with business. As he entered he met a foreman, just taking his departure with, so to speak, his tail between his legs. The man was scarlet to his forehead under the lash of his employer's tongue. It had been administered in the inner room; but the door was open into the large office, and as Mrs. Maitland had not seen fit to modulate her voice, the clerks and some messenger-boys and a couple of traveling-men had had the benefit of it. Ferguson, reporting at that open door, was bidden curtly to come in and sit down. "I'll see you presently," she said, and burst out into the large office. Instantly the roomful of people, lounging about waiting their turn, came to attention. She rushed in among them like a gale, whirling away the straws and chaff before her, and leaving only the things that were worth while. She snapped a yellow envelope from a boy's hand, and even while she was ripping it open with a big forefinger, she was reading the card of an astonished traveling-man:

"No, sir; no, sir; your bid was one-half of one per cent, over Heintz. Your people been customers so long that they thought that I—? I never mix business and friendship!" She stood still long enough to run her eye over the drawing of a patent, and toss it back to the would-be inventor. "No, I don't care to take it up with you. Cast it for you? Certainly. I'll cast anything for anybody"; and the man found his blueprint in his hand before he could begin his explanation. "What? Johnson wants to know where to get the new housing to replace the one that broke yesterday? Tell Johnson that's what I pay him to decide. I have no time to do his business for him—my own is all I can attend to! Mr. Ferguson!" she called out, as she came banging back into the private office, "what about that ore that came in yesterday?" She sat down at her desk and listened intently to a somewhat intricate statement involving manufacturing matters dependent upon the quality of certain shipments of ore. Then, abruptly she gave her orders.

Robert Ferguson, making notes as rapidly as he could, smiled with satisfaction at the power of it all. It was as ruthless and as admirable as a force of nature. She would not pause, this woman, for flesh and blood; she was as impersonal as one of her own great shears that would bite off a "bloom" or a man's head with equal precision, and in doing so would be fulfilling the law of its being. Assuredly she would stop Blair's puppy-love in short order!

Business over, Sarah Maitland leaned back in her chair and laughed. "Did you hear me blowing Dale up? I guess he'll stay put for a while now! But I'm afraid I was angry," she confessed sheepishly; "and there is nothing on earth so foolish as to be angry at a fool."

"There is nothing on earth so irritating as a fool," he said.

"Yes, but it's absurd to waste your temper on 'em. I always say to myself, 'Sarah Maitland, if he had your brains, he'd have your job.' That generally keeps me cool; but I'm afraid I shall never learn to suffer Mr. Doestick's friends, gladly. Read your Bible, and you'll know where that comes from! I tell you, friend Ferguson, you ought to thank God every day that you weren't born a fool; and so ought I. Well what can I do for you?"

"I am bothered about Elizabeth and Blair."

She looked at him blankly for a moment. "Elizabeth? Blair? What about
Elizabeth and Blair?"

"It appears," Robert Ferguson said, and shoved the door shut with his foot, "it appears that there has been some love-making."

"Love-making?" she repeated, bewildered.

"Blair has been talking to Elizabeth," he explained. "I believe they call themselves engaged."

Mrs. Maitland flung her head back with a loud laugh. At the shock of such a sound in such a place, one of the clerks in the other room spun round on his stool, and Mrs. Maitland, catching sight of him through the glass partition, broke the laugh off in the middle. "Well, upon my word!" she said.

"Of course it's all nonsense, but it must be stopped."

"Why?" said Mrs. Maitland. And her superintendent felt a jar of astonishment.

"They are children."

"Blair is sixteen," his mother said thoughtfully; "if he thinks he is in love with Elizabeth, it will help to make a man of him. Furthermore, I'd rather have him make love than make pictures;— that is his last fancy," she said, frowning. "I don't know how he comes by it. Of course, my husband did paint sometimes, I admit; but he never wanted to make a business of it. He was no fool, I can tell you, if he did make pictures!"

Robert Ferguson said dryly that he didn't think she need

worry about Blair. "He has neither industry nor humility," he said, "and you can't be an artist without both of 'em. But as for this love business, they are children!"

Mrs. Maitland was not listening. "To be in love will be steadying him while he's at college. If he sticks to Elizabeth till he graduates, I sha'n't object."

"I shall object."

But she did not notice his protest.

"She has more temper than is quite comfortable," she ruminated; "but, after all, to a young man being engaged is like having a dog; one dog does as well as another; one girl does as well as another. And it isn't as if Blair had to consider whether his wife would be a 'good manager,' as they say; he'll have enough to waste, if he wants to. He'll have more than he knows what to do with!" There was a little proud bridling of her head. She, who had never wasted a cent in her life, had made it possible for her boy to be as wasteful as he pleased. "Yes," she said, with the quick decision which was so characteristic of her, "yes, he can have her."

"No, he can't," said Elizabeth's uncle.

"What?" she said, in frank surprise.

"Blair will have too much money. Inherited wealth is the biggest handicap a man can have."

"Too much money?" she chuckled; "your bearings are getting hot, ain't they? Come, come! I'm not so sure you need thank God. How can a man have too much money? That's nonsense!" She banged her hand down on the call-bell on her desk. "Evans! Bring me the drawings for those channels."

"I tell you I won't have it," Robert Ferguson repeated.

"I mean the blue-prints!" Mrs. Maitland commanded loudly; "you have no sense, Evans!" Ferguson got up; she had a way of not hearing when she was spoken to that made a man hot along his backbone. Robert Ferguson was hot, but he meant to have the last word; he paused at the door and looked back.

"I shall not allow it."

"Good-day, Mr. Ferguson," said his employer, deep in the blue-prints.

Chapter 8

Elizabeth's uncle need not have concerned himself so seriously about the affairs of Elizabeth's heart. The very next day the rift between the lovers began:

"What on earth have you done to your hand?" asked Blair.

"I cut it. I was angry at Uncle, and broke his picture, and—"

Blair shouted with laughter. "Oh, Elizabeth, what a goose you are! That's just the way you used to bite your arm when you were mad. You always did cut off your nose to spite your face! Where is your locket?"

"None of your business!" said Elizabeth savagely. It was easy to be savage with Blair, because David's lack of interest in her affairs had taken the zest out of "being engaged" in the most surprising way. But she had no intention of not being engaged! Romance was too flattering to self-love to be relinquished; nevertheless, after the first week or two she lapsed easily, in moments of forgetfulness, into the old matter-of-fact squabbling and the healthy unreasonableness natural to lifelong acquaintance. The only difference was that now, when she and Blair squabbled, they made up again in new ways; Blair, with gusts of what Elizabeth, annoyed and a little disgusted, called "silliness"; Elizabeth, with strange, half-scared, wholly joyous moments of conscious power. But the "making-up" was far less personal than the fallings-out; these, at least, meant individual antagonisms, whereas the reconciliations were something larger than the girl and boy—something which bore them on its current as a river bears straws upon its breast. But they played with that mighty current as thoughtlessly as all young creatures play with it. Elizabeth used to take her engagement ring from the silk thread about her neck, and, putting it on her finger, dance up and down her room, her right hand on her hip, her left stretched out before her so that she could see the sparkle of the tiny diamond on her third finger. "I'm engaged!" she would sing to herself.

"'Oh, isn't it joyful, joyful, joyful!'

"Blair's in love with me!" The words were so glorious that she rarely remembered to add, "I'm in love with Blair." The fact was, Blair was merely a necessary appendage to the joy of being engaged. When he irritated her by what she called "silliness," she was often frankly disagreeable to him.

As for Blair, he, too, had his ups and downs. He swaggered, and threw his shoulders back, and cast appraising eyes on women generally, and thought deeply on marriage. But of Elizabeth he thought very little. Because she was a girl, she bored him quite as often as he bored her. It was because she was a woman that there came those moments when he offended her; and in those moments she had but little personality to him. In fact, their love-affair, so far as they understood it, apart from its elemental impulses which they did not understand, was as much of a play to them as the apple-tree housekeeping had been.

So Mr. Ferguson might have spared himself the unpleasant interview with Blair's mother. He recognized this himself before long, and was even able to relax into a difficult smile when Mrs. Richie ventured a mild pleasantry on the subject. For Mrs. Richie had spoken to Blair, and understood the situation so well that she could venture a pleasantry. She had sounded him one evening in the darkness of her narrow garden.

David was not at home, and Blair was glad of the chance to wait for him—so long as Mrs. Richie let him lounge on the grass at her feet. His adoration of David's mother, begun in his childhood, had strengthened with his years; perhaps because she was all that his own mother was not.

"Blair," she said, "of course you and I both realize that Elizabeth is only a child, and you are entirely too wise to talk seriously about being engaged to her. She is far too young for that sort of thing. Of course *you* understand that?"

And Blair, feeling as though the sword of manhood had been laid on his shoulder, and instantly forgetting the smaller pride of being "engaged," said in a very mature voice, "Oh, certainly *I* understand."

If, in the dusk of stars and fireflies, with the fragrance of white stocks blossoming near the stone bench that circled the old hawthorn-tree in the middle of the garden—if at that moment Mrs. Richie had demanded Elizabeth's head upon a charger, Blair would have rejoiced to offer it. But this serene and gentle woman was far too wise to wring any promise from the boy, although, indeed, she had no opportunity, for at that moment Mr. Ferguson knocked on the green door between the two gardens and asked if he might come in and smoke his cigar in his neighbor's garden. "I'll smoke the aphids off your rose-bushes," he offered. "You are very careless about your roses!"

"A 'bad tenant'?" said Mrs. Richie, smiling. And poor Blair picked himself up, and went sulkily off.

But Mrs. Richie's flattering assumption that Blair and she looked at things in the same way, and David's apparent indifference to Elizabeth's emotions, made the childish love-affair wholesomely commonplace on both sides. By mid-September it was obvious that the prospect of college was attractive to Blair, and that the moment of parting would not be tragic to Elizabeth. The romance did not come to a recognized end, however, until a day or two before Blair started East. The four friends, and Miss White, had gone out to Mrs. Todd's, where David had stood treat, and after their tumblers of pink and brown and white ice-cream had been emptied, and Mrs. Todd had made her usual joke about "good-looking couples," they had taken two skiffs for a slow drift down the river to Willis's.

When they were rowing home again, the skiffs at first kept abreast, but gradually, in spite of Miss White's desire to be "at her post," and David's entire willingness to hold back, Blair and Elizabeth appropriately fell behind, with only a little shaggy dog, which Elizabeth had lately acquired, to play propriety. In the yellow September afternoon the river ran placidly between the hills and low-lying meadows; here and there, high on a wooded hillside, a maple flamed among the greenness of the walnuts and locusts, or the chestnuts showed the bronze beginnings of autumn. Ahead of them the sunshine had melted into an umber haze, which in the direction of Mercer deepened into a smudge of black. Elizabeth was twisting her left hand about to get different lights on her ring, which she had managed to slip on her finger when Cherry-pie was not looking. Blair, with absent eyes, was singing under his breath:

"'Oh! I came to a river, an' I couldn't get across;
Sing "Polly-wolly-doodle" all the day!
An' I jumped upon a nigger, an' I thought he was a hoss;
Sing Polly-wolly—'

"Horrid old hole, Mercer," he broke off, resting on his oars and letting the boat slip back on the current.

"I like Mercer!" Elizabeth said, ceasing to admire the ring. "Since you've come home from boarding-school you don't like anything but the East." She began to stroke her puppy's head violently. Blair was silent; he was looking at a willow dipping its swaying finger-tips in the water.

"Blair! why don't you answer me?"

Blair, plainly bored, said, "Well, I don't like hideousness and dirt."

"David likes Mercer."

"I bet Mrs. Richie doesn't," Blair murmured, and began to row lazily.

"Oh, Mrs. Richie!" cried Elizabeth; "you think whatever she thinks is about perfect."

"Well, isn't it?"

Elizabeth's lip hardened. "I suppose you think she's perfect too?"

"I do," Blair said.

"She thinks I'm dreadful because, sometimes, I—get provoked,"
Elizabeth said angrily.

"Well, you are," Blair agreed calmly.

"If I am so wicked, I wonder you want to be engaged to me!"

"Can't I like anybody but you?" Blair said, and yawned.

"You can like everybody, for all I care," she retorted. Blair whistled, upon which Elizabeth became absorbed in petting her dog, kissing him ardently between his eyes.

"I hate to see a girl kiss a dog," Blair observed;

"'Sing Polly-wolly-doo—'"

"Don't look, then," said Elizabeth, and kissed Bobby again.

Blair sighed, and gave up his song. Bobby, obviously uncomfortable, scrambled out of Elizabeth's lap and began to stretch himself on the uncertain floor of the skiff.

"Lie down!" Blair commanded, and poked the little creature, not ungently, with his foot. Bobby yelped, gave a flying nip at his ankle, and retreated to the shelter of his mistress's skirts. "Confound that dog!" cried Blair.

"You are a horrid boy!" she said, consoling her puppy with frantic caresses. "I'm glad he bit you!"

Blair, rubbing his ankle, said he'd like to throw the little wretch overboard.

Well, of course, Elizabeth being Elizabeth, the result was inevitable. The next instant the ring lay sparkling in the bottom of the boat. "I break my engagement! Take your old ring! You are a cruel, wicked boy, and I hate you—so there!" "I must say I don't see why you should expect me to enjoy being bitten," Blair said hotly. "Well, all right; throw me over, if you want to. I shall never trust a woman again as long as I live!" He began to row fiercely. "I only hope that darned pup isn't going mad."

"I hope he *is* going mad," said Elizabeth, trembling all over, "and I hope you'll go mad, too. Put me on shore this instant!"

"Considering the current, I fear you will have to endure my society for several instants," Blair said.

"I'd rather be drowned!" she cried furiously, and as she spoke, even before he could raise his hand to stop her, with Bobby in her arms she sprang lightly over the side of the boat into the water. There was a terrific splash—but, alas! Elizabeth, in preferring death to Blair's society, had not calculated upon the September shallows, and even before the horrified boy could drop his oars and spring to her assistance, she was on her feet, standing knee-deep in the muddy current.

The water completely extinguished the fires of wrath. In the hubbub that followed, the ejaculations and outcries, Nannie's tears, Miss White's terrified scolding, Blair's protestations to David that it wasn't his fault—through it all, Elizabeth, wading ashore, was silent. Only at the landing of the toll-house, when poor distracted Cherry-pie bade the boys get a carriage, did she speak:

"I won't go in a carriage. I am going to walk home."

"My lamb! you'll take cold! You mustn't!"

"You look like the deuce," Blair told her anxiously; and David blurted out, "Elizabeth, you can't walk home; you're a perfect object!" Elizabeth, through the mud trickling over her eyes, flashed a look at him:

"*That's* why I'm going to walk!" And walk she did—across the bridge, along the street, a dripping little figure stared at by passers-by, and followed by the faithful but embarrassed four—by five, indeed, for Blair had fished Bobby out of the water, and even stopped, once in a while when no one was looking, to give the maker of all this trouble a furtive and apologetic pat. At Elizabeth's door, in a very scared frame of mind lest Mr. Ferguson should come out and catch him, Blair attempted to apologize.

"Don't be silly," Elizabeth said, muddy and shivering, but just; "it wasn't your fault. But we're not engaged any more." And that was the end of the love-story!

Elizabeth told Cherry-pie that she had "broken with Blair Maitland *forever!*" Miss White, when she went to make her report of the dreadful event to Mr. Ferguson, added that she felt assured the young people had got over their foolishness. Elizabeth's uncle, telling the story of the ducking to David's horrified mother, said that he was greatly relieved to know that Elizabeth had come to her senses.

But with all the "tellings" that buzzed between the three households, nobody thought of telling Mrs. Maitland. Why should they? Who would connect this woman of iron and toil and sweat, of noise and motion, with the sentimentalities of two children? She had to find it out for herself.

At breakfast on the morning of the day Blair was to start East, his mother, looking over the top of her newspaper at him, said abruptly:

"Blair, I have something to say to you before you go. Be at my office at the Works at ten-fifteen." She looked at him amiably, then pushed back her chair. "Nannie! Get my bonnet. Come! Hurry! I'm late!"

Nannie, running, brought the bonnet, a bunch of rusty black

crepe, with strings frayed with many tyings. "Oh, Mamma," she said softly, "do let me get you a new bonnet?"

But Mrs. Maitland was not listening. "Harris!" she called loudly, "tell
Watson to have those roller figures for me at eleven. And I want the linen tracing—Bates will know what I mean—at noon without fail. Nannie, see that there's boiled cabbage for dinner."

A moment later the door banged behind her. The abrupt silence was like a blow. Nannie and Harris caught their breaths; it was as if the oxygen had been sucked out of the air; there was a minute before any one breathed freely. Then Blair flung up his arms in a wordless protest; he actually winced with pain. He glanced around the unlovely room; at the table, with its ledgers and clutter of unmatched china—old Canton, and heavy white earthenware, and odd cups and saucers with splashing decorations which had pleased Harris's eye; at the files of newspapers on the sideboard, the grimy walls, the untidy fireplace. "Thank Heaven! I'm going off to-day. I wish I need never come back," he said.

"Oh, Blair, that is a dreadful thing to say!"

"It may be dreadful, but that's the way I feel. I can't help my feelings, can I? The further mother and I are apart, the better we love each other. Well! I suppose I've got to go and see her bossing a lot of men, instead of sitting at home, like a lady;—and I'll get a dreadful blowing up. Of course she knows about the engagement now, thanks to Elizabeth's craziness."

"I don't believe she knows anything about it," Nannie tried to encourage him.

"Oh, you bet old Ferguson has told her," Blair said, gloomily. "Say, Nannie, if Elizabeth doesn't look out she'll get into awful hot water one of these days with her devil of a temper—and she'll get other people into it, too," he ended resentfully. Blair hated hot water, as he hated everything that was unbeautiful. "Mother is going to take my head off, of course," he said.

But Sarah Maitland, entirely ignorant of what had happened, had no such intention; she had gone over to her office in a glow of personal pleasure that warmed up the details of business. She intended to take Blair that morning through the Works,—not as he had often gone before, tagging after her, a frightened child, a reluctant boy—but as the prince, formally looking over the kingdom into which he was so soon to come! He was in love: therefore he would wish to be married; therefore he would be impatient to get to work! It was all a matter of logical and satisfactory deduction. How many times in this hot summer, when very literally she was earning her son's bread by the sweat of her brow, had she looked at Elizabeth and Blair, and found enjoyment in these deductions! Nobody would have imagined it, but the big, ungainly woman *dreamed!* Dreamed of her boy, of his business success, of his love, of his wife,—and, who knows? perhaps those grimy pink baby socks began to mean something more personal than the missionary barrel. It was her purpose, on this particular morning, to tell him, after they had gone through the Works, just where, when he graduated, he was to begin. Not at the bottom!—that was Ferguson's idea. "He ought to start at the bottom, if he is ever to get to the top," Ferguson had barked. No, Blair need not start at the bottom; he could begin pretty well up at the top; and he should have a salary. What an incentive that would be! First she would tell him that now, when he was going to college, she meant to increase his allowance; then she would tell him about the salary he would have when he got to work. How happy he would be! For a boy to be in love, and have all the pocket-money he wanted, and a great business to look forward to; to have work— work! the finest thing in the world!—all ready to his hand,—what more could a human being desire? At the office, she swept through the morning business with a speed that took her people off their feet. Once or twice she glanced at the clock; Blair was always unpunctual. "He'll get *that* knocked out of him when he gets into business," she thought, grimly.

It was eleven before he came loitering across the Yards. His mother, lifting her head for a moment from her desk, and glancing impatiently out of the dirt-begrimed office window, saw him coming, and caught the gleam of his patent-leather shoes as he skirted a puddle just outside the door. "Well, Master Blair," she said to herself, flinging down her pen, "you'll forget those pretty boots when you get to walking around your Works!"

Blair, dawdling through the outer office, found his way to her sanctum, and sat down in a chair beside her desk. He glanced at her shrinkingly, and looked away. Her bonnet was crooked; her hair was hanging in wisps at the back of her neck; her short skirt showed the big, broad-soled foot twisted round the leg of her chair. Blair saw the muddy sole of that shoe, and half closed his eyes. Then remembering Elizabeth, he felt a little sick; "she's going to row about it!" he thought, and quailed.

"You're late," she said; then, without stopping for his excuses, she proceeded with the business in hand. "I'm going to increase your allowance."

Blair sat up in astonishment.

"I mean while you're at college. After that I shall stop the allowance entirely, and you will go to work. You will go on a salary, like any other man." Her mouth clicked shut in a tight line of satisfaction.

The color flew into Blair's face. "Why!" he said. "You are awfully good, Mother. Really, I—"

"I know all about this business of your engagement to Elizabeth," Mrs. Maitland broke in, "though you didn't see fit to tell me about it yourself." There was something in her voice that would have betrayed her to any other hearer; but Blair, who was sensitive to Mrs. Richie's slightest wish, and careful of old Cherry-pie's comfort, and generously thoughtful even of Harris—Blair, absorbed in his own apprehensions, heard no pain in his mother's voice. "I know all about it," Mrs. Maitland went on. "I won't have you call yourselves engaged until you are out of college, of course. But I have no objection to your looking forward to being engaged, and married, too. It's a good thing for a young man to expect to be married; keeps him clean."

Blair was struck dumb. Evidently, though she did not know what had happened, she did know that he had been engaged. Yet she was not going to take his head off! Instead she was going to increase his allowance because, apparently, she approved of him!

"So I want to tell you," she went on, "though you have not seen fit to tell me anything, that I'm willing you should marry Elizabeth, as soon as you can support her. And you can do that as soon as you graduate, because, as I say, when you are in the Works, I shall pay you"—her iron face lighted—"I shall pay you *a salary!* a good salary."

More money! Blair laughed with satisfaction; the prospect soothed the sting of Elizabeth's "meanness"—which was what he called it, when he did not remember to name it, darkly, "faithlessness." He was so comforted that he had, for the first time in his life, an impulse to confide in his mother; "Elizabeth got provoked at me"—there was a boyish demand for sympathy in his tone; "and —"

But Mrs. Maitland interrupted him. "Come along," she said, chuckling. She got up, pulled her bonnet straight, and gave her son a jocose thrust in the ribs that made him jump. "I can't waste time over lovers' quarrels. Patch it up! patch it up! You can afford to, you

know, before you get married. You'll get your innings later, my boy!"
Still chuckling at her own joke, she slammed down the top of her
desk and tramped into the outer office.

Blair turned scarlet with anger. The personal familiarity
extinguished his little friendly impulse to blurt out his trouble with
Elizabeth, as completely as a gust of wind puts out a scarcely lighted
candle. He got up, his teeth set, his hands clenched in his pockets,
and followed his mother through the Yards—vast, hideous wastes,
scorching in the September heats, full of endless rows of pig, piles of
scrap, acres, it seemed to Blair, of slag. The screeching clamor of the
place reeked with the smell of rust and rubbish and sour earth, and
the air was vibrant with the clatter of the "buggies" on the narrow-
gauge tracks that ran in a tangled network from one furnace to
another. Blair, trudging along behind his mother, cringing at the
ugliness of everything about him, did not dare to speak; he still felt
that dig in the ribs, and was so angry he could not have controlled his
voice.

Mrs. Maitland walked through her Iron Works as some
women walk through a garden:—lovingly. She talked to her son
rapidly; this was so and so; there was such and such a department; in
that new shed she meant to put the draftsmen; over there the
timekeeper;—she paused. Blair had left her, and was standing in an
open doorway of the foundry, watching, breathlessly, a jibcrane
bearing a great ladle full of tons of liquid metal that shimmered above
its white-hot expanse with the shifting blue flames of escaping gas.
Seething and bubbling, the molten iron slopped in a flashing film
over the side of the caldron, every drop, as it struck the black earth,
rebounding in a thousand exploding points of fire. Above the
swaying ladle, far up in the glooms under the roof, the shadows were
pierced by the lurching dazzle of arc-lamps; but when the ladle
tipped, and with a crackling roar the stream of metal flowed into a

mold, the sizzling violet gleam of the lamps was abruptly extinguished by the intolerable glare of light.

"Oh," Blair said breathlessly, "how wonderful!"

"It *is* wonderful," his mother said. "Thomas, here, can move the lever that tips the ladle with his two fingers—and out comes the iron as neatly as cream out of a jug!"

Blair was so entirely absorbed in the fierce magnificence of light, and in the glowing torsos of the molders, planted as they were against the profound shadows of the foundry, that when she said, "Come on!" he did not hear her. Mrs. Maitland, standing with her hands on her hips, her feet well apart, held her head high; she was intensely gratified by his interest. "If his father had only lived to see him!" she said to herself. In her pride, she almost swaggered; she nodded, chuckling, to the molder at her elbow:

"He takes to it like a duck to water, doesn't he, Jim?" "And," said Jim, telling the story afterward, "I allowed I'd never seen a young feller as knowing about castings as him. She took it down straight. You can't pile it on too thick for a woman, about her young 'un."

"Somebody ought to paint it," Blair said, under his breath.

Mrs. Maitland's face glowed; she came and stood beside him a moment in silence, resting her big, dirty hand on his shoulder. Then she said, half sheepishly, "I call that ladle the 'cradle of civilization.' Think what's inside of it! There are rails, that will hold New York and San Francisco together, and engines and machines for the whole world; there are telegraph wires that will bring—think of all the kinds of news they will bring, Blair,—wars, and births of babies! There are bridges in it, and pens that may write—well, maybe love-letters," she said, with sly and clumsy humor, "or even write, perhaps, the liberty of a race, as Lincoln's pen wrote it. Yes!" she said, her face full of luminous abstraction, "the cradle of civilization!"

He could hardly hear her voice in the giant tumult of exploding metal and the hammering and crashing in the adjacent mill; but when she said that, he looked round at her with the astonishment of one who sees a familiar face where he has supposed he would see a stranger. He forgot his shame in having a mother who ran an iron-mill; he even forgot that impudent thrust in the ribs; a spark of sympathy leaped between them as real in its invisibility as the white glitter of the molten iron sputtering over their heads. "Yes," he said, "it's all that, and it is magnificent, too!"

"Come on!" she said, with a proud look. Over her shoulder she flung back at him figures and statistics; she told him of the tons of bridge materials on the books; the rail contract she had just taken was a big thing, very big! "We've never handled such an order, but we can do it!"

They were walking rapidly from the foundry to the furnaces; Sarah Maitland was inspecting piles of pig, talking to puddlers, all the while bending and twisting between her strong fingers, with their blackened nails, a curl of borings, perhaps biting on it, thoughtfully, while she considered some piece of work, then blowing the crumbs of iron out from between her lips and bursting into quick directions or fault-finding. She stood among her men, in her short skirt, her gray hair straggling out over her forehead from under her shabby bonnet, and gave her orders; but for the first time in her life she was self-conscious—Blair was looking on! listening! thinking, no doubt, that one of these days he would be doing just what she was doing! For the moment she was as vain as a girl; then, abruptly, her happy excitement paused. She stood still, flinching and wincing, and putting a hand up to her eye.

"Ach!" she said; "a filing!" she looked with the other sympathetically watering eye at her son. "Here, take this thing out."

"*I*?" Blair said, dismayed. "Oh, I might hurt you." Then, in his helplessness and concern—for, ignorant as he was, he knew enough of the Works to know that an iron filing in your eye is no joke—he turned, with a flurried gesture, to one of the molders. "Get a doctor, can't you? Don't stand there staring!"

"Doctor?" said Mrs. Maitland. She gave her son a look, and laughed. "He's afraid he'll hurt me!" she said, with a warm joyousness in her voice; "Jim, got a jack-knife? Just dig this thing out." Jim came, dirty and hesitating, but prepared for a very common emergency of the Works. With a black thumb and forefinger he raised the wincing lid, and with the pointed blade of the jack-knife lifted, with delicacy and precision, the irritating iron speck from the eyeball. "'Bliged," Mrs. Maitland said. She clapped a rather grimy handkerchief over the poor red eye, and turned to Blair. "Come on!" she said, and struck him on the shoulder so heartily that he stumbled. Her cheek was blackened by the molder's greasy fingers, and so smeared with tears from the still watering eye that he could not bear to look at it. He hesitated, then offered her his handkerchief, which at least had the advantage of being clean. She took it, glanced at its elaborate monogram, and laughed; then she dabbed her eye with it. "I guess I'll have to put some of that cologne of yours on this fancy thing. Remember that green bottle with the calendar and the red ribbons on it, that you gave me when you were a little fellow? I've never had anything of my own fine enough to use the stuff on!"

When they got back to the office again she was very brief and business-like with him. She had had a fine morning, but she couldn't waste any more time! "You can keep all this that you have seen in your mind. I don't know just where I shall put you. If you have a preference, express it." Then she told him what his salary would be when he got to work, and what allowance he was to have for the present.

"Now, clear out, clear out!" she said; "good-by"; and turned her cheek toward him for their semi-annual parting. Blair, with his eyes shut, kissed her.

"Good-by, Mother. It has been awfully interesting. And I am awfully obliged to you about the allowance." On the threshold of the office he halted. "Mother," he said,—and his voice was generous even to wistfulness; "Mother, that cradle thing was stunning."

Mrs. Maitland nodded proudly; when he had gone, she folded his handkerchief up, and with a queer, shy gesture, slipped it into the bosom of her dress. Then she rang her bell. "Ask Mr. Ferguson to step here." When her superintendent took the chair beside her desk, she was all business; but when business was over and he got up, she stopped him: "Tell the bookkeeper to double Blair's allowance, beginning to-day."

Ferguson made a memorandum.

"And Mr. Ferguson, I have told Blair that I consent to his engagement with Elizabeth, and I shall make it possible for them to be married as soon as he graduates—"

"But—"

"I do this," she went on, her satisfaction warm in her voice, "because I think he needs the incentive that comes to a young man when he wants to get married. It is natural and proper. And I will see that things are right for them."

"In the first place," said Robert Ferguson, "I would not permit
Elizabeth to marry Blair; but fortunately we need not discuss that. They have quarreled, and there is no longer any question of such a thing."

"Quarreled! but only this morning, not an hour ago, he let me suppose—" She paused. "Well, I'm sorry." She paused again, and made aimless marks with her pen on the blotter. "That's all this morning, Mr. Ferguson." And though he lingered to tell her, with grim amusement, of Elizabeth's angry bath, she made no further comment.

When he had left the office she got up and shut the door. Then she went back to her chair, and leaning an elbow on her desk, covered her lips with her hand. After she had sat thus for nearly ten minutes, she suddenly rang for an office-boy. "Take this handkerchief up to the house to my son," she said; "he forgot it."

Chapter 9

For the next five or six years Blair was not often at home. At the end of his freshman year he was conditioned, and found a tutor and the seashore and his sketching—for he painted with some enthusiasm just at that time—much more attractive than his mother and Mercer. After that he went to Europe in the long vacations.

"How much vacation have I had since I began to run his business for him?" his mother said once in answer to Nannie's intercession that he might be allowed to travel. But she let him go. She did not know how to do anything else; she always let him do what he pleased, and have what he wanted; she gave him everything, and she exacted no equivalent, either in scholarship or conduct. It never occurred to her to make him appreciate his privileges by paying for them, and so, of course, she pauperized him.

"Blair likes Europe," she said one Sunday afternoon to David Richie, who had come in to see Nannie, "but as for me, I wouldn't take an hour of my good time, or spend a dollar of my good money, to see the best of their cathedrals and statues and things. Do you mean to say there is a cathedral in the world as handsome as my new foundry?"

"Well," David said modestly, "I haven't seen any cathedrals, you know,
Mrs. Maitland."

"It's small loss to you, David," she said kindly. "But I wish I'd thought to invite you to go along with Blair last summer. You might have liked it, though you are a pretty sensible fellow in most things." "Oh, I can't go to Europe till I can earn enough to pay my own way," David replied, and added with a quick look at Nannie, "besides, I like being in Mercer."

"Blair has no need to earn money," said Mrs. Maitland carelessly; then she blew out her lips in a bubbling sigh. "And he would rather see a cathedral than his mother."

The pathos of that pricked even the pleasant egotism of youth; David winced, and Nannie tried to murmur something of her brother's needing the rest.

Mrs. Maitland gave her grunt of amusement. "Rest! What's he ever done to tire him? Well! Clear out, clear out, you two,—if you're going to take a walk. I'm glad *you* came back for your vacation, David, at any rate. Nannie needs shaking up. She sticks at home here with me, and a girl ought to see people once in a while." She glanced at the two young creatures shrewdly. "Why not?" she reflected. She had never thought of it before, but "why not?" It would be a very sensible arrangement. The next moment she had decided that it should be! Nannie's money would be a help to the boy, and he needn't depend on his doctoring business. "I must put it through," she said to herself, just as she might have said that she should put through a piece of work in the office.

This match-making purpose made her invite David to supper very frequently, and every time he came she was apt, after he had taken his departure, to tramp into Nannie's parlor in the hope of being told that the "sensible arrangement" had been made. When she found them together, and caught a word or two about Elizabeth, she had no flash of insight. But, except to her, the situation as regarded David and Elizabeth was perfectly clear.

When, seven years before, the two boys had gone off together to college, Blair had confided to his friend that his faith in women was forever destroyed, "Though I shall love Elizabeth, always," he said.

"Maybe she'll come round?" David tried to comfort him.

"If she doesn't, I shall never love another woman," Blair said darkly.

David was silent. But as he and Blair were just then in the Damon and Pythias stage, and had sworn to each other that "no woman should ever come between them," he gave a hopeless shrug. "That dishes me," he said to himself; "so long as he will never love any other girl, I can't cut in."

It would have been rather a relief to Mrs. Richie to know that her son had reached this artless conclusion, for the last thing she desired was that David's calflove should harden into any real purpose. Elizabeth—sweet-hearted below the careless selfishness of a temper which it never occurred to her must be controlled—was a most kissable young creature to her elders, and Mrs. Richie was heartily fond of her; but all the same she did not want a daughter-in-law with a temper! Elizabeth, on her part, repelled by David's mother's unattainable perfections, never allowed the older woman to feel intimate with her. That first meeting so many years ago, when they had each recoiled from the other, seemed to have left a gulf between them, which had never quite closed up. So Mrs. Richie was just as well pleased that in the next few years David, for one reason or another, did not see his old neighbor very often. By the time he was twenty-four, and well along in his course at the medical school, she had almost forgotten her vague apprehensions. The pause in the intimacy of the mother and son—the inevitable pause that comes between the boy's seventeenth and twentieth years—had ended, and David and his mother were frank and confidential friends again; yet, though she did not know it, one door was still closed between them: "He's forgotten all about it," Mrs. Richie told herself comfortably; and never guessed that in silence he remembered. Of course David's boyish idea of honor was no longer subject to the claim of friendship, for Blair had entirely recovered from his first passion. The only thing he feared now was his own unworth. After all, what had a dumb fellow like himself to offer such a radiant being?

For indeed she was radiant. The girl he had known nearly all his life, impetuous, devoid of self-consciousness, giving her sweet, sexless love with both generous hands, had vanished with the old frank days of dropping an uninvited head on a boy's shoulder. Now, though she was still impetuous, still unconscious of self, she was glowing with womanhood, and ready to be loved. She was not beautiful, except in so far as she was young, for youth is always beautiful; she was tall, of a sweet and delicate thinness, and with the faint coloring of a blush-rose; her dimple was exquisite; her brows were straight and fine, shading eyes wonderfully star-like, but often stormy—eyes of clear, dark amber, which, now that David had come home, were full of dreams.

Before her joyous personality, no wonder poor inarticulate David was torn with apprehensions! He did not share them with his mother, who, with more or less misgiving, began to guess how things were for herself; he knew instinctively that Mrs. Richie's gentle, orderly mind could not possibly understand Elizabeth, still less appreciate the peculiar charm to his inherent reasonableness of her sweet, stormy, undisciplined temperament. Nannie Maitland could not understand either, and yet it was to Nannie—kind, literal little Nannie, who never understood anything abstract, that David revealed his heart. She was intensely sympathetic, and having long ago relinquished the sister-in-law dream, encouraged him to rave about Elizabeth to his heart's content; in fact, for at least a year before Mrs. Maitland had evolved that "sensible arrangement" for her stepdaughter, David, whenever he was at home, used to go to see Nannie simply to pour out his hopes or his dismays. It was mostly dismays, for it seemed to him that Elizabeth was as uncertain as the wind! "She does—she doesn't," he used to say to himself; and then he would question Nannie, who, having received certain confidences from the other side, would reassure him so warmly that he would take heart again.

At the time that he finally dared to put his fate to the touch, Mrs. Maitland's match-making intentions for Nannie had reached a point where she had made up her mind to put the matter through without any more delay. "I'll speak to Mrs. Richie about it, and get the thing settled," she said to herself; "no use dawdling along this way!" But just the day before she found time to speak to Mrs. Richie —it was in David's midwinter recess—something happened.

Elizabeth had accepted—not too eagerly, of course—an invitation to walk with him; and off they went, down Sandusky Street to the river and across the old covered bridge. They stopped to say how do you do to Mrs. Todd, who was peering out from behind the scarlet geraniums in the window of the "saloon." Elizabeth took the usual suggestive joke about a "pretty pair" with a little hauteur, but David beamed, and as he left the room he squeezed Mrs. Todd suddenly round her fat waist, which made her squeak but pleased her very much. "Made for each other!" she whispered wheezily; and David slipped a bill into her hand through sheer joy.

"Better have some ice-cream," the old lady wheedled; "such hot blood needs cooling."

"Oh, Mrs. Todd, *she* is so cool, I don't need ice-cream," the young fellow mourned in her motherly ear.

"Get out with ye! Ain't you got eyes? She's waitin' to eat you up,—and starvin' for ye!" And David hurried after Elizabeth, who had reached the toll-gate and was waiting, if not to eat him, at any rate for his company.

"She's a dear old soul!" he said joyfully.

"I believe you gave her a kiss," Elizabeth declared.

"I gave her a hug. She said things I liked!"

Elizabeth, guessing what the things might have been, swerved away from the subject, and murmured how pretty the country looked. There had been a snow-storm the night before, and the fields were glistening, unbroken sheets of white; the road David chose was followed by a brook, that ran chuckling between the agate strips of ice along its banks; here and there a dipping branch had been caught and was held in a tinkling crystal prison, and here and there the ice conquered the current, and the water could be heard gurgling and complaining under its snowy covering. David thought that all the world was beautiful,—now that Mrs. Todd had bidden him use his eyes!

"Remember when we used to sled down this hill, Elizabeth?"

She turned her cool, glowing face toward him and nodded. "Indeed I do!
And you used to haul my sled up to the top again."

"I don't think I have forgotten anything we did."

Instantly she veered away from personalities. "Isn't it a pity Blair dislikes Mercer so much? Nannie is dreadfully lonely without him."

"She has you; I don't see how she can be lonely."

"Oh, I don't count for anything compared to Blair." Her breath carried quickly. The starry light was in her eyes, but he did not see it. He was not daring to look at her.

"You count for everything to me," he said, in a constrained voice.

She was silent.

"Elizabeth...do you think you could—care? a little?"

She looked away from him without a word. David trembled; "It's all up—" he said to himself; and even as he said it, a small, cold hand was stretched out to him,—a hand that trembled:

"David, I am not good enough. Truly, I'm not."

The very shock of having his doubts and fears crumble so

suddenly, made him stand stock-still; he turned very white. "What!" he said, in a low voice, "You—*care*? Oh no, you don't! You can't. I can't believe it."

Upon which Elizabeth was instantly joyous again. "Well, I won't, if you don't want me to," she said gaily, and walked on, leaving him standing, amazed, in the snow. Then she looked back at him over her shoulder. At that arch and lovely look he bounded to her, stammering something, he did not know what himself; but she laughed, glowing and scolding, swerving over to the other side of the path. "David! We are on a public road. Stop! Please!"

"To think of your caring," he said, almost in a whisper. His face, with its flash of ecstasy, was like wine to her; all her soul spoke fearlessly in her eyes: "Care? Why, David, I was only so awfully afraid you weren't going to ask me!"

His lip trembled. He was quite speechless. But Elizabeth was bubbling over with joy; then suddenly, her exhilaration flagged. "What will your mother say? She doesn't like me."

"Elizabeth! she loves you! How could she help it? How could anybody help it?"

"It's my temper," she said, sighing; "my wicked temper. Of course I never mean anything I say, and I can't imagine why people mind; but they do. Last week I made Cherry-pie cry. Of course she oughtn't to have been hurt;—she knows me. You see I am really a devil, David, to make dear, old Cherry-pie unhappy! But I don't believe I will ever lose my temper again as long as I live. I am going to be good, like your mother." The tears stood in her eyes. "Mrs. Richie is so simply perfect I am sort of afraid of her. I wish she had ever been wicked, like me. David, what shall we do if she won't consent?"

"She'll consent all right," he said, chuckling; and added with the sweet and trusting egotism of youth: "the only thing in the world

Materna wants, you know, is my happiness. But do you suppose it would make any difference if she didn't consent? You are for me," he said with an abrupt solemnity that was almost harsh. "Nothing in the world can take you from me."

And she whispered, "Nothing."

Then David, like every lover who has ever loved, cast his challenge into the grinning face of Fate: "This is forever, Elizabeth."

"Forever, David."

On their way home, as they passed the toll-house, he left her and ran up the path to tap on the window; when Mrs. Todd beamed at him through the geraniums, "*I've got her!*" he cried. And the gay old voice called back, "Glory be!"

On the bridge in the gathering dusk they stood for some time without speaking, looking down at the river. Once or twice a passer-by glanced at the two figures leaning there on the hand-rail, and wondered at the foolishness of people who would stand in the cold and look at a river full of ice; but David and Elizabeth did not see the passing world. The hurrying water ran in a turbulent, foam-streaked flood; great sheets of ice, rocking and grinding against one another, made a continuous soft crash of sound. Sometimes one of them would strike the wooden casing of a pier, and then the whole bridge jarred and quivered, and the cake of ice, breaking and splintering, would heap itself on a long white spit that pushed up-stream through the rushing current. The river was yellow with mud torn up by a freshet back among the hills, but the last rays of the sun,—a disk of copper sinking into the brown haze behind the hills,—caught on the broken edges of the icy snow, and made a sudden white glitter almost from shore to shore.

"Elizabeth," David said, "I want to tell you something. I stood right here, and looked at a raft coming down the river, the evening that Blair told me that you and he—"

"Don't!" she said, shivering.

"I won't," he told her tenderly; "you were only a child; it didn't mean anything. Don't you suppose I understand? But I wanted you to know that it was then, nearly eight years ago, when I was just a boy, that I realized that *I*—" he paused.

She looked at him silently; her lip quivered and she nodded.

"And I have never changed since," he said. "I stood just here, leaning on this railing, and I was so wretched!" he laughed under his breath; "I didn't know what was the matter with me! I was only a cub, you know. But"—he spoke very softly—"all of a sudden I knew. Elizabeth, a woman on the raft looked up at me. There was a little baby.... Dear, it was then that I knew I loved you."

At those elemental words her heart came up into her throat. She could not speak, but suddenly she stooped and kissed the battered hand-rail where he said his hands had rested.

David, horrified, glancing right and left in the dusk and seeing no one, put a swift arm about her in which to whisper a single word. Then, very softly, he kissed her cheek. For a moment she seemed to ebb away from him; then, abruptly, like, the soft surge of a returning wave, she sank against his breast and her lips demanded his....

That night David told his mother. He had been profoundly shaken by Elizabeth's lovely unexpected motion there in the twilight on the bridge; it was a motion so divinely unconscious of the outside world, that he was moved to the point of finding no words to say how moved he was. But she had felt him tremble from head to foot when her lips burned against his,—so she needed no words. His silence still lasted when, after an hour next door with her, he came home and sat down on the sofa beside his mother. He nuzzled his blond head against hers for a moment; then slipped an arm round her waist.

"It's all right, Materna," he said, with a sort of gasp.

"What is, dear?"

"Oh, mother, the idea of asking! The only thing in the world."

"You mean—you and Elizabeth?"

"Yes," he said.

She was silent for a moment; when she spoke her voice broke a little.

"When was it, dear?"

"This afternoon," he said. And once started, he overflowed: "I can't get my breath yet, though I've known it since a quarter past four!"

Mrs. Richie laughed, and then sighed. "David, of course I'm happy, if you are; but—I hope she's good enough for you, dear." She felt him stiffen against her shoulder.

"Good enough? for *me!* Materna, she is perfect! Don't you suppose I know? I've know her nearly all my life, and I can say she is perfect. She is as perfect as you are; she said you were perfect this afternoon. Yes; I never supposed I could say that any woman was as good, and lovely, and pure, as you—"

"David, *please* don't say such things."

David was not listening. "But I can say it of Elizabeth! Oh, what a lucky fellow I am! I always thought Blair would get her. He's such a mighty good fellow,—and so darned good-looking, confound him!" David ruminated affectionately. "And he can talk; he's not bottled up, like me. To think she would look at me, when she could have had him,—or anybody else! It seems kind of mean to cut Blair out, when he isn't here. He hasn't seen her, you know, for about two years."

"Perhaps you would like to call it off until he gets home, and give him a chance?"

David grinned. "No, thank you. Oh, Materna, she is, you

know, really, so—so sort of wonderful! Some time I want to talk to you about her. I don't believe anybody quite understands Elizabeth but me. But to think of her caring for me! To think of my having two such women to care for me." He took her hand gently and kissed it. "Mother," he said—he spoke with almost painful effort; "Mother, I want to tell you something. I want to tell you, because, being what you are, you can't in the least understand what it means; but I do want you to know: I've never kissed any woman but you, Materna, until I kissed—*Her.*"

"Oh," said Helena Richie, in a stifled voice, "don't, David, don't; I can't bear it! And if she doesn't make you happy—"

"Make me happy?" David said. He paused; that unasked kiss burned once more against his lips; he almost shivered at the pang of it. "Materna," he said hoarsely, "if she or I were to die to-night, I, at any rate, have had happiness enough in these few hours to have made it worth while to have lived."

"Love doesn't mean just happiness," she said.

David was silent for a moment; then he said, very gently, "You are thinking of—of your little boy, who died?"

"Yes; and of my marriage; it was not happy, David."

He pressed his cheek against hers, without speaking. The grief of an unhappy marriage he had long ago guessed, and in this moment of his own happiness the remembrance of it was intolerable to him. As for the other grief: "when I think of the baby," he said, softly, "I feel as if that little beggar gave me my mother. I feel as if I had his job; and if I am not a good son—" he stopped, and looked at her, smiling; but something in her face—perhaps the pitiful effort to smile back through the tears of an old, old sorrow, gave him a sudden, solemn thrill; the race pain stirred in him; he seemed to see his own child, dead, in Elizabeth's arms.

"Mother!" he said, thickly, and caught her in his arms. She felt his heart pounding heavily in his side, but she smiled. "Yes," she said, "my little boy gave me another son, though I didn't deserve him! No, no, I didn't," she insisted, laying her soft mother-hand over his protesting lips; "I used to wonder sometimes, David, why God trusted you to me, instead of to a—a better woman—" again she checked his outburst that God had never made a better woman! "Hush, dear, hush. But I didn't mean that love might mean sorrow. There are worse things in the world than sorrow," she ended, almost in a whisper.

"Yes, there are worse things," he said quietly; "of course I know that. But they are not possible things where Elizabeth is concerned. There is only one thing that can hurt us: Death."

"Oh, my dear, my dear! Life can hurt so much more than death! So *much* more."

But David had nothing more to say of life and love. He retreated abruptly to the matter of fact; he had gone to his limit, not only of expression, but of that modesty of soul which forbids exposure of the emotions, and is as exquisite in a young man as physical modesty is in a girl. He was unwilling, indeed he was unable, to show even to his mother, even, perhaps, to Elizabeth, the speechless depths that had been stirred that afternoon by the first kiss of passion, and stirred again that night by the sight of tears for a baby, —a baby dead for almost a quarter of a century! He got up, thrust his hands into his pockets, and whistled. "Heaven knows how long it will be before we can be married! How soon do you think I can count on getting patients enough to get married?"

Mrs. Richie laughed, though there was still a break of pain in her voice. "My dear boy, when you leave the medical school I mean to give you an allowance which,—"

"No, Maternal" he interrupted her; "I am going to stand on my own legs!" David's feeling about self-support gave him a satisfaction out of all proportion to the pain it sometimes gave his mother. She winced now, as if his words hurt her.

"David! All that I have is yours."

"No," he said again. "I couldn't accept anything. I believe if a man can't take care of his wife himself, he has no business to have a wife. It's bad enough for you to be supporting a big, hungry medical student; but I swear you sha'n't feed his wife, too. I can't be indebted, even to you!" he ended, with the laughing cock-sureness of high-minded youth.

"Indebted? Oh, David!" she said. For a moment his words wounded her; but when he had left her to go back to Elizabeth again, and she sat alone by her fireside, she forgot this surface wound in some deeper pain. David had said he had never kissed any woman but her, until he kissed *Her*. He had said that the things that were "worse than death" were not possible to Elizabeth. For a moment this soft mother felt a stab of something like jealousy; then her thought went back to that deeper pain. He had not supposed anybody could be as "perfect" as his mother. Helena Richie cowered, as if the sacred words were whips; she covered her face with her hands, and sat a long time without moving. Perhaps she was thinking of a certain old letter, locked away in her desk, and in her heart,—for she knew every word of it: "My child, your secret belongs to your Heavenly Father. It is never to be taken from His hands, except for one reason: to save some other child of His. Never for any smaller reason of peace of mind to yourself."

When she lifted her bowed head from her hands the fire was out. There were tears upon her face.

Chapter 10

It was the very next afternoon that Mrs. Maitland found time to look after Nannie's matrimonial interests. In the raw December twilight she tramped muddily into Mrs. Richie's firelit parlor, which was fragrant with hyacinths blossoming on every window-sill. Mr. Ferguson had started them in August in his own cellar, for, as any landlord will tell you, it is the merest matter of business to do all you can for a good tenant. Mrs. Maitland found her superintendent and Mrs. Richie just shaking hands on David's luck, Mrs. Richie a little tremulous, and Robert Ferguson a little grudging, of course.

"Well, I hope they'll be happy," he said, sighing; "I suppose some marriages *are* happy, but—"

"Oh, Mr. Ferguson, you are delightful!" Mrs. Richie said; and it was at that moment that Mrs. Maitland came tramping in. Instantly the large, vital presence made the charming room seem small and crowded. There were too many flowers, too many ornaments, too many photographs of David. Mrs. Maitland sat down heavily on a gilded chair, that creaked so ominously that she rose and looked at it impatiently.

"Foolish sort of furniture," she said; "give me something solid, please, to sit on. Well, Mrs. Richie! How do you do?"

"Nannie has told you our great news?" Mrs. Richie inquired.

"Oh, so it's come to a head, has it?" Mrs. Maitland said, vastly pleased. "Of course I knew what was in the wind, but I didn't know it was settled. Fact is, I haven't seen her, except at breakfast, and then I was in too much of a hurry to think of it. Well, well, nothing could be better! That's what I came to see you about; I wanted to hurry things along. What do you say to it, Mr. Ferguson?"

Mrs. Maitland looked positively benign. She was sitting, a

little gingerly, on the edge of the yellow damask sofa at one side of the fireplace, her feet wide apart, her skirt pulled back over her knees, so that her scorching petticoat was somewhat liberally displayed. Her big shoes began to steam in the comfortable heat of a soft-coal fire that was blazing and snapping between the brass jambs.

Mrs. Richie had drawn up a chair beside her, and Robert Ferguson stood with his elbow on the mantelpiece looking down at them. Even to Mr. Ferguson Mrs. Maitland's presence in the gently feminine room was incongruous. There was a little table at the side of the sofa, and Mrs. Maitland, thrusting out a large, gesticulating hand, swept a silver picture-frame to the floor; in the confusion of picking it up and putting it into a safer place the little emotional tension of the moment vanished. Mrs. Richie winked away a tear, and laughed, and said it was too absurd to think that their children were men and women, with their own lives and interests and hopes—and love-affairs!

"But love-making is in the air, apparently," she said; "young Knight is going to be married."

"What, Goose Molly's stepson?" Mrs. Maitland said. "She used to make sheep's-eyes at—at somebody I knew. But she didn't get him! Well, I must give the boy a present."

"And the next thing," Mrs. Richie went on, "will be Nannie's engagement. Only it will be hard to find anybody good enough for Nannie!"

"*Nannie?*" said Mrs. Maitland blankly. "She is to be Elizabeth's bridesmaid, of course,—unless she gets married before our wedding comes off. A young doctor has to have patients before he can have a wife, so I'm afraid the chances are Elizabeth will be Nannie's bridesmaid."

She was so full of these maternal and womanly visions that the sudden slight rigidity of Mrs. Maitland's face did not strike her.

"Nannie has been so interested," Mrs. Richie went on. "David will always be grateful to her for helping his cause. I don't know what he would have done without Nannie to confide in!"

Mrs. Maitland's face relaxed. So Nannie had not been slighted? She herself, Nannie's mother, had made a mistake; that was all. Well, she was sorry; she wished it had been Nannie. Poor 'thing, it was lonely for her, in that big, empty house! But these two people, patting themselves on the back with their personal satisfaction about their children, they must not guess her wish. There was no resentment in her mind; it was one of the chances of business. David had chosen Elizabeth,—more fool David! "for Nannie'll have—" Mrs. Maitland made some rapid calculations; "but it's not my kettle of fish," she reflected; and hoisted herself up from the low, deeply cushioned sofa.

"I hope Elizabeth will put her mind on housekeeping," she said. "A young doctor has to get all the pork he can for his shilling! He needs a saving wife."

"She'll have to be a saving wife, I'm afraid," Mrs. Richie said, with rueful pride, "for that foolish boy of mine declines, if you please, to be helped out by an allowance from me."

"Oh, he'll have more sense when he's more in love," Mrs. Maitland assured her easily. "I never knew a man yet who would refuse honest money when it was offered to him. Well, Mrs. Richie, with all this marrying going on, I suppose the next thing will be you and friend Ferguson." Even as she said it, she saw in a flash an inevitable meaning in the words, and she gave a great guffaw of laughter. "Bless you! I didn't mean *that*! I meant you'd be picking up a wife somewhere, Mr. Ferguson, and Mrs. Richie, here, would be finding a husband. But the other way would be easier, and a very sensible arrangement."

The two victims of her peculiar sense of humor held

themselves as well as they could. Mrs. Richie reddened slightly, but looked blank. Robert Ferguson's jaw actually dropped, but he was able to say casually that of course it would be some time before the young people could be married.

"Well, give my love to Elizabeth," Mrs. Maitland said: "tell her not to jump into the river if she gets angry with David. Do you remember how she did that in one of her furies at Blair, Mr. Ferguson?" She gave a grunt of a laugh, and took herself off, pausing at the front door to call back, "Don't forget my good advice, you people!"

Robert Ferguson, putting on his hat with all possible expedition, got out of the house almost as quickly as she did. "I'd like to choke her!" he said to himself. He felt the desire to choke Mrs. Maitland several times that evening as he sat in his library pretending to read his newspaper. "She ought to be ashamed of herself! Mrs. Richie will think I have been—heaven knows what she will think!"

But the truth was, Mrs. Richie thought nothing at all; she forgot the incident entirely. It was Robert Ferguson who did the embarrassed thinking.

As for Mrs. Maitland, she went home through Mercer's mire and fog, her iron face softening into almost feminine concern. She was saying to herself that if Nannie didn't care, why, she didn't care! "But if she hankers after him"—Mrs. Maitland's face twinged with annoyance; "if she hankers after him, I'll make it up to her in some way. I'll give her a good big check!" But she must make sure about the "hankering." It would not be difficult to make sure. In these silent years together, the strong nature had drawn the weak nature to it, as a magnet draws a speck of iron. Nannie, timid to the point of awe, never daring even in her thoughts to criticize the powerful personality that dominated her daily life, nestled against it, so to speak, with perfect content. Sarah Maitland's esthetic deficiencies which separated her so tragically from her son, did not alienate Nannie. The fact that her stepmother was rich, and yet lived in a poverty-stricken locality; that the inconvenience of the old house amounted to squalor; that they were almost completely isolated from people of their own class;—none of these things disturbed Nannie. They were merely "Mamma's ways," that was all there was to say about them. She was not confidential with Mrs. Maitland, because she had nothing to confide. But if her stepmother had ever asked any personal question, she would have been incapable of not replying. Mrs. Maitland knew that, and proposed to satisfy herself as to the "hankering."

Supper was on the table when she got home, and though while bolting her food she glanced at Nannie rather keenly, she did not try to probe her feelings. "But she looks down in the mouth," Sarah Maitland thought. There must have been delicacy somewhere in the big nature, for she was careful not to speak of Elizabeth's engagement before Harris, for fear the girl might, by some involuntary tremor of lip or eyelid, betray herself.

"I'll look in on you after supper," she said.

Nannie, with a start, said, "Oh, thank you, Mamma."

When Mrs. Maitland, with her knitting and a fistful of unopened letters, came over to the parlor, she had also, tucked into her belt, a check.

It had never occurred to Nannie, in all these years and with a very liberal allowance, to mitigate her parlor. It was still a place of mirrors, grown perhaps a little dim; of chandeliers in balloons of brown paper-muslin, which, to be sure, had split here and there with age, so that a glimmer of cut glass sparkled dimly through the cracks; a place of marble-topped tables, and crimson brocade curtains dingy with age and soot; a place where still the only human thing was Nannie's drawing-board. She was bending over it now, copying with a faithful pencil a little picture of a man and a maid, and a dove and a Love. She was going to give the drawing to Elizabeth; in fact, she had begun it several days ago with joyous anticipation of this happy happening. But now, as she worked, her hand trembled. She had had a letter from Blair, and all her joyousness had fled:

"The Dean is an ass, of course; but mother'll get excited about it, I'm afraid. Do smooth her down, if you can."

No wonder Nannie's hand trembled!

Mrs. Maitland, putting her letters on the table, sat down heavily and began to knit. She glanced at Nannie over her spectacles. "Better get through with it," she said to herself. Then, aloud, "Well, Nannie, so David and Elizabeth have made a match of it?"

For a minute Nannie's face brightened. "Yes! Isn't it fine? I'm so pleased. David has been crazy about her ever since he was a boy."

Well! She was heart-whole! There was no doubt of that; Mrs. Maitland, visibly relieved, dismissed from her mind the whole foolish business of love-making. She began to read her letters, Nannie watching her furtively. When the third letter was taken up—a letter with the seal of the University in the upper left-hand corner of the envelope—Blair's sister breathed quickly. Mrs. Maitland, ripping the envelope open with a thrust of her forefinger, read it swiftly; then again, slowly. Then she said something under her breath and struck her fist on the table. Nannie's fingers whitened on her pencil. Sarah Maitland got up and stood on the hearth-rug, her back to the fire.

"I'll have to go East," she said, and began to bite her forefinger.

"Oh, Mamma," Nannie broke out, "I am sure there isn't anything really wrong. Perhaps he has been—a little foolish. Men are foolish in college. David got into hot water lots of times. But Blair hasn't done anything really bad, and—"

Mrs. Maitland gave her a somber look. "He wrote to you, did

he?" she said. And Nannie realized that she had not advanced her brother's cause. Mrs. Maitland picked up her letters and began to sort them out. "When is he going to grow up?" she said. "He's twenty-four; and he's been dawdling round at college for the last two years! He's not bad; he hasn't stuff enough in him to be bad. He is just lazy and useless; and he's had every chance young man could have!"

"Mamma!" Nannie protested, "it isn't fair to speak that way of Blair, and it isn't true, not a word of it!" Nannie, the 'fraid-cat of twenty years ago,—afraid still of thunder-storms and the dark and Sarah Maitland, and what not,—Nannie, when it came to defending Blair, had all the audacious courage of love. "He is not lazy, he is not useless; he is—he is—" Nannie stammered with angry distress; "he is dear, and good, and kind, and never did any harm in his life. Never! It's perfectly dreadful, Mamma, for you to say such things about him!"

"Well, well!" said Sarah Maitland, lifting an amused eyebrow. It was as if a humming-bird had attacked a steel billet. Her face softened into pleased affection. "Well, stick up for him," she said; "I like it in you, my dear, though what you say is foolish enough. You remind me of your mother. But your brother has brains. Yes, I'll say that for him,—he's like me; he has brains. That's why I'm so out of patience with him," she ended, lapsing into moody displeasure again. "If he was a fool, I wouldn't mind his behaving like a fool. But he has brains." Then she said, briefly, "'Night," and tramped off to the dining room.

The next morning when Nannie, a little pale from a worried night, came down to breakfast, her stepmother's place was empty.

"Yes," Harris explained; "she went off at twelve, Miss Nannie. She didn't let on where. She said you'd know."

"I know," poor Nannie said, and turned paler than ever.

Chapter 11

After Mrs. Maitland had had an interview with the Dean, she went off across the yard, under the great elms dripping in the rainy January thaw. Following his directions, she found her way through the corridors of a new building whose inappropriate expensiveness was obvious at every turn. Blair had rooms there, as had most of the sons of rich fathers. The whole place smelt of money! In Blair's apartment money was less obvious than beauty—but it was expensive beauty. He had a few good pictures, and on one wall a wonderful tapestry of forest foliage and roebucks, that he had picked up in Europe at a price which added to the dealer's affection for traveling Americans. The furnishing was in quiet and, for that period, remarkably good taste; masculine enough to balance a certain delicacy of detail—exquisite Tanagra figures, water-colors and pastels of women in costumes of rose and violet gauze, incense smoldering in an ivory jar, and much small bijouterie that meant an almost feminine appreciation of exquisite and costly prettiness.

Mrs. Maitland came tramping down the hall, her face set and stern; but suddenly, almost at Blair's door, she paused. Some one was singing; she knew the voice—beautiful, joyous, beating and pulsating with life:

"Drink to me only with thine eyes,
And I will pledge with mine."

She moved over to a window that lit the long corridor, and listened:

"Or leave a kiss ... "

Sarah Maitland stared out into the rain; the bare branches of the trees whipped against one another in the wind, but she did not see them. She leaned her forehead on the glass, listening to the golden voice. A warm wave seemed to rise in her breast, a wave of cosmic satisfaction in this vitality that was *hers*, because he was hers! Her eyes blurred so with emotion that she did not see the rocking branches in the rain. All the hardness of her face melted, under those melting cadences into exultant maternity:

"Or leave a kiss but in the cup,
And I'll not look for wine;
The thirst that from the soul—"

She smiled, then turned and knocked peremptorily at her son's door.

Blair, pausing in his song to comment on a thirst that rises otherwhere than in the soul, roared out a jolly command to "come in!" but for an instant he did not realize who stood on the threshold; nor was his mother able to distinguish him in the group of men lounging about a room dim with tobacco smoke. He was standing with his back to the door, pulling a somewhat reluctant cork from a bottle of sherry gripped between his knees.

Blair was immensely popular at college, not only because of the easy generosities of his wealth,—which were often only a pleasant form of selfishness that brought the fellows about him as honey brings flies, but because of a certain sympathetic quality of mind, a genius for companionship that was almost a genius for friendship. Now, his room was full of men. One of his guests was sitting on the window-sill, kicking his heels and swaying rhythmically back and forth to the twang of his banjo. One had begun to read aloud with passionate emphasis a poem, of which happily Mrs. Maitland did not catch the words; all of them were smoking. The door opened, but no one entered. One of the young men, feeling the draught, glanced languidly over his shoulder,—and got on his feet with extraordinary expedition! He said something under his breath. But it was the abrupt silence of the room that made Blair turn round. It did not need his stammering dismay, his half-cringing—"Clear out, will you, you fellows "—to get the men out of the room. They did not know who she was, but they knew she was Somebody. She did not speak, but the powerful personality seemed to sweep in and clear the atmosphere of its sickly triviality. She stood blocking up the doorway, looking at them; they were mostly Seniors, but there was not a man among them who did not feel foolish under that large and quiet look. Then she stepped a little aside. The movement was unmistakable. They jostled one another like a flock of sheep in their effort to get away quickly. Somebody muttered, "Good afternoon—" but the others were speechless. They left a speechless host behind them.

Mrs. Maitland, her rusty bonnet very much on one side, watched them go; then she closed the door behind them, and stood looking at her son who was still holding the corkscrew in his hands. Her feet were planted firmly wide apart, her hands were on her hips; her eyebrow was lifting ominously. "Well?" she said; with the echo of that golden voice still in her ears, her own voice was, even to herself, unexpectedly mild.

"I didn't expect you," Blair managed to say.

"I inferred as much," she said dryly; "so this is the way you keep up with your classes?"

"There are no lectures at this time of day," he said. "If you had been so kind, my dear mother, as to let me know you were coming"—he spoke with that exaggerated and impertinent politeness that confesses fright; "I would have met you. Instead of that, you— you—you burst in—" he was getting whiter and whiter. The thought that the men had seen the unkempt figure, the powerful face, the straggling locks of hair, the bare hands,—seen, in fact, the unlovely exterior of a large and generous nature, a nature which, alas, he, her son, had never seen; that they had seen her, and guessed, of course, that she was his mother, was positively unendurable to Blair. He tried to speak, but his voice shook into silence. His dismay was not entirely ignoble; the situation was excruciating to a man whose feeling for beauty was a form of religion; his mortification had in it the element of horror for a profaned ideal; his mother was an esthetic insult to motherhood.

"I've no fault to find with your friends being here, if they don't interfere with your studies," Mrs. Maitland said.

"Oh," he said rather blankly; then his shame of her stung him into fury: "why didn't you tell me that you—"

"I've been to see the Dean," she said; "sit down there and listen to me. Here, give me a chair; not that pincushion thing! Give me a chair fit for a man to sit on,—if you've got one in this upholstery shop."

Blair, with trembling hands, pushed a mahogany chair to her side. He did not sit down himself. He stood with folded arms and downcast eyes.

She was not unkind; she was not even ungentle. She was merely explicit: *he was a fool.* All this business,—she pointed to the bottle and the empty glasses; all this business was idiotic, it was a boy's foolishness. "It shows how young you are, Blair," she said kindly, "though the Lord knows you are old enough in years to have some sense!" But if he kept the foolishness up, and this other tomfoolery on account of which she had had to leave the Works and spend her valuable time talking to the Dean, why, he might be expelled. He would certainly be suspended. And that would put off his getting into business for still another year. "And you are twenty-four!" she said.

While she talked she looked about her, and the mother-softness began to die out of her eyes. Sarah Maitland had never seen her son's room; she saw, now, soft-green hangings, great bowls of roses, a sideboard with an array of glasses, a wonderfully carved ivory jar standing on a teak-wood table whose costliness, even to her uneducated eyes, was obvious. Suddenly she put on her spectacles, and still talking, rose, and walked slowly about the room glancing at the water-colors. By and by, just at the end of her harangue,—to which Blair had listened in complete silence,—she paused before a row of photographs on the mantelpiece; then, in the midst of a sentence, she broke off with an exclamation, leaned forward, and seizing a photograph, tore it in two, across the smiling face and the bare bosom, across the lovely, impudent line of the thigh, and flung it underfoot. "Shame on you! to let your mother see a thing like that!"

"I didn't ask my mother to see it."

"If you have thoughts like this," she said, "Elizabeth did well to throw you over for David."

Blair lifted one eyebrow with a glimmer of interest. "Oh, David has got her, has he?"

"At any rate, he's a *man!* He doesn't live like this"—she made a contemptuous gesture; "muddling with silks and paintings, and pictures of bad women! What kind of a room is this for a man? Full of flowers and stinking jars, and cushions, and truck? It's more fit for a—a creature like that picture"—she set her heel on the smiling face; "than for a man! I ought never to have sent you here. I ought to have put you to puddling." She looked at him in growing agitation. "My God! Blair, what are you—living this way, with silks and perfumery and clay baby dolls? You've got no guts to you! I didn't mind your making a fool of yourself; that's natural; nobody can get to be a man till he's been a fool; but this—" She stood there, with one hand on the mantelpiece beside the row of photographs and bits of carving and little silver trinkets, and looked at him in positive fright. "And you are *my* son," she said.

The torrent of her angry shame suddenly swept Blair's

manhood of twenty-four years away; her very power stripped him bare as a baby; it almost seemed as if she had sucked his masculinity out of him and incorporated it into herself. He stood there like a cringing schoolboy expecting to be whipped. "One of the men gave me that picture; I—"

"You ought to have slapped his face! Listen to me: you are going to be looked after,—do you hear me? You are going to be watched. Do you understand?" She gathered up the whole row of photographs, innocent and offensive together, and threw them into the fire. "You are going to walk straight, or you are coming home, and going to work."

It was a match to gunpowder; in an instant Blair's temper, the terrific temper of the uniformly and lazily amiable man, flashed into furious words.

Stammering with rage, he told her what he thought of her; to record his opinion is not for edification. Even Sarah Maitland flinched before it. She left him with a bang. She saw the Dean again, and her recommendations of espionage were so extreme and so unwise that he found himself taking Blair's part in his effort to save the young man from the most insolent intrusion upon his privacy. She went back to Mercer in a whirl of anger but in somber silence. She had scorched and stung under the truths her son told her about herself; she had bled under the lies she had told him as to her feeling for him. She looked ten years older for that hour in his room. But she had nothing to say. She told poor, frightened Nannie that she had "seen Master Blair"; she added that he was a fool. To Robert Ferguson she was a little more explicit:

"Blair has not been behaving himself; he's in debt; he has been gambling. See that all these bills are paid. Tell Watson to give him a hundred dollars more a month; I won't have him running in debt in this way. Now what about the Duluth order?"

Chapter 12

Mr. Ferguson made no protest in regard to Blair's increased allowance. "If his mother wants to ruin him, it isn't my business," he said. The fact was, he had not recovered from his astonished resentment at Sarah Maitland's joke in Mrs. Richie's parlor. He thought about it constantly, and asked himself whether he did not owe his neighbor an apology of some kind. The difficulty was to know what kind, for after all *he* was perfectly innocent! "Such an idea never entered my head," he thought angrily; "but of course, if there has been anything in my conduct to put it into Mrs. Maitland's head, I ought to be thrashed! Perhaps I'd better not go in next door more than two or three times a week?" So, for once, Robert Ferguson was distinctly out with his employer, and when she told him to see that Blair had a hundred dollars more a month, he said, in his own mind, "be hanged to him! What difference does it make to me if she ruins him?" and held his tongue—until the next day. Then he barked out a remonstrance: "I suppose you know your own business, but if *I* had a boy I wouldn't increase his allowance because he was in debt."

"I want to keep him from getting in debt again," she explained, her face falling into troubled lines.

"If you will allow me to say so—having been a boy myself, that's not the way to do it."

Sarah Maitland flung herself back in her chair, and struck the desk with her fist. "I am at my wit's end to know what to do about him! My idea has been to make a man of him, by giving him what he wants, not making him fuss over five-cent pieces. He's had everything; he's never heard '*no*' in his life. And yet—look at him!"

"That's the trouble with him. He's had too much. He needs a

few no's. But he's like most rich boys; there isn't one rich man's son in ten who is worth his salt. If he were *my* boy," said Robert Ferguson, with that infallibility which everybody feels in regard to the way other people's children should be brought up, "if he were my son, I'd put him to work this summer."

Mrs. Maitland blew her lips out in a great sigh; then nibbled her forefinger, staring with blank eyes straight ahead of her. She was greatly perplexed. "I'll think it over," she said; "I'll think it over. Hold on; what's your hurry? I want to ask you something: your neighbor there, Mrs. Richie, seems to be a very attractive woman; 'fair and forty,' as the saying is—only I guess she's nearer fifty? But she's mighty good-looking, whatever her age is."

The color came into Robert Ferguson's face; this time he was really offended. Mrs. Maitland was actually venturing—"I have never noticed her looks," he said stiffly, and rose.

"It just struck me when I caught you in there the other day," she ruminated; "what do you know about her?" Buried deep in the casual question was another question, but Robert Ferguson did not hear it; she was *not* going to venture! He was so relieved, that he was instantly himself again. He told her briefly what little he knew: Mrs. Richie was a widow; husband dead many years. "I have an idea he was a crooked stick,—more from what she hasn't said than what she has said. There's a friend of hers I meet once in a while at her house, a Doctor King, and he intimated to me that her husband was a bad lot. It appears he hurt their child, when he was drunk. She never forgave him. I don't blame her, I'm sure; the baby died. It was after the death of the husband that she adopted David. She has no relations apparently; some friends in Old Chester, I believe; this Doctor King is one of 'em."

"Is she going to marry him?" Mrs. Maitland said.

"There might be objections on the part of the present

incumbent," he said, with his meager smile.

Mrs. Maitland admitted that the doctor's wife presented difficulties; "but perhaps she'll die," she said, cheerfully; "I'm interested to know that Mrs. Richie has friends; I was wondering—" She did not say what she wondered. "She's a nice woman, Robert Ferguson, and a good woman, *and* a good-looking woman, too; 'fair and'—well, say 'fifty'! And if you had any sense—"

But this time Robert Ferguson really did get out of the office.

His advice about Blair, however, seemed superfluous. So far as behavior went, Mrs. Maitland had no further occasion to increase his allowance. His remaining months in the university were decorous enough, though his scholarship was no credit to him. He "squeaked through," as he expressed it to his sister, gaily, when she came east to see him graduate, three years behind the class in which he had entered college. But as to his conduct, that domiciliary visit had hardened him into a sort of contemptuous common sense. And his annoyed and humiliated manhood, combined with his esthetic taste, sufficed, also, to keep things fairly peaceful when he was at home, which was rarely for more than a week or two at a time. Quarrels with his mother had become excruciating experiences, like discords on the piano; they set his teeth on edge, though they never touched his heart. To avoid them, he would, he told Nannie, chuckling at her horror,—"lie like the devil!" His lying, however, was nothing more serious than a careful and entirely insincere politeness; but it answered his purpose, and "rows," as he called them, were very rare; although, indeed, his mother did her part in avoiding them, too. To Sarah Maitland, a difference with her son meant a pang at the very center of her being—her maternity; her heart was seared by it, but her taste was not offended because she had no taste. So, for differing reasons, peace was kept. The next fall, after a summer abroad, Blair went back to the university and took two or three special courses;

also he began to paint rather seriously; all of which was his way of putting off the evil day of settling down in Mercer.

Meantime, life grew quite vivid to his sister. Elizabeth had once said that Nannie was "born an old maid"; and certainly these tranquil, gently useless years of being very busy about nothing, and living quite alone with her stepmother, had emphasized in her a simplicity and literalness of mind that was sometimes very amusing to the other three friends. At any rate, hers was a pallid little personality—perhaps it could not have been anything else in the household of a woman like Sarah Maitland, with whom, domestically, it was always either peace, or a sword! Nannie was incapable of anything but peace. "You are a 'fraid-cat," Elizabeth used to tell her, "but you're a perfect dear!" "Nannie is unscrupulously good," Blair said once; and her soft stubbornness in doing anything she conceived to be her duty, warranted his criticism. But during the first year that David and Elizabeth were engaged, her stagnant existence in the silent old house began to stir; little shocks of reality penetrated the gentle primness of her thought, and she came creeping out into the warmth and sunshine of other people's happiness; indeed, her shy appreciation of the lovers' experiences became almost an experience of her own, so closely did she nestle to all their emotions! It was a real blow to her when it was decided that David should enter a Philadelphia hospital as an interne. "Won't he be at home even for the long vacations?" Nannie asked, anxiously; when she was told that hospitals did not give "vacations," her only consolation was that she would have to console Elizabeth.

But when Robert Ferguson heard what was going to happen, he had nothing to console him. "I'll have a love-sick girl on my hands," he complained to Mrs. Richie. "You'll have to do your share of it," he barked at her. He had come in through the green door in the garden wall, with a big clump of some perennial in his hands, and a trowel under one arm. "Peonies have to be thinned out in the fall," he said grudgingly, "and I want to get rid of this lot. Where shall I put 'em?"

It was a warm October afternoon, and Mrs. Richie, who had been sitting on the stone bench under the big hawthorn in her garden, reading, until the dusk hid her page, looked up gratefully. "You are robbing yourself; I believe that is your precious white peony!"

"It's only half of it, and I get as much good out of it here as in my own garden," he grunted (he was sitting on his heels digging a hole big enough for a clump of peonies with a trowel, so no wonder he grunted); "besides, it improves my property to plant perennials; my next tenant may appreciate flowers," he ended, with the reproving significance which had become a joke between them.

"Oh," said Mrs. Richie, sighing, "I don't like to think of that 'next tenant.'"

He looked up at her a little startled. "What do you mean? You are not going to Philadelphia with David next April?"

"Why, you didn't suppose I would let David go alone?"

"What! You will leave Mercer?" he said. In his dismayed astonishment he dropped his trowel and stood up. "Will you please tell me why I should stay in Mercer, when David is in Philadelphia?"

Robert Ferguson was silent; then he tramped the earth in around the roots of the white peony, and said, sullenly, "It never occurred to me that you would go, too."

"You'll have to be extra nice to Elizabeth when we are not here," Mrs.
Richie instructed him. David's mother was very anxious to be nice to Elizabeth herself; which was a confession, though she did not know it,
of her old misgivings as to David's choice.

"Be nice? *I*?" said Mr. Ferguson, and snorted; "did you ever know me 'nice'?"

"Always," she said, smiling.

But he would not smile; he went back to his garden for some more roots; when he returned with a wedge taken from his bed of lemon-lilies, he said crossly, "David can manage his own affairs; he doesn't need apron-strings! I think I've mentioned that to you before?"

"I think I recall some such reference," she admitted, her voice trembling with friendly amusement.

But he went on growling and barking: "Foolish woman! to try the experiment at your age, of living in a strange place!"

At that she laughed outright: "That is the nicest way in the world to tell a friend you will miss her."

Robert Ferguson did not laugh. In fact, as the winter passed and the time drew near for the move to be made, nobody laughed very much. Certainly not the two young people; since David had left the medical school he had worked in Mercer's infirmary, and now they both felt as if the world would end for them when they ceased to see each other several times a day. David did his best to be cheerful about it; in fact, with that common sense of his which his engagement had accentuated, he was almost too cheerful. The hospital service would be a great advantage, he said, So great that perhaps the three years' engagement to which they were looking forward,—because David's finances would probably not be equal to a wife before that; the three years might be shortened to two. But to be parted for two years—it was "practically parting," for visits don't amount to anything; "it's tough," said David. "It's *terrific!*" Elizabeth said.

"Oh, well," David reminded her, "two years is a lot better than three."

It was curious to see how Love had developed these two

young creatures: Elizabeth had sprung into swift and glowing womanhood; with triumphant candor her conduct confessed that she had forgotten everything but Love. She showed her heart to David, and to her little world, as freely as a flower that has opened overnight —a rose, still wet with dew, that bares a warm and fragrant bosom to the sun. David had matured, too; but his maturity was of the mind rather than the body; manhood suddenly fell upon him like a cloak, and because his sense of humor had always been a little defective, it was a somewhat heavy cloak, which hid and even hampered the spontaneous freedom of youth. He was deeply and passionately in love, but his face fell into lines of responsibility rather than passion; lines, even, of care. He grew markedly older; he thought incessantly of how soon he would be able to marry, and always in connection with his probable income and his possible expenses. Helena Richie was immensely proud of this sudden, serious manhood; but Elizabeth's uncle took it as a matter of course:—had he not, himself, ceased to be an ass at twenty? Why shouldn't David Richie show some sense at twenty-five!

As for Elizabeth, she simply adored. Perhaps she was, once in a while, a little annoyed at the rather ruthless power with which David would calmly override some foolish wish of hers; and sometimes there would be a gust of temper,—but it always yielded at his look or touch. When he was not near her, when she could not see the speechless passion in his eyes, or feel the tremor of his lips when they answered the demand of hers, then the anger lasted longer. Once or twice, when he was away from home, his letters, with their laconic taking of her love for granted, made her sharply displeased; but when he came back, and kissed her, she forgot everything but his arms. Curiously enough, the very completeness of her surrender kept him so entirely reverent of her that people who did not know him might have thought him cold—but Elizabeth knew! She knew his love, even when, as she fulminated against the misery of being left alone, David merely said, briefly, "Oh, well, two years is a lot better than three."

The two years of absence were to begin in April. It was in February that Robert Ferguson was told definitely just when his tenant would terminate her lease; he received the news in absolute silence. Mrs. Richie's note came at breakfast; he read it, then went into his library and shut the door. He sat down at his writing-table, his hands in his pockets, an unlighted cigar between his teeth. He sat there nearly an hour. Then, throwing the cigar into his waste-basket, he knocked his glasses off with a bewildered gesture; "Well, I'll be hanged," he said, softly. It was at that moment that he forgave Mrs. Maitland her outrageous joke of more than a year before. "I've always known that woman was no fool," he said, smiling ruefully at the remembrance of his anger at Sarah Maitland's advice. "It was darned good advice!" he said; but he looked positively dazed. "And I've always said I wouldn't give Life the chance to play another trick on me!" he reflected; "well, I won't. This is no silly love-affair; it's good common sense." Ten minutes later, as he started for his office, he caught sight of his face in the mirror in the hall. He had lifted one hand to take his hat from the rack, but as he suddenly saw himself, he stood stock-still, with upraised arm and extended fingers; Robert Ferguson had probably not been really aware of his reflection in a looking-glass for twenty-five years. He saw now a lean, lined, sad face, a morose droop of thin and bitter lips; he saw gray hair standing up stiffly above a careworn forehead; he saw kind, troubled eyes. And as he looked, he frowned. "I'm an ugly cuss," he said to himself, sighing; "and I look sixty." In point of fact, he was nearly fifty. "But so is she," he added, defiantly, and took down his hat. "Only, *she* looks forty." And then he thought of Mrs. Maitland's "fair and fifty," and smiled, in spite of himself. "Yes, she is rather good-looking," he admitted.

And indeed she was; Mrs. Richie's quiet life with her son had kept her forehead smooth, and her eyes—eyes the color of a brook which loiters in shady places over last year's leaves—softly clear. There was a gentle placidity about her; the curious, shy hesitation, the deep, half-frightened sadness, which had been so marked when her landlord knew her first, had disappeared; sometimes she even showed soft gaieties of manner or speech which delighted her moody neighbor to the point of making him laugh. And laughing had all the charm of novelty to poor Robert Ferguson. "I never dreamed of her going away," he said to himself. Well, yes; certainly Mrs. Maitland had some sense, after all. When, a week later, blundering and abrupt, he referred to Mrs. Maitland's "sense," Mrs. Richie could not at first understand what he was talking about. "She 'knew more than you gave her credit for'? I thought you gave her credit for knowing everything! Oh, you don't want me to leave Mercer? I don't see the connection. *I* don't know everything! But you are very flattering, I'm sure. I am a 'good tenant,' I suppose?"

"Please don't go." She laughed at what she thought was his idea of a joke; then said, with half a sigh, that she did not know any one in Philadelphia; "when David isn't at home I shall be pretty lonely," she said.

"Please don't go," he said again, in a low voice. They were sitting before the fire in Mrs. Richie's parlor; the glass doors of the plant-room were open,—that plant-room, which had been his first concession to her; and the warm air of the parlor was fragrant with blossoming hyacinths. There was a little table between them, with a bowl of violets on it, and a big lamp. Robert Ferguson rose, and stood with his hands behind him, looking down at her. His hair, in a stiff brush above his forehead, was quite gray, but his face in its unwonted emotion seemed quivering with youth. He knocked off his glasses irritably. "I never know how to say things," he said, in a low voice; "but—please don't go."

Mrs. Richie stared at him in amazement.

"I think we'd better get married," he said.

"*Mr. Ferguson!*"

"I think I've cared about you ever since you came here, but I am such a fool I didn't know it until Mrs. Maitland said that absurd thing last fall."

"I—I don't know what you mean!" she parried, breathlessly; "at any rate, please don't say anything more about it."

"I have to say something more." He sat down again with the air of one preparing for a siege. "I've got several things to say. First, I want to find out my chances?"

"You haven't any."

His face moved. He put on his glasses carefully, with both hands. "Mrs. Richie, is there any one else? If so, I'll quit. I know you will answer straight; you are not like other women. *Is there anybody else?* That—that Old Chester doctor who comes to see you once in a while, I understand he's a widower now; wife's just died; and if—"

"There is nobody; *never* anybody."

"Ah!" he said, triumphantly; then frowned: "If your attachment to your husband makes you say I haven't any chance—but it can't be that."

Her eyes suddenly dilated. "Why not? Why do you say it can't be that?" she said in a frightened voice.

"I somehow got the impression—forgive me if I am saying anything I oughtn't to; but I had kind of an idea that you were not especially happy with him."

She was silent.

"But even if you were," he went on, "it is so many years; I don't mean to offend you, but a woman isn't faithful to a memory for so many years!" he looked at her incredulously; "not even you, I think."

"Such a thing is possible," she told him coldly; she had grown very pale. "But it is not because of—of my husband that I say I shall never marry again."

He interrupted her. "If it isn't a dead man nor a live man that's ahead of me, then it seems to me you can't say I haven't any chance—unless I am personally offensive to you?" There was an almost child-like consternation in his eyes; "am I? Of course I know I am a bear."

"Oh, please don't say things like that!" she protested. "A bear? You?
Why, you are just my good, kind friend and neighbor; but—"

"Ah!" he said, "that scared me for a minute! Well, when I understood what was the matter with me (I didn't understand until about a week ago), I said to myself, 'If there's nobody ahead of me, that woman shall be my wife.' Of course, I am not talking sentimentalities to you; we are not David and Elizabeth! I'm fifty, and you are not far from it. But I—I—I'm hard hit, Mrs. Richie;" his voice trembled, and he twitched off his glasses with more than usual ferocity.

Mrs. Richie rose; "Mr. Ferguson," she said, gently, "I do appreciate the honor you do me, but—"

"Don't say a thing like that; it's foolish," he interrupted, frowning; "what 'honor' is it, to a woman like you, to have an ugly, bad-mannered fellow like me, want you for a wife? Why, how could I help it! How could any man help it? I don't know what Dr. King is thinking of, that he isn't sitting on your doorsteps waiting for a chance to ask you! I ought to have asked you long ago. I can't imagine why I didn't, except that I supposed we would go on always living next door to each other. And—and I thought anything like *this*, was over for me... . Mrs. Richie, please sit down, and let me finish what I have to say."

"There is no use, Mr. Ferguson," she said; but she sat down, her face falling into lines of sadness that made her look curiously old.

"There isn't anybody ahead of me: so far, so good. Now as to my chances; of course I realize that I haven't any,—to-day. But there's to-morrow, Mrs. Richie; and the day after to-morrow. There's next week, and next year;—and I don't change. Look how slow I was in finding out that I wanted you; it's taken me all these years! What a poor, dull fool I am! Well, I know it now; and you know it; and you don't personally dislike me. So perhaps some day," his harsh face was suddenly almost beautiful; "some day you'll be—*my wife!*" he said, under his breath. He had no idea that he was "talking sentimentalities"; he would have said he did not know how to be sentimental. But his voice was the voice of youth and passion.

She shook her head. "No," she said, quietly; "I can't marry you, Mr.
Ferguson."

"But you are generally so reasonable," he protested, astonished and wistful; "why, it seems to me that you *must* be willing —after a while? Here we are, two people getting along in years, and our children have made a match of it; and we are used to each other, that's a very important thing in marriage. It's just plain common sense, after David is on his own legs in the hospital, for us to join forces. Perhaps in the early summer? I won't be unreasonably urgent. Surely"—he was gaining confidence from his own words—"surely you must see how sensible—"

Involuntarily, perhaps through sheer nervousness, she laughed. "Mrs. Maitland's 'sensible arrangement'? No, Mr. Ferguson; please let us forget all about this—"

He gave his snort of a laugh. "Forget? Now *that* isn't sensible. No, you dear, foolish woman; whatever else we do, we shall neither of us forget this. This is one of the things a man and woman don't forget;" in his earnestness he pushed aside the bowl of violets on the table between them, and caught her hand in both of his. "I'm going to get you yet," he said, he was as eager as a boy.

Before she could reply, or even draw back, David opened the parlor door, and stood aghast on the threshold. It was impossible to mistake the situation. The moment of sharp withdrawal between the two on either side of the table announced it, without the uttering of a word; David caught his breath. Robert Ferguson could have wrung the intruder's neck, but Mrs. Richie clutched at her son's presence with a gasp of relief: "Oh—David! I thought you were next door!"

"I was," David said, briefly; "I came in to get a book for Elizabeth."

"We were—talking," Mrs. Richie said, trying to laugh. Mr. Ferguson, standing with his back to the fire, was slowly putting on his glasses. "But we had finished our discussion," she ended breathlessly.

"For the moment," Mr. Ferguson said, significantly; and set his jaw.

"Well, David, have you and Elizabeth decided when she is to come and see us in Philadelphia?" Mrs. Richie asked, her voice still trembling.

"She says she'll come East whenever Mr. Ferguson can bring her," David said, rummaging among the books on the table. "But it's a pity to wait as long as that," he added, and the hint in his words was inescapable.

Robert Ferguson did not take hints. "I think I can manage to come pretty soon," he retorted.

Chapter 13

When Mr. Ferguson said good night, David, apparently
unable to find the book he had promised to take in to Elizabeth,
made no effort to help his mother in her usual small nightly tasks of
blowing out the lamps, tidying the table, folding up a newspaper or
two. This was not like David, but Mrs. Richie was too absorbed to
notice her son's absorption. Just as she was starting up-stairs, he
burst out: "Materna—"

"Yes? What is it?"

He gave her a keenly searching look; then drew a breath of
relief, and kissed her. "Nothing," he said.

But later, as he lay on his back in bed, his hands clasped
behind his head, his pipe between his teeth, David was distinctly
angry. "Of course she doesn't care a hang for him," he reflected; "I
could see that; but I swear I'll go to Philadelphia right off." Before he
slept he had made up his mind that was the best thing to do. That old
man, gray and granite-faced, and silent, "that old codger," said the
disrespectful cub of twenty-six, "should take advantage of friendship
to be a nuisance,—confound him!" said David. "The idea of his
daring to make love to her! I wanted to show him the door." As for
his mother, even if she didn't "care a hang," he was half shocked, half
hurt; he felt, as all young creatures do, a curious repulsion at the idea
of love-making between people no longer young. It hurt his delicacy,
it almost hurt his sense of reverence for his mother, to think that she
had been obliged to listen to any words of love. "It's offensive," he
said angrily; "yes; we'll clear out! We'll go to Philadelphia the first of
March, instead of April."

The next morning he suggested his plan to his mother.
"Could you pack up in three weeks, Materna?" he said; "I think I'd

like to get you settled before I go to the hospital." Mrs. Richie's instant acceptance of the change of date made him more annoyed than ever. "He has worried her!" he thought angrily; "I wonder how long this thing has been going on?" But he said nothing to her. Nor did he mean to explain to Elizabeth just why he must shorten their last few weeks of being together. It would not be fair to his mother to explain, he said to himself;—he did not think of any unfairness to the "old codger." He was, however, a little uneasy at the prospect of breaking the fact of this earlier departure to Elizabeth without an explanation. Elizabeth might be hurt; she might say that he didn't want to stay with her. "She knows better!" he said to himself, grinning. The honest truth was, and he faced it with placidity, that if things were not explained to Elizabeth, she might get huffy,—this was David's word; but David knew how to check that "huffiness"!

They were to walk together that afternoon, and he manoeuvered for a few exquisite minutes alone before they went out. At first the moments were not very exquisite.

"Well! What happened to you last night? I thought you were going to bring me that book!"

"I couldn't. I had to stay at home."

"Why?"

"Well; Materna wanted me."

Elizabeth murmured a small, cold "Oh." Then she said, "Why didn't you send the book in by Uncle?"

"I didn't think of it," David said candidly.

Elizabeth's dimple straightened. "It would have been polite to have sent me a message."

"I took it for granted you'd know I was detained."

"You take too much for—" she began, but before she could utter the sharp words that trembled on her lips, he caught her in his arms and kissed her; instantly the little flame of temper was blown out.

"That's the worst of walking," David said, as she let him draw her down on the sofa beside him; "I can't kiss you on the street."

"Heavens, I should hope not!" she said. Then, forgetting what she thought was his forgetfulness, she relaxed within his arms, sighing with bliss. "'Oh, isn't it joyful,—joyful,—joyful—'" she hummed softly. "I do love to have you put your arms around me, David! Isn't it wonderful to love each other the way we do? I feel so sorry for other girls, because they aren't engaged to you; poor things! Do you suppose anybody in the world was ever as happy as I am?"

"*You?*" said David, scornfully; "you don't count at all, compared to me!" Then they both laughed for the sheer foolishness of that "joyfulness," which was so often on Elizabeth's lips. But David sighed. "Three years is a devilish long time to wait."

"Maybe it will be only two!" she whispered, her soft lips against his ear. But this was one of David's practical and responsible moments, so he said grimly, "Not much hope of that."

Elizabeth, agreeing sadly, got up to straighten her hat before the mirror over the mantelpiece. "It's hideously long. Oh, if I were only a rich girl!"

"Thank Heaven you are not!" he said, with such sudden cold incisiveness that she turned round and looked at him. "Do you think I'd marry a rich woman, and let her support me?"

"I don't see why she shouldn't, if she loved you," Elizabeth said calmly; "I don't see that it matters which has the money, the man or the girl."

"I see," David said; "I've always felt that way—even about mother. Materna has wanted to help me out lots of times, and I wouldn't let her. I could kick myself now when I think how often I have to put my hand in her pocket."

"I think," cried Elizabeth, "a man might love a girl enough to live on her money!"

"I don't," David said, soberly.

"Well," said Elizabeth, "don't worry. I haven't a cent, so you can't put your hand in my pocket! Come, we must start. I want to go and see Nannie for a minute, and Cherry-pie says I must be in before dark, because I have a cold."

"I like sitting here best," David confessed, but pulled himself up from the sofa, and in another minute Miss White, peering from an upper window, saw them walking off. "Made for each other!" said Cherry-pie, nibbling with happiness.

They had almost reached Nannie's before David said that— that he was afraid he would have to go away a month before he had planned. When he was most in earnest, his usual brevity of speech fell into a curtness that might have seemed, to one who did not know him, indifference. Elizabeth did know him, but even to her the ensuing explanation, which did not explain, was, through his very anxiety not to offend her, provokingly laconic.

"But you don't go on duty at the hospital until April," she said hotly.
 "Why do you leave Mercer the first of March?"

"Materna wants time to get settled."

"Mrs. Richie told me only yesterday that she was going to a hotel," Elizabeth said; "she said she wasn't going to look for a house until the fall, because she will be at the seashore this summer. It certainly doesn't take a month to find a hotel."

"Well, the fact is, there are reasons why it isn't pleasant for Materna to be in Mercer just now."

"Not pleasant to be in Mercer! What on earth do you mean?"

"I'm afraid I can't tell you. It's her affair."

"Oh, I didn't mean to intrude," Elizabeth said coldly.

"Now, Elizabeth," he protested, "that isn't a nice thing to

say."

"Do you think *you've* been saying nice things? I am perfectly certain that you would never hesitate to tell your mother any of my reasons for doing things!"

"Elizabeth, I wouldn't leave Mercer a minute before the first of April, if I wasn't sure it was best for Materna. You know that."

"Oh, go!" she said; "go, and have all the secrets you want. *I* don't care."

"Elizabeth, be reasonable; I—"

But she had left him; they had reached the Maitland house, and, pushing aside his outstretched hand, she opened the iron gate herself, slammed it viciously, and ran up the curving steps to the door. As she waited for Harris to answer her ring, she looked back: "I think you are reasonable enough for both of us; please don't let me ever interfere with your plans!" She paused a minute in the hall, listening for a following step;—it did not come. "Well, if he's cross he can stay outside!" she told herself, and burst into the parlor. "Nannie!" she began,—"Oh, I beg your pardon!" she said. Blair was standing on the hearth-rug, talking vehemently to his sister; at the sound of the opening door he wheeled around and saw her, glowing, wounded, and amazingly handsome. "Elizabeth!" he said, staring at her. And he kept on staring while they shook hands. They were a handsome pair, the tall, dark, well-set-up man, and the girl almost as tall as he, with brown, gilt-flecked hair blowing about a vivid face which had the color, in the sharp February afternoon, of a blush-rose.

"Where's David?" Nannie said.

[Illustration: 'I THINK YOU ARE REASONABLE ENOUGH FOR BOTH OF US']

"I left him at the gate. He's coming in in a minute," Elizabeth said; and turned to Blair: "I didn't know you had come home."

Blair explained that he was only in Mercer for a day. "I'm in a hole," he said drolly, "and I've come home to have Nannie get me out."

"Nannie is always ready to get people out of holes;" Elizabeth said, but her voice was vague. She was listening for David's step, her cheeks beginning to burn with mortification, at his delay.

"Where *is* David?" Nannie demanded, returning from a fruitless search for him in the hall.

"He's a lucky dog," Blair said, looking at the charming, angry face with open and friendly admiration.

Elizabeth shrugged her shoulders. "I don't know about his luck. By the way, he is going to Philadelphia the first of March, Nannie," she said carelessly.

"I thought he didn't have to go until April?" Nannie sympathized.

"So did I. Perhaps he'll tell you why he has changed his mind. He hasn't deigned to give me his reasons yet."

And Blair, watching her, said to himself, "Same old Elizabeth!" He began to talk to her in his gay, teasing way, but she was not listening; suddenly she interrupted him, saying that she must go home. "I thought David was coming in, but I suppose he's walking up and down, waiting for me."

"If he doesn't know which side his bread is buttered, I'll walk home with you," Blair said; "and Nancy dear, while I'm gone, you see Mother and do your best, won't you?"

"Yes," poor Nannie sighed, "but I do wish— "

Blair did not wait to hear what she wished; he had eyes only for this self-absorbed young creature who would not listen when he spoke to her. At the gate she hesitated, looked hurriedly about her, up and down the squalid street; she did not answer, did not apparently hear, some question that he asked. Blair glanced up and down the street, too. "David doesn't appreciate his opportunities," he said.

Elizabeth's lip tightened, and she flung up her head; the rose in her cheeks was drowned in scarlet. She came out of her absorption, and began to sparkle at her companion; she teased him, but not too much; she flattered him, very delicately; she fell into half-sentimental reminiscences that made him laugh, then stabbed him gently with an indifferent word that showed how entirely she had forgotten him. And all the time her eyes were absent, and the straight line in her cheek held the dimple a prisoner. Blair, who had begun with a sort of good-natured, rather condescending amusement at his old playmate, found himself, to his surprise, on his mettle.

"Don't go home yet," he said; "let's take a walk."

"I'd love to!"

"Mercer seems to be just as hideous as ever," Blair said; "suppose we go across the river, and get away from it?"

She agreed lightly: "Horrid place." At the corner, she flashed a glance down the side street; David was not to be seen.

"Will David practise here, when he is ready to put out his shingle?"

"I'm sure I don't know. I can't keep track of David's plans."

"He is just as good as ever, I suppose?" Blair said, and watched her delicate lip droop.

"Better, if anything." And in the dusk, as they sauntered over the old bridge, she flung out gibe after gibe at her lover. Her cheeks grew hotter and hotter; it was like tearing her own flesh. The shame of it! The rapture of it! It hurt her so that the tears stood in her eyes; so she did it again, and yet again. "I don't pretend to live up to David," she said.

Blair, with a laugh, confessed that he had long ago given up any such ambition himself. On the bridge they stopped, and Blair looked back at the town lying close to the water. In the evening dusk lights were pricking out all along the shore; the waste-lands beyond the furnaces were vague with night mists, faintly amethyst in the east, bronze and black over the city. Here and there in the brown distances flames would suddenly burst out from unseen stacks, then sink, and the shadows close again.

"I wish I could paint it," Blair said dreamily; "Mercer from the bridge, at twilight, is really beautiful."

"I like the bridge," Elizabeth said, "for sentimental reasons. (Now," she added to herself, "now, I am a bad woman; to speak of *that* to another man is vile.) David and I," she said, significantly,— and laughed.

Even Blair was startled at the crudeness of the allusion. "I didn't suppose David ever condescended to be spoony," he said, and at the same instant, to his absolute amazement, she caught his arm and pulled his hand from the railing.

"Don't touch that place!" she cried; Blair, amused and cynical, laughed under his breath.

"I see; this is the hallowed spot where you made our friend a happy man?"

"We'll turn back now, please," Elizabeth said, suddenly trembling. She had reached the climax of her anger, and the reaction was like the shock of dropping from a dizzy height. During the walk home she scarcely spoke. When he left her at her uncle's door, she was almost rude. "Goodnight. No; I'm busy. I'd rather you didn't come in." In her own room, without waiting to take off her things, she ran to her desk; she did not even pause to sit down, but bent over, and wrote, sobbing under her breath:

"DAVID: I am just as false as I can be. I ridiculed you to Blair. I lied and lied and lied—because I was angry. I hated you for a little while. I am low, and vulgar, and a blasphemer. *I told him about the bridge.* You see how vile I am? But don't—don't give me up, David. Only—understand just how base I am, and then, if you possibly can, keep on loving me. E.

"P. S. I am not worth loving."

* * * * *

When David read that poor little letter, his face quivered for an instant, then he smiled. "Materna," he said—they were sitting at supper; "Materna, she certainly is perfect!"

His mother laughed, and put out her hand. But he shook his head. "Not even you!" he said.

When he went to see Elizabeth that evening, he found her curiously broken. "David, how could I do it? I made *fun* of you! Do you understand? Yes; I truly did. Oh, how vile I am! And I knew I was vile all the time; that's the queer part of it. But I piled it on! And all the time it seemed as if I was just bleeding to death inside. But I kept on doing it. I loved being false. I loved to blacken myself." She drew away from him, shivering. "No; don't touch me; don't kiss me; I am not worthy. Oh, David, throw me over! Don't marry me, I am not fit—" And as he caught her in his arms, she said, her voice smothered against his breast, "You see, you didn't come in at Nannie's. And it looked as if—as if you didn't care. It was humiliating, David. And last night you didn't bring me the book, or even send any message; and that was sort of careless. Yes, I really think you were a little horrid, David. So I was hurt, I suppose, to start with; and you know, when I am hurt—Oh, yes; it was silly; but —"

He kissed her again, and laughed. "It was silly, dear."

"Well, but listen: I am not excusing myself for this afternoon, but I do want you to understand how it started. I was provoked at your not explaining to me why you go away a whole month earlier than you need; I think any girl would be a little provoked, David. And then, on top of it, you let Blair and Nannie see that you didn't care to walk home with me, and—"

"But good gracious!" said David, amused and tender, "I thought you didn't want me! And it would have been rather absurd to hang round, if I wasn't wanted."

"Oh," she cried, sharply, lifting her wet face from his breast, "don't you see? *I want you to be absurd!* Can't you understand how a girl feels?" She stopped, and sighed. "After all, why should you show Nannie and Blair that you care? Why should you wait? I am not worth caring for, or waiting for, anywhere, any time! Oh, David, my temper—my dreadful temper!"

He lifted her trembling hand and kissed the scar on her left wrist silently.

"I ought not to see you to-night, just to punish myself," she said brokenly. "You don't know how crazy I was when I was talking to Blair. I was *crazy!* Oh, why, when I was a child, didn't they make me control my temper? I suppose I'm like—my mother," she ended in a whisper. "And I can't change, now; I'm too old."

David smiled. "You are terribly old," he said. Like everybody else, save Mrs. Richie, David accepted Elizabeth's temper as a matter of course. "She doesn't mean anything by it," her little world had always said; and put up with the inconvenience of her furies, with the patience of people who were themselves incapable of the irrationalities of temper. "Oh, you are a hardened sinner," David mocked.

"You do forgive me?" she whispered.

At that he was grave. "There is nothing I wouldn't forgive, Elizabeth."

"But I have stabbed you?"

"Yes; a little; but I am yours to stab."

Her eyes filled. "Oh, it is so wonderful, that you go on loving me,
David!"

"You go on loving me," he rallied her; "in spite of my dullness and slowness, and all that."

But Elizabeth was not listening. "Sometimes it frightens me to get so angry," she said, with a somber look. "It was just the same when I was a little girl; do you remember the time I cut off my hair? I think you had hurt my feelings; I forget now what you had done. I was always having my feelings hurt! Of course I was awfully silly. It was a relief then to spoil my body, by cutting off my hair. This afternoon it was a relief to put mud on my soul."

He looked at her, trying to find words tender enough to heal the wounds she had torn in her own heart; not finding them, he was silent.

"Oh, we must face it," she said; "*you* must face it. I am not a good girl; I am not the kind of girl you ought to marry, I'm perfectly sure your mother thinks so. She thinks a person with a temper can't love people."

"I'll not go away in March!" David interrupted her passionately;—of course it might be pleasanter for Materna to get away from old Ferguson; but what is a man's mother, compared with his girl! Elizabeth's pain was intolerable to him. "I won't leave you a day before I have to!"

For a moment her wet eyes smiled. "Indeed you shall; I may be wicked—oh, I am! but I am not really an idiot. Only, David, *don't* take things so for granted, dear; and don't be so awfully sensible, David."

Chapter 14

When the door closed behind Blair and Elizabeth, Nannie set out to do that "best," which her brother had demanded of her. She went at once into the dining-room; but before she could speak, her stepmother called out to her:

"Here! Nannie! You are just the person I want—Watson's late again, and

I'm in a hurry. Just take these letters and sign them 'S. Maitland per N. M.' They must be posted before five. Sit down there at the table."

Nannie could not sign letters and talk at the same time. She got pen and ink and began to write her stepmother's name, over and over, slowly, like a little careful machine: "S. Maitland," "S. Maitland." In her desire to please she discarded her own neat script, and reproduced with surprising exactness the rough signature which she knew so well. But all the while her anxious thoughts were with her brother. She wished he had not rushed off with Elizabeth. If he had only come himself into the detested dining-room, his mother would have bidden him sign the letters; he might have read them and talked them over with her, and that would have pleased her. Nannie herself had no ambition to read them; her eye caught occasional phrases: "Shears for—," "new converter," etc., etc. The words meant nothing to Nannie, bending her blond head and writing like a machine, "S. Maitland," "S. Maitland," ...

"Mamma," she began, dipping her pen into the ink, "Blair has bought a rather expensive—"

Mrs. Maitland came over to the table and picked up the letters. "That's all. Now clear out, clear out! I've got a lot to do!" Then her eye fell on one of the signatures, and she gave her grunt of a laugh. "If you hadn't put 'Per N. M.,' I shouldn't have known that I hadn't signed 'em myself ... Nannie."

"Yes, Mamma?"

"Is Blair going to be at home to supper?"

"I think not. But he said he would be in this evening. And he wanted me to—to ask—"

"Well, perhaps I'll come over to your parlor to see him, if I get through with my work. I believe he goes East again to-morrow?"

"Yes," Nannie said. Mrs. Maitland, at her desk, had begun to write. Nannie wavered for a minute, then, with a despairing look at the back of her stepmother's head, slipped away to her own part of the house. "I'll tell her at supper," she promised herself. But in her own room, as she dressed for tea, panic fell upon her. She began to walk nervously about; once she stopped, and leaning her forehead against the window, looked absently into the dusk. At the end of the cinder path, the vast pile of the foundry rose black against the fading sky; on the left the open arches of the cast-house of the furnace glowed with molten iron that was running into pigs on the wide stretch of sand. The spur track was banked with desolate wastes of slag and rubbish; beyond them, like an enfolding arm, was the river, dark in the darkening twilight. From under half-shut dampers flat sheets of sapphire and orange flame roared out in rhythmical pulsations, and above them was the pillar of smoke shot through with flying billions of sparks; back of this monstrous and ordered confusion was the solemn circling line of hills. It was all hideous and fierce, yet in the clear winter dusk it had a beauty of its own that held Nannie Maitland, even though she was too accustomed to it to be conscious of its details. As she stared out at it with troubled eyes, there was a knock at her door; before she could say "Come in," her stepmother entered.

"Here!" Mrs. Maitland said, "just fix this waist, will you? I can't seem to—to make it look right." There was a dull flush on her cheek, and she spoke in cross confusion. "Haven't you got a piece of lace, or something; I don't care what. This black dress seems—" she broke off and glanced into the mirror; she was embarrassed, but doggedly determined. "Make me look—somehow," she said.

Nannie, assenting, and rummaging in her bureau drawer, had a flash of understanding. "She's dressing up for Blair!" She took out a piece of lace, and laid it about the gaunt shoulders; then tucked the front of the dress in, and brought the lace down on each side. The soft old thread seemed as inappropriate as it would have been if laid on a scarcely cooled steel "bloom."

"Well, pin it, can't you?" Mrs. Maitland said sharply; "haven't you got some kind of a brooch?" Nannie silently produced a little amethyst pin.

"It doesn't just suit the dress, I'm afraid," she ventured.

But Mrs. Maitland looked in the glass complacently. "Nonsense!" she said, and tramped out of the room. In the hall she threw back," —bliged."

"Oh, *poor* Mamma!" Nannie said. Her sympathy was hardly more than a sense of relief; if her mother was dressing up for Blair, she must be more than usually good-natured. "I'll tell her at supper," Nannie decided, with a lift of courage.

But at supper, in the disorderly dining-room, with the farther end of the table piled with ledgers, Mrs. Maitland was more unapproachable than ever. When Nannie asked a timid question about the evening, she either did not hear, or she affected not to. At any rate, she vouchsafed no answer. Her face was still red, and she seemed to hide behind her evening paper. To Nannie's gentle dullness this was no betrayal; it merely meant that Mrs. Maitland was cross again, and her heart sank within her. But somehow she gathered up her courage:

"You won't forget to come into the parlor, Mamma? Blair

wants to talk to you about something that—that—"

"I've got some writing to do. If I get through I'll come. Now clear out, clear out; I'm too busy to chatter."

Nannie cleared out. She had no choice. She went over to her vast, melancholy parlor, into which it seemed as if the fog had penetrated, to await Blair. In her restless apprehension she sat down at the piano, but after the first bar or two her hands dropped idly on the keys. Then she got up and looked aimlessly about. "I'd better finish that landscape," she said, and went over to her drawing-board. She stood there for a minute, fingering a lead pencil; her nerves were tense, and yet, as she reminded herself, it was foolish to be frightened. His mother loved Blair; she would do anything in the world for him —Nannie thought of the lace; yes, anything! Blair was only a little extravagant. And what did his extravagance matter? his mother was so very rich! But oh, why did they always clash so? Then she heard the sound of Blair's key in the lock.

"Well, Nancy!" he said gaily, "she's a charmer."

"Who?" said Nannie, bewildered; "Oh, you mean Elizabeth?"

"Yes; but there's a lot of gunpowder lying round loose, isn't there? She was out with David, I suppose because he didn't show up. In fact, she was so mad she was perfectly stunning. Nancy! I think I'll stick it out here for two or three days; Elizabeth is mighty good fun, and David is in town; we might renew our youth, we four; what do you say? Well!" he ended, coming back to his own affairs, "what did mother say?"

"Oh, Blair, I couldn't!"

"What! you haven't told her?"

"Blair dear, I did my best; but she simply never gave me a chance. Indeed, I tried, but I couldn't. She wouldn't let me open my lips in the afternoon, and at supper she read the paper every minute—

Harris will tell you."

Blair Maitland whistled. "Well, I'll tell her myself. It was really to spare her that I wanted you to do it. I always rile her, somehow, poor dear mother. Nannie, this house reeks of cabbage! Does she live on it?" Blair threw up his arms with a wordless gesture of disgust.

"I'm so sorry," Nannie said; "but don't tell her you don't like it."

The door across the hall opened, and there was a heavy step. The brother and sister looked at each other.

"Blair, *be nice!*" Nannie entreated; her soft eyes under the meekly parted blond hair were very anxious.

He did not need the caution; whenever he was with his mother, the mere instinct of self-preservation made him anxious to "be nice." As Mrs. Maitland had her instinct of self-preservation, too, there had been, in the last year, very few quarrels. Instead there was, on his part, an exaggerated politeness, and on her part, a pathetic effort to be agreeable. The result was, of course, entire absence of spontaneity in both of them.

Mrs. Maitland, her knitting in her hands, came tramping into the parlor; the piece of thread lace was pushed awry, but there had been further preparation for the occasion: at first her son and daughter did not know what the change was; then suddenly both recognized it, and exchanged an astonished glance.

"Mother!" cried Blair incredulously, "*earrings!*"

The dull color on the high cheek-bones deepened; she smiled sheepishly. "Yes; I saw 'em in my bureau drawer, and put 'em on. Haven't worn 'em for years; but Blair, here, likes pretty things." (Her son, under his breath, groaned: "pretty!") "So you are off tomorrow, Blair?" she said, politely; she ran her hand along the yellowing bone needles, and the big ball of pink worsted rolled softly down on to the floor. As she glanced at him over her steel-rimmed spectacles, her eyes softened as an eagle's might when looking at her young. "I wish his father could see him," she thought. "Next time you come home," she said, "it will be to go to work!"

"Yes," Blair said, smiling industriously.

"Pity you have to study this summer; I'd like to have you in the office now."

"Yes; I'm awfully sorry," he said with charming courtesy, "but I feel I ought to brush up on one or two subjects, and I can do it better abroad than here. I'm going to paint a little, too. I'll be very busy all summer."

"Why don't you paint our new foundry?" said Mrs. Maitland. She laughed with successful cheerfulness; Blair liked jokes, and this, she thought, complacently, was a joke. "Well, *I* shall manage to keep busy, too!" she said.

"I suppose so," Blair agreed.

He was lounging on the arm of Nannie's chair, and felt his sleeve plucked softly. "Now," said Nannie.

But Blair was not ready. "You are always busy," he said; "I wish I had your habit of industry."

Mrs. Maitland's smile faded. "I wish you had."

"Oh, well, you've got industry enough for this family," Blair declared.

But the flattery did not penetrate.

"Too much, maybe," she said grimly; then remembered, and began to "entertain" again: "I had a compliment to-day."

Blair, with ardent interest, said, "Really?"

"That man Dolliver in our office—you remember Dolliver?" Blair nodded. "He happened to say he never knew such an honest man as old Henry B. Knight. Remember old Mr. Knight?" She paused, her eyes narrowed into a laugh. "He married Molly

Wharton. I always called her 'goose Molly.' She used to make eyes at your father; but she couldn't get him—though she tried to hard enough, by telling him, so I heard, that the 'only feminine thing about me was my petticoats.' A very coarse remark, in my judgment; and as for being feminine,—when you were born, I thought of inviting her to come and look at you so she could see what a baby was like! She never had any children. Well, old Knight was elder of the Second Church. Remember?"

"Oh yes," Blair said vaguely.

"Dolliver said Knight once lost a trade by telling the truth, 'when he might have kept his mouth shut'—that was Dolliver's way of putting it. 'Well,' I said, 'I hope you think that our Works are just as honestly conducted as the Knight Mills'; fact was, I knew a thing or two about Henry B. And what do you suppose Dolliver said? 'Oh, yes,' he said, 'you are honest, Mrs. Maitland, but you ain't damn-fool honest.'" She laughed loudly, and her son laughed too, this time in genuine amusement; but Nannie looked prim, at which Mrs. Maitland glanced at Blair, and there was a sympathetic twinkle between them which for the moment put them both really at ease. "I got on to a good thing last week," she said, still trying to amuse him, but now there was reality in her voice.

"Do tell me about it," Blair said, politely.

"You know Kraas? He is the man that's had a bee in his bonnet for the last ten years about a newfangled idea for making castings of steel. He brought me his plans once, but I told him they were no good. But last month he asked me to make some castings for him to go on his contrivance. Of course I did; we cast anything for anybody—provided they can pay for it. Well, Kraas tried it in our foundry; no good, just as I said; the metal was full of flaws. But it occurred to me to experiment with his idea on my own hook. I melted my pig, and poured it into his converter thing; but I added some silvery pig I had on the Yard, made when No. 1 blew in, and the castings were as sound as a nut! Kraas never thought of that." She twitched her pink worsted and gave her grunt of a laugh. "Master Kraas hasn't any caveat, and he can't get one on that idea, so of course I can go ahead."

"Oh, Mamma, how clever you are!" Nannie murmured, admiringly.

"Clever?" said Blair; Nannie shook his arm gently, and he recollected himself. "Well, I suppose business is like love and war. All's fair in business."

Mrs. Maitland was silent. Then she said: "Business is war. But —fair?
It is a perfectly legal thing to do."

"Oh, legal, yes," her son agreed significantly; the thin ice of politeness was beginning to crack. It was the old situation over again; he was repelled by unloveliness; this time it was the unloveliness of shrewdness. For a moment his disgust made him quite natural. "It is *legal* enough, I suppose," he said coldly.

Mrs. Maitland did not lift her head, but with her eyes fixed on her needles, she suddenly stopped knitting. Nannie quivered.

"Mamma," she burst in, "Blair wanted to tell you about something very beautiful that he has found, and—" Her brother pinched her, and her voice trailed into silence.

"Found something beautiful? I'd like to hear of his finding something useful!" The ice cracked a little more. "As for your mother's honesty, Blair, if you had waited a minute, I'd have told you that as soon as I found the idea was practical I handed it over to Kraas. *I'm* damn-fool honest, I suppose." But this time she did not laugh at her joke. Blair was instant with apologies; he had not meant —he had not intended— "Of course you would do the square thing," he declared.

"But you thought I wouldn't," she said. And while he was making polite exclamations, she changed the subject for something safer. She still tried to entertain him, but now she spoke wearily. "What do you suppose I read in the paper to-night? Some man in New York—named Maitland, curiously enough; 'picked up' an old master—that's how the paper put it; for $5,000. It appears it was considered 'cheap'! It was 14x18 inches. *Inches*, mind you, not feet! Well, Mr. Doestick's friends are not all dead yet. Sorry anybody of our name should do such a thing."

Nannie turned white enough to faint.

"Allow me to say," said Blair, tensely, "that an 'old master' might be cheap at five times that price!"

"I wouldn't give five thousand dollars for the greatest picture that was ever painted," his mother announced. Then, without an instant's warning, her face puckered into a furious sneeze. "God bless us!" she said, and blew her nose loudly. Blair jumped.

"*I* would give all I have in the world!" he said.

"Well," his mother said, ramming her grimy handkerchief into her pocket, "if it cost all *you* have in the world, it would certainly be cheap; for, so far as I know, you haven't anything." Alas! the ice had given way entirely.

Blair pushed Nannie's hand from his arm, and getting up, walked over to the marble-topped centre-table; he stood there slowly turning over the pages of *The Poetesses of America*, in rigid determination to hold his tongue. Mrs. Maitland's eyebrow began to rise; her fingers tightened on her hurrying needles until the nails were white. Nannie, looking from one to the other, trembled with apprehension. Then she made an excuse to take Blair to the other end of the room.

"Come and look at my drawing," she said; and added under her breath:

"Don't tell her!"

Blair shook his head. "I've got to, somehow." But when he came back and stood in front of his mother, his hands in his pockets, his shoulder lounging against the mantelpiece, he was apparently his careless self again. "Well," he said, gaily, "if I haven't anything of my own, it's your fault; you've been too generous to me!"

The knitting-needles flagged; Nannie drew a long breath.

"Yes, you are too good to me," he said; "and you work so hard! Why do you work like a—a man?" There was an uncontrollable quiver of disgust in his voice.

His mother smiled, with a quick bridling of her head—he was complimenting her! The soreness from his thrust about legality vanished. "Yes; I do work hard. I reckon there's no man in the iron business who can get more pork for his shilling than I can!"

Blair cast an agonized look at Nannie; then set himself to his task again—in rather a roundabout way: "Why don't you spend some of your money on yourself, Mother, instead of on me?"

"There's nothing I want."

"But there are so many things you could have!"

"I have everything I need," said Mrs. Maitland; "a roof, a bed, a chair, and food to eat. As for all this truck that people spend their money on, what use is it? that's what I want to know! What's it worth?"

Blair put his hand in his pocket and pulled out a small beautifully carved jade box; he took off the lid delicately, and shook a scarab into the palm of his hand. "I'll tell you what *that* is worth," he said, holding the dull-blue oval between his thumb and finger; then he mentioned a sum that made Nannie exclaim. His mother put down her knitting, and taking the bit of eternity in her fingers, looked at it silently. "Do you wonder I got that box, which is a treasure in itself, to hold such a treasure?" Blair exulted.

Mrs. Maitland, handing the scarab back, began to knit furiously. "That's what it's worth," he said; he was holding the scarab in his palm with a sort of tenderness; his eyes caressed it. "But it isn't what I paid. The collector was hard up, and I made him knock off twenty-five per cent, of the price."

"Hah!" said Mrs. Maitland; "well; I suppose 'all's fair in love and collections'?"

"What's unfair in that?" Blair said, sharply; "I buy in the cheapest market. You do *that* yourself, my dear mother." When Blair said "my dear mother," he was farthest from filial affection. "Besides," he said, with strained self-control, "besides, I'm like you, I'm not 'damn-fool honest'!"

"Oh, I didn't say you weren't honest. Only, if I was going to take advantage of anybody, I'd do it for something more important than a blue china beetle." "The trouble with you, Mother, is that you don't see anything but those hideous Works of yours!" her son burst out.

"If I did, you couldn't pay for your china beetles. Beetles? You couldn't pay for the breeches you're sitting in!"

"Oh, Mamma! oh, Blair!" sighed poor Nannie.

There was a violent silence. Suddenly Mrs. Maitland brought the flat of her hand furiously down on the table; then, without a word, got on her feet, pulled at the ball of pink worsted which had run behind a chair and caught under the caster; her jerk broke the thread. The next moment the parlor door banged behind her.

Nannie burst out crying. Blair opened and closed his lips, speechless with rage.

"What—what made her so angry?" Nannie said, catching her breath. "Was it the beetle?"

"Don't call it that ridiculous name! I'll have to borrow the $5,000. And where the devil I'll get it I don't know. Nannie, 'goose

Molly' wasn't an entire fool, after all!"

"Blair!" his sister protested, horrified. But Blair was too angry to be ashamed of himself. He could not see that his mother's anger was only the other side of her love. In Sarah Maitland, not only maternity, but pride, the peculiar pride engendered in her by her immense business—pride and maternity together, demanded such high things of her son! Not finding them, the pain of disappointment broke into violent expression. Indeed, had this charming fellow, handsome, selfish, sweet-hearted, been some other woman's son, she would have been far more patient with him. Her very love made her abominable to him. She was furiously angry when she left him there in Nannie's parlor; all the same he did not have to borrow the $5,000.

The next morning Sarah Maitland sent for her superintendent. "Mr. Ferguson," she said—they were in her private office, and the door was shut; "Mr. Ferguson, I think—but I don't know—I think Blair has been making an idiot of himself again. I saw in the paper that somebody called Maitland had been throwing money away on a picture. I don't know what it was, and I don't want to know. It was 14x18 inches; not feet. That was enough for me. Why, Ferguson, those big pictures in my parlor (I bought them when I was going to be married; a woman is sort of foolish then; I wouldn't do such a thing now), those four pictures are 4x6 feet each; and they cost me $400; $100 apiece. But this New York man has paid $5,000 for one picture 14x18 inches! If it was Blair—and it came over me last night, all of a sudden, that it was; he hasn't got any $5,000 to pay for it. I don't want to go into the matter with him; we don't get along on such subjects. But I want you to ask him about it; maybe he'll speak out to you, man fashion. If this 'Maitland' is just a fool of our name so much the better; but if it is Blair, I've got to help him out, I suppose. I want you to settle the thing for me. I—can't." Her voice broke on the last word; she coughed and cleared her throat before she could speak distinctly. "I haven't the time," she said.

Robert Ferguson listened, frowning. "You'll give him money to spend in ways you don't approve of?"

She nodded sullenly. "I have to."

"You don't have to!" he broke out; "for God's sake, Mrs. Maitland, *stop!*"

"What do you mean, sir?"

"I mean … this isn't my business, but I can't see you—Mrs. Maitland, if I get to talking on this subject, we'll quarrel."

The glare of anger in her face died out. She leaned back in her chair and looked at him. "I won't quarrel with you. Go on. Say what you think. I won't say I'll take your advice, but I'll listen to it."

"It's what I have always told you. You are squeezing the life out of Blair by giving him money. You've always done it, because it was the easy thing to do. Let up on him! Give him a chance. Let him earn his money, or go without. Talk about making him independent —you've made him as dependent as a baby! I don't know my Bible as well as you do, but there is a verse somewhere—something about 'fullness of bread and abundance of idleness.' That's what's the trouble with Blair. 'Fullness of bread and abundance of idleness.'"

"But he's been at college; he couldn't work while he was at college," she said, with honest bewilderment.

"Of course he couldn't. But why did you let him dawdle round at college, pretending to special, for a year after he graduated? Of course he *won't* work so long as he doesn't have to. The boy wouldn't be human if he did! You never made him feel he had to get through and to go to work. You've given him everything he wanted, and you've exacted nothing in return; not scholarship, nor even decent behavior. He's gambled, and gone after women, and bought everything on earth he wanted—the only thing he knows how to do is to spend money! He has never done a hand's turn of work in his life. He is just as much a dead beat as any beggar who gets his living out of other people's pockets. That he gets it out of your pocket doesn't alter that; that he doesn't wear rags and knock at back doors doesn't alter it. He's a dead beat! Any man is, who takes and doesn't give anything in return. It's queer you can't see that, Mrs. Maitland."

She was silent.

"Why, look here: I've heard you say, many a time, that the best part of your life was when you had to work hardest. Isn't that so?" She nodded. "Then why in thunder won't you let Blair work? Let him work, or go without!"

Again she did not speak.

"For Heaven's sake, give him a chance, before it's too late!"

Mrs. Maitland got up, and stood with her back to him, looking out of the smoke-grimed window. Presently she turned round. "Well, what would you do now—supposing he did buy the picture?"

"Tell him that he has overdrawn his allowance, and that if he wants the picture he must earn the money to pay for it. Say you'll advance it, if instead of going to Europe this summer he'll stay at home and go to work. Of course he can't earn five thousand dollars. I doubt if he can earn five thousand cents! But make up a job—just for this once; and help him out. I don't believe in made-up jobs, on principle; but they're better than nothing. If he won't work, darn the picture! It can be resold."

She blew her lips out in a bubbling sigh, and began to bite her forefinger. Robert Ferguson had said his say. He gathered his papers together and got on his feet.

"Mr. Ferguson ..." He waited, his hand on the knob.

"Yes?"

"'Bliged to you. But for the present—"

"Very well," Robert Ferguson said shortly.

"Just put through the business of the picture. Hereafter—"
Ferguson shrugged his shoulders.

Chapter 15

After his first spasm of angry disgust, when he declared he would go East the next morning, Blair's fancy for "hanging round Mercer" hardened into purpose; but he did not "hang round" his mother's house. "The hotel is pretty bad," he told Nannie, "but it's better than *this*." So he took the most expensive suite in the big, dark old River House that in those days was Mercer's best hotel. Its blackened facade and the Doric columns of its entrance gave it a certain exterior dignity; and its interior comfort, combined with the reviving associations of youth, lengthened Blair's two or three days to a week, then to a fortnight.

The day after that distressing interview with his mother, he went gaily round to Mrs. Richie's to pound David on the back, and say "Congratulations, old fellow! Why in thunder," he complained, "didn't I come back before? You've cut me out, you villain!"

David grinned.

"'Before the devil could come back,
  The angel had the inside track,'"

he admitted.

"Well, if you'll take my advice, you won't be too angelic," Blair said a little dryly. "She always had a touch of the other thing in her, you know."

"You think I'd better cultivate a few vices?" David inquired amiably;

"I'm obliged for an example, anyhow!"

But Blair did not keep up the chaffing. The atmosphere of Mrs. Richie's house dominated him as completely as when he was a boy. He looked at her serene face, her simple, feminine parlor, the books and flowers and pictures,—and thought of his mother and his mother's house. Then, somehow, he was ashamed of his thoughts, because this dear lady said in her gentle way:

"How happy your mother must be to have you at home again, Blair. You won't rush right off and leave us, will you?"

"Well," he hesitated, "of course I don't want to"—he was surprised at the ring of truth in his voice; "but I am going to paint this summer. I am going to be in one of the studios in Paris."

"Oh, I'm sorry," she said simply. And Blair had an instant of uncertainty, although a moment before his "painting" had seemed to him necessary, because it facilitated another summer away from home; and after the interview with his mother's general manager, a summer away from home was more than ever desirable.

Mr. Ferguson had handed over the five thousand dollars, and then freed his mind. Blair listened. He heard that he was a sucker, that he was a poor stick, that he wasn't fit to black his mother's boots. "They need it," he said, chuckling; and Robert Ferguson nearly burst with anger!

Yet when the check was on its way to New York, and the picture had been shipped to Mercer, Blair still lingered at the River House. The idea of "renewing their youth" had appealed to all four friends. In the next two or three weeks they were constantly together at either one house or the other, or at some outside rendezvous arranged by Blair—a drive down to Willis's, a theater party and supper, a moonlight walk. Once David suggested "ice-cream at Mrs. Todd's." But this fell through; Blair said that even his sentimentality could not face the blue paper roses, and when David urged that the blue paper roses were part of the fun, Blair said, "Well, *I'll* match you for it. All important decisions ought to be left to chance, to avoid the burden of responsibility!" A pitched penny favored Blair, and Mrs. Todd did not see the 'handsome couples.' It was at the end of the first week, when they were all dining with Mrs. Richie—the evening meal was beginning to be called dinner nowadays in Mercer; that Mrs. Richie's soft eyes, which took duty and energy and ability so sweetly and trustingly for granted,—Mrs. Richie's believing eyes did for Blair what Robert Ferguson's vociferating truthfulness had not been able to accomplish. It was after dinner, and she and Blair had gone into the little plant-room, where the air was sweet with hyacinths and the moist greenness of ferns.

"Blair," she said, putting her soft hand on his arm; "I want to say something. You won't mind?"

"Mind anything *you* say? I should think not!"

"It is only that I want you to know that, when the time comes, I shall think it very fine in you, with your tastes and temperament, to buckle down at the Works. I shall admire you very much then, Blair."

He gave her a droll look. "Alas, dear Mrs. Richie," he began; but she interrupted him.

"Your mother will be so proud and happy when you get to work; and I wanted you to know that I, too—"

He took her hand from his arm and lifted it to his lips; there was a courtliness about Blair, and a certain gravity, which at moments gave him positive distinction. "If there is any good in me," he said, "you would bring it out." Then he smiled. "But probably there isn't any."

"Nonsense!" she cried, and hesitated; he saw that her leaf-brown eyes were wet. "You must make your life worth while, Blair. You must! It would be such a dreadful failure if you didn't do anything but enjoy yourself." He was keenly touched. He did not kiss her hand again; he just put his arm around her, as David might have done, and gave her a hug. "Mrs. Richie! I—I *will* brace up!"

"You are a dear fellow," she said, and kissed him. Then they went back to the other three, to find Elizabeth in a gale of teasing merriment because, she said, David was so "terribly talkative"!

"He has sat there like a bump on a log for fifteen minutes," she complained. "Say something, dummy!" she commanded.

David only chuckled, and pulled Blair into a corner to talk. "You girls keep on your own side; don't interrupt serious conversation," he said. "Blair, I want to ask you—" And in a minute the two young men were deep in their own affairs. It was amusing to see how quickly all four of them fell back into the comfortable commonplace of old friendship, the men roaring over some college reminiscences, and the two girls grumbling at being left out. "Really," said Mrs. Richie, "I should think none of you were more than fifteen!"

That night, when he took his sister home, Blair was very silent. Her little trickle of talk about David and Elizabeth was apparently unheard. As they turned into their own street, the full moon, just rising out of the river mists, suddenly flooded the waste-lands beyond the Works; the gaunt outlines of the Foundry were touched with ethereal silver, and the Maitland house, looming up in a great black mass, made a gulf of shadow that drowned the dooryard and spread half-way across the squalid street. Beyond the shadow, Shantytown, in the quiet splendor of the moon, seemed as intangible as a dream.

"Beautiful!" Blair said, involuntarily. He stood for a silent moment, drinking the beauty like wine, perhaps it was the exhilaration of it that made him say abruptly: "Perhaps I'll not go abroad. Perhaps I'll pitch in."

Nannie fairly jumped with astonishment. "Blair! You mean to go into the Works? This summer? Oh, how pleased Mamma would be! It would be perfectly splendid. *Oh!*" Nannie gave his arm a speechless squeeze.

"If I do, it will be because Mrs. Richie bolstered me up. Of course I would hate it like the devil; but perhaps it's the decent thing to do? Oh, well; don't say anything about it. I haven't made up my mind—this is an awful place!" he said, with a shiver, looking across at Shantytown and remembering what was hidden under the glamor of the moon. "The smell of it! Democracy is well enough, Nancy—until you smell it."

"But you could live at the hotel," Nannie reminded him, as he pulled out his latch-key.

"You bet I would," her brother said, laughing. "My dear, not even your society could reconcile me to the slums. But I don't know whether I can screw myself up to the Works, anyhow. David won't be in town, and that would be a nuisance. Well, I'll think it over; but if I do stay, I tell you what it is!—you two girls will have to make things mighty agreeable, or I'll clear out."

He did think it over; but Blair had never been taught the one regal word of life, he had never learned to say "I *ought*." Therefore it needed more talks with Mrs. Richie, more days with Elizabeth— David, confound him! wouldn't come, because he had to pack, but Nannie tagged on behind; it needed the "bolstering up" of much approval on the part of the onlookers, and much self-approval, too, before the screwing-up process reached a point where he went into his mother's office in the Works and told her that if she was ready to take him on, he was ready to go to work.

Mrs. Maitland was absolutely dumb with happiness. He wanted to go to work! He asked to be taken on! "What do you say *now*, friend Ferguson?" she jeered; "you thought he was going to play at his painting for another year, and you wanted me to put his nose to the grindstone, and make him earn the money to pay for that fool picture. Isn't it better to have him come to it of his own accord? I'd pay for ten pictures, if they made him want to go to work. As for his painting, it will be his father over again. My husband had his fancies about it, too, but he gave it all up when he married me; marriage always gives a man common sense,—marriage and business. That's how it's going to be with Blair," she ended complacently. "Blair has brains; I've always said so."

Robert Ferguson did not deny the brains, but he was as astonished as she.

"I believe," he challenged Mrs. Richie, "*you* put him up to it? You always could wind that boy round your finger."

"I did talk to him," she confessed; it was their last interview, for she and David were starting East that night, and Mr. Ferguson had come in to say good-by. "I talked to him—a little. Mrs. Maitland's disappointment about him went to my heart. Besides, I am very fond of Blair; there is a great deal of good in him. You are prejudiced."

"No I'm not. I admit that as his mother says, 'he's no fool'; but that only makes his dilly-dallying so much the worse. Still, I believe that if she were to lose all her money, and he were to fall very much in love and be refused, he might amount to something. But it would need both things to make a man of him."

Robert Ferguson sighed, and Mrs. Richie left the subject of the curative effect of unsuccessful love, with nervous haste. "I am going to charge Elizabeth and Nannie to do all they can to make it pleasant for him, so that he won't find the Works too terrible," she said. At which reflection upon the Works, Mr. Ferguson barked so fiercely that she felt quite at ease with him. But his barking did not prevent her from telling the girls that business would be very hard for Blair, and they must cheer him up: "Do try to amuse him! You know it is going to be very stupid for him in Mercer."

Nannie, of course, needed no urging; as for Elizabeth, she was a little contemptuous. Oh yes; she would do what she could, she said. "Of course, I'm awfully fond of Blair, but—"

The fact was, she was contrasting in her own mind the man who had to be "amused" to keep him at his work, with David —"working himself to death!" she told Nannie, proudly. And Nannie, quick to feel the slur in her words, said:

"Yes, but it is quite different with Blair. Blair doesn't *have* to do anything, you know."

Still, thanks to Mrs. Richie, he was at least going to pretend to do something. And so, at a ridiculously high salary, he entered, as he told Elizabeth humorously, "upon his career." The only thing he did to make life more tolerable for himself was to live in the hotel instead of in his mother's house. But it was characteristic of him that he left the wonderful old canvas—the "fourteen by eighteen inch" picture, hanging on the wall in Nannie's parlor. "You ought to have something fit for a civilized eye to rest upon," he told her, "and I can see it when I come to see you." If his permanent departure for the River House wounded his mother, she made no protest; she only lifted a pleased eyebrow when he dropped in to supper, which, she noticed, he was apt to do whenever Elizabeth happened to take tea with Nannie. When he did come, Sarah Maitland used to look about the dining-room table, with its thick earthenware dishes—the last of the old Canton service had found its way to the ash-barrel; she used to glance at the three young people with warm satisfaction. "Like old times!" she would say kindly; "only needs David to make it complete."

Mrs. Maitland was sixty-two that spring, but there was no stoop of the big shoulders, no sign of that settling and shrinking that age brings. She was at the full tide of her vigor, and her happiness in having her son beside her in the passion of her life, which was second only to her passion for him, showed itself in clumsy efforts to flaunt her contentment before her world. Every morning, with varying unpunctuality, Blair came into her office at the Works where she had

had a desk placed for him. He was present, because she insisted that he should be, at the regular conferences which she held with the heads of departments. She made a pretense of asking his advice, which was as amusing to Mr. Ferguson and the under-superintendents as it was tiresome to Blair. For after his first exhilaration in responding to Mrs. Richie's high belief in him, the mere doing of duty began gradually to pall. Her belief helped him through the first four or five months, then the whole thing became a bore. His work was ludicrously perfunctory, and his listlessness when in the office was apparent to everybody. At the bottom of her heart, Sarah Maitland must have known that it was all a farce. Blair was worth nothing to the business; his only relation to it was the weekly drawing of an unearned "salary." Perhaps if Mrs. Richie had been in Mercer, to make again and again the appeal of confident expectation, that little feeble sense of duty which had started him upon his "career," might have struck a root down through feeling, into the rock-bed of character. But as it was, not even the girls' obedience to her order, "to amuse Blair," made up for the withdrawal of her own sustaining inspiration.

But at least Nannie and Elizabeth kept him fairly contented out of business hours; and so long as he was contented, things were smooth between him and his mother. There was, as Blair expressed it, "only one rumpus" that whole summer, and it was a very mild one, caused by the fact that he did not go to church. On those hot July Sunday mornings, his mother in black silk, and Nannie in thin lawn, sat in the family pew, fanning themselves, and waiting; Nannie, constantly turning to look down the aisle; Sarah Maitland intent for a familiar step and a hand upon the little baize-lined door of the pew. The "rumpus" came when, on the third Sunday, Blair was called to account.

It was after supper, in the hot dusk in Nannie's parlor;

Elizabeth was there, and the two girls, in white dresses, were fanning themselves languidly; Blair, at the piano, was playing the Largo, with much feeling. The windows were open. It was too warm for lamps, and the room was lighted only by the occasional roar of flames, breaking fan-like from the tops of the stacks in the Yards. Suddenly, in the midst of their idle talk, Mrs. Maitland came in; she paused for a moment before the dark oblong of canvas on the wall beside the door. Of course, in the half-light, the little dim Mother of God—immortal maternity!—could scarcely be seen.

"Umph," she said, "a dirty piece of canvas, at about twenty dollars a square inch!" No one spoke. "Let's see;" she calculated; —"ore is $10 a ton; 20 tons to a car; say one locomotive hauls 25 cars. Well, there you have it: a trainload of iron ore, to pay for *this*!" she snapped a thumb and finger against the canvas. Blair jumped—then ran his right hand up the keyboard in a furious arpeggio. But he said nothing. Mrs. Maitland, moving away from the picture, blew out her lips in a loud sigh. "Well," she said; "tastes differ, as the old woman said when she kissed her cow."

Still no one spoke, but Elizabeth rose to offer her a chair. "No," she said, coming over and resting an elbow on the mantelpiece, "I won't sit down. I'm going in a minute."

As she stood there, unrest spread about her as rings from a falling stone spread on the surface of a pool. Blair yawned, and got up from the piano; Elizabeth fidgeted; Nannie began to talk nervously.

"Blair," said his mother, her strident voice over-riding the girls' chatter, "why don't you come to church?"

His answer was perfectly unevasive and entirely good-natured. "Well, for one thing, I don't believe the things the church teaches."

"What do you believe?" she demanded. And he answered

carelessly, that really, he hardly knew.

It was, of course, the old difference of the generations; but it was more marked because these two generations had never spoken the same language, therefore quiet, sympathetic disagreement was impossible. It was impossible, too, because the actual fact was that neither her belief nor his disbelief were integral to their lives. Her creed was a barbarous anthropomorphism, which had created an offended and puerile god—a god of foreign missions and arid church-going and eternal damnation. The fear of her god (such as he was) would, no doubt, have protected her against certain physical temptations, to which, as it happened, her temperament never inclined; but he had never safeguarded her from the temptation of cutthroat competition, or even of business shrewdness which her lawyer showed her how to make legal. Blair, on the contrary, had long ago discarded the naive brutalities of Presbyterianism; church-going bored him, and he was not interested in saving souls in Africa. But, like most of us—like his mother, in fact, he had a god of his own, a god who might have safeguarded him against certain intellectual temptations; cheating at cards, or telling the truth, if the truth would compromise a woman. But as he had no desire to cheat at cards, and the women whom he might have compromised did not need to be lied about, his god was of as little practical value to him as his mother's was to her. So they were neither of them speaking of realities when Mrs. Maitland said: "What do you believe? What have you got instead of God?"

"Honor," Blair said promptly. "What do you mean by honor?" she said, impatiently.

"Well," her son reflected, "there are things a man simply can't do; that's all. And that's honor, don't you know. Of course, religion is supposed to keep you from doing things, too. But there's this difference: religion, if you pick pockets—I speak metaphorically;

threatens you with hell. Honor threatens you with yourself." As he spoke he frowned, as if a disagreeable idea had occurred to him.

His mother frowned, too. That hell and a man's self might be the same thing had never struck Sarah Maitland. She did not understand what he meant, and feeling herself at a disadvantage, retaliated with the reproof she might have administered to a boy of fifteen: "You don't know what you are talking about!"

The man of twenty-five laughed lazily. "Your religion is very amusing, my dear mother."

Her face darkened. She took her elbow from the mantelpiece, and seemed uncertain what to do. Blair sprang to open the door, but she made an irritated gesture. "I know how to open doors," she said. She threw a brief "good-night" to Elizabeth, and turned a cheek to Nannie for the kiss that had fallen there, soft as a little feather, in all the nights of all the years they had lived together. "'Night, Blair," she said shortly; then hesitated, her hand on the door-knob. There was an instant when the command "*Go to church!*" trembled upon her lips, but it was not spoken. "I advise you," she said roughly, "to get over your conceit, and try to get some religion into you. Your father and your grandfather didn't think they could get along without it; they went to church! But you evidently think you are so much better than they were that you can stay away."

The door slammed behind her. Blair whistled. "Poor dear mother!" he sighed; and turned round to listen to the two girls. "Can you be ready to start on the first?" Elizabeth was asking Nannie, evidently trying to cover up the awkwardness of that angry exit.

"Start where?" Blair asked.

"Why, East! You know. I told you ages ago," Nannie explained.

"Elizabeth and I are going to stay with Mrs. Richie at the seashore."

"You never said a word about it," Blair said disgustedly. His annoyance knew no disguise. "I call it pretty shabby for you two to go off! What's going to happen to me?"

"Business, Blair, business!" Elizabeth mocked. But Nannie was plainly conscience-stricken. "I'll not go, if you'd rather I didn't, Blair."

"Nonsense!" her brother said shortly, "of course you must go, but—" He did not finish his thought, whatever it was; he went back to the piano and began to drum idly. His face was sharply annoyed. That definition of his god which he had made to his mother, had aroused a nameless uneasiness. It occurred to him that perhaps he was "picking a pocket," in finding such emphatic satisfaction in Elizabeth's society. Now, abruptly, at the news of her approaching absence, the uneasiness sharpened into faintly recognizable outlines.

He struck a jarring chord on the piano, and told himself not to be a fool. "She's mighty good fun. Of course I shall miss her or any other girl, in this Godforsaken hole! That's all it amounts to. Anyhow, she's dead in love with David." Sitting there in the hot dusk, listening to the voices of the girls, Blair felt suddenly irritated with David. "Darn him, why does he go off and leave her in this way? Not but what it is all right so far as I am concerned; only—" Then, wordlessly, his god must have accused him, for he winced. "I am *not*, not in the least!" he said. The denial confessed him to himself, and there was an angry bang of discordant octaves. The two girls called out in dismay.

"Oh, *do* stop!" Elizabeth said. Blair got up from the piano-stool and came over to them silently. His thoughts were in clamoring confusion. "I am *not*," he said again to himself. "I like her, but that's all." There was a look of actual panic on his lazily charming face. He glanced at Elizabeth, who, her head on Nannie's shoulder, was humming softly: "'Oh, won't it be joyful—joyful-joyful—'" and clenched his hands.

He was very silent as he walked home with her that night. When they reached her door, Elizabeth looked up at the closed shutters of Mrs. Richie's house, and sighed. "How dreary a closed house looks!" she said. "I almost wish Uncle would rent it, but he won't. *I* think he is keeping it for Mrs. Richie to live in when David and I settle down in Philadelphia."

Blair was apparently not interested in Mrs. Richie's future. "I wish," he said, "that I'd gone to Europe this summer."

"Well, that's polite, considering that Nannie and I have spent our time making it agreeable for you."

"I stayed in Mercer because I thought I'd like a summer with Nannie," he defended himself; he was just turning away at the foot of the steps, but he stopped and called back: "with Nannie-*and you.*"

Elizabeth, from the open door, looked after him with frank astonishment. "How long since Nannie and I have been so much appreciated?"

"I think I began to appreciate you a good while ago, Elizabeth," he said, significantly; but she did not hear him. "Perhaps it's just as well she's going," he told himself, as he went slowly back to the hotel. "Not that I'm smitten; but I might be. I can see that I might be, if I should let myself go." But he was confident that allegiance to his god would keep him from ever letting himself go.

The girls went East that week, and when they did, Blair took no more meals in the office-dining-room.

It was a very happy time that the inland girls spent with Mrs. Richie, in her small house on the Jersey shore. It happened that neither of them had ever seen the ocean, and their first glimpse of it was a great experience. Added to that was the experience, new to both of them, of daily companionship with a serene nature. Mrs. Richie was always a little remote, a little inclined to keep people at arm's-length; there were undercurrents of sadness in her talk, and she was perhaps rather absorbed in her own supreme affair, maternal love. Also, her calm outlook upon heavenly horizons made the affairs of the girls seem sometimes disconcertingly small, and to realize the smallness of one's affairs is in itself an experience to youth. But in spite of the ultimate reserves they felt in her, Mrs. Richie was sympathetic, and full of soft gaieties, with endless patience for people and events. Elizabeth's old uneasy dislike of her had long since yielded to the fact that she was David's mother, and so must be, and in theory was, loved. But the love was really only a faint awe at what she still called "perfection"; and during the two months of living under the same roof with her, Elizabeth felt at times a resentful consciousness that Mrs. Richie was afraid of that ungovernable temper, which, the girl used to say, impatiently, "never hurts anybody but myself!" Like most high-tempered people, Elizabeth, though penitent and more or less mortified by her outbursts of fury, was always a little astonished when any one took them seriously; and Mrs. Richie took them very seriously.

Nannie, being far simpler than Elizabeth, was less impressed by Mrs. Richie than by her surroundings;—the ocean, the whole gamut of marine sights and happenings; Mrs. Richie's housekeeping; the delicate food and serving (what would Harris have thought of that table!)-all these things, as well as David's fortnightly visits, and Elizabeth's ardors and gay coldnesses, were delights to Nannie. Both girls had an absorbingly good time, and when the last day of the last week finally arrived, and Mr. Robert Ferguson appeared to escort them home, they were both of them distinctly doleful.

"Every perfect thing stops!" Elizabeth sighed to David. They had left the porch, and gone down on to the sands flooded with moonlight and silence. The evening was very still and warm, and the full blue pour of the moon made everything softly unreal, except the glittering path of light crossing the breathing, black expanse of water. David had hesitated when she had suggested leaving the others and coming down here by themselves,—then he had looked at Nannie, sitting between Robert Ferguson and his mother, and seemed to reassure himself; but he was careful to choose a place on the beach where he could keep an eye on the porch. He was talking to Elizabeth in his anxious way, about his work, and how soon his income would be large enough for them to marry. "The minus sign expresses it now," he said; "I could kick myself when I think that, at twenty-six, my mother has to pay my washwoman!" Their engagement had continued to accentuate the difference in the development of these two; David's manhood was more and more of the mind; Elizabeth's womanhood was most exquisitely of the body. When he spoke of his shame in being supported by his mother, she leaned her cheek on his shoulder, careless of the three spectators on the porch, and said softly, "David, I love you so that I would like to scrub floors for you." He laughed; "I wouldn't like to have you scrub floors, thank you! Why in thunder don't I get ahead faster," he sighed. Then he told her that the older men in the profession were "so darned mean, even the big fellows, 'way up," that they kept on practising when they could just as well sit back on their hind legs and do nothing, and give the younger men a chance.

"They are nothing but money-grabbers," Elizabeth agreed, burning with indignation at all successful physicians. "But David, we can live on very little. Corn-beef is very cheap, Cherry-pie says. So's liver."

Up on the porch the conversation was quite as practical as it was down by the moonlit water:

"Elizabeth is to have a little bit of money handed over to her on her next birthday," Mr. Ferguson was saying; then he twitched the black ribbon of his glasses and brought them tumbling from his nose;

"it's an inheritance from her father."

"Oh, how exciting!" said Nannie. "Will it make it possible for them to be married any sooner?"

"They can't marry on the interest on it," he said, with his meager laugh; "it's only a nest-egg."

Mrs. Richie sighed. "Well, of course they must be prudent, but I am sorry to have them wait. It will be some time before David's practice is enough for them to marry on. He is so funny in planning their housekeeping expenses," she said, with that mother-laugh of mockery and love. "You should hear the economies they propose!" And she told him some of them. "They make endless calculations as to how little they can possibly live on. You would never suppose they *could* be so ignorant as to the cost of things! Of course I enlighten them when they deign to consult me. I do wish David would let me give him enough to get married on," she ended, a little impatiently.

"I think he's right not to," Robert Ferguson said.

"David is so queer about money," Nannie commented; and rose, saying she wanted to go indoors to the lamplight and her book.

"Pity Blair hasn't some of David's 'queerness,'" Mr. Ferguson barked, when she had vanished into the house.

Mrs. Richie looked after her uneasily, missing her protecting presence. But in Mr. Ferguson's matter-of-fact talk he seemed just the same harsh, kind, unsentimental neighbor of the last seventeen years; "he's forgotten his foolishness," she thought, and resigned herself, comfortably, to Nannie's absence. "Does Elizabeth know about the legacy?" she asked.

"No, she hasn't an idea of it. I was bound that the expectation of money shouldn't spoil her."

"Well," she jeered at him, "I do hope you are satisfied *now*, that she is not spoiled by money or anything else! How afraid you were to let yourself really love the child—poor little Elizabeth!"

"I had reason," he insisted doggedly. "Life had played a trick on me once, and I made up my mind not to build on anybody again, until I was sure of them." Then, without looking at her, he said, as if following out some line of thought, "I hope you have come to feel that you will marry me, Mrs. Richie?"

"*Oh!*" she said, in dismay.

"I don't see why you can't make up your mind to it," he continued, frowning; "I know"—he stopped, and put on his glasses carefully with both hands—"I know I am a bear, but—"

"You are not!"

"Don't interrupt. I am. But not at heart. Listen to me, at my age, talking about 'hearts'!" They both laughed, and then Mr. Ferguson gave a snort of impatience. "Look at those two youngsters down there, engaged to be married, and swearing by the moon that nobody ever loved as they do. How absurd it is! A man has to be fifty before he knows enough about love to get married."

"Nonsense!"

"I cannot take youth seriously," he ruminated; "its behavior, yes; that may be serious enough! Youth is always firing the Ephesian dome; but youth itself, and its opinions, always seem to me a little ridiculous. Yet those two infants seem to think that they have discovered love! Well," he interrupted himself, in sudden somber memory, "I felt that way once myself. And yet *now*, I know—"

Mrs. Richie said hurriedly something about its being too damp for
Elizabeth on the sand. "Do call them in!"

He laughed. "No; you don't need 'em. I won't say any more —to-night."

"Here they come!" Mrs. Richie said in a relieved voice.

A minute before, David, looking up at the porch, and

discovering Nannie's absence, had said, "Let's go in." "Oh, must we?" Elizabeth said, reluctantly. "I'd so much rather sit down here and have you kiss me." But she came, perforce, for David, in his anxiety not to leave his mother alone with Mr. Ferguson, was already halfway up the beach.

"Do tell Elizabeth about the money now," Mrs. Richie said.

"I will," said Robert Ferguson; but added, under his breath, "I sha'n't give up, you know." Mrs. Richie was careful not to hear him.

"Elizabeth!" she said, eagerly. "Your uncle has some news for you." And Mr. Ferguson told his niece briefly, that on her birthday in December she would come into possession of some money left her by her father.

"Don't get up your expectations, it's not much," he said, charily, "but it's something to start on."

"Oh, Uncle! how splendid!" she said, and caught David's hand in both of hers. "David!"—her face was radiantly unconscious of the presence of the others: "perhaps we needn't wait two years?"

"I'm afraid it won't make much difference." David spoke rather grimly; "I must be able to buy your shoestrings myself, you know, before we can be married."

Elizabeth dropped his hand, and the dimple straightened in her cheek.

Mrs. Richie smiled at her. "Young people have to be prudent, dear child."

"How much money shall I have, Uncle?" Elizabeth asked coldly.

He told her. "Not a fortune; but David needn't worry about your shoestrings."

"Yes, I will," he broke in, with a laugh. "She'll have to go barefoot, if I can't get 'em for her!"

Elizabeth exclaimed, with angry impatience, and Robert Ferguson, chuckling, struck him lightly on the shoulder. "Look out you don't fall over backward trying to stand up straight!" he said.

The possibility of an earlier wedding-day was not referred to again. The next morning they all went up to town together in the train, and Elizabeth, who had recovered from her momentary displeasure, did no more than cast glowing looks at David—lovely, melting looks of delicate passion, as virginal as an opening lily— looks that said, "I wish we did not have to wait!" For her part, she would have been glad "to go barefoot," if only they might the sooner tread the path of life together.

When they got into Mercer, late in the evening, who should meet them at the station but Blair. Robert Ferguson, with obvious relief, immediately handed his charges over to the young man with a hurried explanation that he must see some one on business before going to his own house. "Take the girls home, will you, Blair?" Blair said that that was what he was there for. His method of taking them home was to put Nannie into one carriage, and get into another with Elizabeth, who, a little surprised, asked where Nannie was.

"It would delay you to go round to our house first," Blair explained. "You forget we live in the slums. And Nannie's in a hurry, so I sent her directly home. She doesn't mind going by herself, you know. Look here, you two girls have been away an abominably long time! I've been terribly lonely—without Nannie."

He had indeed been lonely "without Nannie." In these empty, meaningless weeks at the Works, Blair Maitland had suddenly stumbled against the negations of life. Hitherto, he had known only the easy and delightful assents of Fate; this was his first experience with the inexorable *No*. A week after the girls went East, he admitted to himself that, had David been out of the way, he would undoubtedly have fallen in love with Elizabeth. "As it is, of course I haven't," he declared. Night after night in those next weeks, as he idled moodily about Mercer's streets, or, lounging across the bridge, leaned on the handrail and watched the ashes from his cigar flicker down into the unseen current below, he said the same thing: "I am not in love with her, and I sha'n't allow myself to be. I won't let it go any farther. But David is no man for a girl like Elizabeth to marry." Then he would fall to thinking just what kind of man Elizabeth ought to marry. Such reflections proved, so he assured himself, how entirely he knew that she belonged to David. Sometimes he wondered sullenly whether he had not better leave Mercer before she came back? Perhaps it was his god who made this suggestion; if so, he did not recognize a divine voice. He always decided against such a course. It would be cowardly, he told himself, to keep away from Elizabeth. "I will see her when she gets home, just as usual. To stay away might make her think that I was—afraid. And I am not in the least, because I am not in love with her, and I shall not allow myself to be." He was perfectly sure of himself, and perfectly sincere, too; what lover has ever understood that love has nothing to do with volition!

Now, alone with her in the old depot carriage, his sureness permitted him to say, significantly,

``I have been terribly lonely—without Nannie.''

``I thought you were absorbed in business cares,'' she told him drolly.

``How do you like business, Blair, really?''

``Loathe it,'' he said succinctly. ``Elizabeth, come and take dinner with us to-morrow evening?''

``Oh, Nannie's had enough of me. She's been with me for nearly two months.''

``I haven't been with you for two months. Be a good girl, and do some missionary work. Slumming is the fashion, you know. Come and cheer me up. It's been fiendishly stupid without you.''

She laughed at his sincerely gloomy voice.

``Come,'' he urged; ``we'll have dinner in the back parlor. Do you remember that awful dinner-party?'' He laughed as he spoke, but—being 'sure';—in the darkness of the shabby hack he looked at her intently.... . Oh, if David were only out of the way!

``Remember it? I should think I did!'' There was no telltale flicker on her smooth cheek; even in the gloom of the carriage he could see that the dark amber of her eyes brimmed over with amusement, and the dimple deepened entrancingly. ``How could I forget it? Didn't I wear my first long dress to that dinner-party—oh, and my six-button gloves?''

``I—'' said Blair, and paused. ``I remember other things than the gloves and long dress, Elizabeth.'' (Why shouldn't he say as much as that? He was certain of himself, and David was certain of her, so why not speak of what it gave him a rapturous pang to remember?)

But at his words the color whipped into her cheek; her clear brows drew together into a slight frown. ``How is your mother, Blair?'' she said coldly. "Oh, very well. Can you imagine Mother anything but well? The heat has nearly killed me, but Mother is iron."

"She's perfectly wonderful!"

"Yes; wonderful woman," he agreed carelessly. "Elizabeth, promise you'll come to-morrow evening?"

"Cherry-pie would think it was horrid in me not to stay with her, when
I've been away so long."

"I think it's horrid in you not to stay with me."

She laughed; then sighed. "David is working awfully hard, Blair."

"Darn David!" he retorted, laughing. "So am I, if that's any reason for your giving a man your society."

"You! You couldn't work hard to save your life."

"I could, if I had somebody to work for, as David has."

"You'd better get somebody," she said gaily.

"I don't want any second-bests," he declared.

"Donkey!" Elizabeth said good-naturedly. But she was a little surprised, for whatever else Blair was, he was not stupid—and such talk is always stupid. That it had its root in anything deeper than chaffing never occurred to her. They were at her own door by this time, and Blair, helping her out of the carriage, looked into her face, and his veins ran hot.

The next morning, when he went to see Nannie, he was absorbed and irritable. "Girls are queer," he told her; "they marry all kinds of men. But I'll tell you one thing: David is the last man for a girl like Elizabeth. He is perfectly incapable of understanding her."

That was the first day that he did not assure himself that he "was not in love."

Chapter 16

That autumn, with its heats and brown fogs and sharp frosts, was the happiest time in Sarah Maitland's life—the happiest time, at least, since those brief months of marriage;—*Blair was in the Business!* "If only his father could see him!" she used to say to herself. Of course, she had moments of disappointment; once or twice moments of anger, even; and once, at any rate, she had a moment of fright. She had summoned her son peremptorily to go with her to watch a certain experiment. Blair appeared, shrinking, bored, absent-minded, nearly an hour later than the time she had set. That put her in a bad humor to start with; but as they were crossing the Yards, her irritation suddenly deepened into dismay: Blair, his lip drooping with disgust at the sights and sounds about him, his hands in his pockets, was lounging along behind her, and she, realizing that he was not at her side, stopped and looked back. He was standing still, looking up, his eyes radiant, his lips parted with delight.

"What is it?" she called. He did not hear her; he stood there, gazing at three white butterflies that were zigzagging into a patch of pale blue sky. How they had come into this black and clamorous spot, why they had left their fields of goldenrod and asters farther down the river, who can say? But here they were, darting up and up, crossing, dipping, dancing in the smoky sunshine that flooded thinly the noisy squalor of the Yards. Blair, looking at them, said, under his breath, in pure delight, "Yes, just like the high notes. A flight of violin notes!"

"Blair!" came the impatient voice; "what's the matter with you?"

"Nothing, nothing."

"I was just going to tell you that a high silicon pig—"

"My dear mother," he interrupted wearily, "there is something else in the world than pig. I saw three butterflies—"

"Butterflies!"

She stood in the cinder pathway in absolute consternation. Was her son a fool? For a moment she was so startled that she was not even angry. "Come on," she said soberly; and they went into the Works in silence.

That evening, when he dropped into supper, she watched him closely, and by and by her face lightened a little. Of course, to stop and gape up into the air was silly; but certainly he was talking intelligently enough now,—though it was only to Elizabeth Ferguson, who happened to be taking supper with them. Yes, he did not look like a fool. "He *has* brains," she said to herself, frowning, "but why doesn't he use 'em?" She sighed, and called out loudly, "Harris! Corn-beef!" But as she hacked off a slab of boiled meat, she wondered why on earth Nannie asked Elizabeth to tea so often, and especially why she asked her on those evenings when Blair happened to be at home. "Elizabeth is such a little blatherskite," she reflected, good-naturedly, "the boy doesn't get a chance to talk to me!" Then it occurred to her that perhaps he came because Elizabeth came? for it was evident that she amused him. Well, Sarah Maitland had no objection. To secure her son for her dingy supper table she was willing to put up with Elizabeth or any other girl. But certainly Nannie invited her very often. "I'll come in to-night, if you'll invite Elizabeth," Blair would bribe her. And Nannie, like Mrs. Maitland herself, would have invited anybody to gain an hour of her brother's company.

Those four weeks had committed Blair Maitland to his first real passion. He was violently in love, and now he acknowledged it. The moment had come when his denials became absurd, even to himself, so he no longer said he did not love her; he merely said he would never let her know he loved her. "If she doesn't know it, I am square with David," he argued. Curiously enough, when he said "David," he always thought of David's mother. He was profoundly unhappy, and yet exhilarated—there is always exhilaration in the aching melancholy of hopeless love; but somewhere, back in his mind, there was probably the habit of hope. He had always had everything he wanted, so why should not fate be kind now?—of course without any questionable step on his part. "I will never tell her," he assured himself; the words stabbed him, but he meant them. He only wished, irrationally enough, that Mrs. Richie might know how agonizingly honorable he was.

Elizabeth herself did not know it; she had not the slightest idea that he was in love with her. There were probably two reasons for an unconsciousness which was certainly rather unusual, for a woman almost always knows. Some tentacles of the soul seem brushed by the brutalities of the material fact, and she knows and retreats—or advances. Elizabeth did not know, and so did not retreat. Perhaps one reason for her naive stupidity was the commonplaceness of her relations with Blair. She had known him all her life, and except for that one childish playing at love, which, if she ever remembered it, seemed to her entirely funny, she had never thought of him in any other way than as "Nannie's brother"; and Nannie was, for all practical purposes, her sister. Another reason was her entire absorption in her own love-affair. Ever since she had learned of the little legacy, the ardent thought had lurked in her mind that it might, somehow, in spite of David's absurd theories about shoestrings, hasten her marriage. "With all this money, why on earth should we wait?" she fretted to Nannie.

"My dear! you couldn't live on the interest of it!"

"I don't know why not," Elizabeth said, wilfully.

"Goose!" Nannie said, much amused. "No; the only thing

you could do would be to live on your principal. Why don't you do that?"

Elizabeth looked suddenly thoughtful. When she went home she repeated Nannie's careless words to Miss White, who nibbled doubtfully, and said she never heard of such a thing. But after that, for days, they talked of household economies, and with Cherry-pie's help Elizabeth managed to pare down those estimates which had so diverted her uncle and Mrs. Richie. With such practical preoccupations no wonder she was unconscious of the change in Blair. Suddenly, like a stone flung through the darkness at a comfortably lighted domestic window, she saw, with a crash of fright, a new and unknown Blair, a man who was a complete and dreadful stranger.

It was dusk; she had come in to see Nannie and talk over that illuminating suggestion: *why not live on the principal?* But Nannie was not at home, so Elizabeth sat down in the firelight in the parlor to wait for her. She sat there, smiling to herself, eager to tell Nannie that she had argued Cherry-pie into admitting that the plan of "living on the principal" was at least feasible; and also that she had sounded her uncle, and believed that if she and David and Cherry-pie attacked him, all together, they could make him consent!—"But of course David will simply have to insist," she thought, a little apprehensively, "for Uncle Robert is so awfully sensible." Then she began to plan just how she must tell David of this brilliant idea, and make him understand that they need not wait; "as soon as he really understands it, he won't listen to any 'prudence' from Uncle!" she said, her eyes crinkling into a laugh. But how should she make him understand? She must admit at once (because he was so silly and practical) that, of course, the interest on her money would not support them. Then she must show him her figures—David was always crazy about figures! Well, she had them; she had brought them with her to show Nannie;

they proved conclusively that she and David could live on her capital for at least two years. It would certainly last as long as that, perhaps even for two years and a half! When they had exhausted it, why, then, David's income from his profession would be large enough; large enough even if—she blushed nobly, sitting there alone looking into the fire; "even if!" Thinking this all out, absorbed and joyous, a little jealous because this practical idea had come to Nannie and not to her, she did not hear Blair enter. He stood beside her a moment in silence before she was aware of his presence. Then she looked up with a start, and leaning back in her chair, the firelight in her face, smiled at him: "Where's Nannie?"

"I don't know. Church, I think. But I am glad of it. I would rather—see you alone." His voice trembled.

He had come in, in all the unrest of misery; he had said to himself that he was going to "tell Nannie, anyhow." The impulse to "tell" had become almost a physical necessity, and when he came into the room, the whole unhappy, hopeless business was hot on his lips. The mere unexpectedness of finding her here, alone, was like a touch against that precariously balanced sense of honor, which was his god, and had so far kept him, as he expressed it to himself, "square with David."

To Elizabeth, sitting there in friendly idleness by the fire, the thrill in his voice was like some palpable touch against her breast. Without knowing why, she put her hand up, as if warding something off. She was bewildered; her heart began to beat violently. Instantly, at the sight of the lovely, startled face, the rein broke. He forgot David, he forgot his god, with whom he had been juggling words for the last two months, he forgot everything, except the single, eternal, primitive purpose: *there was the woman he wanted*. And all his life, if he had wanted anything, he had had it. With a stifled cry, he caught her hand: "Elizabeth—I love you!"

"Stop!" she said, outraged and astounded; "stop this instant!"

"I *must* speak to you."

"You shall not speak to me!" She was on her feet, trying with trembling fingers to put on her hat.

"Elizabeth, wait!" he panted, "wait; listen—I must speak—" And before she knew it, he had caught her in his arms, and she felt his breath on her mouth. She pushed him from her, gasping almost, and looking at him in anger and horror.

"How dare you?"

"Listen; only one minute!"

"I will not listen one second. Let me out of this room—out of this house!"

"Elizabeth, forgive me! I am mad!"

"You *are* mad. I will never forgive you. Stand aside. Open the door."

"Elizabeth, I love you! I love you! Won't you listen—?"

But she had gone, flaming with anger and humiliation.

When Nannie came in an hour later, her brother was sitting with his head bowed in his hands. The room was quite dark; the fire had died down. The fire of passion had died down, too, leaving only shame and misery and despair. His eyes, hidden in his bent arms, were wet; he was shaken to the depths of his being. For the first time in his life he had come against a thwarted desire. The education that should have been spread over his whole twenty-five years, an education that would have taught him how to meet the negations of life, of duty, of pity even, burst upon him now in one shattering moment. He had broken his law, his own law; and, mercifully, his law was breaking him. When he rose to his feet as his sister came into the room, he staggered under the shock of such concentrated education.

"Blair! What *is* it?" she said, catching his arm.

"Nothing. Nothing. I've been a fool. Let me go."

"But tell me! I'm frightened. Blair!"

"It's nothing, I tell you. Nannie! Will she ever look at me again? Oh no, no; she will never forgive me! Why was I such a fool?"

"What *are* you talking about?" poor Nannie said. It came into her head that he had suddenly gone out of his senses.

Blair sank down again in a heap on his chair.

"I've been a damned fool. I'm in love with Elizabeth, and—and I told her so."

Chapter 17

Of course, with that scene in the parlor, all the intimacies of youth were broken short off; although between the two girls some sort of relationship was patched up. Nannie, thrown suddenly into the whirlpool of her brother's emotions, was almost beside herself with distress; she was nearly twenty-eight years old, but this was her first contact with the primitive realities of life. With that contact,—which made her turn away her horrified, virginal eyes; was the misery of knowing that Blair was suffering. She was ready to annihilate David, had such a thing been possible, to give her brother what he wanted. As David could not be made non-existent, she did her best to comfort Blair by trying to make Elizabeth forgive him. The very next day she came to plead that Blair might come himself to ask for pardon. Elizabeth would not listen:

"Please don't speak of it."

"But Elizabeth—"

"I am perfectly furious, and I am very disgusted. I never want to see
 Blair again!"

At which Blair's sister lifted her head.

"Of course, he ought not to have spoken to you, but I think you forget that he loved you long before David did."

"Nonsense!" Elizabeth cried out impatiently.

But Nannie's tears touched her. "Nannie, I can't see him, and I won't; but I'll come and see you when he is not there." At which Nannie flared again.

"If you are angry at my brother, and can't forgive just a momentary, a passing feeling,—which, after all, Elizabeth, *is* a compliment; at least everybody says it's a compliment to have a man say he loves you—"

"Not if you're engaged to another man!" Elizabeth burst in, scarlet to her temples.

"Blair loved you before David thought of you."

"Now, Nannie, don't be silly."

"If you can't overlook it, because of our old friendship, you will have to drop me, too, Elizabeth."

Nannie was so pitiful and trembling that Elizabeth put her arms around her. "I'll never drop you, dear old Nannie!"

So, as far as the two girls were concerned, the habit of affection persisted; but Mrs. Maitland was not annoyed by having Elizabeth present when Blair came to supper.

Blair did not come to supper very often now; he did not come to the

Works. "Is your brother sick?" Sarah Maitland asked her stepdaughter

three or four days later. "He hasn't been at his desk since Monday. What's the matter with him?"

"He is worried about something, Mamma."

"Worried? What on earth has *he* got to worry him?" she grunted. In her own worry she had come across the hall to speak to Nannie, and find out, if she could, something about Blair. As she turned to go back to the dining-room, a little more uneasy than when she came in, her eye fell on that picture which Blair had left, a small oasis in the desert of Nannie's parlor, and with her hand on the door-knob she paused to look at it. The sun was lying on the dark oblong, and in those illuminated depths maternity was glowing like a jewel. Sarah Maitland saw no art, but she saw divine things. She bent forward and looked deep into the picture; suddenly her eyes smiled until her whole face softened. "Why, look at his little foot," she said, under her breath; "she's holding it in her hand!" She was silent for a moment; then she spoke as if to herself: "When Blair was as big as that, I bought him a pair of green morocco slippers. I don't suppose you remember them, Nannie? They buttoned round the ankle; they had white china buttons. He used to try to pick the buttons off." She smiled again vaguely; then blinked as if awakening from a dream, and blew a long bubbling sigh through her closed lips; "I can't imagine why he doesn't come to the office!"

In the dining-room, as she took up her pen, she frowned. "Debt again?" she asked herself. But when, absorbed and irritable, Blair came into her office at the Works, and sat down at his desk to write endless letters that he tore up as soon as they were written, she did not ask for any explanation. She merely told Robert Ferguson to tell the bookkeeper to make a change in the pay-roll. "I'm going to raise Blair's salary," she said. Money was the only panacea Mrs. Maitland knew anything about.

That next fortnight left its marks on Blair Maitland. People who have always had what they want, have a sort of irrational certainty of continuing to have what they want. It makes them a little unhumanly young. Blair's face, which had been as irresponsible as a young faun's, suddenly showed those scars of thwarted desire which mean age. There was actual agony in his sweet, shallow eyes, and with it the half-resentful astonishment of one who, being unaccustomed to suffering, does not know how to bear it. He grew very silent; he was very pale; in his pain he turned to his sister with an openness of emotion which frightened and shamed her; he had no self-control and no dignity.

"I must see her. I must, I must! Go and ask her to see me for a moment. I've disgusted her"—Nannie blushed; "but I'll make her forgive me." Sometimes he burst out in rages at David: "What does *he* know about love? What kind of a man is he for Elizabeth? She's a girl now, but if he gets her, God help him when she wakes up, a woman! Not that *I* mean to try to get her. Understand that. Nothing is farther from my mind than that. She belongs to him; I play fair. I don't pretend to be a saint, but I play fair. I don't cut in, when the man's my friend. No; I just want to see her and ask her to forgive me. That's all. Nannie, for God's sake ask her if she won't see me, just for five minutes!"

He quivered with despair. Twice he went himself to Mr. Ferguson's house. The first time Miss White welcomed him warmly, and scuttled up-stairs saying she would "tell Elizabeth." She came down again, very soberly. "Elizabeth is busy, Blair, and she says she can't see you." The next time he called he was told at the door that "Miss Elizabeth asks to be excused." Then he wrote to her: "All I ask is that you shall see me, so that I can implore you to pardon me."

Elizabeth tore the letter up and threw it into the fire. But she softened a little. "Poor Blair," she said to herself, "but of course I shall never forgive him."

She had not told David what Blair had done. "He would be furious," she thought. "I'll tell him later—when we are married"; at the word, the warm, beautiful wave of young love rose in her heart; "later, when I belong to him, I will tell him everything!" She would tell him everything just as she would give him everything; not that she had much to give him—only herself and her little money. That blessed money, on which he and she could live for two years,—she was going to give him that! For she and Nannie and Cherry-pie had decided that if the money were *his*, by a gift, then David, who was perfectly crazy and noble about independence, would feel that he and Elizabeth were living on his money, not hers. It was an artless and very feminine distinction, but serious enough to the three women who were all so young—Elizabeth, in fact, being the oldest, and Cherry-pie, at sixty-three, the youngest. And not only had they discovered this way of overcoming David's scruples about a shorter engagement, but Elizabeth had had another inspiration: why not be married on the very day that the money came into her possession? "Oh, splendid!" said Nannie; but she spoke with an effort, remembering Blair. A little timidly, Elizabeth had told her uncle of this wonderful plan about the money. He snorted with amusement at her way of whipping the devil round the stump by a "gift" to David; but after a rather startled moment, although he would not commit himself to a date, he was inclined to think an earlier marriage practicable. We are selfish creatures at best, all of us: Elizabeth's way of being happy herself opened a possibility of happiness for her uncle. "Mrs. Richie can't make David an excuse for saying 'no,' if the boy gets a home of his own," he thought; and added to himself, "of course, when the child's money is used up, I'll help them out." But to his niece he only barked warningly: "Well, let's hear what David has to say; *he* has some sense."

"Do you think there's much doubt as to what he'll say?" Elizabeth said; and the dimple deepened so entrancingly that Robert Ferguson gave her a meager kiss. After securing this somewhat tentative consent, Elizabeth and Cherry-pie decided that the next thing to do was to "make David write to uncle, and simply *insist* that the wedding shall be next month!" Her plan was very simple: when David came to Mercer to spend her birthday, he should receive, at the same moment, her money and herself.

That future time of sacramental giving and of complete taking was in her thoughts with tenderness and shame and glory, as it is in the thought of every woman who loves and forgets herself. Yes, he could have her now; but he must take her money! That was the price he had to pay—the taking of her money. That it would be a high price to a man with his peculiarly intense feeling about independence, Elizabeth knew; but he would be willing to pay it! Elizabeth could not doubt that. No price could be too high, he loved her so! She shivered with happiness at the thought of how he loved her; some soft impulse of passion made her lift her round wrist,—that bitten wrist! to her mouth, and kiss it, hard. David had kissed it, many times! Yes; she was his if he would pay the price! She was going to tell him so, and then wait, glowing, and shrinking, and eager, for him to come and "take her."

It was so true, so limpid, this noble flame that burned in her, that she almost forgot Blair's behavior; the only thing she thought of was her plan, and the difficulty of putting it into the cold limits of pen and ink! But with much joyous underlining of important words she did succeed in stating it to him. She told him, not only the practical details, but with a lovely, untrammelled outpouring of her soul which was sacrificial, she told him that she wanted to be his wife. She had no reserves; it was an elemental moment, and the matter of what is called modesty had no place in her ardent purity. It rarely has a place in organic impulses. In connection with death, or birth, or love, modesty is only a rather puerile self-consciousness. So Elizabeth, who had never been self-conscious in her life, told David, with perfect simplicity, that she "wanted to be married." She said she had "worked the money part of it out," and according to her latest estimate of how much, or rather how little, they could live on, it was possible. "You will say, we haven't even as much as this," she wrote, after she had stated what seemed to be the minimum income; then, triumphantly: "*we have!*the money Uncle is going to give me on my birthday! If we live on it, instead of hoarding it up, it will last *at least* two years! I've talked to Uncle about it, and I'm pretty sure he will consent; but you'd better write and urge him,—*just insist!*" Then she approached the really difficult matter of making David agree to live on money that was not his. She admitted that she knew how he felt on such matters. "And you are all wrong," she declared candidly, "wrong, and a goose. But, so long as you do feel so, why, you needn't any longer. For I am going to give the money to you. It is to be yours, *not mine*. You can't refuse to use the money that is *yours*, that comes to you as a 'gift'? It will be as much *yours* as if somebody left it to you in their will, and you can burn it up, if you want to!" And when "business" had been written out, her heart spoke:

"Dear" (she stopped to kiss the paper), "dear, I hope you won't burn it up, because I am tired of waiting, and I hope you are too;"—when she wrote those last words, she was suddenly shy; "Uncle is to give me the money on my birthday—let us be married that day. I *want* to be married. I am all yours, David, all my soul, and all my mind, and all my body. I have nothing that is not yours to take; so the money is yours. No, I will not even give it to you! it belongs to you already—as I do. Dear, come and take it—and me. I love you—love you—love you. *I want you to take me.* I want to be your wife. Do you understand? I *want* to belong to you. I *am* yours."

So she tried, this untutored creature, to put her soul and body into words, to write the thing that cannot even be spoken, whose utterance is silence. The mailing of the letter was a rite in itself; in the dusk, as she held the green lip of the post-box open, she kissed the envelope, as she had kissed the glowing sheet an hour before. She said to herself that she was "too happy to live!" As she said it, a wave of pity blotted out her usual shamed resentment at that poor mother of hers who had not been happy;—and whose lack of self-control was, Elizabeth believed, her legacy to her child. But her gravity was only for a moment; forgetting Blair, and the possible chance of meeting him, she flew down to Nannie's to tell her that the die had been cast —the letter had been written! Nannie, sitting by herself in the parlor, brooding over her brother's troubles, was trying to draw; but Elizabeth brushed aside pencils and crusts of bread and india-rubbers, and flung her arms about her, pressing her face against hers and pouring the happy secret into her ear:

"Oh, Nannie—I've told him! We'll be married on my birthday. Go ahead and get your dress!" she said, breathlessly, and Nannie tried her best to be happy, too.

For the next three days Elizabeth moved about in a half-dream, sometimes reddening suddenly; sometimes breathing a little quickly, with a faint fright in her eyes,—had she said too much? would he understand? Then a gush of confident love filled her like music. "I couldn't say too much! I want him to know that I feel— that way."

When David read that throbbing letter, he grew scarlet to his temples. There had been many moments during their engagement when Elizabeth, in slighter ways, had bared her soul to him, and always he had had the impulse to cover his eyes, as in a holy of holies. He had never, in those moments, dared to take advantage of such divine nakedness, even by a kiss. But she had never before trusted her passion to the coldness of pen and ink; it had had the accompaniment of eyes and lips, and eager, breaking voice. Perhaps if the letter had come at a different moment, he could more easily have called up that voice, and those humid eyes; he might have felt again the rose-pressure of the soft mouth. As it was, he read it in troubled preoccupation; then reddened sharply: he was a worthless cuss; he couldn't stand on his own legs and get married like a man; his girl had to urge her uncle to let her support her lover! "Damn," said David softly.

A letter is a risky thing; the writer gambles on the reader's frame of mind. David's frame of mind when he read those words about urging Robert Ferguson, was not hospitable to other people's generosity, for Elizabeth's hot letter came on what had been, figuratively speaking, a very cold day. In the morning he had been reprimanded by the House officer for some slight forgetfulness—a forgetfulness caused by his absorption in planning an experiment in the laboratory. At noon he made the experiment, which, instead of crowning a series of deductions with triumphant proof, utterly failed. Then he had had pressing reminders of bills, still unpaid, for a pair of trousers and a case of instruments, and he had admitted to himself that he would have to ask his mother for the money to meet them. "I am a fizzle, all round," he had told himself grimly. "Can't remember anything overnight. Can't count on a doggone reaction. Can't pay for my own pants! I won't be able to marry for ten years. If Elizabeth is wise, she will throw me over. She'll be tired of waiting for me, before I can earn enough to buy my instruments — let alone the shoe-strings Mr. Ferguson talked about!"

Then her letter came. It was a spur on rowelled flesh. Elizabeth *was* tired of waiting! She said so. But she would help him; she had induced her uncle to consent that she should "give" him money; that she should, in fact, support him! — just as his mother had been doing all his life. He was sore with disappointment at himself, yet, when he answered her letter his eyes stung at the thought of the loveliness of her love! He held her letter in his hand as he wrote, and once he put it to his lips. All the same he wrote, as he had to write, laconically:

"DEAR ELIZABETH, — I'm sure Mr. Ferguson will agree with me that your money cannot be mine, by any gift. Calling it so won't make it so. Anyhow, it would not support us two years. By that time, as things look now, I shall probably not be earning any kind of an income. I am sorry you are tired of waiting, but I can't let you be imprudent. And apart from prudence, I could not respect myself if you supported me. It has been misery to me to have Materna saddled with a big, lazy brute of a fellow like me, who ought by this time to be taking care of you both. I am sure, if you think it over, you would be ashamed of me if I asked your uncle to help me out by letting you marry me now. Anyhow, I should be ashamed of myself. Well, the Lord only knows when I will come up to time! You might as well make up your mind to it that I'm a fizzle. I am discouraged with myself and everything else, and I see you are too; Heaven knows I don't blame you. I know you think it is an awfully long time to wait, but it isn't as long to you as it is to me. Dear, I love you; I can't tell you how I love you. I haven't words, as you have, but you know I do—and yet sometimes I feel as if I oughtn't to marry you."

Elizabeth, running down the steps to meet the postman, saw a familiar imprint on the corner of an envelope, and drew it from the pack before the good-natured man could hand it to her.

"Guess you don't want no Philadelphia letter?" he said slyly.

"Of course I don't!" she retorted; and the trudging postman smiled for a whole block because of the light in her face. In the house, the letter in her hand, she stopped to hug Miss White. "Cherry-pie! the letter has come. I'm to be married on my birthday!"

"Oh, my lamb," said Cherry-pie, "however shall I get things ready in time!" Elizabeth did not wait to help her in her housekeeping anxieties. She fled singing up to her room.

"Oh, that will be joyful, joyful, joyful,
Oh, that will be joyful,
To meet to part no more!"

Then she opened the letter.... She read the last lines with unseeing eyes; the first lines were branding themselves into her soul. She folded the brief sheet with deliberation, and slowly put it back into the envelope. Then the color began to fall out of her face. Her eyes smoldered, glowed, then suddenly blazed: "He is sorry I am tired waiting."

Something warm, like a lifting tide of heat, was rising just below her breast-bone; it rose, and rose, and surged, until she gasped, and cried out hoarsely: "If 'I think it over,' I'll be 'ashamed,' will I? 'Couldn't respect himself'? What about me respecting myself?" And the intolerable wave of heat still rose, swelling and bursting until it choked her; she was strangling! She clutched at her throat, then flung out clenched hands. "He 'can't let' me marry him? It's 'a long time for *me* to wait'! I must 'make up my mind to it'! I hate him—I want to kill him—I want to tear him! What did I tell him? 'to come and take me'? And he doesn't want me! And Nannie knows I told him to come, and Miss White and Uncle know it. And they will know he didn't want me. Oh, how could I have told him I wanted him? I must kill him. I must kill myself—" Her wild outpouring of words was without sense or meaning to her. She shuddered violently, something crimson seemed to spread before her eyes, but the pallor of her face was ghastly. She began to pace up and down the room. Once she unfolded the letter, and glancing again at those moderate words, laughed loudly. "'His,'" she said, "I told him I was 'his'? I must have been out of my head. Well, I'll 'think it over!' I'll 'think it over!'—he needn't worry about that. Oh, I could kill myself! And I told Cherry-pie I was going to be—" she could not speak the word. She stood still and gasped for breath.

The paroxysm was so violent, and so long in coming to its height before there could be any ebb, that suddenly she reeled slightly. A gray mist seemed to roll up out of the corners of the room. She sank down on the floor, crumpling up against her bed. When she opened her eyes, the mist had gone, and she felt very stiff and a little sick. "Why, where am I?" she said aloud, "what's the matter with me?" Then, dully, she remembered David's letter. "I was so angry I fainted," she thought, in listless astonishment. For the moment she was entirely without feeling, neither angry, nor wounded, nor ashamed. Then, little by little, the dreadful wave, which had ebbed, began to rise again. But now it was cold, not hot. She said to herself, quietly, that she would write to David Richie, and tell him she *had* 'thought it over'; and that neither she nor her money was his, or any further concern of his. "He needn't trouble himself; there would be no more 'imprudence.' Oh, fool! fool! immodest fool! to have told him he 'could have her for the taking,' and he said it was 'long' for *her* to wait!" It was an unbearable recollection. "His," she had said; "soul and body." She saw again the written words that she had kissed, and she had an impulse to tear the flesh of the lovely young body she had offered this man, and he had—declined. "*His?*" She blushed until she had to put her cold hands on her cheeks and forehead to ease the scorch. The modesty which a great and simple moment had obliterated came back with intolerable sharpness.

By and by she got on her feet and dragged herself to a chair; she looked very wan and languid. For the moment the fire was out. It had burned up precious things.

"I'll write to him to-morrow," she thought. And through the cold rage she felt a hot stab of satisfaction; her letter—"a rather different letter, this time!" would make him suffer! But not enough. Not enough. She wished she could make him die, as she was dying. But she could not write at that moment; the idea of taking up a pen turned her sick with the remembrance of what her pen had written three days before. Instead of writing, she would go out and walk, and walk, and walk, and think how she could punish him—how she could *kill* him! Where should she go? Never mind! anywhere; anywhere. Just let her get out, let her be alone, where nobody could speak to her. How could she ever speak to people again?—to Miss White, who was down in the dining-room, now, planning for the— wedding! To Nannie, who knew that David had been summoned, and who must be told that he refused to come; to Blair, who would guess—she paused, remembering that she was angry with Blair. There was a perceptible instant before she could recollect why; when she did, she felt a pang of relief in her agony of humiliation. Blair, whatever else he was, was a *man*, a man who could love a woman! It occurred to her that the girl Blair loved would not be thought immodest if she showed him how much she loved him.

She began to put on her things to go out, and as she fastened her hat she looked at herself in the glass. "I have a wicked sort of face," she thought, with a curious detachment from the situation which was almost that of an outside observer. She packed a small hand-bag, and then opened her purse to see if she had money enough to carry out a vague plan of going somewhere to spend the night, "to get away from people." It was noon when she went down-stairs; in the hall she called to Miss White that she was going out.

"But it's just dinner-time, my lamb," Miss White called back from the dining-room; "and I must talk to you about—"

"I—I want to see Nannie," Elizabeth said, in a smothered voice. It occurred to her that, later, she would go and tell Nannie that she had broken her engagement; it would be a satisfaction to do that, at any rate!

"Oh, you're going to take dinner with her?" Miss White said, peering out into the hall; "well, tell her to come in this afternoon and let us talk things over. There is so much to be done between now and the wedding," Cherry-pie fretted happily.

"*Wedding!*" Elizabeth said to herself; then slipped back the latch of the front door: "I sha'n't come back until to-morrow."

"Oh, my lamb!" Miss White remonstrated, "I *must* ask you some questions about the wedding!" Then she remembered more immediate questions: "Is your satchel packed? Have you plenty of clean pocket-handkerchiefs? Elizabeth! be careful not to take cold, and ask Nannie how many teaspoons she can lend us—" The door slammed. It seemed to Elizabeth that she could never look Cherry-pie in the face again. She had a frantic feeling that if she could not escape from that intolerable insistence on the—the wedding, she would die. In the street, the mere cessation of Miss White's joyous twittering was a relief. Well, she must go where she could be alone. She walked several blocks before she thought of Willis's; it would take at least two hours to get there, and she could think things over without interruption. She would think how she could save her self-respect before Miss White and her uncle and Nannie; and she would also think of some dreadful way, some terrible way to punish David Richie! Yes; she would walk out to Willis's... .

"Elizabeth!" some one said, at her elbow, and with a start she turned to see Blair. As they looked at each other, these two unhappy beings, each felt a faint pity for the other. Blair's face was haggard; Elizabeth's was white to the point of ghastliness, but there was a smudge of crimson just below the glittering amber of her eyes. "Elizabeth!" he said, shocked, "what is it? You are ill! What has happened?"

"Nothing. I—am tired." She was so unconscious of everything but the maelstrom realization that she hated David that she did not remember that the hesitating man beside her was under the ban of her displeasure. Her only thought was that she wished he would leave her to herself.

"Dark day, isn't it?" Blair said; but his voice broke in his throat.

"I think we are going to have rain," Elizabeth answered, mechanically. She was perfectly unaware of what she said, for at that moment she saw, on the other side of the street, the friendly postman who two hours ago had brought her David Richie's insult; now, his empty pouch over his shoulder, he was trudging back to the post-office. Against the clamoring fury of her thoughts and the instant vision of David's letter, Blair's presence was no more to her than the brush of a wing across the surface of a torrent.

As for Blair, he was dazed, and then ecstatic. She had not sent him away! She was perfectly matter-of-fact! "'*I think we are going to have rain.*'" She must have forgiven him! "May I walk home with you, Elizabeth?" he said breathlessly.

"I'm not going home. I am—just walking."

"So am I," he said. He had got himself in hand by this time; every faculty was alert; he had his chance to ask for pardon! "Come out to Mrs. Todd's, and have some pink ice-cream. Elizabeth, do you remember the paper roses on those dreadful marble-topped tables that were sort of semi-transparent?"

Elizabeth half smiled. "I had forgotten them; how horrid they were!" With the surface of her mind she was conscious that his presence was a relief; it was like a veil between her and the flames.

Blair, watching her furtively, said: "I'll treat. Come along, let's have a spree!"

"You always did do the treating," she said absently. Blair laughed. The primitive emotions are always naked; but how inevitably most of us try to cover them with the fig-leaf of trivial speech—a laugh, perhaps, or a question about the weather; somehow, in some way, the nakedness must be covered! So now, Love and Hate, walking side by side in Mercer's murky noon, were for the moment hidden from each other. Blair laughed, and said he would make her "treat" for a change, and she replied that she couldn't afford it.

At the toll-house he urged again, with gay obstinacy. "Oh, come in! You needn't eat the stuff, but just for the fun of the thing; Mrs. Todd will be charmed to see us, I'm sure."

"Well," Elizabeth agreed; for a moment the vapid talk was like balm laid upon burnt flesh. Then suddenly she remembered how David had sprung up that snowy path to the toll-house, to knock on the window and cry, "I've got her!" Ah, he was a little too sure; a *little* too sure! She was not so easy to get as all that, not so cheap as he seemed to think—though she had offered herself; had even told him she was "tired of waiting"! (And at home Cherry-pie was counting the teaspoons for the wedding breakfast.)

Blair heard that fierce intake of her breath, and quivered without knowing why. "Yes, let us go!" Elizabeth said fiercely. At least this chuckling old woman should see that David had not "got her"; she should see her with Blair, and know that there were men in the world who cared for her, if David Richie did not.

Mrs. Todd was not at home; perhaps, if she had been... .

But instead of the big, motherly old figure, beaming at them from the toll-house door, a slatternly maid-servant said her mistress was out. "We ain't doin' much cream now," she said, wrapping her arms in her apron and shivering; "it's too cold. I ain't got anything but vanilla."

"We'll have vanilla, then," Blair said, in his rather courtly way, and the girl, opening the door of the "*saloon*," scurried off. "By Jove!" said Blair, "I believe these are the identical blue paper roses— look at them!"

She sat down wearily. "I believe they are," she said, and began to pull off her gloves. Outside in the tollhouse garden the frosted stems of last summer's flowers stood upright in the snow. She remembered that Mrs. Todd's geraniums had been glowing in the window that winter day when David had shouted his triumphant news. Probably they were dead now. Everything else was dead.

"Still the tissue-paper star on the ceiling!" Blair cried, gaily, "yes, everything is just the same!" And indeed, when the maid, glancing with admiring eyes at the handsome gentleman and the cross-looking lady, put down on the semi-translucent marble top of the table two tall glasses of ice-cream, each capped with its dull and dented spoon, the past was completely reproduced. As the frowsy little waitress left them, they looked at the pallid, milky stuff, and then at each other, and their individual preoccupations thinned for a moment. Blair laughed; Elizabeth smiled faintly:

"You don't expect me to eat it, I hope?"

"I won't make you eat it. Let's talk."

But Elizabeth took up her gloves. "I must go, Blair."

He pushed the tumblers aside and leaned toward her; one hand gripped the edge of the table until the knuckles were white: the other was clenched on his knee. "Elizabeth," he said, in a low voice, "have you forgiven me?"

"Forgiven you? What for?" she said absently; then remembered and looked at him indifferently. "Oh, I suppose so. I had forgotten."

"I wouldn't have done it if I hadn't loved you. You know that."

She was silent.

"Do you hate me for loving you?" On Elizabeth's cheeks the smudge of crimson began to flame into scarlet. "I don't hate you. I think you were a fool to love me. I think anybody is a fool to love anybody."

In a flash Blair understood. *She had quarrelled with David!*

It seemed as if all the blood in his body surged into his throat; he felt as if he were suffocating; but he spoke quietly. "Don't say I was a fool; say I am a fool, if you want to. Because I love you still. I love you now. I shall never stop loving you."

Elizabeth glanced at him with a sort of impersonal interest. So *that* was the way a man might love? "Well, I am sorry for you, Blair. I'm sorry, because it hurts to love people who don't love you. At least, I should think it did. I don't love anybody, so I don't know much about it."

"You have broken with David," he said slowly.

"How did you know?" she said, with a surprised look; then added listlessly, "Yes; I've done with David. I hate him." She looked blankly down at her muff, and began to stroke the fur. It occurred to her that before going to Willis's she must see Nannie, or else she would have told Miss White a lie; again the double working of her mind interested her; rage, and a desire to be truthful, were like layers of thought. She noted this, even while she was saying again, between set teeth, "I hate him."

"He has treated you badly," Blair said.

"How did you know?" she said, startled.

"I know David. What does a man like David know about loving a woman? He would talk his theories and standards to her, when he could be silent—in her arms!" He flung out his hand and caught her roughly by the wrist. "Elizabeth, for God's sake, *marry me.*"

[Illustration: "ELIZABETH, MARRY ME!"]

He had risen and was leaning toward her, his fingers gripped her wrist like a trap, his breath was hot against her neck, his eyes glowed into hers. "Marry—me, Elizabeth."

The moment was primal; the intensity of it was like a rapier-thrust, down through her fury to the quick of womanly consciousness; she shrank back. "Don't," she said, faintly; "don't—" For one instant she forgot that she hated David. Instantly he was tender.

"Dearest, dearest, I love you. Be my wife. Elizabeth, I have always loved you, always; don't you remember?" He was kneeling beside her, lifting the hem of her skirt and kissing it, murmuring crazy words; but he did not touch her, which showed that the excuse of passion was not yet complete. And indeed it was not, for somewhere in the tumult of his mind he was defending himself—perhaps to his god: "*I have the right.* It's all over between them. Any man has the right now." Then, aloud: "Elizabeth, I love you. I shall love you forever. Marry me. Now. To-night." When he said that, it was as if he had struck his god upon the mouth—for the accusing Voice ceased. And when it ceased, he no longer defended himself. Elizabeth looked at him, dazed. "No, I know you don't care for me, now," he said. "Never mind that! I will teach you to care; I will teach you—" he whispered: "the meaning of love! *He* couldn't teach you; he doesn't know it himself; he doesn't"—he was at a loss for a word; some instinct gave him the right one—"want you."

It was the crack of the whip! She answered it with a look of hate. But still she was silent.

"You love him," he flung at her.

"I do not. I hate him! hate him! hate him! I wish he were dead in this room, so I could trample on him!" Even in the scorch of that insane moment, Blair Maitland flinched at such a declaration of hate. Hate like that is the left hand of Love. He had sense enough left in his madness to know that, and he could have killed David because he was jealous of such precious hate.

"You'll get over that," he assured her; neither of them saw in such an assurance the confession that he knew she loved David still. And still his smitten god was silent! "You—you hate him because he slighted you," Blair said, stammering with passion. "But for God's sake, Elizabeth, *show* him that you hate him. Since he despises you, despise him! Will you let him slap you in the face, and still love him?"

"I do not love him."

They were both standing; Elizabeth, staring at him with unseeing eyes, seemed to be answering some fierce interrogation in her own thought: What? was *this* the way to kill David Richie? That it would kill her, too, never occurred to her. If it had occurred to her, it would have seemed worth while—well worth while!

"Then why do you let him think you love him?" Blair was insisting, in a violent whisper, "why do you let him think you are under his heel still? Show him you hate him—if you do hate him? Marry me, *that will show him.*"

They were standing, now, facing each other—Love and Hate. Love, radiant, with glorious eyes, with beautiful parted lips, with outstretched hands that prayed, and threatened, and entreated: "Come! I must have you,—God, I *must!*" And Hate, black-browed, shaking from head to foot, with dreadful set stare, and hands clenched and trembling; hands that reached for a dagger to thrust, and thrust again! Hands reaching out and finding the dagger in that one, hot, whispered word: "Come." Yes; that would "show him"!

"When?" she said, trembling.

And he said, "Now."

Elizabeth flung up her head with a look of burning satisfaction.

"*Come!*" she said; and laughing wildly, she struck her hand into his.

Chapter 18

When Robert Ferguson came in to luncheon the next day, he asked for Elizabeth. "She hasn't come home yet from Nannie's," Miss White told him; "I thought she would be here immejetly after breakfast. I can't imagine what keeps her, though I suppose they have a great deal to talk over!"

"Well, she'll have to wait for her good news," Mr. Ferguson said; and handed a telegram to Miss White. "Despatch from David. He's bringing a patient across the mountains to-night; says he'll turn up here for breakfast. He'll have to go back on the ten-o'clock train, though."

Cherry-pie nibbled with excitement; "I guess he just had to come and talk the arrangements over with her!"

"What arrangements?" Mr. Ferguson asked, vaguely; when reminded by Miss

White, he looked a little startled. "Oh, to be sure; I had forgotten." Then he smiled:

"Well, I suppose I shall have to say 'yes.' I think I'll go East myself next week!" he added, fatuously; but the connection was not obvious to Miss White.

"Elizabeth got a letter from him yesterday," she said, beaming; "they've decided on her birthday—if you are willing."

"Willing? I guess it's a case of 'he had to be resigned!'" said Robert

Ferguson—thinking of that trip East, he was positively gay. But Cherry-pie's romance lapsed into household concerns: "We must have

something the boy likes for breakfast."

"Looking at Elizabeth will be all the breakfast he wants,"

Elizabeth's uncle said, with his meager chuckle. "David's as big a donkey as any of 'em, though he hasn't the gift of gab on the subject."

When he had gone to his office, Miss White propped the telegram up on the table, so that Elizabeth's eyes might brighten the moment she opened the front door But to her dismay, Elizabeth did not open the door all that afternoon. Instead came a note, plainly in her hand, addressed to Mr. Ferguson. "Why! she is sending word that she's going to stay all night *again* with Nannie," Miss White thought, really disturbed. If such a thing had been possible, Cherry-pie would have been vexed with her beloved "lamb," for after all, Elizabeth really ought to be at home attending to things! Miss White herself had spent every minute since the wonderful news had been flung at her, in attending to things. She had made a list of the people who must be invited to the wedding, she had inspected the china-closet, she had calculated how many teaspoons would be needed,—"Better borrow some forks from Nannie, too," she said, beginning, like every good housekeeper, to look careworn. "There's so much to be done!" said Cherry-pie, excitedly. Yet this scatter-brain girl evidently meant to stay away from home still another night. "Well, she can't, that's all there is to it!" Miss White said, decidedly; "she must come home, so as to be here in the morning when David arrives. Perhaps I'd better go down to Mrs. Maitland's and take her the despatch."

She was getting ready to go, when the first rumble of the hurricane made itself heard. Nannie dropped in, and—

"'Where's Elizabeth?' I'm sure I don't know. Isn't she at home? 'Stayed with me last night?' Why, no, she didn't. I haven't seen Elizabeth for two days, and—"

Nannie sprang to catch poor old Miss White, who reeled, and then tried, as she sank into a chair, to speak: "What? *What?* Not with you last night? Nannie! She must have been. She told me she was going—" Miss White grew so ghastly that Nannie, in a panic, called a servant.

"Send for her uncle!" the poor lady stammered. "Send—send. Oh, what has happened to my child?" Then she remembered the letter addressed to Mr. Ferguson, lying on the table beside David's telegram. "Perhaps that will say where she is. Oh, tell him to *hurry!*"

When Robert Ferguson reached home he found the two pallid, shaking women waiting for him in the hall. Miss White, clutching that unopened letter, tried to tell him: Elizabeth had not been at Nannie's; she had not come home; she had—

"Give me the letter," he said. They watched him tear it open and run his eye over it; the next instant he had gone into his library and slammed the door in their faces.

Outside in the hall the trembling women looked at each other in silence. Then Nannie said with a gasp, "She must have gone to—to some friend's."

"She has no friend she would stay all night with but you."

"Well, you see she has written to Mr. Ferguson, so there can't be anything much the matter; he'll tell us where she is, in a minute! If he can't, I'll make Blair go and look for her. Dear, *dear* Miss White, don't cry!"

"There has been an accident. Oh, how shall we tell David? He's coming to-morrow to talk over the wedding, and—"

The library door opened: "Miss White."

"Mr. Ferguson! Where—? What—?"

"Miss White, that—creature, is never to cross my threshold again. Do you understand me? Never again. Nannie, your brother is a scoundrel. Read that." He flung the letter on the floor between them, and went back to his library. They heard the key turn in the lock. Miss White stared at the shut door blankly; Nannie picked up the letter. It was headed "The Mayor's Office," and was dated the day before; no address was given.

"Dear Uncle Robert: I married Blair Maitland this afternoon. David did not want me. E.F."

They read it, looked at each other with astounded eyes, then read it again. Nannie was the first to find words:

"I—don't understand." Miss White was dumb; her poor upper lip quivered wildly.

"She and David are to be married," Nannie stammered. "How can she marry—anybody else? I don't understand."

Then Miss White broke out, "*I* understand. Oh, wicked boy! My child, my lamb! He has killed my child Elizabeth!"

"Who has? What do you mean? What *are* you talking about!"

"He has lured her away from David," the old woman wailed shrilly. "Nannie, Nannie, your brother is an evil, cruel man—a false man, a false friend. Oh, my lamb! my girl!"

Nannie, staring at her with horrified eyes, was silent. Miss White sank down on the floor, her head on the lowest step of the staircase; she was moaning to herself: "They quarrelled about something, and this is what she has done! Oh, she was mad, my lamb, my poor lamb! She was crazy; David made her angry; I don't know how. And she did this frightful thing. Oh, I always knew she would do some terrible thing when she was angry!"

Nannie looked at the closed door of the library, then at Miss White, lying there, crying and moaning to herself with her poor old head on the stairs; once she tried to speak, but Miss White did not hear her; it was intolerable to see such pain. Blair's sister, ashamed with his shame, stammered something, she did not know what, then opening the front door, slipped out into the dusk. The situation was so incredible she could not take it in. Blair and Elizabeth—*married?* She kept saying it over and over. But it was impossible! Elizabeth was to marry David on her birthday. "I feel as if I were going out of my mind!" Nannie told herself, hurrying down into Mercer's black, noisy heart. When she reached the squalor of Maitland's shantytown and saw the great old house on the farther side of the street, looming up on its graded embankment, black against a smoldering red sunset, she was almost sobbing aloud, and when Harris answered her ring, she was in such tension that she burst out at him: "Harris! where is Mr. Blair? Do you know? Have you heard—anything?" She seized the old man's arm and held on to it. "Where is Mr. Blair, Harris?"

"My laws, Miss Nannie! how do I know? Ain't he at the hotel? There's a letter come for you; it come just after you went out. Looks like it was from him. There, now, child! Don't you take on like that! I guess if Mr. Blair can write letters, there ain't much wrong with him."

When he brought her the letter, she made him wait there in the dimly lighted hall until she opened it, she had a feeling that she could not read it by herself, "Oh, Harris!" she said, and began to tremble; "it's true! He did.... They are—oh, Harris!" And while the old man drew her into the parlor, and scuffled about to light the gas and bring her a glass of water, she told him, brokenly—she had to tell somebody—what had happened. Harris's ejaculations were of sheer amazement, untouched by disapproval: "Mr. Blair? Married to Miss Elizabeth? My land! There! He always did git in ahead!" His astounded chuckle was as confusing as all the rest of it. Nannie, standing under the single flaring jet of gas, read the letter again. It was, at any rate, more enlightening than Elizabeth's to her uncle:

"Dear Nannie: Don't have a fit when I tell you Elizabeth and I are married. She had a row with David, and broke her engagement with him. We were married this afternoon. I'm afraid mother won't like it, because, I admit, it's rather sudden. But really it is the easiest way all round, especially for—other people. It's on the principle of having your tooth pulled *quick*!—if you have to have it pulled, instead of by degrees. I'll amount to something, now, and that will please mother. You tell her that I will amount to something now! I want you to tell her about it before I write to her myself—which, of course, I shall do to-morrow—because it will be easier for her to have it come from you. Tell her marrying Elizabeth will make a business man of me. You must tell her as soon as you get this, because probably it will be in the newspapers. I feel like a cur, asking you to break it to her, because, of course, it's sort of difficult. She won't like it, just at first; she never likes anything I do. But it will be easier for her to hear it first from you. Oh, you dear old Nancy!—I am nearly out of my head, I'm so happy.… .

"P.S. We are going off for a month or so. I'll let you know where to address us when I know myself."

Nannie dropped down into a chair, and tried to get her wits together. If Elizabeth had broken with David, why, then, of course, she could marry Blair; but why should she marry him right away? "It isn't—decent!" said Nannie. And when did she break with David? Only day before yesterday she was expecting to marry him. "It is horrible!" said Nannie; and her recoil of disgust for a moment included Blair. But the habit of love made her instant with excuses: "It's worse in Elizabeth than in him. Mamma will say so, too." Then she felt a shock of terror: "Mamma!" She smoothed out the letter, crumpled in her shaking hand, and read it again: "'I want you to tell her—' Oh, I *can't!*" Nannie said; "'it will be easier for her to have it come from you—' And what about me?" she thought, with sudden, unwonted bitterness; "it won't be 'easy' for me."

She began to take off her things; then realized that she was shivering. The few minutes of stirring the fire which was smoldering under a great lump of coal between the brass jambs of the grate, gave her the momentary relief of occupation; but when she sat down in the shifting firelight, and held her trembling hands toward the blaze, the shame and fright came back again. "Poor David!" she said; but even as she said it she defended her brother; "if Elizabeth had broken with him, of course Blair had a right to marry her. But how *could* Elizabeth! I can never forgive her!" Nannie thought, wincing with disgust. "To be engaged to David one day, and marry Blair the next! —Oh, Blair ought not to have done it," she said, involuntarily; and hid her face in her hands. But it was so intolerable to her to blame him, that she drove her mind back to Elizabeth's vulgarity; she could bear what had happened if she thought of Blair as a victim and not as an offender.

"I can never feel the same to Elizabeth again," she said. Then she remembered what her brother had bidden her do, and quailed. For a moment she was actually sick with panic. Then she, too, knew the impulse to get the tooth pulled "quick." She got up and went swiftly across the hall to the dining-room. It was empty, except for Harris, who was moving some papers from the table to set it for supper.

"Oh, Harris," she said, with a gasp of relief, "she isn't here! Harris,

I have got to tell her. You don't think she'll mind much, do you?"

But by this time Harris's chuckling appreciation of Mr. Blair's cleverness in getting in ahead had evaporated. "My, my, my, Miss Nannie!" he said, his weak blue eyes blinking with fright, "*I* wouldn't tell her, not if you'd gimme the Works!"

"Harris, if you were in my place, would you try to, at supper?"

"Now, Miss, how can I tell? She'll be wild; my, my; wild!"

"I don't see why. Mr. Blair had a right to get married."

"He'd ought to have let on to her about it," Harris said.

For a few minutes Nannie was stricken dumb. Then she sought encouragement again: "Perhaps if you had something nice for supper, she'd be—pleased, you know, and take it better?"

"There's to be cabbage. Maybe that will soften her up. She likes it; gor, how she likes cabbage!" said Harris, almost weeping.

"Harris, how do you think she'll take it?"

"She won't take it well," the old man said. "Miss Elizabeth was Mr. David's girl. When I come to think it over, I don't take it well myself, Miss Nannie. Nor you don't, neither. No, she won't take it well."

"But Miss Elizabeth had broken with Mr. David," Nannie defended her brother; "Mr. Blair had a right—" then she shivered. "But *I've* got to tell her! Oh, Harris, I think she wouldn't mind so much, if he told her himself?"

Harris considered. "Yes, Miss, she would. Mr. Blair don't put things right to his ma. He'd say something she wouldn't like. He'd say something about some of his pretty truck. Them things always make her mad. That picture he bought—the lady nursin' the baby, in your parlor; she ain't got over that yet. Oh, no, she'll take it better from you. You be pretty with her, Miss Nannie. She likes it when you're pretty with her. I once seen a chippy sittin' on a cowcatcher; well, it made me think o' you and her. You be pretty to her, and then tell her, kind of—of easy," Harris ended weakly.

Easy! It was all very well to say "*easy*"; Harris might as well say knock her down "easy." At that moment the back door banged.

Mrs. Maitland burst into the room in intense preoccupation; the day had been one of absorbing interest, culminating in success, and she was alert with satisfaction. "Harris, supper! Nannie, take my bonnet! Is your brother to be here to-night? I've something to tell him! Where's the evening paper?"

Nannie, breathless, took the forlorn old bonnet, and said, "I —I think he isn't coming, Mamma." Harris came running with the newspaper; they exchanged a frightened glance, although the mistress of the house, with one hand on the carving-knife, was already saying, "Bless, O Lord—"

At supper Mrs. Maitland, eating—as the grocer said so long ago, "like a day-laborer"—read her paper. Nannie watching her, ate nothing at all and said nothing at all.

When the coarse, hurried meal was at an end, and Harris, blinking with horrified sympathy, had shut himself into his pantry, Nannie said, faintly, "Mamma, I have something to tell you."

"I guess it will keep, my dear, I guess it will keep! I'm too busy just now to talk to you." She crumpled up her newspaper, flung it on the floor, and plunged over to her desk.

Nannie looked helplessly at the back of her head, then went off to her parlor. She sat there in the firelit darkness, too distracted and frightened to light the gas, planning how the news must be told. At eight o'clock there was a fluttering, uncertain ring at the front door, and Cherry-pie came quivering in: had Nannie heard anything more? Did she know where *they* were? "I asked her uncle to come down here and see if Mrs. Maitland had heard anything, but—he was dreadful, Nannie, dreadful! He said he would see the whole family in —I can't repeat where he said he would see them!" She broke down and cried; then, crouching at Nannie's side, she read Blair's letter by the uncertain light of the fire. After that, except for occasional whispered ejaculations of terror and pain, they were silent, sitting close together like two frightened birds; sometimes a lump of coal split apart, or a hissing jet of gas bubbled and flamed between the bars of the grate, and then their two shadows flickered gigantic on the wall behind them; but except for that the room was very still. When the older woman rose to go, Nannie clung to her:

"Oh, won't you tell her? Please—please!" Poor old Miss White could only shake her head:

"I can't, my dear, I *can't!* It would not be fitting. Do it now, my dear; do it immejetly, and get it over."

When Cherry-pie had wavered back into the night, Nannie gathered up her courage to "get it over." She went stealthily across the hall; but at the dining-room door she stood still, her hand on the knob, not daring to enter. Strangely enough, in the midst of the absorbing distress of the moment, some trick of memory made her think of the little 'fraid-cat, standing outside that door, trying to find the courage to open it and get for Blair—for whose sake she stood there now—the money for his journey all around the world! In spite of her terror, she smiled faintly; then she opened the door and looked in. Mrs. Maitland was still at work, and she retreated noiselessly. At eleven she tried again.

Except for the single gas-jet under a green shade that hung above the big desk, the room was dark. Mrs. Maitland was in her chair, writing rapidly; she did not hear Nannie's hesitating footstep, or know that she was in the room, until the girl put her hand on the arm of her chair.

"Mamma."

"Yes?"

"Mamma, I have something to—to tell you."

Mrs. Maitland signed her name, put her pen behind her ear, flung a blotter down on the heavily written page, and rubbed her fist over it. "Well?" she said cheerfully; and glanced up at her stepdaughter over her steel-rimmed spectacles, with kind eyes; "what are you awake for, at this hour?" Then she drew out a fresh sheet of paper, and began to write: "My dear Sir:—Yours received, and con —"

"Mamma ... Blair is married."

The pen made a quick, very slight upward movement; there was a spatter of ink; then the powerful, beautiful hand went on evenly "—tents noted." She rubbed the blotter over this line, put the pen in a cup of shot, and turned around. "What did you say?"

"I said ... Blair is married."

Silence.

"He asked me to tell you."

Silence.

"He hopes you will not be angry. He says he is going to be a —a tremendous business man, now, because he is so happy."

Silence. Then, in a loud voice: "How long has this been going on?"

"Oh, Mamma, not any time at all, truly! I am perfectly sure it —it was on the spur of the moment."

"Married, 'on the spur of the moment'? Good God!"

"I only mean he hasn't been planning it. He—"

"And what kind of woman has married him, 'on the spur of the moment'?"

"Oh,—Mamma ... "

Her voice was so terrified that Mrs. Maitland suddenly looked at her. "Don't be frightened, Nannie," she said kindly. "What is it? You have something more to tell me, I can see that. Come, out with it! Is she bad?"

"Oh, *Mamma!* don't! don't! It is—she is—Elizabeth—"

Then she fled.

That night, at about two o'clock, Mrs. Maitland entered her stepdaughter's room. Nannie was dozing, but started up in her bed, her heart in her throat at the sight of the gaunt figure standing beside her. Blair's mother had a candle in one hand, and the other was curved about it to protect the bending flame from the draught of the open door; the light flickered up on her face, and Nannie was conscious of how deep the wrinkles were on her forehead and about her mouth.

"Nannie, tell me everything."

She put the candle on the table at the head of the bed, and sat down, leaning forward a little, as if a weight were resting on her shoulders. Her clasped hands, hanging loosely between her knees, seemed, in the faint light of the small, pointed flame, curiously shrunken and withered. "Tell me," she said heavily.

Nannie told her all she knew. It was little enough.

"How do you know that Elizabeth had broken with David Richie?" her stepmother said. Nannie silently handed her Blair's letter. Mrs. Maitland took up her candle, and holding it close to the flimsy sheet, read her son's statement. Then she handed it back. "I see; some sort of a squabble; and Blair—" She stopped, almost with a groan. "His *friend,*" she said, and her chin shook; "your father's son!" she said brokenly.

"Mamma!" Nannie protested—she was sitting up in bed, her hair in its two braids falling over her white night-dress, her eyes, so girlish, so frightened, fixed on that quivering iron face; "Mamma! remember, he was in love with Elizabeth long ago, before David ever thought—"

"In love with Elizabeth? He was never in love with anybody but himself."

"Oh, Mamma, please forgive him! It's done now, and it can't be undone."

"What has my forgiveness got to do with it? It's done, as you say. It can't be undone. Nothing can be undone. Nothing; nothing. All the years that remain cannot undo the years that I have been building this up."

Nannie stared at her blankly. And suddenly the hard face softened. "Lie down. Go to sleep." She put her big roughened hand gently on the girl's head. "Go to sleep, my child." She took up her candle, and a moment later Nannie heard the stairs creak under her heavy tread.

Sarah Maitland did not sleep that night; but after the first outburst, when Nannie had panted out, "It is—Elizabeth," and then fled, there had been no anger. When the door closed behind her stepdaughter, Blair's mother put her hand over her eyes and sat perfectly still at her desk. *Blair was married.* And he had not told her, —that was the first thought. Then, into the pitiful, personal dismay of mortification and wounded love, came the sword-thrust of a second thought: he had stolen his friend's wife.

It was not a moment for nice discriminations; the fact that Elizabeth had not been married to David seemed immaterial. This was because, to Sarah Maitland's generation, the word, in this matter of getting married, was so nearly as good as the bond, that a broken engagement was always a solemn, and generally a disgraceful thing. So, when she said that Blair had "stolen David's wife," she cringed with shame. What would his father say to such conduct! In what had she been wanting that Herbert's son could disgrace his father's name —and hate his mother? For of course he must hate her to shut her out of his life, and not tell her he was going to get married! Her mind seemed to oscillate between the abstraction of his dishonor and a more intimate and primitive pain,—the sense of personal slight. "Oh, my son, my son, my son," she said. She was bending over, her elbows on her knees, her furrowed forehead resting on her clenched hands; her whole big body quivered. He had shut her out.... He hated her.... He had never loved her.... "My son! my son!" Then a sharp return of memory to the shame of his conduct whipped her to her feet and set her walking about the room. It was long after midnight before she said to herself that the first thing to do was to learn exactly what had happened. Nannie must tell her. It was then that she went up to her stepdaughter's room.

When Nannie had told her, or rather when Blair's letter had made the thing shamefully clear, she went down-stairs and faced the situation. Who was responsible for it? Who was to blame—before she could add, in her mind, "Elizabeth or Blair?" some trick of memory finished her question: who was to blame—"*this man or his parents?*" The suggestion of personal responsibility was like a blow in the face. She flinched under it, and sat down abruptly, breathing hard. How could it be possible that she was to blame? What had she left undone that other mothers did? She had loved him; no mother could have loved him more than she did!—and he had never cared for her love. In what had she been lacking? He had had a religious bringing up; she had begun to take him to church when he was four years old. He had had every educational opportunity. All that he wanted he had had. She had never stinted him in anything. Could any mother have done more? Could Herbert himself have done more? No; she could not reproach herself for lack of love. She had loved him, so that she had spared him everything—even desire! All that he could want was his before he could ask for it.

In the midst of this angry justifying of herself, tramping up and down the long room, she stopped suddenly and looked about her; where was her knitting? Her thoughts were in such a distracted tangle that the accustomed automatic movement of her fingers was imperative. She tucked the grimy pink ball of zephyr under her arm, and tightening her fingers on the bent and yellowing old needles, began again her fierce pacing up and down, up and down. But the room seemed to cramp her, and by and by she went across the hall into Nannie's parlor, where the fire had sprung into cheerful flames; here she paused for a while, standing with one foot on the fender, knitting rapidly, her unseeing eyes fixed on the needles. Yes; Blair had had no cares, no responsibilities,—and as for money! With a wave of resentment, she thought that she would find out in the morning from her bookkeeper just how much money she had given him since he was twenty-one. It was then that a bleak consciousness, like the dull light of a winter dawn, slowly began to take possession of her: *money*. She had given him money; but what else had she given him? Not companionship; she had never had the time for that; besides, he would not have wanted it; she knew, inarticulately, that he and she had never spoken the same language. Not sympathy in his endless futilities; what intelligent person could sympathize with a man who found serious occupation in buying—well, china beetles? Or pictures! She glanced angrily over at that piece of blackened canvas by the door, its gold frame glimmering faintly in the firelight. He had spent five thousand dollars on a picture that you could cover with your two hands! Yes; she had given him money; but that was all she had given him. Money was apparently the only thing they had in common.

Then came another surge of resentment,—that pitiful resentment of the wounded heart; Blair had never cared how hard she worked to make money for him! It occurred to her, perhaps for the first time in her life, that she worked very hard; she said to herself that sometimes she was tired. Yes, she had never thought of it before, but she was sometimes very tired. But what did Blair care for that? What did he care how hard she worked? Even as she said it, with that anger which is a confession of something deeper than anger, her mind retorted that if he had never cared how hard she worked for their money, she had never cared how easily he spent it. She had been irritated by his way of spending it, and she had been contemptuous; but she had never really cared. So it appeared that they did not have even money in common. The earning had been all hers; the spending had been all his. If she had liked to buy gimcracks, they would have had that in common, and perhaps he would have been fond of her? "But I never knew how to be a fool," she thought, simply. Yes; she didn't know how to spend, she only knew how to earn. Of course, if he had had to earn what he spent, they would have had work as a bond of sympathy. Work! Blair had never understood that work was the finest thing in the world. She wondered why he had not understood it, when she herself had worked so hard—worked, in fact, so that he might be beyond the need of working. As she said that, her fingers were suddenly rigid on her needles; it seemed as if her soul had felt a jolt of dismay; why didn't her son understand the joy of work? Because she had spared him all necessity for it!—for the work she had given him to do was not real, and they both knew it. Spared him? Robbed him! "*Who hath sinned, this man or his parents?*" "This man," her selfish, indolent, dishonorable son, or she herself, whose hurry to possess the one thing she wanted, that finest thing in the world, Work!—had pushed him into the road of pleasant, shameful idleness, the road that always leads to dishonor? Good God! what a fool she had been not to make him work.

Sarah Maitland, tramping back and forth, the ball of pink worsted dragging behind her in a grimy tangle, thought these things with a sledge-hammer directness that spared herself nothing. She wanted the truth, no matter how it made her cringe to find it! She would hammer out her very heart to find the truth. And the truth she found was that she had never allowed Blair to meet the negations of life—to meet those *No's*, which teach the eternal affirmations of character. He had had everything; he had done nothing. The result was as inevitable as the action of a law of nature! In the illuminating misery of this terrible night, she saw that she had given her son, as Robert Ferguson had said to her once, "fullness of bread and abundance of idleness." And now she was learning what bread and idleness together must always make of a man.

Walking up and down the dimly lighted room, she had a vision of her sin that made her groan. *She* had made Blair what he was: because it had been easy for her to make things easy for him, she had given him his heart's desire, and brought leanness withal to his soul. In satisfying her own hunger for work, she had forgotten to give it to him, and he had starved for it! She had left, by this time, far behind her the personal affront to her of his reserves; she took meekly the knowledge that he did not love her: she even thought of his marriage as unimportant, or as important only because it was a symptom of a condition for which she was responsible. And having once realized and accepted this fact, there was only one solemn question in her mind:

"What am I going to do about it?"

For she believed, as other parents have believed before her— and probably will go on believing as long as there are parents and sons—she believed that she could, in some way or other, by the very strength of her agonizing love, force into her son's soul from the outside that Kingdom of God which must be within. "Oh, what am I going to do?" she said to herself.

She stood still and covered her face with her hands. "God," she said, "don't punish him! It's my fault; punish me."

Perhaps she had never really prayed before.

Chapter 19

Robert Ferguson, in his library, and poor Miss White in the hall, listened with tense nerves for the wheels of the carriage that was to bring David Richie "to breakfast."

"Send him in to me," Mr. Ferguson had said; and then had shut himself into his library.

Miss White was quivering with terror when at last she heard the carriage door bang. David came leaping up the steps, his face rosy as a girl's in the raw morning air—it was a lowering Mercer morning, with the street lamps burning at eight o'clock in a murk of smoke and fog. He raked the windows with a smiling glance, and then stood, laughing for sheer happiness, waiting for *her* to open the door to him.

David had had a change of spirit, if not of mind, since he wrote his eminently sensible letter to Elizabeth. He had been able to scrape up enough money of his own to pay at least one of his bills, and things had gone better with him at the hospital, so he no longer felt the unreasonable humiliation which Elizabeth's proposal had accentuated in him. The reproach which his mood had read into her letter had vanished after a good night's sleep and a good day's work; now, it seemed to him only an exquisite expression of most lovely love, which brought the color into his face, and made his lips burn at the thought of her lips! Of course her idea of marrying on her little money was not to be thought of—he and Mr. Ferguson would laugh over it together; but what an angel she was to think of it! All that night, in the journey over the mountains, he had lain in his berth and looked out at the stars, cursing himself joyously for a dumb fool who had had no words to tell her how he loved her for that sweet, divinely foolish proposal, which was "not to be thought of"! "But when I see her, I'll make her understand; when I hold her in my arms

—" he told himself, with all the passion of twenty-six years which had no easy outlet of speech.

When Robert Ferguson's door opened, his heart was on his lips. "Eliz—" he began, and stopped short. "Oh, Miss White. Good morning, Miss White!" And before poor Cherry-pie knew it, he had given her a great hug; "Where is Elizabeth? Not out of bed yet? Oh, the lazybones!" He was so eager that, until he was fairly in the hall, with the front door shut, and his overcoat almost off, he did not notice her silence. Then he gave her a startled look. "Miss White! is anything the matter? Is Elizabeth ill?"

"No; oh, no," she said breathlessly; "but—Mr. Ferguson will tell you.
No, she is not sick. Go, he will tell you. In the library."

The color dropped out of his face as a flag drops to half-mast. "She is dead," he said, with absolute finality in his voice. "When did she die?" He stood staring straight ahead of him at the wall, ghastly with fright.

"No! no! She is not dead; she is well. Quite well; oh, very well. Go, David, my dear boy—oh, my *dear* boy! Go to Mr. Ferguson. He will tell you. But it is—terrible, David."

He went, dazed, and saying, "Why, but what is it? If she is not—not—"

Robert Ferguson met him on the threshold of the library, drew him in, closed the door, and looked him full in the face. "No, she isn't dead," he said; "I wish to God she were." Then he struck him hard on the shoulder. "David," he said harshly, "be a man; they've played a damned dirty trick on you. Yesterday she married Blair Maitland.... Take it like a man, and be thankful you are rid of her." He wheeled about and stood with his back to his niece's lover. He had guided the inevitable sword, but he could not witness the agony of the wound. There was complete stillness in the room; the ticking of the clock suddenly hammered in Robert Ferguson's ears; a cinder fell softly from the grate. Then he heard a long-drawn breath:

"Tell me, if you please, exactly what has happened."

Elizabeth's uncle, still with his back turned, told him what little he knew. "I don't know where they are," he ended; "I don't want to know. The scoundrel wrote to Nannie, but he gave no address. Elizabeth's letter to me is on my table; read it."

He heard David move over to the library table; he heard the rustle of the sheet of paper as it was drawn out of the envelope. Then silence again, and the clamor of the clock. He turned round, in time to see David stagger slightly and drop into a chair; perspiration had burst out on his forehead. He was so white around his lips that Robert Ferguson knew that for a moment his body shared the awful astonishment of his soul. "There's some whiskey over there," he said, nodding toward a side table. David shook his head. Then, still shuddering with that dreadful sickness, he spoke.

"She ... has married—Blair? *Blair?*" he repeated, uncomprehendingly. He put his hand up to his head with that strange, cosmic gesture which horrified humanity has made ever since it was capable of feeling horror.

"Yes," Mr. Ferguson said grimly; "yes, Blair—your friend! Well, you are not the first man who has had a sweetheart—and a 'friend.' A wife, even—and a 'friend.' And then discovered that he had neither wife nor friend. Damn him."

"Damn him?" said David, and burst into a scream of laughter. He was on his feet now, but he rocked a little on his shaking legs. "Damnation is too good for him; may God—" In the outburst of fury that followed, even Robert Ferguson quailed and put up a protesting hand.

"David—David," he stammered, actually recoiling before that storm of words. "David, he will get what he deserves. She was worthless!" David stopped short. At the mention of Elizabeth, his hurricane of rage dropped suddenly into the flat calm of absolute bewilderment. "Do not speak of Elizabeth in that way, in my presence," he said, panting.

"She is her mother's daughter! She is bad, through and through. She—"

"Stop!" David cried, violently; "what in hell do you keep on saying that for? I will not listen—I will not hear." ... He was beside himself; he did not know what he said.

But Robert Ferguson was silenced. When David spoke again, it was in gasps, and his words came thickly as if his tongue were numb: "What—what are we to do?"

"Do? There is nothing to do, that I can see."

"She must be taken away from him!"

"Nobody knows where they are. But if I did know, I wouldn't lift my hand to get her away. She has made her bed—she can lie in it, so far as I am concerned."

"But she didn't!" David groaned; "you don't understand. I am the one to curse, not Elizabeth."

"What are you talking about?"

"I did it."

The older man looked at him with almost contemptuous incredulity. "My dear fellow, what is the use of denying facts? You can't make black white, can you? Day before yesterday you loved this—this," he seemed to search for some epithet; glanced at David, and said, almost meekly: "girl. Day before yesterday she expected to marry you. To-day she is the wife of another man. Have you committed any crime in the last three days which justifies that?"

"Yes," David said, in a smothered voice, "I have." Then he handed back to the shamed and angry man the poor, pitiful little letter. "Don't you see? She says, 'David didn't want'"—he broke off, unable to speak. A moment later he added, "'E. *F.*' She isn't used to the—the other, yet," he said, again with that bewildered look.

But Elizabeth's uncle was too absorbed in his own humiliation to see confession in that tragic initial. "What is that nonsense about your not wanting her?"

"She thought so. She had reason to think so."

"You had better explain yourself, David."

"She wrote to me," David said, after a pause; "she told me she would have that money of hers on her birthday. She said we could be married then." He reddened to his temples. "She asked me to marry her that day; *asked* me, you understand." He turned on his heel and went over to the window; he stood there for some minutes with his back to Robert Ferguson. The green door in the wall between the two gardens was swinging back and forth on sagging hinges; David watched it with unseeing eyes; suddenly a sooty pigeon came circling down and lit just inside the old arbor, which was choked with snow shovelled from the flagstones of the path. Who can say why, watching the pigeon's teetering walk on the soot-specked snow, David should smell the fragrance of heliotrope hot in the sunshine, and see Elizabeth drawing Blair's ring from her soft young bosom? He turned back to her uncle, with a rigid face: "Well, *I*—I said—'no' to her letter. Do you understand? I told her 'no.' '*No*,' to a girl like Elizabeth! Because, in my—my filthy pride—" he paused, picked up a book, turned it over and over, and then put it straight edge to edge with the table. His hand was trembling violently. When he could speak again it was in a whisper. "My cursed pride. I didn't want to marry until I could do everything. I wasn't willing to be under obligations; I told her so. I said—'no.' It made her angry. It would make any girl angry,—but Elizabeth! Why, she used to bite herself when she was angry. When she is angry, she will do—anything. *She has done it.* My God!"

Robert Ferguson could not look at him. He made a pretense of taking up some papers from his desk, and somehow or other got himself out of the room. He found Miss White in the hall, clasping and unclasping her little thin old hands.

"How did he—?" she tried to say, but her poor nibbling lip could not finish the question.

"How does a man usually take a stab in the back?" he flung at her. "Don't be a—" He stopped short. "I beg your pardon, Miss White." But she was too heartbroken to resent the rudeness of his suffering.

After that they stood there waiting, without speaking to each other. Once Mr. Ferguson made as if he would go back to the library, but stopped with his hand on the door-knob; once Miss White said brokenly, "The boy *must* have some breakfast"; but still they left him to himself.

After a while, Cherry-pie sat down on the stairs and cried softly. Robert Ferguson walked about; now out to the front door, with a feint of looking at the thermometer in the vestibule; now the length of the hall, into which the fog had crept until the gas burned in a hazy ring; now into the parlor—from which he instantly fled as if a serpent had stung him: her little basket of embroidery, overflowing with its pretty foolishness, stood on the table.

When David Richie opened the library door and came into the hall he was outwardly far steadier than they. "I think I'll go to the depot now, sir. No, thank you, Miss White; I'll get something to eat there."

"Oh, but my dear boy," she said, trying to swallow her tears, "now do—now don't—I can have your breakfast ready immejetly, and—"

"Let him alone," Mr. Ferguson said; "he'll eat when he feels like it."

David, must you go back this morning? I wish you'd stay."

"I have to go back, thank you, sir."

"You may find a letter from her at home; she didn't know you were to be here to-day."

"I may," David said; and some dull note in his voice told Robert
Ferguson that the young man's youth was over.

"My boy," he said, "forget her! You are well rid of—" he stopped short, with an apprehensive glance; but David made no protest; apparently he was not listening.

"I shall take the express," he said; "I must see my mother, before I go to the hospital to-night. She must be told. She will be—sorry."

"Your mother!" said Robert Ferguson. "Well, David, thank God you have loved one woman who is good!"

"I have loved *two* women who are good," David said. He turned and took
Miss White's poor old, shaking hands in his. "When she comes back —"

"Comes back?" the older man cried out, furiously; "she shall never come back to this house!"

David did not notice him: "Miss White, listen. When you see her, tell her I understand. Just tell her, 'David says, "I understand."' And Miss White, say: 'He says, try to forgive him.'"

She sobbed so, that instinctively, but without tenderness, he put his arm about her; his face was dull to the point of indifference. "Don't cry, Miss White. And be good to her; but I know you will be good to her!" He picked up his hat, put his coat over his arm, and stretched out his hand to Robert Ferguson with a steady smile. "Good-by, sir." Then the smile dropped and left the amazed and naked face quivering before their eyes. Through the wave of merciful numbness which had given him his hard composure, agony stabbed him. "For God's sake, don't be hard on her. She has enough to bear! And blame me—*me*. I did it—"

He turned and fled out of the house, and the two unhappy people who loved Elizabeth looked at each other speechlessly.

Chapter 20

Except in his gust of primitive fury when he first knew that he had been robbed, and in that last breaking down in the hall, David knew what had happened to him only, if one may say so, with the outside of his mind. Even while he was talking with comparative calmness to Mr. Ferguson, his thoughts were whirling, and veering, in dizzying circles—bewildered rage, pity, fright, revolt,—and then back again to half-dazed fury. But each time he tried to realize exactly what had happened, something in him seemed to swerve, like a shying horse; he could not get near enough to the fact, to understand it. In a numb way he must have recognized this, because in those moments by himself in the library he deliberately shut a door upon the blasting truth. Later, of course, he would have to open it and look in upon the ruin of his life. Somewhere back in his thoughts he was aware that this moment of opening the Door would come, and come soon. But while he talked to Robert Ferguson, and tried, dully, to comfort Miss White, and even as he went down the steps up which he had bounded not an hour before, he was holding that moment off. His one clear feeling was a desire to be by himself. Then, he promised himself, when he was alone, he would open the Door, and face the Thing that lay behind it. But as he walked along the street, the Door was closed, bolted, locked, and his back was against it. "Elizabeth has married Blair," he said to himself, softly. The words seemed to have no meaning. "Elizabeth has married Blair," he insisted again; but was only cognizant that the blur of fog around a street-lamp showed rainbow lines in a wonderful pattern. "They are all at right angles," he said; "that's interesting," and looked ahead to see if the next light repeated the phenomenon. Then automatically he took out his watch: "Nine-thirty. Elizabeth has married Blair. The train leaves at ten. I had better be going to the depot. *Elizabeth has married Blair.*" And he walked on, looking at the lamps burning in the fog. Then suddenly, as if the closed Door showed a crack of light, he decided that he would not go back on the express; an inarticulate impulse pierced him to the quick,—the impulse to resist, to fight, to save himself and her! But almost with the rending pang, the Door slammed to again and the impulse blurred —like the street-lamps. Still, the impetus of it was sufficient to keep him from turning toward the railroad station.

"Hello!" some one said; Harry Knight was standing, grinning, directly in front of him; "you needn't run down a friend of your youth, even if you don't condescend to live in Mercer any more!"

"Oh, hello," David heard himself say.

"When did you come to town? I'd ask you to lunch with me, but I suppose your lady-love would object. Wait till you get to be an old married man like me; then she'll be glad to get rid of you!" David knew that he gave the expected laugh, and that he said it was a foggy day, and Philadelphia had a better climate than Mercer; ("he hasn't heard it yet," he was saying to himself) "yes, dark old hole; I'm going back to-night. Yes; awfully sorry I can't—good-by—good-by. (He'll know by to-night.") He did not notice when Knight seemed to melt into the mist; nor was he conscious that he had begun to walk again —on, and on, and on. Suddenly he paused before the entrance of a saloon, which bore, above "XXX Pale Ale," in gilt letters on the window, the sign "Landis' Hotel."

He was aware of overpowering fatigue. Why not go in here and sit down? He would not meet any one he knew in such a place. "Better take a room for an hour or two," he thought. He knew that he must be alone to open that Door, but he did not say so; instead his mind, repeating, parrot-like, "Elizabeth has married Blair," made its arrangements for privacy, as steadily as a surgeon might make arrangements for a mortal operation.

As he entered the hotel, a woman on her hands and knees, slopping a wet cloth over the black and white marble floor of the office, looked up at him, and moved her bucket of dirty water to let him pass. "Huh! He's got a head on him this morning," she thought knowingly. But the clerk at the desk gave him an uneasy glance. Men with tragic faces and bewildered eyes are not welcomed by hotel clerks.

"Say," he said, pleasantly enough, as he handed out a key, "don't you want a pick-me-up? You're kind o' white round the gills."

David nodded. "Where's the bar?" he said thickly. He found his way to it, and while he waited for his whisky he lifted a corkscrew from the counter and looked at it closely. "That's something new, isn't it?" he said to the man who was rinsing out a glass for him; "I never saw a corkscrew (Elizabeth has married Blair) with that hook thing on the side." He took his two fingers of whisky, and followed the bell-boy to a room.

"I don't like that young feller's looks," the clerk told the scrub-woman; "we don't want any more free reading notices in the papers of this hotel being a roadhouse on the way to heaven." And when the bell-boy who had shown the unwelcome guest to his room came back to his bench in the office, he interrogated him, with a grin that was not altogether facetious: "Any revolvers lyin' round up in No. 20, or any of those knobby blue bottles?"

"Naw," said the bell-boy, disgustedly, "ner no dimes, neither."

David, in the small, unfriendly hotel bedroom that looked out upon squalid back yards and smelled as if its one window had not been opened for a year, was at last alone. Down in the alley, a hand-organ was shrilling monotonously: Kafoozleum—Kafoozleum.

He looked about him for a minute, then tried to open the window, but the sash stuck; he shook it violently, then shoved it up with such force that a cracked pane of glass clattered out; a gust of raw air came into the stagnant mustiness of the narrow room. After that he sat down and drew a long breath. Then he opened the Door....

Down-stairs the clerk was sharing his uneasiness with the barkeeper. "He came in looking like death. Wild-eyed he was. Mrs. Maloney there will tell you. She came up to me and remarked on it. No, sir, men, like that ain't healthy for this hotel."

"That's so," the barkeeper agreed. "Why didn't you tell him you were full up?"

"Well, he seemed the gentleman," the clerk said. "I didn't just see my way—"

"Huh!" the other flung back at him resentfully. "'Tain't only a poor man that puts his hand in the till, and then hires a room in a hotel"—he made a significant gesture and rolled up his eyes.

"He didn't register," the clerk said. "Only wanted the room for a couple of hours."

"A couple of hours is long enough to—" said the barkeeper.

"Good idea to send a boy up to ask if he rung?"

"*I'd* have sent him ten minutes ago," the barkeeper said scornfully.

So it was that David, staring in at his ruin, was interrupted more than once that morning: "No, I didn't ring. Clear out." And again: "No; I'm not waiting for anybody. Shut that door." But the third time he was frantic: "Damn it, if you knock on my door again I'll kick you down-stairs! Do you understand?" And at that the office subsided.

"They don't do it when they're swearing mad," the barkeeper

said. "I guess his girl has given him the mitten. You ladies are always making trouble for us, Mrs. Maloney. You drive us to suicide for love of you!" Mrs. Maloney simperingly admitted her baleful influence. "As for you," he jeered at the clerk, "you're fresh, I guess. That little affair in 18 got on your nerves."

"Well, if you'd found him as I did, I guess it would 'a' got on your nerves," the clerk said, affrontedly; he added under his breath that they could kill themselves all over the house, and he wouldn't lift a finger to stop 'em. "You don't get no thanks," he told himself gloomily. But after that, No. 20 was not disturbed.

At first, when David opened his closed Door and looked in, there had been the shock again. He was stunned with incredulous astonishment. Then his mind cleared. With the clearing came once more that organic anger of the robbed man; an anger that has in it the uncontrollable impulse to regain his property. It could not be—this thing that had happened. It should not be!

He would see her; he would take her. As for *him*—David's sinewy fingers closed as talons might close into the living flesh of a man's neck. He knew the lust of murder, and he exulted in it. Yet even as he exulted, the baseness of what Blair had done was so astounding, that, sitting there in the dreary room, his hands clenched in his pockets, his legs stretched out in front of him, David Richie actually felt a sort of impersonal amazement that had nothing to do with anger. For one instant the unbelievableness of Blair's dishonor threw him back into that clamoring confusion from which he had escaped since he opened the Door. Blair must have been in love with her! Had Elizabeth suspected it? She certainly had never hinted it to him; why not? Some girlish delicacy? But Blair—Blair, a dishonorable man? In the confounding turmoil of this uprooting of old admirations, he was conscious of the hand-organ down in the alley, pounding out its imbecile refrain. He even found himself repeating the meaningless words:

"In ancient days there lived a Turk,
A horrid beast within the East, ...
Oh, Kafoozleum, Kafoozleum" —

His mind righted itself; he came back to facts, and to the simple incisive question: what must he do? It was not until the afternoon that, by one tortuous and torturing line of reasoning after another, he came to know that, as her uncle had said, for the present he could do nothing.

"Nothing?" At first, David had laughed savagely; he would turn the world upside down before he would leave her in her misery! For that she was in misery he never doubted; nor did he stop to ask himself whether she had repented her madness, he only groaned. He saw, or thought he saw, the whole thing. There was not one doubt, not one poisonous suspicion of Elizabeth herself. That she was disloyal to him never entered his head. To David she was only in a terrible trap, from which, at any cost, she must be rescued. That her own mad temper had brought her to such a pass was neither here nor there; it had nothing to do with the matter in hand, namely her rescue —and then the killing of the man who had trapped her! It came into David's head—like a lamp moving toward him through a mist—that perhaps she had written to him? He had not really grasped the idea when Robert Ferguson suggested it; but now he was suddenly certain that a letter must be awaiting him in Philadelphia! Perhaps in it she called on him to come and help her? The thought was like a whip. He forgot his desire to kill Blair; he leaped to his feet, fumbling in his pocket for a time-table; then realized that there was no train across the mountains until night. Should he telegraph his mother to open any letter from Elizabeth, and wire him where she was? No; even in the whirl of his perplexity, he knew he could not let any other eyes than his own see what, in her abasement, Elizabeth must have written. He began to pace frantically up and down; then stood and looked out of the window, beating his mind back to calmness,—for he must be calm. He must think what could be done. He would get the letter as soon as he reached home; until he got it and learned where she was, the only thing to do was to decide how she should be saved.

And so it was that, not allowing himself to dip down into that elemental rage of the wronged man, not even daring to think of his own incredible blunder which had kindled her crazy anger, still less venturing to let his thought rest on the suffering that had come to her, he kept his mind steadily on that one imperative question: *what was to be done?* At first the situation seemed almost simple: she must leave Blair instantly. "To-day!" he said to himself, striking the rickety table before him with his fist; "to-day!" Next, the marriage must be annulled. That was all; annulled! These were the premises from which he started. All that long, dark morning, well into the afternoon, he followed blind alleys of thought, ending always in the same *impasse*—there was nothing he could do. He did not even know where she was, until the letter in Philadelphia should tell him,—at that thought he looked at his watch again. Oh, how many endless hours before he could go and get that letter! And after all, she was Blair Maitland's wife. Suppose she did leave him, would the swine give her her freedom? Not without long, involved processes of law; he knew his man well enough to know that. Yes, there would have to be dreadful publicity, heart-breaking humiliation for his poor, mad darling. She would have to face those things. Oh, if he only knew where she was, so that he could go that moment and help her to take that first step of flight. She must go at once to his mother. Yes, his mother would shelter her from the beast. If he could only get word to her, to go, *instantly*, to his mother. But he did not know where she was! He cursed himself for not having taken the ten o'clock express!

He could have been at home that night, had her letter, and started out again to go to her. As it was, nothing could be done until to-morrow morning. Then he would know what to do, because then he would know where she was. But meantime—meantime...

There is no doubt that when the frantic man realized his befogging ignorance, and found himself involved in this dreadful delay, the hotel clerk's apprehensions were, at least for wild moments, justified. But only for moments—Elizabeth was to be rescued! David could not consider escape from his own misery until that task had been accomplished. Yet consider: his girl, his woman— another man's; and he helpless! And suppose he did rescue her; suppose he did drag her from the arms of the thief who had been his friend—could it ever be the same? Never. Never. Never. His Elizabeth was dead. The woman whom he meant to have yet— somehow, sometime, somewhere; the woman whom Blair Maitland had filched from him, was not his Elizabeth. The rose, trampled in the mire, may be lifted, it may be revived, it may be fragrant—but it has known the mire!

There were, in the early darkening afternoon, crazy moments for David Richie. Moments of murderous hate of Blair, moments of unbearable consciousness of his own responsibility, moments of almost repulsion for the tragic, marred creature he loved; and at this last appalling revelation to himself of his own possibilities—moments of absolute despair. And when one of those despairing moments came, he put his head down on the table, on his folded arms, and cried for his mother. He cried hard, like a child: "Materna!"

And so it was that he arose and went to his mother.

Chapter 21

When, after his interview with David, Robert Ferguson went into Mrs. Maitland's office at the Works, he looked older by twenty years than when he had left it the night before. Sarah Maitland, sitting at her desk, heard his step, and wheeled round to greet him.

"Better shut that door," she said briefly; and he gave the door in the glass partition a shove with his foot. Then they looked at each other. "Well," she said; and stretched out her hand. "We're in the same box. I guess we'd better shake hands." She grinned with pain, but she forced her grunt of a laugh. "What's your story? Mine is only his explanation to Nannie."

"Mine isn't even that. She merely wrote me she had married him; that was all. Miss White told me what he wrote to Nannie. What do you know about it?"

"That's all I know," she said, and gave him Blair's note.

He read it, and handed it back in silence.

"Well, what are you going to do?" she asked.

"Do? There's nothing to do. I'm done with her!"

"He's my son," Sarah Maitland said. "I have got to do something."

"But there's nothing to be done," he pointed out; it was not like this ruthless woman to waste time crying over spilt milk. "They are both of age, and they are married; that's all there is to it. I went into the mayor's office and found the registry. The marriage is all right so far as that goes. As for David—men don't go out with a gun or a horsewhip in these fine times. He won't do anything. For that matter, he is well rid of her. I told him so. I might have added that the best thing a jilted man can do is to go down on his knees and thank God that he's been jilted; I know what I'm talking about! As for your son—" he stopped.

"Yes," she said, "*my son?*" And even in his fury, Robert Ferguson felt a pang at the sight of her torn and ravaged face that quivered so that he turned his eyes away out of sheer decency. "I must do something for my son. And I think I know what it will be." She bit her forefinger, frowning with thought. "I think I know ... I have not done right by Blair."

"No, you haven't," he said dryly. "Have you just discovered that? But I don't see what you or I or God Almighty can do *now*! They're married."

"Oh, I can't do anything about this marriage," she said, with a gesture of indifference; "but that's not the important thing."

"Not important? What do you mean?"

"I mean that the important thing is to know what made Blair behave in this way; and then cure him."

"Cure him! There's no cure for rottenness." He was so beside himself with pain that he forgot that she was a woman, and Blair's mother.

"I blame myself for Blair's conduct," she said.

"Oh, Elizabeth is as bad as he is!" But he waited for her contradiction.

It did not come. "Probably worse." Involuntarily he raised a protesting hand.

"But I mean to forgive her," said Sarah Maitland, with cold determination.

"Forgive Elizabeth?" he said, angrily, and his anger was the very small end of the wedge of his own forgiveness; "forgive *her*? It strikes me the boot is on the other leg, Mrs. Maitland."

"Oh, well," she said, "what difference does it make? I guess it's a case of the pot and the kettle. I'm not blaming your girl overmuch; although a bad woman is always worse than a bad man. In this case, Elizabeth acted from hate, and Blair from love; the result is the same, of course, but one motive is worse than the other. But never mind that—Blair has got her, and he will be faithful to her; for a while, anyhow. And Elizabeth will get used to him—that's Nature, and Nature is bigger than a girl's first fancy. So if David doesn't interfere—you think he won't? you don't know human nature, Friend Ferguson! David isn't a saint—at least I hope he isn't; I don't care much about twenty-seven-year-old male saints. David may not be able to interfere, but he'll try to, somehow. You wait! As for Blair, as I say, if David doesn't put his finger in the pie, Blair isn't hopeless."

"I'm glad you think so."

"I *do* think so. Blair is young yet; and if she costs him something, he may value her—and I think I can manage to make her cost him something! A man doesn't value what comes cheap; and all his life everything has come cheap to Blair."

"I don't see what you're driving at."

"Just this," she explained; "Blair has had everything he wanted,—oh, yes, yes; it's my fault!" she struck an impatient fist upon the arm of her chair. "I told you it was my fault. Don't take precious time to argue over that. It is *all* my fault. There! will that satisfy you? I've given him everything. So he thought he could have everything. He doesn't know the meaning of 'no.' He has got to learn. I shall teach him. I have thought it all out. I'm going to make a man of him."

"How?" said Robert Ferguson.

"I haven't got the details clear in my mind yet, but this is the gist of it: *NO money but what he earns.*"

"No money?"

"After this, it will be 'root, hog, or die.'"

"But Blair can't root," her superintendent said, fair in spite of himself. And at that her face lighted with a sort of awful purpose.

"Then he must die! Ferguson, don't you see—*he has begun to die already?*" Again her face quivered. "Look at this business of taking David's wife—oh, I know, they weren't married yet, but the principle is the same; what do you call that but dying? Look at his whole life: what has he done? Received—received! Given nothing. Ferguson, you can't fool God: you've got to give something! A privilege means an obligation—the obligation of sweat! Sweat of your body or your brains. Blair has never sweated. He's always had something for nothing. That is the one immorality that damns. It has damned Blair. Of course, I ought to have realized it before, but I—I suppose I was too busy. Yes; I tell you, if Blair had had to work for what he's got, as you and I have worked for what we've got, he wouldn't be where he is to-day. You know that! He'd have had something else to think of than satisfying his eyes, or his stomach, or his lust. He'd have been decent."

"He might have been," Robert Ferguson said drearily, "but I doubt it. Anyway, you can't, by making him earn or go without, or anything else, give David's girl back to him."

"No," she said heavily, and for a moment her passion of hope flagged; "no, I can't do that. But I shall try to make it up to David in some way, of course. Where is he?" she broke off.

He told her briefly of David's arrival and departure. "He's gone back to his mother," he ended; "she'll comfort him." Then, with a bark of anger, he added, "Mrs. Richie was always saying that Elizabeth would turn out well. I wonder what she will say now? I knew better; her mother, my brother Arthur's wife, was—no good. Yet I let Mrs. Richie bamboozle me into building on her. I always said Life shouldn't play the same trick on me twice—but it has done it! It has done it. My heart was set on Elizabeth. Yes, Mrs. Maitland, I've been fooled again—but so have you."

"Nothing of the kind! I never was fooled before," Sarah Maitland said; "and I sha'n't be again. I am going to make a man of my son! As for your girl, forgive her, Ferguson. Don't be a fool; you take it out of yourself when you refuse forgiveness."

"I'll never forgive her," said Robert Ferguson; "she's hurt the woman I—I have a regard for; she's made David's mother suffer. I'm done with her!"

Chapter 22

When, on drunken and then on leaden feet, there came to Elizabeth the ruthless to-morrow of her act, her first clear thought was to kill herself ....

After the marriage in the mayor's office—where they paused long enough to write the two notes that were received the next day—Blair had fled with her up into the mountains to a little hotel, where they would not, he felt certain, encounter any acquaintances.

Elizabeth neither assented nor objected. From the moment she had struck her hand into his, there in the tawdry "saloon" of the toll-house, and cried out, "*Come!*" she let him do as he chose. So he had carried her away to the city hall, where, like any other unclassed or unchurched lovers, they were married by a hurried city official. She had had one more crisis of rage, when in the mayor's office, as she stood at a high wall desk and wrote with an ink-encrusted pen that brief note to her uncle, she said to herself that, as to David Richie, he could hear the news from her uncle—or never hear it; she didn't care which. Then for an instant her eyes glittered again; but except for that one moment, she seemed stunned, mind and body. To Blair, her silent acquiescences had been signs that he had won something more than her consent to revenge herself upon David,—and he wanted more! In all his life he had never deeply cared for anybody but himself; but now, under the terrible selfishness of his act, under the primitive instinct that he called love, there was, trembling in the depths of his nature, *Love*. It had been born only a little while ago, this new, naked baby of Love. It had had no power and no knowledge; unaided by that silent god of his, it had not been strong enough to save him from himself, or save Elizabeth from him. But he did love her, in spite of his treason to her soul, for he was tender with her, and almost humble; yet his purpose was inflexible. It seemed to him it must find response in her. Such purpose might strike fire from the most unbending steel—why not from this yielding, silent thing, Elizabeth's heart? But numb and flaccid, perfectly apathetic, stunned by that paroxysm of fury, she no more responded to him than down would have responded to the blow of flint ...

It was their second day in the mountains. Blair, going down-stairs very early in the morning, stopped in the office of the hotel to write a brief but intensely polite note to his mother, telling her of his marriage. "Nannie will have broken it to her—poor, dear old Nannie!" he said to himself, pounding a stamp down on the envelope, "but of course it's proper to announce it myself." Then he dropped the "announcement" into the post-bag, and went out for a tramp in the woods. It was a still, furtive morning of low clouds, with an expectancy of snow in the air. But it was not cold, and when, leaving the road and pushing aside the frosted ferns and underbrush, he found himself in the silence of the woods, he sat down on a fallen tree trunk to think.... The moment had come when the only god he knew would no longer be denied.

"I might as well face it," he said; and slowly lit a cigar. But instead of "facing it," he began to watch the first sparse and fitful beginnings of snow—hesitant flakes that sauntered down to rest for a crystal moment on his coat sleeve. Suddenly he caught his thoughts together with a jerk: "I've *got* to think it out!" he said. Curiously enough, when he said this his thought did not turn with any especial distinctness to David Richie.

Instead, in the next hour of reasonings and excuses, there was always, back in his mind, one face—scornful, contemptuous even; a face he had known only as gentle, and sometimes tender; the face of David's mother. Once he swore at himself, to drive that face out of his mind. "What a fool I am! Elizabeth had broken her engagement with him. I had the right to speak before the thing was smoothed over again. Anybody would say so, even—even Mrs. Richie if she could really understand how things were. But of course she will only see *his* side." All his excuses for his conduct were in relation to David Richie; he did not think of Elizabeth. He honestly did not know that he had wronged her. He loved her so crazily that he could not realize his cruelty.

It was snowing steadily now; he could hear the faint patter of small, hard flakes on the dry oak leaves over his head. Suddenly some bleached and withered ferns in front of him rustled, and he saw wise, bright eyes looking at him. "I wish I had some nuts for you, bunny," he said—and the bright eyes vanished with a furry whirl through the ferns. He picked up the empty half of a hickory-nut, and turning it over in his fingers, looked at the white grooves left by small sharp teeth. "You little beggars must get pretty hungry in the winter, bunny," he said; "I'll bring a bag of nuts out here for you some day." But while he was talking to the squirrel, he was wrestling with his god. It was characteristic of him that never once in that struggle to justify himself did he use the excuse of Elizabeth's consent. His code, which had allowed him to injure a woman, would not permit him to blame her—even if she deserved it. Instead, over and over he heaped up his own poor defense: "If I had waited, he might have patched it up with her." Over and over the defense crumbled before his eyes: "it was contemptible not to give him the chance to patch it up." Then would come his angry retort: "That's nonsense! Besides it is better, infinitely better, for her to marry me than a poor man like him. I can give her everything,—and love her! God, how I love her. Apart from any selfish consideration, it is a thousand times better for her." For an instant his marrying her seemed actually chivalrous; and at that his god laughed. Blair reddened sharply; to recognize his hypocrisy was the "touch on the hollow of the thigh; and the hollow of the thigh was out of joint"! He pitched the nut away with a vicious fling, and knew, inarticulately, that there was no use lying to himself any longer.

With blank eyes he watched the snow piling up on a withered stalk of goldenrod. "I wish it hadn't happened in just the way it did," he conceded;—his god was beginning to prevail!—"but if I had waited, I might have lost her." Then a thought stabbed him: suppose that he should lose her anyhow? Suppose that when she came to herself—the phrase was a confession! suppose she should want to leave him? It was an intolerable idea. "Well, she can't," he told himself, grimly, "she can't, now." His face was dusky with shame, yet when he said that, his lip loosened in a furtively exultant smile. Blair would have been less, or more, than a man if, at that moment, in spite of his shame, he had not exulted. "She's my wife!" he said, through those shamed and smiling lips. Then his eyes narrowed: "And she doesn't care a damn for me."

So it was that as he sat there in the snow, watching the puff of white deepen on the stalk of goldenrod, his god prevailed yet a little more, for, so far as Elizabeth was concerned, he did not try to fool himself: "she doesn't care a damn." But when he said that, he saw the task of his life before him—to make her care! It was like the touch of a spur; he leaped to his feet, and flung up his arms in a sort of challenge. Yes; he *had* "done the thing a man can't do." Yes; he ought not to have taken advantage of her anger. Yes; his honor was smirched, grant it all! grant it all! "I was mad," he said, stung by this intolerable self-knowledge; "I was a cur. I ought to have waited; I know it. I admit it. But what's the use of talking about it now? It's done; and by God, she shall love me yet!"

So it was that his god blessed him, as the best that is in us, always blesses us when it conquers us: the blessing was the revelation of his own dishonor. It is a divine moment, this of the consciousness of having been faithless to one's own ideals. And Blair Maitland, a false friend, a selfish and cruel lover, was not entirely contemptible, for his eyes, beautiful and evasive, confessed the shock of a heavenly vision.

As he walked home, he laid his plans very carefully: he must show her the most delicate consideration; he must avoid every possible annoyance; he must do this, he must not do that. "And I'll buy her a pearl necklace," he told himself, too absorbed in the gravity of the situation to see in such an impulse the assertion that he was indeed his mother's son! But the foundation of all his plans for making Elizabeth content, was the determination not to admit for a single instant, to anybody but himself, that he had done anything to be ashamed of. Which showed that his god was not yet God.

When he got back to the hotel, he found that Elizabeth had not left her room; and rushing up-stairs two steps at a time, he knocked at her door.... . She was sitting on the edge of her bed, her lips parted, her eyes staring blindly out of the window at the snow. The flakes were so thick now that the meadow on the other side of the road and the mountain beyond were blurred and almost blotted out; there was a gray pallor on her face as if the shadow of the storm had fallen on it. Instantly Blair knew that she "had come to herself." As he stood looking at her, something tightened in his throat; he broke out into the very last thing he had meant to say: "Elizabeth?- forgive me!"

"I ought to die, you know," she said, without turning her eyes from the window and the falling snow.

He came and knelt down beside her, and kissed her hand. "Elizabeth, dearest! When I love you so?"

He kissed her shoulder. She shivered.

"My darling," he said, passionately.

She looked at him dully; "I wish you would go away."

"Elizabeth, let me tell you how I love you."

"Love me?" she said; "*me?*"

"Elizabeth!" he protested; "you are an angel, and I love you —no man ever loved a woman as I love you."

In her abasement she never thought of reproaching him, of saying "if you loved me, why did you betray me?" She had not gone as far as that yet. Her fall had been so tremendous that if she had any feeling about him, it was nothing more than the consciousness that he too, had gone over the precipice. "Please go away," she said.

"Dearest, listen; you are my wife. If—if I hurried you too much, you will forgive me because I loved you so? I didn't dare to wait, for fear—" he stumbled on the confession which his god had wrung from him, but which must not be made to her. Elizabeth's heavy eyes were suddenly keen.

"Fear of what?"

"Oh, don't look at me that way! I love you so that it kills me to have you angry at me!"

"I am not angry with you," she said, faintly surprised; "why should I be angry with *you*? Only, you see, Blair, I—I can't live. I simply can't live."

"You have got to live!—or I'll die," he said. "I love you, I tell you I love you!" His outstretched, trembling hands entreated hers, but she would not yield them to his touch; her shrinking movement away from him, her hands gripped together at her throat, filled him with absolute terror: "Elizabeth! *don't*—" She glanced at him with stony eyes. Blair was suffering. Why should *he* suffer? But his suffering did not interest her. "Please go away," she said, heavily.

He went. He dared not stay. He left her, going miserably down-stairs to make a pretense of eating some breakfast. But all the while he was arranging entreaties and arguments in his own mind. He went to the door of their room a dozen times that morning, but it was locked. No, she did not want any breakfast. Wouldn't she come out and walk? No, no, no. Please let her alone. And then in the afternoon; "Elizabeth, I *must* come in! You must have some food."

She let him enter; but she was indifferent alike to the food and to the fact that by this time there was, of course, a giggling consciousness in the hotel that the "bride and groom had had a rumpus." ... "A nice beginning for a honeymoon," said the chambermaid, "locking that pretty young man out of her room!— and me with my work to do in there. Well, I'm sorry for him; I bet you she's a case."

Blair, too, was indifferent to anything ridiculous in his position; the moment was too critical for such self-consciousness. When at last he took a little tray of food to his wife, and knelt beside her, begging her to eat, he was appalled at the ruin in her face. She drank some tea to please him; then she said, pitifully:

"What shall we do, Blair?" That she should say "we" showed that these hours which had plowed her face had also sowed some seed of unselfishness in her broken soul.

"Darling," he said, tenderly, "have you forgiven me?"

At this she meditated for a minute, staring with big, anguished eyes straight ahead of her at nothing; "I *think* I have, Blair. I have tried to. Of course I know I was more wicked than you. It was more my doing than yours. Yes. I ought to ask you if you would forgive me."

"Elizabeth! Forgive you? When you made me so happy! Am I to forgive you for making me happy?"

"Blair," she said—she put the palms of her hands together, like a child; "Blair, please let me go." She looked at him with speechless entreaty. The old dominant Elizabeth was gone; here was nothing but the weak thing, the scared thing, pleading, crouching, begging for mercy. "Please, Blair, *please—*"

But the very tragedy of such humbleness was that it made an

appeal to passion rather than to mercy. It made him love her more, not pity her more. "I can't let you go, Elizabeth," he said, hoarsely; "I can't; I love you—I will never let you go! I will die before I will let you go!"

With that cry of complete egotism from him, the storm which her egotism had let loose upon their little world broke over her own head. As the sense of the hopelessness of her position and the futility of her struggle dawned upon her, she grew frightened to the point of violence. She was outrageous in what she said to him—beating against the walls of this prison-house of marriage which she herself had reared about them, and crying wildly for freedom. Yet strangely enough, her fury was never the fury of temper; it was the fury of fear. In her voice there was a new note, a note of entreaty; she demanded, but not with the old invincible determination of the free Elizabeth. She was now only the woman pleading with the man; the wife, begging the husband.

Through it all, her jailer, insulted, commanded, threatened, never lost a gentleness that had sprung up in him side by side with love. It was, of course, the gentleness of power, although he did not realize that, for he was abjectly frightened; he never stopped to reassure himself by remembering that, after all, rave as she might, she was his! He was incredibly soft with her—up to a certain point: "I will never let you go!" If his god spoke, the whisper was drowned in that gale of selfishness. Elizabeth, now, was the flint, striking that she might kindle in Blair some fire of anger which would burn up the whole edifice of her despair. But he opposed to her fiercest blows of terror and entreaty nothing but this softness of frightened love and unconscious power. He cowered at the thought of losing her; he entreated her pity, her mercy; he wept before her. The whole scene in that room in the inn, with the silent whirl of snow outside the windows, was one of dreadful abasement and brutality on both sides.

"I am a bad woman. I will not stay with you. I will kill myself first.

I am going away. I am going away to-night."

"Then you will kill me. Elizabeth! Think how I love you; think! And—*he* wouldn't want you, since you threw him over. You couldn't go back to him."

"Go back to David? now? How can you say such a thing! I am dead, so far as he is concerned. Oh—oh—oh,—why am I not dead? Why do I go on living? I will kill myself rather than stay with you!" It seemed to Elizabeth that she had forgotten David; she had forgotten that she had meant to write him a terrible letter. She had forgotten everything but the blasting realization of what had happened to her. "Do not dare to speak his name!" she said, frantically. "I cannot bear it! I cannot bear it! I am dead to him. He despises me, as I despise myself. Blair, I can't—I can't live; I can't go on—"

In the end he conquered. There were two days and nights of struggle; and then she yielded. Blair's reiterated appeal was to her sense of justice. Curiously, but most characteristically, through all the clamor of her despair at this incredible thing that she had done, justice was the one word which penetrated to her consciousness. Was it fair, she debated, numbly, in one of their long, aching silences, was it just, that because she had ruined herself, she should ruin him?

She had locked herself in her room, and was sitting with her head on her arms that were stretched before her on a little table. Blair had gone out for one of his long, wretched walks through the snow; sometimes he took the landlord's dog along for company, and on this particular morning, a morning of brilliant sunshine and cold, insolent wind, he had stopped to buy a bag of nuts for the hungry squirrels in the woods. As he walked he was planning, planning, planning, how he could make his misery touch Elizabeth's heart; he was all unconscious that her misery had not yet touched his heart. But Elizabeth, locked in her room, was beginning to think of his misery. Dully at first, then with dreary concentration, she went over in her mind his arguments and pleadings: he was satisfied to love her even if she didn't love him; he had known what stakes he played for, and he was willing to abide by them; she ought to do the same; she had done this thing—she had married him, was it fair, now, to destroy him, soul and body, just because she had acted on a moment's impulse? In a crisis of terror, his primitive instinct of self-preservation had swept away the acquired instinct of chivalry, and like a brutal boy, he had reminded her that she was to blame as well as he. "You did it, too," he told her. sullenly. She remembered that he had said he had not fully understood that it was only impulse on her part; "I thought you cared for me a little, or else you wouldn't have married me." In the panic of the moment he really had not known that he lied, and in her absorption in her own misery she did not contradict him. She ought, he said, to make the best of the situation; or else he would kill himself. "Do you want me to kill myself?" he had threatened. If she would make the best of it, he would help her. He would do whatever she wished; he would be her friend, her servant,—until she should come to love him.

"I shall never love you," she told him. "I will always love you! But I will not make you unhappy. Let me be your servant; that's all I ask."

"I love David. I will always love him."

He had been silent at that; then broke again into a cry for mercy. "I don't care if you do love him! Don't destroy me, Elizabeth."

He had had still one other weapon: *they were married*. There was no getting round that. The thing was done; except by Time and the outrageous scandal of publicity, it could not be undone. But this weapon he had not used, knowing perfectly well that the idea of public shame would be, just then, a matter of indifference to Elizabeth?-perhaps even a satisfaction to her, as the sting of the penitential whip is a satisfaction to the sinner. All he said was summed up in three words: "Don't destroy me."

There was no reply. She had fallen into a silence which frightened him more than her words. It was then that he went out for that walk on the creaking snow, in the sunshine and fierce wind, taking the bag of nuts along for the squirrels. Elizabeth, alone, her head on her arms on the table, went over and over his threats and entreaties, until it seemed as if her very mind was sore. After a while, for sheer weariness, she left the tangle of motives and facts and obligations, and began to think of David. It was then that she moaned a little under her breath.

Twice she had tried to write to him to tell him what had happened. But each time she cringed away from her pen and paper. After all, what could she write? The fact said all there was to say, and he knew the fact by this time. When she said that, her mind, drawn by some horrible curiosity, would begin to speculate as to how he had heard the fact? Who told him? What did he say? How did he—? and here she would groan aloud in an effort *not* to know "how" he took it! To save herself from this speculation which seemed to dig into a grave, and touch and handle the decaying body of love, she would plan what she should say to him when, after a while, "to-morrow," perhaps, she should be able to take up her pen: "David,—I was out of my head. Think of me as if I were dead." ... "David,—I don't want you to forgive me. I want you to hate me as I hate myself." ... "David,—I was not in my right mind—forgive me. I love you just the same. But it is as if I were dead." Again and again she had thought out long, crying, frightened letters to him; but she had not written them. And now she was beginning to feel, vaguely, that she would never write them. "What is the use? I am dead." The idea of calling upon him to come and save her, never occurred to her. "I am dead," she said, as she sat there, her face hidden in her arms; "there is nothing to be done."

After a while she stopped thinking of David and the letter she had not been able to write; it seemed as if, when she tried to make it clear to herself why she did not write to him, something stopped in her mind—a cog did not catch; the thought eluded her. When this happened—as it had happened again and again in these last days; she would fall to thinking, with vague amazement, that this irremediable catastrophe was out of all proportion to its cause. It was monstrous that a crazy minute should ruin a whole life—two whole lives, hers and David's. It was as if a pebble should deflect a river from its course, and make it turn and overflow a landscape! It was incredible that so temporary a thing as an outbreak of temper should have eternal consequences. She gasped, with her face buried in her arms, at the realization—which comes to most of us poor human creatures sooner or later—that sins may be forgiven, but their results remain. As for sin—but surely that meaningless madness was not sin? "It was insanity," she said, shivering at the memory of that hour in the toll-house—that little mad hour, that brought eternity with it! She had had other crazy hours, with no such weight of consequence. Her mind went back over her engagement: her love, her happiness—and her tempers. Well, nothing had come of them. David always understood. And still further back: her careless, fiery girlhood— when the knowledge of her mother's recreancy, undermining her sense of responsibility by the condoning suggestion of heredity, had made her quick to excuse her lack of self-control. Her girlhood had been full of those outbreaks of passion, which she "couldn't help"; they were all meaningless, and all harmless, too; at any rate they were all without results of pain to her.

Suddenly it seemed to her, as she looked across the roaring gulf that separated her from the past, that all her life had been just a sunny slope down to the edge of the gulf. All those "harmless" tempers which had had no results, had pushed her to this result!

Her poor, bright, shamed head lay so long and so still on her folded arms that one looking in upon her might have thought her dead. Perhaps, in a way, Elizabeth did die then, when her heart seemed to break with the knowledge that it is impossible to escape from yesterday. "Oh," she said, brokenly, "why didn't somebody tell me? Why didn't they stop me?" But she did not dwell upon the responsibility of other people. She forgot the easy excuse of 'heredity.' This new knowledge brought with it a vision of her own responsibility that filled her appalled mind to the exclusion of everything else. It is not the pebble that turns the current—it is the easy slope that invites it. All her life Elizabeth had been inviting this moment; and the moment, when it came, was her Day of Judgment. What she had thought of as an incredible injustice of fate in letting a mad instant turn the scales for a whole life, was merely an inevitable result of all that had preceded it. When this fierce and saving knowledge came to her, she thought of Blair. "I have spoiled my own life and David's life. I needn't spoil Blair's. He said if I left him, it would destroy him.... Perhaps if I stay, it will be my punishment. I can never be punished enough."

When Blair came home, she was standing with her forehead against the window, her dry eyes watching the dazzling white world.

Coming up behind her, he took her hand and kissed it humbly. She turned and looked at him with somber eyes.

"Poor Blair," she said.

And Blair, under his breath, said, "Thank God!"

Chapter 23

The coming back to Mercer some six weeks later was to Blair a miserable and skulking experience. To Elizabeth it was almost a matter of indifference; there is a shame which goes too deep for embarrassment. The night they arrived at the River House, Nannie and Miss White were waiting for them, tearful and disapproving, of course, but distinctly excited and romantic. After all, Elizabeth was a "bride!" and Cherry-pie and Nannie couldn't help being fluttered. Blair listened with open amusement to their half-scared gossip of what people thought, and what the newspapers had said, and how "very displeased" his mother had been; but Elizabeth hardly heard them. At the end of the call, while Blair was bidding Nannie tell his mother he was coming to see her in the morning. Miss White, kissing her "lamb" good night, tried to whisper something in her ear: "*He* said to tell you—" "No—no—no,—I can't hear it; I can't bear it yet!" Elizabeth broke in; she put her hands over her eyes, shivering so that Cherry-pie forgot David and his message, and even her child's bad behavior.

"Elizabeth! you've taken cold?"

Elizabeth drew away, smiling faintly. "No; not at all. I'm tired.
Please don't stay." And with the message still unspoken, Miss White and
Nannie went off together, as fluttering and frightened as when they came.

The newspaper excitement which had followed the announcement of the elopement of Sarah Maitland's son, had subsided, so there was only a brief notice the morning after their arrival in town, to the effect that "the bride and groom had returned to their native city for a short stay before sailing for Europe." Still, even though the papers were inclined to let them alone, it would be pleasanter, Blair told his wife, to go abroad.

"Well," she said, dully. Elizabeth was always dull now. She had lifted herself up to the altar, but there was no exaltation of sacrifice; possibly because she considered her sacrifice a punishment for her sin, but also because she was still physically and morally stunned.

"Of course there is nobody in Mercer for whose opinion I care a copper," Blair said. They were sitting in their parlor at the hotel; Elizabeth staring out of the window at the river, Blair leaning forward in his chair, touching once in a while, with timid fingers, a fold of her skirt that brushed his knee. "Of course I don't care for a lot of gossiping old hens; but it will be pleasanter for you not to be meeting people, perhaps?" he said gently.

There was only one person whom he himself shrank from meeting—his mother. And this shrinking was not because of the peculiar shame which the thought of Mrs. Richie had awakened in him that morning in the woods, when the vision of her delicate scorn had been so unbearable; his feeling about his mother was sheer disgust at the prospect of an interview which was sure to be esthetically distressing. While he was still absent on what the papers called his "wedding tour," Nannie had written to him warning him what he might expect from Mrs. Maitland:

"Mamma is terribly displeased, I am afraid, though she hasn't said a word since the night I told her. Then she said very severe things —and oh, Blair, dear, why *did* you do it the way you did? I think Elizabeth was perfectly—" The unfinished sentence was scratched out. "You *must* be nice to Mamma when you come home," she ended.

"She'll kick," Blair said, sighing; "she'll row like a puddler!"

In his own mind, he added that, after all, no amount of kicking would alter the fact. And again the little exultant smile came about his lips. "As for being 'nice,' Nannie might as well talk about being '*nice*' to a circular saw," he said, gaily. His efforts to be gay, to amuse or interest Elizabeth, were almost pathetic in their intensity. "Well! the sooner I'll go, the sooner I'll get it over!" he said, and reached for his hat; Elizabeth was silent. "You might wish me luck!" he said. She did not answer, and he sighed and left her.

As he loitered down to Shantytown, lying in the muddy drizzle of a midwinter thaw, he planned how soon he could get away from the detestable place. "Everything is so perfectly hideous," he said to himself, "no wonder she is low-spirited. When I get her over in Europe she'll forget Mercer, and—everything disagreeable." His mind shied away from even the name of the man he had robbed.

At his mother's house, he had a hurried word with Nannie in the parlor: "Is she upset still? She mustn't blame Elizabeth! It was all my doing. I sort of swept Elizabeth off her feet, you know. Well—it's another case of getting your tooth pulled quickly. Here goes!" When he opened the dining-room door, his mother called to him from her bedroom: "Come in here," she said; and there was something in her voice that made him brace himself. "I'm in for it," he said, under his breath.

For years Sarah Maitland's son had not seen her room; the sight of it now was a curious shock that seemed to push him back into his youth, and into that old embarrassment which he had always felt in her presence. The room was as it had been then, very bare and almost squalid; there was no carpet on the floor, and no hint of feminine comfort in a lounge or even a soft chair. That morning the inside shutters on the lower half of the uncurtained windows were still closed, and the upper light, striking cold and bleak across the dingy ceiling, glimmered on the glass doors of the bookcases behind which, in his childhood, had lurked such mysterious terrors. The narrow iron bed had not yet been made up, and the bedclothes were in confusion on the back of a chair; the painted pine bureau was thick with dust; on it was the still unopened cologne bottle, its kid cover cracked and yellow under its faded ribbons, and three small photographs: Blair, a baby in a white dress; a little boy with long trousers and a visored cap; a big boy of twelve with a wooden gun. They were brown with time, and the figures were almost undistinguishable, but Blair recognized them,—and again his armor of courage was penetrated.

"Well, Mother," he said, with great directness and with at least an effort at heartiness, "I am afraid you are rather disgusted with me."

"Are you?" she said; she was sitting sidewise on a wooden chair—what is called a "kitchen chair"; she had rested her arm along its back, and as Blair entered, her large, beautiful hand, drooping limply from its wrist, closed slowly into an iron fist.

"No, I won't sit down, thank you," he said, and stood, lounging a little, with an elbow on the mantelpiece. "Yes; I was afraid you would be displeased," he went on, good-humoredly; "but I hope you won't mind so much when I tell you about it. I couldn't really go into it in my letter. By the way, I hope my absence hasn't inconvenienced you in the office?"

"Well, not seriously," she said dryly. And he felt the color rise in his face. That he was frightfully ill at ease was obvious in the elaborate carelessness with which he began to inquire about the Works. But her only answer to his meaningless questions was silence. Blair was conscious that he was breathing quickly, and that made him angry. "Why *am* I such an ass?" he asked himself; then said, with studied lightness, that he was afraid he would have to absent himself from business for still a little longer, as he was going abroad.

Fortunately—here the old sarcastic politeness broke into his really serious purpose to be respectful; fortunately he was so unimportant that his absence didn't really matter. "You *are* the Works, you know, Mother."

"You are certainly unimportant," she agreed. He noticed she had not taken up her knitting, though a ball of pink worsted and a half-finished baby sock lay on the bureau near her; this unwonted quiet of her hands, together with the extraordinary solemnity of her face, gave him a sense of uneasy astonishment. He would almost have welcomed one of those brutal outbursts which set his teeth on edge by their very ugliness. He did not know how to treat this new dignity.

"I would like to tell you just what happened," he began, with a seriousness that matched her own. "Elizabeth had made up her mind not to marry David Richie. They had had some falling out, I believe. I never asked what; of course that wasn't my business. Well, I had been in love with her for months; but I didn't suppose I had a ghost of a chance; of course I wouldn't have dreamed of trying to— to take her from him. But when she broke with him, why, I felt that I had a—a right, you know."

His mother was silent, but she struck the back of her chair softly with her closed fist: her eyebrow began to lift ominously.

"Well; we thought—I mean I thought; that the easiest way all round was to get married at once. Not discuss it, you know, with people; but just—well, in point of fact, I persuaded her to run off with me!" He tried to laugh, but his mother's face was rigid. She was looking at him closely, but she said nothing. By this time her continued silence had made him so nervous that he went through his explanation again from beginning to end. Still she did not speak. "You see, Mother," he said, reddening with the discomfort of the moment, "you see it was best to do it quickly? Elizabeth's engagement being broken, there was no reason to wait. But I do regret that I could not have told you first. I fear you felt—annoyed."

"Annoyed?" For a moment she smiled. "Well, I should hardly call it 'annoyed.'" Suddenly she made a gesture with her hand, as if to say, stop all this nonsense! "Blair," she said, "I'm not going to go into this business of your marriage at all. It's done." Blair drew a breath of astonished relief. "You've not only done a wicked thing, which is bad; you've done a fool thing, which is worse. I have some sort of patience with a knave, but a fool—'annoys' me, as you express it. You've married a girl who loves another man. You may or may not repent your wickedness—you and I have different ideas on such subjects; but you'll certainly repent your foolishness. When you are eaten up with jealousy of David, you'll wish you had behaved decently. I know what I'm talking about"—she paused, looking down at her fingers picking nervously at the back of the chair; "I've been jealous," she said in a low voice. Then, with a quick breath: "However, wicked or foolish, or both, it's *done*, and I'm not going to waste my time talking about it."

"You're very kind," he said; he was so bewildered by this unexpected mildness that he could not think what to say next. "I very much appreciate your overlooking my not telling you about it before I did it. The—the fact was," he began to stammer; her face was not reassuring; "the fact was, it was all so hurried, I—"

But she was not listening. "You say you mean to go to Europe; how?"

"How?" he repeated. "I don't know just what you mean. Of course I shall be sorry to leave the Works, but under the circumstances—"

"It costs money to go to Europe. Have you got any?"

"My salary—"

"How can you have a salary when you don't do any work?"

Blair was silent; then he said, frowning, something about his mother's always having been so kind—

"Kind?" she broke in, "you call it kind? Well, Blair, I am going to be kind now—another way. So far as I'm concerned, you'll not have one dollar that you don't earn."

He looked perfectly uncomprehending.

"I've done being 'kind,' in the way that's ruined you, and made you a useless fool. I'm going to try another sort of kindness. You can work, my son, or you can starve." Her face quivered as she spoke.

"What do you mean?" Blair said, quietly; his embarrassment fell from him like a slipping cloak; he was suddenly and ruthlessly a man.

She told him what she meant. "This business of your marrying Elizabeth isn't the important thing; that's just a symptom of your disease. It's the fact of your being the sort of man you are, that's important." Blair was silent. Then Sarah Maitland began her statement of the situation as she saw it; she told him just what sort of a man he was: indolent, useless, helpless, selfish. "Until now I've always said that at any rate you were harmless. I can't say even that now!" She tried to explain that when a man lives on money he has not earned, he incurs, by merely living, a debt of honor;—that God will collect. But she did not know how to say it. Instead, she told him he was a parasite;—which loathsome truth was like oil on the flames of his slowly gathering rage. He was a man, she said, whose business in life was to enjoy himself. She tried to make clear to him that after youth,—perhaps even after childhood,—enjoyment, as the purpose of effort, was dwarfing. "You are sort of a dwarf, Blair," she said, with curiously impersonal brutality. Any enjoyment, she insisted, that was worthy of a man, was only a by-product, as you might call it, of effort for some other purpose than enjoyment. "One of our puddlers enjoys doing a good job, I guess;—but that isn't why he does it," she said, shrewdly. Any man whose sole effort was to get pleasure is, considering what kind of a world we live in, a poor creature. "That's the best that can be said for him," she said; "as for the worst, we won't go into that. You know it even better than I do." Then she told him that his best, which had been harmlessness, and his worst, which they "would not go into"—were both more her fault than his. It was her fault that he was such a poor creature; "a pithless creature; I've made you so!" she said. She stopped, her face moving with emotion. "I've robbed you of incentive; I see that now. Any man who has the need of work taken away from him, is robbed. I guess enjoyment is all that is left for him. I ask your pardon." Her humility was pitiful, but her words were outrageous. "You are young yet," she said; "I *think* what I am going to do will cure you. If it doesn't, God knows what will become of you!" It was the cure of the surgeon's knife, ruthless, radical; it was, in fact, kill or cure; she knew that. "Of course it's a gamble," she admitted, and paused, nibbling at her finger; "a gamble. But I've got to take it." She spoke of it as she might of some speculative business decision. She looked at him as if imploring comprehension, but she had to speak as she thought, with sledgehammer directness. "It takes brains to make money—I know because I've made it; but any fool can inherit it, just as any fool can accept it. I'm going to give you a chance to develop some brains. You can work or you can starve. Or," she added simply, "you can beg. You have begged practically all your life, thanks to me."

If only she could have said it all differently! But alas! yearning over him with agonized consciousness of her own wrong-doing, and with singular justice in regard to his, she approached his selfish heart as if it were one of her own "blooms," and she a great engine which could mold and squeeze it into something of value to the world. She flung her iron facts at him, regardless of the bruises they must leave upon that most precious thing, his self-respect. Well; she was going to stop her work of destruction, she said. Then she told him how she proposed to do it: he had had everything—and he was nothing. Now he should have nothing, so that he might become something.

There was a day, many years ago, when this mother and son, standing together, had looked at the fierce beauty of molten iron; then she had told him of high things hidden in the seething and shimmering metal—of dreams to be realized, of splendid toils, of vast ambitions. And as she spoke, a spark of vivid understanding had leaped from his mind to hers. Now, her iron will, melted by the fires of love, was seething and glowing, dazzlingly bright in the white heat of complete self-renunciation; it was ready to be poured into a torturing mold to make a tool with which he might save his soul! But no spark of understanding came into his angry eyes. She did not pause for that; his agreement was a secondary matter. The habit of success made her believe that she could achieve the impossible—namely, save a man's soul in spite of himself; "make," as she had told Robert Ferguson, "a man of her son." She would have been glad to have his agreement, but she would not wait for it.

Blair listened in absolute silence. "Do I understand," he said when she had finished, "that you mean to disinherit me?"

"I mean to give you the finest inheritance a young man can have: *the necessity for work!*—and work for the necessity. For, of course, your job is open to you in the office. But it will be at an honest salary after this; the salary any other unskilled man would get."

"Please make yourself clear," he said laconically; "you propose to leave me no money when you die?"

"Exactly."

"May I ask how you expect me to live?"

"The way most decent men live—*by work*. You can work; or

else, as I said, you can starve. There's a verse in the Bible—you don't know your Bible very well; perhaps that's one reason you have turned out as you have; but there's a verse in the Bible that says if a man won't work, he sha'n't eat. That's the best political economy I know. But I never thought of it before," she said simply; "I never realized that the worst handicap a young man can have in starting out in life is a rich father—or mother. Ferguson used to tell me so, but somehow I never took it in."

"So," he said—he was holding his cane in both hands, and as he spoke he struck it across his knees, breaking it with a splintering snap; "so, you'll disinherit me because I married the girl I love?"

"No!" she said, eager to make herself clear; "no, not at all! Don't you understand? (My God! how can I make him understand?) I disinherit you to make a man of you, so that your father won't be ashamed of you—as I am. Yes, I owe it to your father to make a man of you; if it can be done."

She rose, with a deep breath, and stood for an instant silent, her big hands on her hips, her head bent. Then, solemnly: "That is all; you may go, my son."

Blair got on to his feet with a loud laugh—a laugh singularly like her own. "Well," he said, "I *will* go! And I'll never come back. This lets me out! You've thrown me over: I'll throw you over. I think the law will have something to say to this disinheritance idea of yours; but until then—take a job in your Works? I'll starve first! So help me God, I'll forget that you are my mother; it will be easy enough, for the only womanly thing about you is your dress"—she winced, and flung her hand across her face as if he had struck her. "If I can forget that I am your son, starvation will be a cheap price. We've always hated each other, and it's a relief to come out into the open and say so. No more gush for either of us!" He actually looked like her, as he hurled his insults at her. He picked up his coat and left the room; he was trembling all over.

She, too, began to tremble; she looked after him as he slammed the door, half rose, bent over and lifted the splintered pieces of his cane; then sat down, as if suddenly weak. She put her hands over her face; there was a broken sound from behind them.

That night she came into Nannie's parlor and told her, briefly, that she meant to disinherit Blair. She even tried to explain why, according to her judgment, she must do so. But Nannie, appalled and crying, was incapable of understanding.

"Oh, Mamma, don't—don't say such things! Tell Blair you take it back. You don't mean it; I know you don't! Disinherit Blair? Oh, it isn't fair! Mamma, please forgive him, please—please—"

"My dear," said Sarah Maitland patiently, "it isn't a question of forgiving Blair; I'm too busy trying to forgive myself." Nannie looked at her in bewilderment. "Well, well, we won't go into that," said Mrs. Maitland; "you wouldn't understand. What I came over to say, especially, was that if things can go back into the old ways I shall be glad. I reckon Blair won't want to see me for a while, but if Elizabeth will come to the house as she used to, I sha'n't rake up unpleasant subjects. She is your brother's wife, and shall be treated with respect in my house. Tell her so. 'Night."

But Nannie, with a soft rush across the room, darted in front of her and stood with her back against the door, panting. "Mamma! Wait. You must listen to me!" Her stepmother paused, looking at her with mild astonishment. She was like another creature, a little wild creature standing at bay to protect its young. "You have no right," Nannie said sternly, "you have no right, Mother, to treat Blair so. Listen to me: it was not—not nice in him to run away with Elizabeth; I know that, though I think it was more her fault than his. But it wasn't wicked! He loved her."

"My dear, I haven't said it was wicked," Blair's mother tried to explain; "in fact, I don't think it was; it wasn't big enough to be wicked. No, it was only a dirty, contemptible trick." Nannie cringed back, her hand gripping the knob behind her. "If Blair had been a hard-working man, knocking up against other hard-working men, trying to get food for his belly and clothes for his nakedness, he'd have been ashamed to play such a trick—he'd have been a man. If I had loved him more I'd have made a man of him; I'd have made work real to him, not make-believe, as I did. And I wouldn't have been ashamed of him, as I am now."

"I think," said Nannie, with one of those flashes of astuteness so characteristic of the simple mind, "that a man would fall in love just as much if he were poor as if he were rich; and—and you ought to forgive him, Mamma."

Mrs. Maitland half smiled: "I guess there's no making you understand, Nannie; you are like your own mother. Come! Open this door! I've got to go to work."

But Nannie still stood with her hand gripping the knob. "I must tell you," she said in a low voice: "I must not be untruthful to you, Mamma: I will give Blair all I have myself. The money my father left me shall be his; and—and everything I may ever have shall be his." Then she seemed to melt away before her stepmother, and the door banged softly between them.

"Poor little soul!" Sarah Maitland said to herself, smiling, as she sat down at her desk in the dining-room. "Exactly like her mother! I must give her a present."

The next day she sent for her general manager and told him what course she had taken with her son. He was silent for a moment; then he said, with an effort, "I have no reason to plead Blair's cause, but you're not fair, you know."

"So Nannie has informed me," she said dryly. Then she leaned back in her chair and tapped her desk with one big finger. "Go on; say what you like. It won't move me one hair."

Robert Ferguson said a good deal. He pointed out that she had no right, having crippled Blair, to tell him to run a race. "You've made him what he is. Well, it's done; it can't be undone. But you are rushing to the other extreme; you needn't leave him millions, of course; but leave him a reasonable fortune."

She meditated. "Perhaps a very small allowance, in fact, to make my will sound I may have to. I must find out about that. But while I'm alive, not one cent. I never expected to be glad his father died before he was born, and so didn't leave him anything, but I am. No, sir; my son can earn what he wants or he can go without. I've got to do my best to make up to him for all the harm I've done him, and this is the way to do it. Now, the next thing is to make my will *sound*. He says he'll contest it"—she gave her grunt of amusement. "Pity I can't see him do it! I'd like the fun of it. It will be cast-iron. If there was any doubt about it, I would realize on every security I own to-morrow and give it all away in one lump, now, while I'm alive—if I had to go hungry myself afterward! Will you ask Howe and Marston to send their Mr. Marston up here to draw up a new will for me? I want to go to work on it to-night. I've thought it out pretty clearly, but it's a big job, a big job! I don't know myself exactly how much I'm worth—how much I'd clean up to, at any rate. But I've got a list of charities on my desk as long as your arm. Nannie will be the residuary legatee; she has some money from her father, too, though not very much. The Works didn't amount to much when my husband was alive; he divided his share between Nannie and me; he —"; she paused, reddening faintly with that strange delicacy that lay hidden under the iron exterior; "he didn't know Blair was coming along. Well, I suppose Nannie will give Blair something. In fact, she as good as warned me. Think of Nannie giving *me* notice! But as I say, she won't have any too much herself. And, Mr. Ferguson, I want to tell you something: I'm going to give David some money now. I mean in a year or two. A lot."

Robert Ferguson's face darkened. "David doesn't take money very easily."

Mrs. Maitland did not ask him to explain. She was absorbed in the most tremendous venture of her life—the saving of her son, and her plan for David was comparatively unimportant. She put through the business of her will with extraordinary despatch and precision, and with a ruthlessness toward Blair that took her lawyer's breath away; but she would not hear one word of protest.

"Your business, sir, is to see that this instrument is unbreakable," she said, "not to tell me how to leave my money."

The day after the will was executed she went to Philadelphia. "I am going to see David," she told her general superintendent; "I want to get this affair off my mind so I can settle down to my work, but I've got to square things up first with him. You'll have to run the shop while I'm off!"

She had written to David briefly, without preface or apology:

"DEAR DAVID,—Come and see me at the Girard House Tuesday morning at 7.45 o'clock."

Chapter 24

Nearly two months had passed since that dreadful day when David Richie had gone to his mother to be comforted. In his journey back across the mountains his mind and body were tense with anticipation of the letter which he was confident was awaiting him in Philadelphia. He was too restless to lie down in his berth. Once he went into the day coach and wandered up and down the aisle between the rows of huddled and uncomfortable humanity. Sometimes a sleepy passenger, hunched up on a plush seat, would swear at him for jostling a protruding foot, and once a drearily crying baby, propped against a fat and sleeping mother, clutched with dirty fingers at his coat. At that little feeble pull he stopped and looked down at the small, wabbling head, then bent over and lifted the child, straightening its rumpled clothes and cuddling it against his shoulder. The baby gurgled softly in his ear—and instantly he remembered the baby he had seen on the raft the night that he first knew he was in love with Elizabeth. When he went back to the smoking-compartment and sat down, his hands deep in his pockets, his head sunk between his shoulders, his hat pulled down over his eyes, he thought of that raft baby and wondered if it were alive. But such thoughts were only in the moments when his bruised mind could not steady itself on what had happened to him. Most of the time he was saying, over and over, just what he was going to do the next morning: he would get into the station; take a cab; drive to the hospital—a dozen times that night his thumb and finger sought his waistcoat pocket for a bill to hasten the driver of that cab! leap out, run up the stairs to the mail-rack beside the receiving clerk's desk, seize Elizabeth's letter—here the pause would come, the moment when his body relaxed, and something seemed to melt within him: suppose the letter was not there? Very well: back to the cab! another tip; hurry! hurry! hurry! His mother's house, the steps, his key in the lock— again and again his fingers closed on the key-ring in his pocket! letters on the hall table awaiting him—*her* letter. Then again the relaxing shock: suppose it was not there? The thought turned him sick; after the almost physical recoil from it, came brief moments of longing for his mother's tender arms, or the remembrance of that baby on the raft. But almost immediately his mind would return to the treadmill of expectation; get into the station—take a cab—rush— So it went, on and on, until, toward dawn, through sheer exhaustion he slept.

That next day was never very clear in David's memory. Only one fact stood out distinctly in the mists: there was no letter. Afterward, when he tried to recall that time of discovering that she had not written, he was confused by the vision of his mother smiling down at him from the head of the stairs and calling to an unseen maid, "Bring the doctor a cup of coffee, Mary!" He could remember that he stood sorting out the letters on the hall table, running them over swiftly, then going through them slowly, one by one, scanning each address, each post-mark; then, with shaking hands, shuffling and sorting them like a pack of cards, and going through them again. *She had not written.* He could remember that he heard the blood beating in his ears, and at the same time his mother's voice: "Bring the doctor a cup of coffee." … She had not written.

For months afterward, when he tried to recall that morning, the weak feeling in his knees, the way the letters that were not from her shook in his hand, the sound of his mother's joyous voice—these things would come into his mind together. They were all he could remember of the whole day; the day when the grave closed over his youth.

After that came hours of expectation, of telegrams back and

forth: "Have you heard where they are?" And: "No news." Weeks of letters between Robert Ferguson and his mother: "It is what I have always said, she is her mother's daughter." And: "Oh, don't be so hard on her—and on her poor, bad mother. Find out where she is, and go and see her." And: "I will never see her. I'm done with her." But among all the letters, never any letter from Elizabeth to David.

In those first days he seemed to live only when the mail arrived; but his passion of expectation was speechless. Indeed his inarticulateness was a bad factor when it came to recovery from the blow that had been dealt him. At the moment when the wound was new, he had talked to his mother; but almost immediately he retreated into silence. And in silence the worst things in his nature began to grow. Once he tried to write to Elizabeth; the letter commenced with frantic directions to come to his mother "at once!" Then his pen faltered: perhaps she did not care to come? Perhaps she did not wish to leave "him"?—and the unfinished letter was flung into the fire. With suspicion of Elizabeth came a contemptuous distrust of human nature in general, and a shrinking self-consciousness, both entirely foreign to him. He was not only crushed by loss, but he was stinging with the organic mortification of the man who has not been able to keep his woman. It was then that Helena Richie first noticed a harshness in him that frightened her, and a cynical individualism that began to create its own code of morals, or at any rate of responsibilities. But before he shut himself into all this misery, not only of loss, but of suspicion and humiliation, he did say one thing:

"I'm not going to howl; you needn't be afraid. I shall do my work. You won't hear me howl." There were times when she wished he would! She wished it especially when Robert Ferguson wrote that Elizabeth and Blair were going to return to Mercer, that they would live at the River House, and that it was evident that the "annulment," to which at first David's mind had turned so incessantly, was not being thought of. "I understand from Miss White (of course I haven't heard from or written to Mrs. Blair Maitland) that she does not wish to take any steps for a separation," Elizabeth's uncle wrote.

"He *must* see her when she gets back," Helena Richie said, softly; but David said nothing at all. At that moment his suspicion became a certainty; yes, she had loved the fellow! It had been something else than one of her fits of fury! It had been *love*. ... No wonder, with this poison working in him, that he shut even his mother out of his heart. At times the pitying tenderness of her eyes was intolerable to him; he thought he saw the same pity in everybody's eyes; he felt sure that every casual acquaintance was thinking of what had happened to him: he said to himself he wished to God people would mind their business, and let him mind his! "I'm not howling," he told himself. He was like a man whose skin has been taken off; he winced at everything, but all the same, he did his work in the hospital with exhausting thoroughness; to be sure he gave his patients nothing but technical care. Whether they lived or died was nothing to David; whether he himself lived or died was still less to him—except, perhaps, that in his own case he had a preference. But work is the only real sedative for grief, and the suffering man worked himself callous, so he had dull moments of forgetfulness, or at any rate of comparative indifference, Yet when he received that note from Mrs. Maitland summoning him to her hotel he flinched under the callousness. However, at a little before eight o'clock on Tuesday morning, he knocked at her bedroom door.

The Girard House knew Sarah Maitland's eccentricities as well as her credit; she always asked for a cheap room, and was always put up under the roof. She had never learned to use her money for her own comfort, so it never occurred to her to have a parlor for herself; her infrequent callers were always shown up here to the top of the house.

On this especial morning she had come directly from the train, and when David arrived she was pacing up and down the narrow room, haggard and disheveled from a night in the sleeping-car; she had not even taken off her bonnet. She turned at his step and stopped short in her tracks—he was so thin, so grim, so old! "Well, David," she said; then hesitated, for there was just an instant's recoil in David. He had not realized the fury that would leap up and scorch him like a flame at the sight of Blair's mother.

"David, you'll—you'll shake hands with me, won't you?" she said timidly. At the sound of her voice his anger died out; only the cold ashes of misery were left.

"Why, Mrs. Maitland!" he protested, and took her big, beautiful, unsteady hand in both of his.

For a moment neither of them spoke. It was a dark, cold morning; far below them stretched the cheerless expanse of snow-covered roofs; from countless chimneys smoke was rising heavily to the lowering sky, and soot was sifting down; the snow on the window-sill was speckled with black. Below, in the courtyard of the hotel, ice-carts rumbled in and out, and milk-cans were banged down on the cobblestones; a dull day, an empty sky, a futile interview, up here in this wretched little room under the eaves. David wondered how soon he could get away.

"David," Mrs. Maitland said, "I know I can't make it up to you in any way. But I'd like to."

"You are very kind," he said coldly, "but we won't go into that, if you please, Mrs. Maitland."

"No, we won't talk about it," she said, with evident relief; "but David, I came to Philadelphia to say that I want you to let me be of help to you in some way."

"Help to me?" he repeated, surprised. "I really don't see—"

"Why," she explained, "you want to begin to practise; you don't want to drudge along at a hospital under some big man's thumb. I want to set you up!"

David smiled involuntarily, "But the hospital is my greatest chance, Mrs. Maitland. I'm lucky to have these three years there. But it's kind in you to think of giving me a hand."

"Nonsense!" she said, quite missing the force of what he said. "You ought to put out your own shingle. David, you can have all the money you need; it's yours to take."

David started as if she had struck him: "*yours to take*." Oh, that had been said to him before! "No, I can't, I couldn't take money! You don't understand. I couldn't take money from— anybody!" he said with a gasp.

She looked at him helplessly, then stretched out her empty hands. "David," she said pitifully, "money is all I've got. Won't you take it?" The tears were on her cheeks and the big, empty hands shook. "I haven't got anything but money, David," she entreated.

His face quivered; he said some broken, protesting word; then suddenly he put his arms round her and kissed her. Her gray head, in the battered old bonnet, rested a moment on his shoulder, and he felt her sob. "Oh, David," she said, "what shall I do? He—he hates me. He said the only womanly thing about me was ... Oh, can I make a man of him, do you think?" She entirely forgot David's wrongs in her cry for comfort, a cry that somehow penetrated to his benumbed heart, for in his effort to comfort her he was himself vaguely comforted, For a minute he held her tightly in his arms until he was sure he could command himself. When he let her go, she put her hand up in a bewildered way and touched her cheek; the boy had kissed her! But by that time she was able to go back to the purpose that had brought her here; she told him to sit down and then began, dogmatically, to insist upon her plan.

David smiled a little as he explained that, quite apart from any question of income, the hospital experience was valuable to him. "I wouldn't give it up, Mrs. Maitland, if I had a million dollars!" he said, with a convincing exaggeration that was like the old David. "But it's mighty kind in you. Please believe I do appreciate your kindness."

"No kindness about it," she said impatiently; "my family is in your debt, David." At which he hardened instantly.

"Well," she said; and was silent for awhile, biting her finger and looking down at her boots. Suddenly, with a grunt of satisfaction, she began to hit the arm of her chair softly with her closed fist. "I've got it!" she said. "I suppose you wouldn't refuse the trusteeship of a fund, one of these days, to build a hospital? Near my Works, maybe? I'm all the time having accidents. I remember once getting a filing in my eye, and—and somebody suggested a doctor to take it out. A doctor for a filing! I guess *you'd* have been equal to that job—young as you are? Still, it wouldn't be bad to have a doctor round, even if he was young, if anything serious happened. Yes, a hospital near the Works—first for my men and then for outsiders. It is a good idea! I suppose you wouldn't refuse to run such a hospital, and draw your wages, like a man?"

"Well, no, I wouldn't refuse that," he said, smiling. It was many weeks since David had smiled so frankly. A strange thing had happened in that moment when he had forgotten himself in trying to comfort Blair's mother—his corroding suspicion of Elizabeth seemed to melt away! In its place was to come, a little later, the dreadful but far more bearable pain of enduring remorse for his own responsibility for Elizabeth's act. But just then, when he tried to comfort that poor mother, there was only a breaking of the ice about his own heart in a warm gush of pity for her.... "I don't see that there's much chance of funds for hospitals coming my way," he said, smiling.

"You never can tell," said Mrs. Maitland.

Chapter 25

The morning Blair heard his sentence from his mother,
Elizabeth spent in her parlor in the hotel, looking idly out of the
window at the tawny current of the river covered with its slipping
sheen of oil. Steamboats were pushing up and down or nosing into
the sand to unload their cargoes; she could hear the creak of hawsers,
the bang of gangplanks thrown across to the shore, the cries and
songs of stevedores sweating and toiling on the wharf that was piled
with bales of cotton, endless blue barrels of oil, and black avalanches
of coal. She did not think of Blair's ordeal; she was not interested in
it. She was not interested in anything. Sometimes she thought
vaguely of the letter which had never been and would never be
written to David, and sometimes of that message from him which she
had not yet been able to hear from Miss White's lips; but for the most
part she did not think of anything. She was tired of thinking. She sat
huddled in a chair, staring dully out of the window; she was like a
captive bird, moping on its perch, its poor bright head sinking down
into its tarnished feathers. She was so absorbed in the noise and
confusion of traffic that she did not hear a knock. When it was
repeated, she rose listlessly to answer it, but before she reached the
door it opened, and her uncle entered. Elizabeth backed away
silently. He followed her, but for a moment he was silent, too—it
seemed to Robert Ferguson as if youth had been wiped out of her
face. Under the shock of the change in her, he found for a moment
nothing to say. When he spoke his voice trembled—with anger, she
thought. "Mrs. Richie wrote me that I must come and see you. I told
her I would have nothing to do with you."

Elizabeth sat down without speaking.

"I don't see what good it does to come," he said, staring at the tragic face. "Of course you know my opinion of you." She nodded. "So why should I come?"

"I don't know."

"Well, I—I'm here. And you may come home sometimes, if you want to.
Miss White is willing to see you, I believe."

"Thank you, Uncle Robert."

As she spoke the door of the elevator in the hall clanged shut, and the next moment Blair entered. He carried a loose twist of white paper in his arms, and when, at the sight of Robert Ferguson, he tossed it down on the table it fell open, and the fragrance of roses overflowed into the room. Raging from the lash of his mother's tongue, he had rushed back to the hotel to tell Elizabeth what had happened, but in spite of his haste he stopped on the way to get her some flowers. He did not think of them now, nor even of his own wrongs, for here was Robert Ferguson attacking her! "Mr. Ferguson," he said, quietly, but reddening to his temples, "of course you know that in the matter of Elizabeth's hasty marriage I am the only one to blame. But though you blame me, I hope you will believe that I will do my best to make her happy."

[Illustration: "OF COURSE YOU KNOW MY OPINION OF YOU"]

"I believe," said Elizabeth's uncle, "that you are a damned scoundrel." He took up his hat and began to smooth the nap on his arm; then he turned to Elizabeth—and in his heart he damned Blair Maitland more vigorously than before: the lovely color had all been washed away by tears, the amber eyes were dull, even the brightness of her hair seemed dimmed. It was as if something had breathed upon the sparkle and clearness; it was like seeing her through a mist. So, barking fiercely to keep his lip from shaking, he said: "And I hope you understand, Elizabeth, I have no respect for you, either."

She looked up with faint surprise. "Why, of course not."

"I insist," Blair said, peremptorily, "that you address my wife with respect or leave her presence."

Mr. Ferguson put his hat down on the table, not noticing that the roses spotted it with their wet petals, and stared at him. "Well, upon my word!" he said. "Do you think I need *you* to instruct me in my duty to my niece?" Then, with sudden, cruel insight, he added, "David Richie's mother has done that." As he spoke he bent over and kissed Elizabeth. Instantly, with a smothered cry, she clung to him. There was just a moment when, her head on his breast, he felt her soft hair against his cheek—and a minute later, she felt something wet on her cheek. They had both forgotten Blair. He slunk away and left them alone.

Robert Ferguson straightened up with a jerk. "Where—where —where's my hat!" he said, angrily; "she said I was hard. She doesn't know everything!" But Elizabeth caught his hand and held it to her lips.

When Blair came back she was quite gentle to him; yes, the roses were very pretty; yes, very sweet. "Thank you, Blair," she said; but she did not ask him about his interview with his mother; she had forgotten it. He took the stab of her indifference without wincing; but suddenly he was comforted, for when he began to tell her what his mother was going to do, she was sharply aroused. She lifted her head—that spirited head which in the old days had never drooped; and looked at him in absolute dismay. Blair was being punished for a crime that was more hers than his!

"Oh," she said, "it isn't fair! I'm the one to blame; it isn't fair!"

The indignation in her voice made his heart leap. "Of course it isn't fair. But Elizabeth, I would pay any price to know that you were my wife." He tried to take her hand, but she pushed him aside and began to pace about the room.

"It isn't right!" she said; "she sha'n't treat you so!" She was almost like the old, furious Elizabeth in that gust of distress at her own responsibility for an injustice to him. But Blair dared to believe that her anger was for his sake, and to have her care that he should lose money made the loss almost welcome. He felt, through his rage at his mother, a thrill of purpose, a desire to amount to something, for Elizabeth's sake—which, if she could have known it, might have comforted Sarah Maitland, sitting in her dreary bedroom, her face hidden in her hands.

"Dearest, what do I care for her or her money?" he cried out; "*I have you!*"

Elizabeth was not listening to him; she was thinking what she could do to save him from his mother's displeasure. "I'll go and see her, and tell her it was my fault," she said to herself. She had a vague feeling that if she could soften Mrs. Maitland she and Blair would be quits.

She did not tell him of her purpose, but the mere having a purpose made her face alert, and it seemed to him that she identified herself with him and his interests. His eager denial of her self-accusation that she had injured him, his ardent impulse to protect her from any remorse, to take all the blame of a possible "mistake" on his own shoulders, brought an astonishing unselfishness into his face. But Elizabeth would not let him blame himself.

"It was all my fault," she insisted. "I was out of my head!"

At that he frowned sharply—"when you are eaten up with jealousy," his mother had said. Oh, he did not need his mother to tell him what jealousy meant: Elizabeth would not have married him if she had not been 'out of her head'! "She still thinks of him," he said to himself, as he had said many, many times in these two months of marriage—months of alternate ecstasies and angers, of hopes and despairs. As for her indignation at the way he had been treated, it meant nothing personal, after all. In his disappointment he went out of the room in hurt silence and left her to her thoughts of "him." This was the way most of their talks ended.

But Elizabeth's indignation did not end. In the next two days, while Mrs. Maitland was in Philadelphia making her naive offer to David, she brooded over the situation. "I won't have Blair punished for my sins," she said to herself; "I won't have it!" Her revolt at an injustice was a faint echo of her old violence. She had no one to talk to about it; Nannie was too shy to come to see her, and Miss White too tearful to be consulted. But she did not need advice; she knew what she must do. The afternoon following Mrs. Maitland's return from Philadelphia she went to see her.... She found Nannie in the parlor, sitting forlornly at her drawing-board. Nannie had heard, of course, from Blair, the details of that interview with his mother, and in her scared anger she planned many ways of "making Mamma nice to Blair," but she had not thought of Elizabeth's assistance. She took it for granted that Elizabeth would not have the courage to "face Mamma."

"I have come to see Mrs. Maitland," Elizabeth said. "Is she in the dining-room?"

Nannie quailed. "Oh, Elizabeth! How do you dare? But do go; and make her forgive him. She wouldn't listen to me. And after all, Elizabeth, you know that *you*—"

"Yes, I'm the one," Elizabeth said, briefly; and went swiftly across the hall. She stood for a moment by Sarah Maitland's desk unnoticed. "Mrs. Maitland!" Elizabeth's voice was peremptory. Blair's mother put her pen down and looked up over her spectacles. "Oh—Elizabeth?"

"Mrs. Maitland, I came to tell you that you must not be angry at Blair.

It was all my fault."

"I guess, as I told your uncle, it was the pot and the kettle, Elizabeth."

"No, no! I was angry, and I was—willing."

"Do you think it excuses Blair if you did throw yourself at his head?"

Elizabeth, who had thought that no lesser wound than the one she had dealt herself could hurt her, flinched. But she did not defend herself. "I think it does excuse him to some extent, and that is why I have come to ask you to forgive him."

"Oh," said Mrs. Maitland, and paused; then with most disconcerting suddenness, sneezed violently and blew her nose; "bless you, I've forgiven him."

"Then," said Elizabeth, with a gasp of relief, "you won't disinherit him!"

"Disinherit him? What's that got to do with forgiving him? Of course I will disinherit him,—or rather, I have. My will is made; signed, sealed. I've left him an income of a thousand dollars a year. That will keep you from starvation. If Blair is worth more he'll earn more. If he isn't, he can live on a thousand dollars—as better men than he have done. Or he can go to the workhouse;—your uncle can take care of you. I reckon I've paid taxes in this county long enough to entitle my son to go to the workhouse if he wants to."

"But Mrs. Maitland," Elizabeth protested, hotly, "it isn't fair, just because I—I let him marry me, to punish him—"

Mrs. Maitland struck her fist on the arm of her chair. "You don't know what you are talking about! I am not 'punishing' him; that's the last thing I was thinking of. If there's any 'punishing' going on, I'm the one that's getting it. Listen, Elizabeth, and I'll try to explain—you look as if you had some sense, so maybe you can understand. Nannie couldn't; she has no brains. And Blair wouldn't

—I guess he has no heart. But this is how it is: Blair has always been a loafer—that's why he behaved as he did to you. Satan finds some mischief still, you know! So I'm cutting off his allowance, now, and leaving him practically penniless in my will, to stop his loafing. To make him work! He'll have to work, to keep from starving; and work will make a man of him. As for you, you've done an abominable thing, Elizabeth; but it's *done*! Now, turn to, and pay for your whistle: do your duty! Use your influence to induce Blair to work. That's the best way to make up for the injury you've done him. As for the injury he's done you, I hope the Lord will send you some children to make up for that. Now, my—my dear, clear out! clear out! I've got my work to do."

Elizabeth went back to Nannie's parlor, stinging under her mother-in-law's candor. That she was able to feel it showed that her apathy was wearing off. At any rate, the thought of the "injury" she had done Blair, which she took to be the loss of fortune, strengthened her sometimes wavering resolution to stay with him. She did not tell him of this interview, or of its effect upon her, but she told her uncle —part of it. She went to him that night, and sitting down on a hassock at his feet, her head against his knee, she told him how Blair was to be punished for her crime—she called it a crime. Then, in a low voice, she told him, as well as she could, just how the crime had been committed.

"I guessed how it was," he said. And they were silent for a while. Then he broke out, huskily: "I don't care a hang about Blair or his mother's will. He deserves all he gets—or won't get, rather! But, Elizabeth, if—if you want to be free—"

"Uncle Robert, what I want isn't of any importance any more."

"I talked it over as a supposititious case with Howe the other day, and he said that if Blair would agree, possibly—mind you, only *possibly*;—a divorce could be arranged."

She sunk her head in her hands; then answered in a whisper: "Uncle, I did it. I've got to see it through."

After a minute's silence he put his hand on her soft hair. "Bully for you, Elizabeth," he said, brokenly. Then, to escape from the emotional demand of the moment, he began to bark: "You are outrageously careless about money. How on earth a girl, who has been brought up by a man, and so might be expected to have some sense in such matters, can be so careless, I don't understand! You've never asked me about that legacy. I've put the money in the bank. Your bank-book is there on my table."

Elizabeth was silent. That money! Oh, how could she ever touch it? But in view of Mrs. Maitland's decision it was perfectly obvious that ultimately she would have to touch it. "Blair can live on it." she thought—it was a relief to her to stab herself with words; —"*Blair* 'can live on it for two years.'"

Chapter 26

Of course, after a while, as time passed, all the people who had been caught in the storm the two reckless creatures had let loose, shook down again into their grooves, and the routine of living went on. There are few experiences more bewildering to the unhappy human heart than this of discovering that things do go on. Innumerable details of the unimportant flood in and fill up the cracks and breaches that grief has made in the structure of life; we continue to live, and even to find life desirable!

Miss White had been the first to realize this; her love for Elizabeth, being really (poor old maid!) maternal, was independent of respect, so almost the next day she had been able to settle down with complete happiness into the old habit of loving. Blair's mother was the next to get into the comfortable track of routine; the very day after she came back from that trip to Philadelphia she plunged into business. She did, however, pause long enough to tell her superintendent how she was going to "even things up with David."

"I am going to give him a lot of money for a hospital," she said. "I'm not going to leave it to him; I'm only sixty-two, and I don't propose to die yet awhile. When I do Blair will probably contest the will. He can't break it. It's cast-iron. But I don't want David to wait until I'm dead and gone, and Blair has given up trying to break my will, and the estate is settled. I'm going to give it to him before I die. In a year or two, maybe. I'm realizing on securities now —why don't I give him the securities? My dear sir, what does a doctor know about securities? Doctors have no more financial sense than parsons—at least, not much more," she added, with relenting justice. "No; David is to have his money, snug in the bank—that new bank, on Federal Street. I told the president I was rolling up a nest-egg for somebody—I could see he thought it was for Blair! I didn't enlighten him, because I don't want the thing talked about. When I get the amount I want, I'll hand Master David a bank certificate of deposit, and with all his airs about accepting money, he won't be able to help himself! He'll have to build his hospital, and draw his wages. It will make him independent of his outside customers, you see. Yes, I guess I can whip the devil round the stump as well as the next person!" she said, bridling with satisfaction. So, with an interest and a hope, Sarah Maitland, like Miss White, found life worth living.

With David's mother the occupation of trying to help David made living desirable. It also made her a little more remote from other people's interests. Poor Robert Ferguson discovered this to his cost: it had occurred to him that now, when they were all so miserable, she might perhaps "be willing." But she was not. When, a day or two after he had gone to see Elizabeth, he went to Philadelphia, Mrs. Richie was tremulously glad to see him, so that she might pour out her fears about David and ask advice on this point and that. "Being a man, you understand better than I do," she acknowledged meekly; then broke down and cried for her boy's pain. And when the kind, barking old friend, himself blinking behind misty spectacles, said, "Oh, now, my dear, don't cry," she was so comforted that she cried some more, and for a single minute found her head most unexpectedly on his shoulder. But all the same, she was not "willing."

"Don't ask me, dear Mr. Ferguson," she said, wiping her eyes. "We are such good friends, and I'm so fond of you, don't let's spoil it all."

"I believe you are fond of me," he said, "and that is why it's so unreasonable in you not to marry me. I don't ask—impossibilities. But you do like me; and I love you, you dear, good, foolish woman; —so good that you couldn't see badness when it lived next door to you!"

"Don't be so hard on people who do wrong," she pleaded; "you make me afraid of you when you are so hard."

"I'm not hard; Elizabeth is her mother's daughter; that's all."
"Oh!" she cried, with sudden passion, "that poor mother! Can't you forgive her?"

"No," he said; "I can't."

"You ought to forgive Elizabeth, at any rate," she insisted, faintly; "and you ought to go and see her."

"Have you forgiven her?" he parried.

She hesitated. "I think I have. I've tried to; but I don't understand her. I can understand doing something—wicked, for love; but not for hate."

He gave his meager laugh. "If forgiveness was a question of understanding, I'm afraid you'd be as hard on her mother as I am."

"On the contrary," she said, vehemently, "if I forgive Elizabeth, it is for her mother's sake." Then she broke out, almost with tears: "Oh, how can you be so unkind as not to go and see the child? The time we need our friends most is when we have done wrong!"

He was silent.

"Sometimes," she said, "sometimes I wish you would do something wrong yourself, just to learn to be pitiful!"

"You wish I would do wrong? I'm *always* doing wrong! I did wrong when I growled so. But—" he paused; "I believe I *have* seen Elizabeth," he said sheepishly; "I believe we kissed and made up." At which even poor, sad Helena laughed.

But these two old friends discovered, just as Miss White and Blair's mother had discovered, that life was not over for them, because the habit of friendship persisted. And by and by, nearly a year later, David—even David! began to find a reason for living, in his profession. The old, ardent interest which used to make his eyes dim with pity, or his heart leap with joy at giving help, was gone; he no longer cared to cuddle the babies he might help to bring into the world; and a death-bed was an irritating failure rather than any more human emotion. So far as other people's hopes and fears went, he was bitter or else callous, but he began to forget his humiliation, and he lost his self-consciousness in the serious purpose of success. He did not talk to his mother of the catastrophe of his life; but he did talk of other things, and with the old friendly intimacy. She was his only intimate friend.

Thus, gradually, the little world that loved Elizabeth and Blair fell back, after the storm of pain and mortification, into the merciful commonplace of habit and of duty to be done.

But for Elizabeth and Blair there was no going back; they had indeed fired the Ephesian dome! The past now, to Elizabeth, meant David's message,—to which, finally, she had been able to listen: "Tell her I understand; ask her to forgive me." In Blair's past there was nothing real to which he could return; for him the reality of life had begun with Love; and notwithstanding the bite of shame, the battle with his sense of chivalry, that revolted (now and then) at the thought of holding an unwilling woman as his wife, and the constant dull ache of jealousy, he had madly happy moments that first year of his marriage. Elizabeth was his! That was enough for him. His circumstances, which would have caused most men a good deal of anxiety, were, thanks to his irresponsibility, very little in his thought. There was still a balance at his bank which made it possible, without encroaching on Elizabeth's capital—which he swore he would not do —to live at the old River House "fairly decently." He was, however, troubled because he could not propitiate Elizabeth with expensive gifts; and almost immediately after that interview with his mother, he began to think about an occupation, merely that he might have more money to spend on his wife. "If I could only buy her some jewels!" he used to say to himself, with a worried look. "I want to get you everything you want, my darling," he told her once.

She made no answer; and he burst out in sudden angry pain: "You don't care what I do!" Still she did not speak. "You—you are thinking of him still," he said between set teeth. This constant corroding thought did not often break through his studied purpose to win her by his passionately considerate tenderness; when it did, it always ended in bitterness for him.

"Of course I am thinking of him," she would say, dully; "I never stop thinking of him."

"I believe you would go back to him now!" he flung at her

"Go back to him? I would go back to him on my hands and knees if he would take me."

Words like that left him speechless with misery; and yet he was happy—she was his wife!

When his bank account began to dwindle, he found it easy to borrow; the fact that he was the son of his mother (and consequently his bills had always been paid) was sufficient collateral. That he borrowed at a ruinous interest was a matter of indifference to a man who, having never earned a dollar, had not the slightest idea of the value of a dollar. At the end of the first year of his marriage, jewels for Elizabeth seemed less important to him than her bread and butter; and it was then that with real anxiety he tried to find something to do. Again "Sarah Maitland's son" found doors open to him which the ordinary man, inexperienced and notoriously idle, would have found closed; but none of them offered what he thought a sufficient salary; and by and by he realized that very soon he would be obliged, as he expressed it, "to sponge on Elizabeth"; for, reckless as he was, he knew that his borrowing capacity must come to an end. When the "sponging" finally began, he was acutely uncomfortable, which was certainly to his credit. At any rate, it proved that he was enough of a man to be miserable under such conditions. When a husband who is young and vigorous lives idly on his wife's money one of two things happens: he is miserable, or he degenerates into contentment. Blair was not degenerating—consequently he was honestly wretched.

His attempts to find something to do were not without humor to his mother, who kept herself informed, of course, of all his "business" ventures. "What! he wants the Dalzells to take him on? What for? Errand-boy? That's all he's good for. But I'm afraid two dollars and a half a week won't buy him many china beetles!" When Blair essayed a broker's office she even made an ancient joke to her superintendent: "If Blair could buy himself for what he is worth to Haines, and sell himself for what he thinks he's worth, he might make a fair profit,—and pick up some more old masters."

But she was impatient for him to get through with all this nonsense of dilly-dallying at making a living by doing things he knew nothing about! How soon would he get down to hard-pan and knock at her door at the Works and ask for a job, man-fashion? "That's what I want to know!" she used to tell Mr. Ferguson, who was silent. He did not want to know anything about Blair; all he cared for was to help his girl bear the burden of her folly. He called it "folly" now, and Miss White used to nod her old head in melancholy agreement. It was only to Robert Ferguson that Mrs. Maitland betrayed her constant anxiety about her son; and it was that anxiety which made her keenly sensitive to Elizabeth's deepening depression. For as the excitement of sacrifice and punishment wore off, and the strain of every-day living began to tell, Elizabeth's depression was very marked. She was never angry now—she had not the energy for anger; and she was never unkind to Blair; perhaps her own pain made her pitiful of his. But she was always, as Cherry-pie expressed it, "under a cloud." Mrs. Maitland, watching her, wondered if she was moody because funds were getting low. How intensely she hoped that was the reason! "I reckon that money of hers is coming to an end," she used to think, triumphantly—for she had known, through Nannie, just when Blair had reached the point at which he had been obliged to use his wife's capital. Whenever she saw Elizabeth—who for want of anything better to do came constantly to see Nannie: she would drop a word or two which she thought might go back to her son: "We need an extra hand in the office." Or: "How would Blair like to travel for the Works? We can always take on a traveling man."

She never had the chance to drop her hints to Blair himself. In vain Nannie urged upon her brother her old plea: "Be nice to Mamma. Do come and see her. Everything will be all right again if you will only come and see her!" Nothing moved him. If his mother could be firm, so could he; he was never more distinctly her son than in his obstinacy.

"If she alters her will," he said, briefly, "I will alter my behavior.
She's not my mother so long as she casts off her son."

Mrs. Maitland seemed to age very much that second year. Her business was still a furious interest; she stormed her way through every trade obstacle, occasionally bargaining with her conscience by increasing her donations to foreign missions; but there was this change of suddenly apparent age. Instead of the old, clear-eyed, ruthless joy in work, there was a look of furtive waiting; an anxiety of hope deferred, that grooved itself into her face. And somewhere in the spring of the third year, the hoped-for moment approached— necessity began to offer its beneficent opportunity to her son. In spite of experiments in prudence in borrowing and in earning, the end of Elizabeth's money was in sight. When the end was reached, there would be nothing for Blair Maitland but surrender.

"Shall I cave in now?" he vacillated; he was wandering off

alone across the bridge, fairly aching with indecision, and brooding miserably, not only over the situation, but over his helplessness to buy his way into Elizabeth's affections. "She ought to have a carriage; it is preposterous for my wife to be going round in streetcars. If I could give her a carriage and a pair of horses!" But of course it was ridiculous to think of things like that. He could not buy a carriage for Elizabeth out of her own money—besides, her money was shrinking alarmingly. It was this passionate desire to propitiate her, as well as the recognition of approaching necessities, that brought him to the point where he saw capitulation ahead of him. "I wish I could make up my mind," he thought, wearily. "Well, if I don't get something to do pretty soon, it will be made up for me,—I'll *have* to eat crow! I'll have to go to the Works and ask for a job. But I swear I won't speak to—*her!* It is damnable to have to cave in; I'd starve before I'd do it, if it wasn't for Elizabeth."

But before the time for eating crow arrived, something happened.

Chapter 27

Mrs. Maitland and Nannie were having their supper at the big, cluttered office table in the shabby dining-room—shabbier now by twenty years than when Blair first expressed his opinion of it. In the midst of the silent meal Sarah Maitland's eye fell on her stepdaughter, and hardened into attention. Nannie looked pale, she thought; and frowned slightly. It occurred to her that the girl might be lonely in the long evenings over there in the parlor, with nothing to do but read foolish little stories, or draw foolish little pictures, or embroider foolish little tidies and things. "What a life!" she said to herself; it was a shame Blair did not come in and cheer his sister up. Yes; Nannie was certainly very solitary. What a pity David Richie had no sense! "Now that he can't get Elizabeth, nothing could be more sensible," she said to herself; then sighed. Young men were never very sensible in regard to matrimony. "I suppose I ought to do something myself to cheer her up," she thought—a little impatiently, for really it was rather absurd to expect a person of her quality to cheer Nannie! Still, she might talk to her. Of course they had only one topic in common:

"Seen your brother lately?"

"No, Mamma. He went East day before yesterday."

"Has he found anything to do?" This was the usual weary question;

Nannie gave the usual scared answer:

"I *think* not; not yet. He is going to look up something in New York,

Elizabeth says."

"Tell Elizabeth I will take him on at the Works, whenever he is ready to come. His belly will bring him to it yet!" she ended, with the old, hopeful belief that has comforted parents ever since the fatted calf proved the correctness of the expectation. Nannie sighed. Mrs. Maitland realized that she was not "cheering" her very much. "You ought to amuse yourself," she said, severely; "how do you amuse yourself?"

"I—draw," Nannie managed to say; she really could not think of any other amusement.

Then her stepmother had an inspiration: "Would you like to come over to the furnace and see the night cast? It's quite a sight, people say."

Nannie was dumfounded at the attention. Mamma offering to take her to the Works! To be sure, it was the last thing on earth she would choose to do, but if her stepmother asked her, of course she could not say no. She said "yes," reluctantly enough, but Mrs. Maitland did not detect the reluctance; she was too pleased with herself at having thought of some way of entertaining the girl.

"Get your bonnet on, get your bonnet on!" she commanded, in high good humor. And Nannie, quailing at the thought of the Works at night—"it's dreadful enough in the daytime," she said to herself—put on her hat, in trembling obedience. "Yes," Mrs. Maitland said, as she tramped down the cinder path toward the mills, Nannie almost running at her heels—"yes, the cast is a pretty sight, people say. Your brother once said that it ought to be painted. Well, I suppose there are people who care for pictures," she said, incredulously. "I know I'm $5,000 out of pocket on account of a picture," she ended, with a grim chuckle.

As they were crossing the Yards, the cavernous glooms of the Works, under the vast stretch of their sheet-iron roofs, were lighted for dazzling moments by the glow of molten metal and the sputtering roar of flames from the stacks; a network of narrow-gauge tracks spread about them, and the noises from the mills were deafening.

Nannie clutched nervously at Mrs. Maitland's arm, and her stepmother grunted with amusement. "Hold on to me," she shouted —she had to shout to make herself heard; "there's nothing to hurt you. Why, I could walk around here with my eyes shut!"

Nannie clung to her frantically; if she protested, the soft flutter of her voice did not reach Mrs. Maitland's ears. A few steps farther brought them into the comparative silence of the cast-house of the furnace, and here they paused while Sarah Maitland spoke to one of the keepers. Only the furnace itself was roofed; beyond it the stretch of molded sand was arched by the serene and starlit night.

"That's the pig bed out there," Mrs. Maitland explained, kindly; "see, Nannie? Those cross-trenches in the sand they call sows; the little hollows on the side are the pigs. When they tap the furnace, the melted iron will flow down into 'em; understand?"

"Mamma, I'd—I'd like to go home," poor Nannie managed to say; "it scares me!"

Mrs. Maitland looked at her in astonishment. "Scares you? What scares you?"

"It's so—dreadful," Nannie gasped.

"You don't suppose I'd bring you anywhere where you could get hurt?" her stepmother said, incredulously. She was astonished to the point of being pained. How could Herbert's girl be such a fool? She remembered that Blair used to call his sister the "'fraid-cat." "Good name," she thought, contemptuously. She made no allowance for the effect of this scene of night and fire, of stupendous shadows and crashing noises, upon a little bleached personality, which for all these years, had lived in the shadow of a nature so dominant and aggressive that, quite unconsciously, it sucked the color and the character out of any temperament feebler than itself. Sarah Maitland frowned, and said roughly, "Oh, you can go home, if you want to; Mr. Parks!" she called to the foreman; "just walk back to the house, if you please, with my daughter;" then she turned on her heel and went up to the furnace.

Nannie, clutching Parks's hand, stumbled out into the darkness. "It's perfectly awful!" she confided to the good-natured man, when he left her at her back door.

"Oh, you get used to it," he said, kindly. "You'd 'a knowed," he told one of his workmen afterward, "that there wasn't hide nor hair of her that belonged to the Old One. A slip of a thing, and scared to death of the noise."

The "Old One," after Nannie had gone, poked about for a moment or two, — "she noses into things, to save two cents," her men used to say, with reluctant admiration of the ruthless shrewdness that was instant to detect their shortcomings; then she went down the slight incline from the furnace hearth to the open stretch of molding-sand; there was a pile of rusty scrap at one side, and here, in the soft April darkness under the stars, she seated herself, looking absently at the furnace and the black, gnome-like figures of the helpers. She was thinking just what Parks had thought, that Nannie had none of her blood in her. "Afraid!" said Sarah Maitland. Well, Blair had never been afraid, she would say that for him; he was a fool, and pig-headed, and a loafer; but he wasn't a coward. He had even thought it fine, that scene of power, where civilization made itself before his very eyes! When would he think it fine enough to come in and go to work? Come in, and take his part in making civilization? Then she noticed the bending figure of the keeper opening the notch of the furnace; instantly there was a roar of sparks, and a blinding white gush of molten iron flowing like water down into the sand runner. The sudden, fierce illumination drowned the stars overhead, and brought into clear relief her own figure, sitting there on the pile of scrap watching the flowing iron. Tiny blue flames of escaping gas danced and shimmered on its ineffable rippling brightness, that cooled from dazzling snow to rose, then to crimson, and out in the sand, to glowing gray. Blair had called it "beautiful." Well, it was a pretty sight! She wished she had told him that she herself thought it pretty; but the fact was, it had never struck her before. "I suppose I don't notice pretty things very much," she thought, in some surprise. "Well, I've never had time for foolishness. Too busy making money for Blair." She sighed; after all, he wasn't going to have the money. She had been heaping up riches, and had not known who should gather them. She had been too busy to see pretty things. And why? That orphan asylums and reformatories—and David Richie's hospital —should have a few extra thousands! A month ago the fund she was making for David had reached the limit she had set for it, and only to-day she had brought the bank certificate of deposit home with her. She had felt a little glow of satisfaction when she locked it into the safe in her desk; she liked the consciousness of a good job finished. She was going to summon the youngster to Mercer, and tell him how he was to administer the fund; and if he put on any of his airs and graces about accepting money, she would shut him up mighty quick! "I'll write him to-morrow, if I've time," she had said. At the moment, the sense of achievement had exhilarated her; yet now, as she sat there on the heap of scrap, bending a pliant boring between her fingers, her pillar of fire roaring overhead from the chimneys of the furnaces, the achievement seemed flat enough. Why should she, to build a hospital for another woman's son, have worked so hard that she had never had time to notice the things her own son called "pretty"? Not his china beetles, of course, or truck like that; but the shimmering flow of her iron,—or even that picture, for which she was out of pocket $5,000. "I can see you might call it pretty, if it hadn't cost so much," she admitted. Yes, she had worked, she told herself, "as hard as a man," to earn money for Blair!—only to make him idle and to have him say that thing about her clothes which Goose Molly had said before he was born. "Wonder if I've been a fool?" she ruminated.

It was at that moment that she noticed, at one side of the furnace, between two bricks of the hearth, a little puff of white vapor; instantly she leaped, shouting, to her feet. But it was too late. The molten iron, seeping down through some crack in the furnace, creeping, creeping, beneath the bricks of the pavement, had reached some moisture...The explosion, the clouds of scalding steam, the terror of the flowing, scattering fire, drowned her voice and hid her frantic gestures of warning....

"Killed?" she said, furiously, as some one helped her up from the scrap-heap against which she had been hurled; "of course not! I don't get killed." Then suddenly the appalling confusion was dominated by her voice:

"*Look after those men.*"

She stood there in the center of the horror, reeling a little once or twice, holding her skirt up over her left arm, and shouting her quick orders. "Hurt?" she said again to a questioning helper. "I don't know. I haven't time to find out. That man there is alive! Get a doctor!" She did not leave the Works until two badly burned men had been carried away, and two dead bodies lifted out of the reek of steam and the spatter of half-chilled metal. Then, still holding her skirt over her arm, she went alone, in the darkness, up the path to her back door.

"No! I don't want anybody to go home with me," she said, angrily; "look after things here. Notify Mr. Ferguson. I'll come back." When she banged open her own door, she had only one question: "Is—Nannie—all—right?" Harris, gaping with dismay, and stammering, "My goodness! yes'm; yes'm!" followed her to the dining-room, where she crashed down like a felled tree, and lay unconscious on the floor.

When she began to come to herself, a doctor, for whom

Harris had fled, was binding up her torn arm, which, covered with blood, and black with grit and rust, was an ugly sight. "Where's Blair?" she said, thickly; then came entirely to her senses, and demanded, sharply, "Nannie all right?" Reassured again on this point, she looked frowningly at the doctor. "Come, hurry! I want to get back to the Works."

"Back to the Works! To-night? Impossible! You mustn't think of such a thing," the young man protested. Mrs. Maitland looked at him, and he shifted from one foot to the other. "It—it won't do, really," he said, weakly; "that was a pretty bad knock you got on the back of your head, and your arm—"

"Young man," she said, "you patch this up, *quick*. I've got to see to my men. That's my business. You 'tend to yours."

"But my business is to keep you here," he told her, essaying to be humorous. His humor went out like a little candle in the wind: "Your business is to put on bandages. That's all I pay you for."

And the doctor put on bandages with expedition. In the front hall he spoke to Nannie. "Your mother has a very bad arm, Miss Maitland; and that violent blow on her head may have done damage. I can't tell yet. You must make her keep still."

"*Make!*—Mamma?" said Nannie.

"She says she's going over to the Works," said the doctor, shrugging his shoulders; "when she comes home, get her to bed as quickly as you can. I'll come in and see her in the morning, if she wants me. But if she won't do what I say about keeping quiet, I'd rather you called in other advice." When Nannie tried to "make Mamma" keep still, the only reply she received was: "You showed your sense in going home, my dear!" And off she went, Harris, at Nannie's instigation, lurking along behind her. "If Herbert's girl had been hurt!" she said, aloud, staggering a little as she walked, "my God, what would I have done?"

Afterward, they said it was astounding that she had been able to go back to the Works that night. She must have been in very intense pain. When she came home, the pain conquered to the extent of sending her, at midnight, up to her stepdaughter's room; she was red with fever, and her eyes were glassy. "Got any laudanum, or stuff of that kind?" she demanded. And yet the next day, when the bandages had been changed and there was some slight relief, she persisted in going to the Works again. But the third day she gave up, and attended to her business in the dining-room.

"If only Blair would come home," Nannie said, "I think, perhaps, she would be nice to him. Haven't you any idea where he is, Elizabeth?"

"Not the slightest," Elizabeth said, indifferently. She herself came every day, and performed what small personal services Mrs. Maitland would permit. Nannie did not amount to much as a nurse, but she was really helpful in writing letters, signing them so exactly in Sarah Maitland's hand that her stepmother was greatly diverted at her proficiency. "I shall have to look after my check-book," she said, with a chuckle.

It was not until a week later that they began to be alarmed. It was Harris who first discovered the seriousness of her condition; when he did, the knowledge came like a blow to her household and her office. It was late in the afternoon. Earlier in the day she had had a violent chill, during which she sat crouching and cowering over the dining-room fire, refusing to go to bed, and in a temper that scared Nannie and Harris almost to death. When the chill ceased, she went, flushed with fever, to her own room, saying she was "all right," and banging the door behind her. At about six, when Harris knocked to say that supper was ready, she came out, holding the old German cologne bottle in her hand. "*He* gave me that," she said, and fondled the bottle against her cheek; then, suddenly she pushed it into

Harris's face. "Kiss it!" she commanded, and giggled shrilly.

Harris jumped back with a screech. "*Gor!*" he said; and his knees hit together. The slender green bottle fell smashing to the floor. Mrs. Maitland started, and caught her breath; her mind cleared instantly.

"Clean up that mess. The smell of the cologne takes my breath away.
I—I didn't know I had it in my hand."

That night Elizabeth sent a peremptory letter into space, telling Blair that his mother was seriously ill, and he really ought to be at home. But he had left the hotel to which she sent it, without giving any address, so it lay in a dusty pigeonhole awaiting his return a week later.

The delirium came again the next day; then Sarah Maitland cried, because, she said, Nannie had hidden the Noah's ark; "and Blair and I want to play with it," she whined. But a moment afterward she looked at her stepdaughter with kind eyes, and said, as she had said a dozen times in the last ten days, "Lucky you went home that night, my dear."

Of course by this time the alarm was general. The young doctor was supported, at Robert Ferguson's insistence, by an old doctor, who, if he was awed by his patient, at least did not show it. He was even courageous enough to bring a nurse along with him.

"Miss Baker will spare your daughter," he said, soothingly, when Sarah Maitland, seeing the strange figure in her bedroom, had declared she wouldn't have a fussing woman about. "Miss Nannie needs help," the doctor said. Mrs. Maitland frowned, and yielded.

But the nurse did not have a good time. In her stiffly starched skirt, with her little cap perched on her head, she went fluttering prettily about, watched all the while by the somber, half-shut eyes. She moved the furniture, she dusted the bureau, she arranged the little row of photographs; and then she essayed to smooth Mrs. Maitland's hair—it was the last straw. The big, gray head began to lift slowly; a trembling finger pointed at the girl; there was only one word:

"*Stop.*"

The startled nurse stopped,—so abruptly that she almost lost her balance.

"Clear out. You can sit in the hall. When I want you, I'll let you know."

Miss Baker fled, and Mrs. Maitland apparently forgot her. When the doctor came, however, she roused herself to say: "I won't have that fool girl buzzing round. I don't like all this highfalootin' business of nurses, anyhow. They are nothing but foolish expense." Perhaps that last word stirred some memory, for she added abruptly: "Nannie, bring me that—that picture you have in the parlor. The Virgin Mary, you know. Rags of popery, but I want to look at it. No; I can't pay $5,000 for 14 X 18 inches of old master, and hire nurses to curl my hair, too!" But nobody smiled at her joke.

When Nannie brought the picture, she bade her put it on a chair by the bedside, and sometimes the two girls saw her look at it intently. "I think she likes the child," Elizabeth said, in a low voice; but Nannie sighed, and said, "No; she is provoked because Blair was extravagant." After Miss Baker's banishment, Elizabeth did most of the waiting on her, for Nannie's anxious timidity made her awkward to the point of being, as Mrs. Maitland expressed it, wearily, "more bother than she was worth." Once she asked where Blair was, and Elizabeth said that nobody knew. "He heard of some business opening, Mrs. Maitland, and went East to see about it."

"Went East? What did he go East for? He's got a business opening at home, right under his nose," she said, thickly.

After that she did not ask for him. But from her bed in her

own room she could see the dining-room door, and she lay there watching it, with expectation smoldering in her half-shut eyes. Once, furtively, when no one was looking, she lifted the hem of the sheet with her fumbling right hand and wiped her eyes. For the next few days she gained, and lost, and gained again. There were recurrent periods of lucidity, followed by the terrible childishness that had been the first indication of her condition. At the end of the next week she suddenly said, in a loud voice, "I won't stay in bed!" And despite Nannie's pleadings, and Miss Baker's agitated flutterings, she got up, and shuffled into the dining-room; she stood there, clutching with her uninjured hand a gray blanket that was huddled around her shoulders. Her hair was hanging in limp, disordered locks about her face, which had fallen away to the point of emaciation. She was leaning against the table, her knees shaking with weakness. But it was evident that her mind was quite clear. "Bed is a place to die in," she said; "I'm well. Let me alone. I shall stay here." She managed to get over to her desk, and sank into the revolving chair with a sigh of relief. "Ah!" she said, "I'm getting out of the woods. Harris! Bring me something to eat." But when the food was put before her, she could not touch it.

Robert Ferguson, who almost lived at the Maitland house that week, told her, soothingly, that she really ought to go back to bed, at which she laughed with rough goodnature. "Don't talk baby-talk. I'm getting well. But I've been sick; I've had a scare; so I'm going to write a letter, in case—Or here, you write it for me."

"To Blair?" he said, as he took his pen out of his pocket.

"Blair? No! To David Richie about that money. Don't you remember I told you I was going to give him a lot of money for a hospital? That I was going to get a certificate of deposit"—her voice wavered and she seemed to doze. A moment later, when her mind cleared again, her superintendent said, with some effort: "Aren't you going to do something for Blair? You will get well, I'm sure, but—in case—Your will isn't fair to the boy; you ought to do something for him."

Instantly she was alert: "I have. I've done the best thing in the world for him; I've thrown him on his own legs! As for getting well, of course I'm going to get well. But if I didn't, everything is closed up; my will's made; Blair is sure of poverty. Well; I guess I won't have you write to David to-day; I'm tired. When I'm out again, I'll tell Howe to draw up a paper telling him just what the duties of a trustee are.... Why don't you ... why don't you marry his mother, and be done with it? I hate to see a man and woman shilly-shally."

"She won't have me," he said, good-naturedly; in his anxiety he was willing to let her talk of anything, merely to amuse her.

"Well, she's a nice woman," Sarah Maitland said; "and a good woman; I was afraid *you* were doing the shilly-shallying. And any man who would hesitate to take her, isn't fit to black her boots. Friend Ferguson, I have a contempt for a man who is more particular than his Creator." Robert Ferguson wondered what she was driving at, but he would not bother her by a question.

"What was that I used to say about her?" the sick woman ruminated, with closed eyes; "'fair and—What was it? Forty? No, that wasn't it."

"Fifty," he suggested, smiling.

She shook her head peevishly. "No, that wasn't it. 'Fair, and, and'—what was it? It puts me out of patience to forget things! 'Fair and—*frail*!' That was it; frail! 'Fair and frail.'" She did not pause for her superintendent's gasp of protest. "Yes; first time I saw her, I thought there was a nigger in the woodpile. She won't marry you, friend Ferguson, because she has something on her conscience. Tell her I say not to be a fool. The best man going is none too good for her!"

Robert Ferguson's heart gave a violent plunge in his breast, but before his angry denial could reach her brain, her thought had wandered. "No! no! no! I won't go to bed. Bed is where people die." She got up from her chair, to walk about and show how well she was; but when she reached the center of the room she seemed to crumple up, sinking and sliding down on to the floor, her back against one of the carved legs of the table. Once there, she would not get up. She became so violently angry when they urged her to let them help her to her feet, that they were obliged to yield. "We will do more harm by irritating her," the doctor said, "than any good we could accomplish by putting her back to bed forcibly." So they put cushions behind her, and there she sat, staring with dim, expectant eyes at the dining room door; sometimes speaking with stoical endurance, intelligently enough; sometimes, when delirious, whimpering with the pain of that terrible arm, swollen now to a monstrous mass of agony.

Late in the afternoon she said she wanted to see '"that picture"; and Elizabeth knelt beside her, holding the little dark canvas so that she could look at it; she sat staring into it for a long time. "Mary didn't try to keep her baby from the cross," she said, suddenly; "well, I've done better than that; I brought the cross to my baby." Her face fell into wonderfully peaceful lines. Just at dusk she tried to sing.

"'Drink to me only with thine eyes'"

she quavered; "my boy sings that beautifully. I must give him a present. A check. I must give him a check."

But when Nannie said, eagerly, "Blair has written Elizabeth that he will be at home to-morrow; I'll tell him you want to see him; and oh, Mamma, won't you please be nice to him?"—she looked perfectly blank. Toward morning she sat silently for a whole hour sucking her thumb. When, abruptly, she came to herself and realized what she had been doing, the shamed color rose in her face. Nannie, kneeling at her side, caught at the flicker of intelligence to say, "Mamma, would you like to see the Rev. Mr. Gore? He is here; waiting in the parlor. Sha'n't I bring him in?"

Mrs. Maitland frowned. "What does he come for now? I'm sick. I can't see people. Besides, I sent him a check for Foreign Missions last month."

"Oh, Mamma!" Nannie said, brokenly, "he hasn't come for money; I—I sent for him."

Sarah Maitland's eyes suddenly opened; her mind cleared instantly. "Oh," she said; and then, slowly: "Um-m; I see." She seemed to meditate a moment; then she said, gravely: "No, my dear, no; I won't see little Gore. He's a good little man; a very good little man for missions and that sort of thing. But when it comes to *this*—" she paused; "I haven't time to see to him," she said, soberly. A minute later, noticing Nannie's tears, she tried to cheer her: "Come, come! don't be troubled," she said, smiling kindly, "I can paddle my own canoe, my dear." After that she was herself for nearly half an hour. Once she said. "My house is in order, friend Ferguson." Then she lost herself again. To those who watched her, huddled on the heap of cushions, mumbling and whimpering, or with a jerk righting her mind into stony endurance, she seemed like a great tower falling and crumbling in upon itself. At that last dreadful touch of decay, when she put her thumb in her mouth like a baby, her stepdaughter nearly fainted.

All that night the mists gathered, and thinned, and gathered again. In the morning, still lying on the floor, propped against all the pillows and cushions of the house, she suddenly looked with clear eyes at Nannie.

"Why!" she said, in her own voice, and frowning sharply, "that certificate of deposit! I got it from the Bank the day of the accident, but I haven't indorsed it! Lucky I've got it here in the house. Bring it to me. It's in the safe in my desk. Take my keys."

Nannie, who for the moment was alone with her, found the key, and opening the little iron door in the desk, brought the certificate and a pen dipped in ink; but even in those few moments of preparation, the mist had begun to settle again: "I told the cashier it was a present I was going to make," she chuckled to herself; "said *he'd* like to get a present like that. I reckon he would. Reckon anybody would." Her voice lapsed into incoherent murmurings, and Nannie had to speak to her twice before her eyes were intelligent again; then she took the pen and wrote, her lips faintly mumbling: "Pay to the order of—what's the date?" she said, dully, her eyes almost shut. "Never mind; I don't have to date it. But I was thinking: Blair gave me a calendar when he was a little boy. Blair—Blair—" And as she spoke his name, she wrote it: "*Blair Maitland.*" But just as she did so, her mind cleared, and she saw what she had written. "Blair Maitland?" she said, and smiled and shook her head. "Oh, I've written that name too many times. Too many times. Got the habit." She lifted her pen heavily, perhaps to draw it through the name, but her hand sagged.

"Aren't you going to sign it, Mamma?" Nannie asked, breathlessly; and her stepmother turned faintly surprised eyes upon her. Nannie, kneeling beside her, urged again: "Mamma, you want to give it to Blair! Try, do try—" But she did not hear her.

At noon that day, through the fogged and clogging senses, there was another outburst of the soul. They had been trying to give her some medicine, and each time she had refused it, moving her head back and side-wise, and clenching her teeth against the spoon. Over and over the stimulant was urged and forced upon her; when suddenly her eyes flashed open and she looked at them with the old power that had made people obey her all her life. The mind had been insulted by its body beyond endurance; she lifted her big right hand and struck the spoon from the doctor's fingers: "*I have the right to die.*"

Then the flame fluttered down again into the ashes.

When Blair reached the house that afternoon, she was unconscious. Once, at a stab of pain, she burst out crying with fretful wildness; and once she put her thumb into her mouth.

At six o'clock that night she died.

Chapter 28

When the doctor came to tell Nannie that Sarah Maitland was dead, he found her in the parlor, shivering up against her brother. Blair had come to his mother's house early that afternoon; a note from Elizabeth, awaiting him at the River House, had told him of the gravity of Mrs. Maitland's condition, and bidden him "come instantly." As he read it, his face grew tense. "Of course I must go," he said; but there was no softening in his eyes. In all these months, in which his mother's determination had shown no weakening, his anger had deepened into the bitterest animosity. Yet curiously enough, though he hated her more, he disliked her less. Perhaps because he thought of her as a Force rather than as a mother; a power he was fighting—force against force! And the mere sense of the grapple gave him a feeling of equality with her which he had never had. Or it may have been merely that his eyes and ears did not suffer constant offense from her peculiarities. He had not forgotten the squalor of the peculiarities, but they did not strike him daily in the face, so hate was not made poignant by disgust. But neither was it lessened by the possibility of her death.

"I wonder if she has changed her will?" he said to himself, with fierce curiosity. But whether she had done so or not, propriety demanded his presence in her house if she were dying. As for anything more than propriety,—well, if by destroying her iniquitous will she had showed proper maternal affection, he would show proper filial solicitude. It struck him, as he stepped into a carriage to drive down to Shanty town, that such an attitude of mind on his part was pathetic for them both. "She never cared for me," he thought; and he knew he had never cared for her. Yes, it was pathetic; if he could have had for a mother such a woman as—he frowned; he would not name David Richie's mother even in his thoughts. But if he could have had a gentle and gracious woman for a mother, how he would have loved her! He had always been motherless, he thought; it was not today which would make him so. Still, it was strangely shaking, this idea of her death. When Nannie came into the parlor to greet him, he was silent while she told him, shivering and crying, the story of the last two weeks.

"She hasn't been conscious since noon," she ended, "but she may call for you; and oh, if she does. Blair, you will be lovely to her, won't you?"

His grave silence seemed an assent.

"Will you go in and see her?" she said, weeping. But Blair, with the picture she had given him of that awful figure lying on the floor, shook his head.

"I will wait here.—I could not bear to see it," he added, shuddering.

"Elizabeth is with her," Nannie said, "so I'll stay a little while with you. I don't believe it will be before morning."

Now and then they spoke in whispers; but for the most part they were silent, listening to certain sinister sounds that came from the room across the hall.

It was a warm May twilight; above the gaunt outline of the foundry, the dim sickle of a young moon hung in a daffodil sky; the river, running black between banks of slag and cinders, caught the sheen of gold and was transfigured into glass mingled with fire. Through the open windows, the odor of white lilacs and the acrid sweetness of the blossoming plum-tree, floated into the room. The gas was not lighted; sometimes the pulsating flames, roaring out sidewise from under the half-shut dampers of the great chimneys, lighted the dusk with a red glare, and showed Blair's face set in new lines. He had never been so near the great Reality before; never been in a house where, on the threshold, Death was standing; his personal affairs, angers or anxieties, dropped out of his mind. So sitting and listening and not speaking, the doctor found them.

"She has gone," he said, solemnly. Nannie began to cry; Blair stood up, then walked to the window and looked out at the Yards. *Dead?* For a moment the word had no meaning. Then, abruptly, the old, elemental meaning struck him like a blow; that meaning which the animal in us knows, before we know the acquired meanings which grief and faith have put into the word: his mother "was not." It was incredible! He gasped as he stood at the window, looking out over the blossoming lilacs at the Works, black against a fading saffron sky. Ten minutes ago his mother was in the other room, owning those Works; now—? The sheer impossibility of imagining the cessation of such a personality filled him with an extraordinary dismay. He was conscious of a bewildered inability to believe what had been said to him.

Mr. Ferguson, who had been with Sarah Maitland when the end came, followed the doctor into the parlor; but neither he nor Blair remembered personalities. They stood together now, listening to what the doctor was saying; Blair, still dazed and unbelieving, put his arm round Nannie and said, "Don't cry, dear; Mr. Ferguson, tell her not to cry!" And the older man said, "Make her sit down, Blair; she looks a little white." Both of them had forgotten individual resentments or embarrassments.

When some people die, it is as if a candle flame were gently blown out; but when, on the other side of the hall, this big woman lay dead on the floor, it seemed to the people who stood by as if the whole machinery of life had stopped. It was so absorbing in its astonishment that everything else became simple. Even when Elizabeth entered, and came to put her arms around Nannie, Blair hardly noticed her. As the doctor and Robert Ferguson spoke together in low tones, of terrible things they called "arrangements," Sarah Maitland's son listened, and tried to make himself understand that they were talking of—his mother!

"I shall stay until everything has been done," Mr. Ferguson said, after the doctor left them. "Blair, you and Elizabeth will be here, of course, to-night? Or else I'll stay. Nannie mustn't be alone."

Blair nodded. "Of course," he said. At which Nannie, who had been crying softly to herself, suddenly looked up.

"I would rather be by myself. I don't want any one here. Please go home with Elizabeth, Blair. Please!"

"But Nannie dear, I want to stay," Blair began, gently; she interrupted him, almost hysterically:

"No! *Please!* It troubles me. I would rather you didn't. I—I want to be alone."

"Well," Blair said, vaguely; he was too dazed to protest.

Robert Ferguson yielded too, though with a little surprise at her vehemence. Then he turned to Blair; "I'll give you some telegrams that must be sent," he said, in the old friendly voice. It was only when he wrote a despatch to David's mother that the world was suddenly adjusted to its old levels of anger and contempt. "I'll send this myself," he said, coldly. Blair, with instant intuition, replied as coldly, "Oh, very well."

He and Elizabeth went back to the hotel in silence, each deeply shaken by the mere physical fact of death. When they reached the gloomy granite columns of the old River House, Blair left his wife, saying briefly something about "walking for a while." He wanted to be alone. This was not because he felt any lack of sympathy in Elizabeth; on the contrary, he was nearer to her than at any time since their marriage; but it was a moment that demanded solitude. So he wandered about Mercer's streets by himself until after midnight—down to the old covered bridge, past Mrs. Todd's ice-cream saloon, out into the country, where the wind was rising, and the tree-tops had begun to sway against the sky.

There is a bond, it appears, between mother and child which endures as long as they do. It is independent of love; reason cannot weaken it; hate cannot destroy it. When a man's mother dies, something in the man dies, too. Blair Maitland, walking aimlessly about in the windy May midnight, standing on the bridge watching the slipping twinkle of a star in the inky ripples below him, was vaguely conscious of this. He thought, with a reluctance that was almost repulsion, of her will. He did not want to think of it, it was not fitting! Yet he knew, back in his mind, that within a few days, as soon as decency permitted, he would take the necessary steps to contest it. Nor did he think definitely of her; certainly not of all the unbeautiful things about her, those acute, incessant trivialities of ugliness which had been a veil between them all his life. Now, the veil was rent, and behind it was a holy of holies,—the inviolable relation of the child and the mother. It was of this that he thought, inarticulately, as he stood on the bridge, listening to the rush of the wind; this, and the bare and unbelievable fact that she "was not." As he struggled to realize her death, he was aware of a curious uneasiness that was almost fright.

When he came to Nannie the next morning, he was still deeply absorbed; and when she put something into his hands and said it was from his mother, he suddenly wept.

* * * * *

They had respected Nannie's desire to be alone that night, but it was nearly twelve before she was really left to herself, and the house was silent. Robert Ferguson had made her go up-stairs to bed, and bidden the worn-out nurse sleep in the room next to her so that she would not be so entirely solitary. He himself did not go home until those soft and alien footsteps that cross our thresholds, and dare as business the offices that Love may not essay, had at last died away. Nannie, in her bedroom, sat wide-eyed, listening for those footsteps. Once she said to herself: "When *they* have gone—" and her heart pounded in her throat. At last "they" went; she heard the front door close; then, out in the street, another door banged softly; after that there was the sound of wheels.

"Now!" she said to herself. But still she did not move…. Was the nurse asleep? Was Harris up in his room in the garret? Was there any one downstairs—except Death? Death in Mrs. Maitland's bedroom. "For God's sake, *lock her door!*" Harris had said. And they locked it. We generally lock it. Heaven knows why! Why do we turn the key on that poor, broken, peaceful thing, as if it might storm out in the night, and carry us back with it into its own silence?

It was almost dawn—the high spring dawn that in May flushes even Mercer's skies at three o'clock in the morning, when, lamp in hand, Nannie Maitland opened her bedroom door and peered into the upper hall. Outside, the wind, which had begun to blow at sunset, was roaring around the old house; it rumbled in the chimneys, and a sudden gust tore at a loose shutter, and sent it banging back against the bricks. But in the house everything was still. The window over the front door was an arch of glimmering gray barred by the lines of the casement; but toward the well of the staircase there was nothing but darkness. Nannie put a hesitating foot across her own threshold, paused, then came gliding out into the hall; at the head of the stairs she looked down into a gulf of still blackness; the close, warm air of the house seemed to press against her face. She listened intently: no sound, except the muttering indifference of the wind about the house. Slowly, step by step, shivering and shrinking, she began to creep down-stairs. At the closed door of the dining-room—next to that other room which Harris had bidden them lock up; she stood for a long time, her fingers trembling on the knob; her lamp, shaking in her hand, cast a nimbus of light around her small gray figure. It seemed to her as if she could not turn that knob. Then, with gasp of effort, it was done, and she entered. Her first look was at that place on the floor, where for the last two days the pillows had been piled. The pillows were not there now; the room was in new, bleak order. Instantly, after that shrinking glance at the floor, she looked toward Mrs. Maitland's room, and her hand went to her throat as if she could not breathe. A moment afterward she began to creep across the floor, one terrified step dragging after another; she walked sidewise, always keeping her head turned toward that silent room. Just as she reached the big desk, the wind, sucking under the locked door, shook it with sly insinuation;—instantly she wheeled about, and stood, swaying with fright, her back against the desk. She stood there, panting, for a full minute. The terror of that furtively shaken door was agonizing. Then, very slowly, with a sidewise motion so that she could look toward the room, she put her lamp down on the top of the desk, and began, with constant bird-like glances over her shoulder, to search…. Yes; there it was! just where she herself had put it, slipped between the pages of a memorandum-book, so that if, in another gleam of consciousness, Blair's mother should ask for it, there need be no delay in getting it. When her fingers closed on it, she turned, swiftly, so that the room might not be behind her. Always watching the locked door, she groped for pen and ink and some sheets of paper, which she carried over to the table. Then she drew up a chair, folded back the sleeves of her wrapper, propped the memorandum-book—which had on the inside page the flowing signature of its owner—open before her. Then, slowly and steadily, she began to do the thing she had come to do. Instantly she was calmer. When a great gust of wind rumbled suddenly in the chimney, and a wraith of ashes blew out of the fireplace, she did not even raise her eyes; but once she looked over toward the room, and smiled, as if to say "It is all right. I am making it all right!"

It took her a long time, this business that would make it "all right," this business that brought her, a creature who all her life had been afraid of her own shadow, creeping down to the dining-room, creeping past the room into which Death had been locked, creeping over to the desk, to that unsigned indorsement which had been meant for Blair! It took a long time. Sheet after sheet of paper was scrawled over, held up beside the name in the notebook, then tossed into the empty grate. At last she did it:

Sarah Maitland

When she had finished, her relief, in having done what she could to carry out the purpose of the dying hand, was so great that she was able, without once looking over her shoulder, to put the pen and ink back into the desk and set a match to the papers in the fireplace. Indeed, as she took up her lamp to creep up-stairs again, she even stopped and touched the knob of the locked door with a sort of caress.

But when, with a last breathless rush across the upper hall, she regained her own room, she bolted her door with furious panic-stricken hands, then sank, almost fainting, upon her bed.

Chapter 29

The Maitland Works were still. High in the dusty gloom of the foundry, a finger of sunshine pointing down from a grimy window touched the cold lip of a cupola and traveled noiselessly over rows of empty molds upon the blackened floor. The cast-house was silent. The Yards were deserted. The pillar of fire was out; the pillar of smoke had faded away.

In the darkened parlor of her great house, Sarah Maitland was still, too. Lines of sunshine fell between the bowed shutters, and across them wavering motes swam noiselessly from gloom to gloom. The marble serenities of death were without sound; the beautiful, powerless hands were empty, even of the soft futility of flowers; some one had placed lilies-of-the-valley in them, but her son, with new, inarticulate appreciation, lifted them and took them away. The only sound that broke the dusky stillness of the room was the subdued brush of black garments, or an occasional sigh, or the rustle of a furtively turned page of a hymn-book. Except when, standing shoulder to shoulder in the hall, her business associates, with hats held decorously before whispering lips, spoke to each other of her power and her money,—who now had neither money nor power,— the house was profoundly still. Then, suddenly, from the head of the stairs, a Voice fell into the quietness:

"*Lord, let me know mine end and the number of my days, that I may be certified how long I have to live. When thou with rebukes dost chasten man for sin, thou makest his beauty to consume away, like as it were a moth fretting a garment: every man, therefore, is vanity. For man walketh in a vain show, and disquieteth—*" the engine of a passing freight coughed, and a cloud of smoke billowed against the windows; the strips of sunshine falling between the shutters were blotted out; came again—went again. Over and over the raucous running jolt of backing cars, the rattling bump of sudden breaks, swallowed up the voice, declaring the eternal silence: "... *glory of the celestial is one, and the glory of the terrestrial is ... of the sun, and another glory of the moon, for one star differeth from ... Dust to dust, ashes to ashes ...* "

Out in the street the shadow of her house fell across the meager dooryard, where, on its blackened stems, the pyrus japonica showed some scattered blood-red blossoms; it fell over Shantytown, that packed the sidewalk and stared from dingy doors and windows; it fell on her men, standing in unrebuked idleness, their lowered voices a mutter of energy held, for this waiting moment, in leash. A boy who had climbed up the lamp-post announced shrilly that "It" was coming. Some girls, pressing against the rusted iron spears of the fence, and sagging under the weight of babies almost as big as themselves, called across the street to their mothers, "Here she is!"

And so she came. No squalor of her surroundings could mar the pomp of her approach. The rumble of her men's voices ceased before it; Shantytown fell silent. Out from between the marble columns of her doorway, out from under the twisted garland of wistaria murmurous with bees, down the curving steps, along the path to the crowded, curious sidewalk, she came. Out of the turmoil and the hurry of her life, out of her triumphs and arrogances and ambitions, out of her careless generosities and her extraordinary successes, she came. And following her, with uncovered head, came the sign and symbol of her failure—her only son.

Up-stairs, in the front hall, standing a little back from the wide arched window, Nannie,—forbidden by the doctor, because of her fatigue, to go to the grave; and Elizabeth and Miss White, who would not leave her alone,—looked down on the slowly moving crowd. When Sarah Maitland's men closed in behind her, nearly a thousand strong, and the people in twos and threes began to file out of the house, Nannie noiselessly turned a slat of the Venetian blind. Why! there were those Maitlands from the North End. "I didn't suppose they remembered our existence," she said, her breath still catching in a sob; "and there are the Knights," she whispered to Elizabeth. "Do you see old Mrs. Knight? I don't believe she's been to call on Mamma for ten years. I never supposed she'd come."

Miss White, wiping her eyes as she peered furtively through the blinds, said in a whisper that there was So-and-so, and that such and such a person was evidently going out to the cemetery. "Mrs. Knight is dreadfully lame, isn't she?" Nannie said. "Poor Mamma always called her Goose Molly. It was nice in her to come, wasn't it?"

"Nannie," some one said, softly. And turning, she saw Mrs. Richie. "I came on last night, Nannie dear. She was a good, kind friend to me. And David is here, too. He hopes you will feel like seeing him. He was very fond of her." Then she looked at Elizabeth: "How do you do? How is Blair?" she said, calmly.

The moment was tense, yet of the four women, Elizabeth felt it least.

David was in the house! She could not feel anything else.

"Oh, Mrs. Richie—poor Mamma!" Nannie said; and with Mrs. Richie's kind arm about her, she retreated to her own room.

Miss White went hurrying down-stairs—Elizabeth knew why! As for her, she stood there in the empty hall, quite alone. She heard the carriage doors closing out in the street, the sound of horses' feet, the drag of wheels—even the subdued murmur of Shantytown looking on at the show.... David was in the house.

She went to the end of the hall and stood leaning over the banisters; she could hear Miss White's flurried voice; then, suddenly, he spoke. It was only some grave word,—she did not catch the sense of it, but the sound—the sound of his voice! It turned her dizzy. Before she knew it she sank down on the top step of the stairs, her head against the banisters. She sat there, her face haggard with unshed tears, until Mrs. Richie came out of Nannie's room and found her. It was then that David's mother, who thought she had done her best in the courteous commonplace of how-do-you-do—suddenly did better; she stooped down and kissed Elizabeth's cheek.

"You poor child!" she said; "oh, you *poor* child!" The pity of the slender, crouching figure touched even Helena Richie's heart,—that heart of passionate and resentful maternity; so she was able to kiss her, and say, with wet eyes, "poor child!"

Elizabeth could not speak. Later, when the mother and son had left the house, Miss White came upstairs and found her still sitting dumb and tearless, on the top step. She clutched at Cherry-pie's skirt with shaking hands: "Did he say—anything?"

"Oh, my poor lamb," old Miss White said, nibbling and crying, "how could he, *here?*"

David, coming with his mother over the mountains to be present at Mrs. Maitland's funeral, thought to himself how strange it was that it had taken death to bring him to Mercer. In all those long months of bewildered effort to adjust himself to the altered conditions of life, there had been an undercurrent of purpose: *he would see Elizabeth.* He would know from her own lips just how things were with her. It seemed to David that if he could do that, if he could know beyond doubt—or hope—that she was happy, he would himself be cured of the incessant, dull ache of remorse, which quickened sometimes into the stabbing suspicion that she had never really loved him. ... If she was happy, then he need no longer blame himself for injuring her. The injury he had done himself, he must bear, as men before him had borne, and as men after him would bear, the results of their own sins and follies. He had, of course, long since lost the wincing self-consciousness of the jilted man, just as he had lost the expectation that she would send for him, summon him to storm her prison and carry her away to freedom! That was a boy's thought, anyhow. It was when that hope had completely faded, that he began to say he must see for himself that she was happy and that she did not wish to leave the man who had, at any rate, been man enough to take her, and whom now, very likely, she loved. It was the uncertainty about her happiness that was so intolerable to him. Far more intolerable, he thought, than would be the knowledge that she was content, for that he would deserve, and to the honest mind there is a certain satisfaction in receiving its deserts. But his hatred of Blair deepened a little at the mere suggestion of her contentment. Those evil moments of suspecting her loyalty to him at the time of her marriage were very rare now; though the evil moments of speculating as to how God—or he himself, would finally punish Blair Maitland, were as frequent as ever. During the last six months the desire to know how things were with Elizabeth had been at times almost overwhelming. Once he went so far as to buy his railroad ticket; but though his feet carried him to the train, his mind drove him away from it, and the ticket was not used. But when the news came of Sarah Maitland's death, he went immediately to the station and engaged his berth. Then he went home and asked his mother if she were going to the funeral; "I am," he said. He spoke with affection of Mrs. Maitland, but so far as his going to Mercer went, her funeral was entirely incidental. Her death had ended his uncertainty: he would see Elizabeth!

"And when I see her," he said to himself, "the moment I see her,—I will know." He debated with himself whether he should speak of the catastrophe of their lives, or wait for her to do so. As he thought of putting it into words, he was aware of singular shyness, which showed him with startling distinctness how far apart he and she were. Just how and when he would see her he had not decided; probably it could not be on the day Mrs. Maitland was buried; but the next day? "How shall I manage it?" he asked himself—then found that it had been managed for him.

When they came back from the cemetery, Mrs. Richie went to Robert Ferguson's. "You are to come home and have supper with me," he had told her; "David can call for you when he gets through his gallivanting about the town." (David had excused himself, on the ground of seeing Knight and one or two of the fellows; he had said nothing of his need to walk alone over the old bridge, out into the country, and, in the darkness, round and round the River House.) So, in the May twilight of Robert Ferguson's garden, the two old neighbors paced up and down, and talked of Sarah Maitland.

"I've got to break to David that apparently he isn't going to get the fund for his hospital," Mr. Ferguson said. "There is no mention of it in her will. She told me once, about two years ago, that she was putting money by for him, and when she got the amount she wanted she was going to give it to him. But she left no memorandum of it. I'm afraid she changed her mind." His voice, rather than his words, caught her attention; he was not speaking naturally. He seemed to talk for the sake of talking, which was so unlike him that Mrs. Richie looked at him with mild curiosity. "Mrs. Maitland had a perfect right to change her mind," she said; "and really David never counted very much on the hospital. She spoke of it to him, I know, but I think he had almost forgotten it—though I hadn't," she confessed, a little ruefully. She smiled, and Robert Ferguson, fiercely twitching off his glasses, tried to smile back; but his troubled eyes lingered questioningly on her serene face. It was almost a beautiful face in its peace. What was it Mrs. Maitland had said about her looks? "Fair and—" He was so angry at remembering the word that he swore softly at himself under his breath, and Helena Richie gave him a surprised look. He had sworn at himself several times in these five days since Sarah Maitland, half delirious, wholly shrewd, had said those impossible things about David's mother. Under his concern and grief, under his solemn preoccupations, Robert Ferguson had felt again and again the shock of the incredible suggestion: "*something on her conscience.*" Each time the words thrust themselves up through his absorbed realization of Mrs. Maitland's death, he pushed them down savagely: "It is impossible!" But each time they rose again to the surface of his mind. When they did, they brought with them, as if dredged out of the depths of his memory, some sly indorsement of their truth... . She never says anything about her husband. "Why on earth should she? He was probably a bad egg; that friend of hers, that Old Chester doctor, hinted that he was a bad egg. Naturally he is not a pleasant subject of conversation for his wife." ... Her only friends, except in his own little circle, were two old men (one of them dead now), in Old Chester. "Well, Heaven knows a parson and a doctor are about as good friends as a woman can have." ... But no *women* friends belonging to her past. "Thank the Lord! If she had a lot of cackling females coming to see her, *I* wouldn't want to!" ... She is always so ready to defend Elizabeth's wicked mother.

"She has a tender heart; she's not hard like the rest of her sex."

No, Life had not played another trick on him! Mrs. Maitland was out of her head, that was all. As for him, somebody ought to boot him for even remembering what the poor soul had said. And so, disposing of the intolerable suspicion, he would draw a breath of relief—until the whisper came again: "*something on her conscience?*"

He was so goaded by this fancy of a dying woman, and at the same time so shaken by her death, that, as his guest was quick to see, he was entirely unreal; almost—if one can say such a thing of Robert Ferguson, artificial. He was artificial when he spoke of David and the money he was not to have; the fact was, he did not at that moment care, he said to himself, a hang about David, or his money either!

"You see," he said, as they came to the green door in the brick wall, and went into the other garden, "you see, your house is still empty?"

"Dear old house!" she said, smiling up at the shuttered windows.

He looked into her face, and its entire candor made him suddenly and sharply angry at Sarah Maitland. It was the old friendly anger, just as if she were not dead; and he found it curiously comforting. ("She ought to be ashamed of herself to have such an idea of Mrs. Richie. I'll tell her so—oh, Lord! what am I saying? Well, well; she was dying; she didn't know what she was talking about.") ... "We could pull down some partitions and make the two houses into one," he said, wistfully.

But she only laughed and shook her head. "I want to see if my white peony is going to blossom; come over to the stone seat."

"You always shut me up," he said, sulkily; and in his sulkiness he was more like himself than he had been for days. Sitting by her side on the bench under the hawthorn, he let her talk about her peony or anything else that seemed to her a safe subject; for himself, all he wanted was the comfort of looking into her comforting eyes, and telling himself that he insulted her when he even denied those poor, foolish, dying words. When a sudden soft shower drove them indoors to his library he came back with a sigh to Mrs. Maitland; but this time he was quite natural: "The queer part of it is, she hadn't changed her mind about David's money up to within two days of her death. She meant him to have it when she spoke to me of writing to him; and her mind was perfectly clear then; at least"—he frowned; "she did wander for a minute. She had a crazy idea—"

"What?" said Mrs. Richie, sympathetically.

"Nothing; she was wandering. But it was only for a minute, and except for that she was clear. When I urged her to make some provision for Blair, she was perfectly clear. Practically told me to mind my own business! Just like her," he said, sighing.

"It would have been a great deal of money," Mrs. Richie said; "probably David is better off without it." But he knew she was disappointed; and indeed, after supper, in his library, she admitted the disappointment frankly enough. "He has changed very much; his youth is all gone. He is more silent than ever. I had thought that perhaps the building of this hospital would bring him out of himself. You see, he blames himself for the whole thing."

"He is still bitter?"

"Oh, I'm afraid so. He very rarely speaks of it. But I can see that he blames himself always. I wish he would talk freely."

"He will one of these days. He'll blurt it out and then he'll begin to get over it. Don't stop him, and don't get excited, no matter what absurd things he says. He'll be better when he has emptied his heart. I was, you know, after I talked to you and told you that I'd been—jilted."

"I'm afraid it's gone too deep for that with David," she said, sadly.

"It couldn't go deeper than it did with me, and yet you—you taught me to forgive her. Yes, and to be glad, too; for if she hadn't thrown me over, I wouldn't have known you."

"Now *stop!*" Mrs. Richie said, with soft impatience.

"For a meek and mild looking person," said Robert Ferguson, twitching off his glasses, "you have the most infernally strong will. I hate obstinacy."

"Mr. Ferguson, be sensible. Don't talk—that way. Listen: David must see Elizabeth while he is here. This situation has got to become commonplace. I meant to go home to-morrow morning, but if you will ask us all to luncheon—"

"'Dinner'! We don't have your Philadelphia airs in Mercer."

"Well, 'dinner,'" she said, smiling; "we'll stay over and take the evening train.

"I won't ask Blair!"

"I hate obstinacy," Mrs. Richie told him, drolly. "Well, I am not so very anxious to see Blair myself. But I do want Elizabeth and David to meet. You see, David means to practise in Mercer—"

"What! Then you will come here to live? When will you come?"

"Next spring, I hope. And it is like coming home again. The promise of the hospital was a factor in his decision, but, even without it, I think he will want to settle in Mercer"; she paused and sighed.

Her old landlord did not notice the sigh. "I'll get the house in order for you right off!" he said, beaming. "I suppose you'll ask for all sorts of new-fangled things! A tenant is never satisfied." He was so happy that he barked and chuckled at the same time.

"I hope it's wise for him to come," Mrs. Richie said, anxiously; "I confess I don't feel quite easy about it, because— Elizabeth will be here; and though, of course, nobody is going to think of how things might have been, still, it will be painful for them both just at first. That's why I want you to invite us to dinner,—the sooner they meet, the sooner things will be commonplace."

"When a man has once been in love with a woman," Robert Ferguson said, putting on his glasses carefully, "he can hate her, but she can never be commonplace to him."

And before she knew it she said, impulsively, "Please don't ever hate me."

He laid a quick hand on hers that was resting in her lap. "I'll never hate you and you'll never be commonplace. Dear woman— can't you?"

She shook her head; the tears stood suddenly in her leaf-brown eyes.

"Helena!" he said, and there was a half-frightened violence in his voice; "*what* is it? Tell me, for Heaven's sake; what is it? Do you hate me?"

"No—no—no!"

"If you dislike me, say so! I think I could bear it better to believe you disliked me."

"Robert, how absurd you are! You know I could never dislike you. But our—our age, and David, and—"

He put an abrupt hand on her shoulder and looked hard into her eyes; then for a single minute he covered his own. "Don't talk about age, and all that nonsense. Don't talk about little things, Helena, for God's sake! Oh, my dear—" he said, brokenly. He got up and went across the room to a bookcase; he stood there a moment or two with his back to her. Helena Richie, bewildered, her eyes full of tears, looked after him in dismay. But when he took his chair again, he was "commonplace" enough, and when, later, David came in, he was able to talk in the most matter-of-fact way. He told the young man that evidently Mrs. Maitland had changed her mind about a hospital. "Of course some papers may turn up that will entitle you to your fund, but I confess I'm doubtful about it. I'm afraid she changed her mind."

"Probably she did," David said, laconically; "well, I am glad she thought of it,—even if she didn't do it. She was a big person, Mr. Ferguson; I didn't half know how big a person she was!" For a moment his face softened until his own preoccupations faded out of it.

"Nobody knew how big she was—except me," Robert Ferguson said. Then he began to talk about her.... It was nearly midnight when he ended; when he did, it was with an outburst of pain and grief: "Nobody understood her. They thought because she ran an iron-works, that she wasn't—a woman. I tell you she was! I tell you her heart was a woman's heart. She didn't care about fuss and feathers, and every other kind of tomfoolery, like all the rest of you, but she was as—as modest as a girl, and as sensitive. You needn't laugh—"

"Laugh?" said Helena Richie; "I am ready to cry when I think how her body misrepresented her soul!"

He nodded; his chin shook. "Big, generous, incapable of meanness, incapable of littleness!—and now she's dead. I believe her disappointment about Blair really killed her. It cut some spring. She has never been the same woman since he—" He stopped short, and looked at David; no one spoke.

Then Mrs. Richie asked some casual question about the Works, and they began to talk of other things. When his guests said good-night, Robert Ferguson, standing on his door-step, called after them: "Oh, hold on: David, won't you and your mother come in to dinner to-morrow? Luncheon, your mother calls it. She wants us to be fashionable in Mercer! Nobody here but Miss White and Elizabeth."

"Yes, thank you; we'll come with pleasure," Mrs. Richie called back, and felt the young man's arm grow rigid under her hand.

The mother and son walked on in silence. It had stopped raining, but the upper sky was full of fleecy clouds laid edge to edge like a celestial pavement; from between them sometimes a serene moon looked down.

"David, you don't mind staying over for a day?"

"Oh no, not at all. I meant to."

"And you don't mind—seeing Elizabeth?"

"I want to see her. Will he be there?"

"Blair? No! Certainly not. It wouldn't be pleasant for—for —"

"For him?" David said, dryly. "I should think not. Still, I am sorry. I have rather a curiosity to see Blair."

"Oh, David!" she protested, sadly.

"My dear mother, don't be alarmed. I have no intention of calling him out. I am merely interested to know how a sneak-thief looks when he meets—" he laughed; "the man he has robbed. However, it might not be pleasant for the rest of you."

His mother was silent; her plan of making things "commonplace" was not as simple as she thought.

Robert Ferguson, on his door-step, looked after them, his face falling abruptly into stern lines. When he went back to his library he stood perfectly still, his hands in his pockets, staring straight ahead of him. Once or twice his whole face quivered. Suddenly he struck his clenched fist hard on the table: "Well!" he said, aloud, violently, "what difference does it make?" He lit a cigar and sat down, his legs stretched out in front of him, his feet crossed. He sat there for an hour, biting on his extinguished cigar. Then he said in an unsteady voice, "She is a heavenly creature." The vigil in his library, which lasted until the dawn was white above Mercer's smoke, left Robert Ferguson shaken to the point of humility. He no longer combated Mrs. Maitland's wandering words; they did not matter. What mattered was the divine discovery that they did not matter! Or rather, that they opened his eyes to the glory of the human soul. To a man of his narrow and obstinate council of perfection, the realization, not only that it was possible to enter into holiness through the door of sin—that low door that bows the head that should be upright—but that his own possibilities of tenderness were wider than he knew,—such a realization was conversion. It was the recognition that in the matter of forgiveness he and his Father were one. Helena might or might not "have something on her conscience." If she had, then it proved that she in her humility was a better woman than, with nothing on his conscience, he in his arrogance was a man; and when he said that, he began to understand, with shame, that in regard to other people's wrong-doing he had always been, as Sarah Maitland expressed it, "more particular than his Creator." He thought of her words now, and his lean face reddened. "She hit me when she said that. I've always set up my own Ebenezer. What a fool I must have seemed to a woman like Helena.... . She's a heavenly creature!" he ended, brokenly; "what difference does it make how she became so? But if *that's* the only reason she keeps on refusing me—"

When Elizabeth and David met in Mr. Ferguson's library at noon the next day, everybody was, of course, elaborately unconscious.

Elizabeth came in last. As she entered, Miss White, nibbling speechlessly, was fussing with the fire-irons of a grate filled with white lilacs. Mrs. Richie, turning her back upon her son, began to talk entirely at random to Robert Ferguson, who was rapidly pulling out books from the bookcase at the farther end of the room. David was the only one who made no pretense. When he heard the front door close and knew that she was in the house, he stood staring at the library door. Elizabeth, entering, walked straight up to him, and put out her hand.

"How are you, David?" she said.

David, taking the small, cold hand in his, said, calmly, "How're you, Elizabeth?" Then their eyes met. Hers held steadfast; it was his which fell.

"Have you seen Nannie?" she said.

And he: "Yes; poor Nannie!"

"Hullo, Elizabeth," her uncle called out, carelessly; and Mrs. Richie came over and kissed her.

So that first terrible moment was lived through. During luncheon, they hardly spoke to each other. Elizabeth, with obvious effort, talked to Mrs. Richie of Nannie and Mrs. Maitland; David talked easily and (for him) a great deal, to Robert Ferguson; he talked politics, and disgusted his iron-manufacturing host by denouncing the tariff; he talked municipal affairs, and said that Mercer had a lot of private virtue, but no public morals. "Look at your streets!" said the squirt. In those days, the young man who criticized the existing order was a squirt; now he is a cad; but in the nostrils of middle age, he is as rankly unpleasant by one name as by the other. Elizabeth's uncle was so annoyed that he forgot the embarrassment of the occasion, and said, satirically, to Mrs. Richie: "Well, well! 'See how we apples swim'!" which made her laugh, but did not disturb David in the least. The moment luncheon was over, Elizabeth rose.

"I must go and see Nannie," she said; and David, opening the door for her, said, "I'll go along with you." At which their elders exchanged a startled look.

Out in the street they walked side by side—these two between whom there was a great gulf fixed. By that time the strain of the occasion had begun to show in Elizabeth's face; she was pale, and the tension of her set lips drew the old dimple into a livid line. David was apparently entirely at ease, speaking lightly of this or that; Elizabeth answered in monosyllables. Once, at a crossing, he laid an involuntary hand on her arm—but instantly lifted it as if the touch had burnt him! "Lookout!" he said, and for the first time his voice betrayed him. But before the clattering dray had passed, his taciturn self-control had returned: "you can hardly hear yourself think, in Mercer," he said. Elizabeth was silent; she had come to the end of effort.

It was not until they reached the iron gate of Mrs. Maitland's house that he dragged his quivering reality out of the inarticulate depths, but his brief words were flat and meaningless to the strained creature beside him.

"I was glad to see you to-day," he said.

And she, looking at him with hard eyes, said that it was very kind in him and in his mother to come on to Mrs. Maitland's funeral. "Nannie was so touched by it," she said. She could not say another word; not even good-by. She opened the gate and fled up the steps to the front door.

David, so abruptly deserted, stood for a full minute looking at the dark old house, where the wistaria looping above the pillared doorway was blossoming in wreaths of lavender and faint green.

Then he laughed aloud. "What a fool I am," he said.

Chapter 30

When Nannie Maitland, trembling very much, pressed into her brother's hand that certificate for what was, in those days, a very considerable fortune, Blair had been deeply moved. It came after a night, not of grief, to be sure, but of what might be called cosmic emotion,—the child's realization of the parent's death. When he saw the certificate, and knew that at the last moment his mother's ruthless purpose had flagged, her iron will had bent, a wave of something like tenderness rose above his hate as the tide rises above wrecking rocks. For a moment he thought that even if she had carried out her threat of disinheriting him he would be able to forgive her. But as inevitably the wave of feeling ebbed, and he saw again those black rocks of hate below the moving brightness of the tide, he reminded himself that this gift of hers was only a small part of what belonged to him. In a way it was even a confession that she had wronged him. She had written his name, Nannie told him with a curious tremor in her hands and face, "just at the last. It was that last morning," Nannie said, huskily, trying to keep her voice steady; "she hadn't time to change her will, but this shows she was sorry she made it."

"I don't know that that follows," Blair said, gravely. It was not until the next day that he referred to it again: "After all, Nannie, if her will is what she said it would be, it is—outrageous, you know. This money doesn't alter that."

Yet somehow, in those days before the funeral, whenever he thought of breaking the will, that relenting gift seemed to stay his hand. The idea of using her money to thwart her purpose, of taking what she had given him, from affection and a tardy sense of justice, to insult her memory, made him uncomfortable to the point of irritability. It was esthetically offensive. Once he sounded Elizabeth on the subject, and her agreeing outcry of disgust drove him into defending himself: "Of course we don't know yet what her will is; but if she has done what she threatened, it is abominable; and I'll break it—"

"With the money she gave you?" she said.

And he said, boldly, "Yes!"

But he was not really bold; he was perplexed and unhappy, for his hope that his mother had not disinherited him was based on something a little finer than his wish to come into his own; it was a real reluctance to do violence to a relationship of which he had first become conscious the night she died. But with that reluctance, was also the instinct of self-defense: "I have a right to her money!"

The day after the funeral he went to Mrs. Maitland's lawyers with a request to see the will.

"Certainly," the senior member of the firm said; "as you are a legatee a copy has already been prepared for you. I regret, Blair, that your mother took the course she did. I cannot help saying to you that we ventured to advise against it.

"I was aware of my mother's purpose," Blair said, briefly; and added, to himself, "she has done it! ... I shall probably contest the will," he said aloud.

Sarah Maitland's old friend and adviser looked at him sympathetically.

"No use, my boy; it's cast-iron. That was her own phrase, 'cast-iron.'"

Then, really sorry for him, he left him in the inner office so that he might read that ruthless document alone.

Mrs. Maitland had said it was a pity she could not live to see Blair fight her will; she "would like the fun of it." She would not have found any food for mirth if she could have seen her son in that law-office reading with set teeth, her opinion of himself, her realization of her responsibility in making him what he was, and her reason for leaving him merely a small income from a trust fund. Had it not been for the certificate—in itself a denial of her cruel words—lying at that moment in his breast pocket, he would have been unable to control his fury. As it was, underneath his anger was the consciousness that she had made what reparation she could.

When he folded the copy of the will and thrust it into his pocket his face was very pale, but he could not resist saying to old Mr. Howe as he passed him in the outer office, "I hope you will be pleased, sir, in view of your protest about this will, to know that my mother regretted her course toward me, and left a message to that effect with my sister."

"I am glad to hear it," the astonished lawyer said, "but— "

Blair did not wait to hear the end of his sentence. He said to himself that even before he made up his mind what to do about the will he must get possession of his money— "or the first thing I know some of their confounded legal quibbles will make trouble for me," he said.

Certainly there was no trouble for him as yet; the process of securing his mother's gift involved nothing more than the depositing of the certificate in his own bank. The cashier, who knew Sarah Maitland's name very well indeed on checks payable to her son, ventured to offer his condolences: "Your late mother was a very wonderful woman, Mr. Maitland. There was no better business man this side of the Alleghanies than your mother, sir."

Blair bowed; he was too absorbed to make any conventional reply. The will: should he or should he not contest it? His habit of indecision made the mere question—apart from its gravity—acutely painful; not even the probabilities of the result of such a contest helped him to decide what to do. The probabilities were grimly clear. Blair had, perhaps, a little less legal knowledge than the average layman, but even he could not fail to realize that Sarah Maitland's will was, as Mr. Howe had said, "iron." Even if it could be broken, it might take years of litigation to do it. "And a 'bird in the hand'!" Blair reminded himself cynically. "But," he told Nannie, a week or two later when she was repeating nervously, for the twentieth time, just how his mother had softened toward him,—"but those confounded orphan asylums make me mad! If she wanted orphans, what about you and me? Charity begins at home. I swear I'll contest the will!"

Nannie did not smile; she very rarely smiled now. Miss White thought she was grieving over her stepmother's death; and Elizabeth said, pityingly, "I didn't realize she was so fond of her." Perhaps Nannie did not realize it herself until she began to miss her stepmother's roughness, her arrogant generosity, her temper,—to miss, even, the mere violence of her presence; then she began to grieve softly to herself. "Oh, Mamma, I wish you hadn't died," she used to say, over and over, as she lay awake in the darkness. She lay awake a great deal in those first weeks.

All her life Nannie had been like a little leaf whirled along by a great gale of thundering power and purpose which she never attempted to understand, much less contend with; now, abruptly, the gale had dropped, and all her world was still. No wonder she lay awake at night to listen to such stillness! Apart from grief the mere shock of sudden quietness might account for her nervousness, Robert Ferguson said; but he was perplexed at her lack of interest in her own affairs. She seemed utterly unaware of the change in her circumstances. That she was a rich woman now was a matter of indifference to her. And she seemed equally unconscious of her freedom. Apparently it never occurred to her that she could alter her mode of life. Except that, at Blair's insistence, she had a maid, and that Harris had cleared the office paraphernalia from the dining-

362

room table, life in the stately, dirty, melancholy old house still ran in those iron grooves which Mrs. Maitland had laid down for herself nearly thirty years before. Nannie knew nothing better than the grooves, and seemed to desire nothing better. She was indifferent to her surroundings, and what was more remarkable, indifferent to Blair's perplexities; at any rate, she was of no assistance to him in making up his mind about the will. His vacillations hardly seemed to interest her. Once he said, suppose instead of contesting it, he should go to work? But she only said, vaguely, "That would be very nice."

Curiously enough, in the midst of his uncertainties, a little certainty had sprung up: it was the realization that work, merely as work, might be amusing. In these months of tormenting jealousy, of continually crushed hope that Elizabeth would begin to care for him, of occasional shamed consciousness of having taken advantage of a woman—Blair Maitland had had very little to amuse him. So, in those hesitating weeks that followed his mother's death, work, which her will necessitated, began to interest him. Perhaps the interest, if not the amusement, was enhanced by one or two legal opinions as to the possibility of breaking the will. Harry Knight read it, and grinned:

"Well, old man, as you wouldn't give me the case anyhow, I can afford to be perfectly disinterested and tell you the truth. In my opinion, it would put a lot of cash into some lawyer's pocket to contest this will; but I bet it would take a lot out of yours! You'd come out the small end of the horn, my boy."

But Knight was young, Blair reflected, and perhaps his opinion wasn't worth anything. "He's 'Goose Molly's' son," he said to himself, with a half-laugh; it was strange how easily he fell into his mother's speech sometimes! With a distrust of Harry Knight's youth as keen as her own might have been, Blair stated his case to a lawyer in another city.

"Before reading the will," said this gentleman, "let me inquire, sir, whether there is any doubt in your mind of your mother's mental capacity at the time the instrument was drawn?"

"My mother was Sarah Maitland, of the Maitland Works," said Blair, briefly; and the lawyer's involuntary exclamation of chagrin would have been laughable, if it had not been so significant. "But we should, of course, be glad to represent you, Mr. Maitland," he said. Blair, remembering Harry Knight's disinterested remark about pockets, said, dryly, "Thanks, very much," and took his departure. "He must think I'm Mr. Doestick's friend," he told himself. The old joke was his mother's way of avoiding an emphatic adjective when she especially felt the need of it; but he had forgotten that she had ever used it.

As he walked from the lawyer's office to his hotel, he was absorbed to the point of fatigue in his effort to make up his mind, but it was characteristic of him that even in his absorption he winced at the sight of a caged robin, sitting, moping on its perch, in front of a tobacconist's. He had passed the poor wild thing and walked a block, before he turned impulsively on his heel, and came back to interview the shopkeeper. "How much will you sell him for?" he said, with that charming manner that always made people eager to oblige him. The robin, looking at him with lack-luster eyes, sunk his poor little head down into his dulled feathers; there was something so familiar in the movement, that Blair cringed.

"I want to buy the little beggar," he said, so eagerly that the owner mentioned a preposterous price. Blair took the money out of his pocket, and the bird out of the cage. For a minute the captive hesitated, clinging with terrified claws to his rescuer's friendly finger. "Off with you, old fellow!" Blair said, tossing the bird up into the air; and the unused wings were spread! For a minute the eyes of the two men followed the joyous flight over the housetops; then the tobacconist grinned rather sheepishly: "Guess you've struck oil, ain't you?—or somebody's left you a fortune."

Blair chuckled. "Think so?" he said. But as he walked on down the street, he sighed; how dull the robin's eyes had been. Elizabeth's eyes looked like that sometimes. "What a donkey I am," he said to himself; "ten dollars! Well, I'll *have* to contest the will and get that fortune, or I can't keep up the liberator role!" Then he fell to thinking how he must invest what fortune he had—anything to get that confounded robin out of his head! "I'm not going to keep all my money in a stocking in the bank," he told himself. The idea of investment pleased him; and when he got back to Mercer he devoted himself to consultations with brokers. After some three months of it, he found the 'work,' as he called it, distinctly amusing. "It's mighty interesting," he told his wife once; "I really like it."

Elizabeth said, languidly, that she hoped he would go into business because it would have pleased his mother. Since Mrs. Maitland's death, Elizabeth had not seemed well; no one connected her languor with that speechless walk with David to Nannie's door, or her look into his eyes when she bade farewell to a hope that she had not known she was cherishing. But the experience had been a profound shock to her. His entire ease, his interest in other matters than the one matter of her life, and most of all his casual "glad to see you," meant that he had forgiven her, and so no longer loved her,—for of course, if he loved her he would not forgive her! In these two years she had told herself with perfect sincerity, a thousand times, that he had ceased to love her; but now it seemed to her that, for the first time, she really knew it. "He doesn't even hate me," she thought, bleakly. For sheer understanding of suffering she grew a little gentler to Blair; but her sympathy, although it gave him moments of hope, did not reach the point of helping him to decide what to do about the will. So, veering between the sobering reflection that litigation was probably useless, and the esthetically repulsive idea of using his mother's confession of regret to fight her, he reached no decision. Meantime, "investment" slipped easily into speculation,—speculation which, by that strange tempering of the wind that sometimes comes before the lamb is shorn, was remarkably successful.

It was gossip about this speculation that made Robert Ferguson prick up his ears: "Where in thunder does he get the money to monkey with the stock-market?" he said to himself; "he hasn't any securities to put up, and he can't borrow on his expectations any more,—everybody knows she cut him off with a shilling!" He was concerned as well as puzzled. "I'll have him on my hands yet," he thought, morosely. "Confound it! It's hard on me that she disinherited him. He'll be a millstone round my neck as long as he lives." Robert Ferguson had long ago made up his mind—with tenderness—that he must support Elizabeth, "but I won't supply that boy with money to gamble with! And if he goes on in this way, of course he'll come down on me for the butcher's bill." That was how he happened to ask Elizabeth about Blair's concerns. When he did, the whole matter came out. It was Sunday morning. Elizabeth, starting for church, had asked Blair, perfunctorily, if he were going. "Church?" he said—he was sitting at his writing-table, idly spinning a penny; "not I! I'm going to devote the Sabbath day to deciding about the will." She had made no comment, and his lip hardened. "She doesn't care what I do," he said to himself, gloomily; yet he believed she would be pleased if he refused to fight. "Heads or tails," he said, listening to her retreating step; "suppose I say 'heads, bird in the hand;—work. Tails, bird in the bush;—fight.' Might as well decide it this way if she won't help me."

She had never thought of helping him; instead she stopped at her uncle's and went out into the garden with him to watch him feed his pigeons. When that was over, they came back together to the library, and it was while she was standing at his big table buttoning her gloves that he asked her if Blair was speculating.

Yes; she believed he was. No; not with her money; that had been just about used up, anyhow; although he had paid it all back to her when he got his money. "Will you invest it for me, Uncle Robert?" she said.

"Of course; but mind," he barked, with the old, comfortable crossness, "you won't get any crazy ten per cent out of my investments! You'll have to go to Blair Maitland's wildcats for that. But if he isn't using your money, how on earth can he speculate? What do you mean by 'his' money?"

"Why," she explained, surprised, "he has all that money Mrs. Maitland gave him the day she died."

"What!"

"Didn't you know about the check?" she said; she had not mentioned it to him herself, partly because of their tacit avoidance of Blair's name, but also because she had taken it for granted that he was aware of what Mrs. Maitland had done. She told him of it now, adding, in a smothered voice, "She forgave him for marrying me, you see, at the end."

He was silent for a few moments, and Elizabeth, glancing at the clock, was turning to go, but he stopped her. "Hold on a minute. I don't understand this business. Tell me all about it, Elizabeth."

She told him what little she knew, rather vaguely: Mrs. Maitland had drawn a check—no: she believed it was called a bank certificate of deposit. It was for a great deal of money. When she told him how much, Robert Ferguson struck his fist on the arm of his chair. "That's it!" he said. "That is where David's money went!"

"*David's* money?" Elizabeth said, breathlessly.

"I see it now," he went on, angrily; "she had the money on hand; that's why she tried to write that letter. How Fate does get ahead of David every time!"

"Uncle! What do you mean?"

He told her, briefly, of Mrs. Maitland's plan. "She said two years ago that she was going to give David a lump sum. I didn't know she had got it salted down—she was pretty close-mouthed about some things; but I guess she had. Well, probably, at the last minute, she thought she had been hard on Blair, and decided to hand it over to him, instead of giving it to David. She had a right to, a perfect right to. But I don't understand it! The very day she spoke of writing to David, she told me she wouldn't leave Blair a cent. It isn't like her to whirl about that way—unless it was during one of those times when she wasn't herself. Well," he ended, sighing, "there is nothing to be done about it, of course; but I'll see Nannie, and get at the bottom of it, just for my own satisfaction."

Elizabeth's color came and went; she reminded herself that she must be fair to Blair; his mother had a right to show her forgiveness by leaving the money to him instead of David. Yes; she must remember that; she must be just to him. But even as she said so she ground her teeth together.

"Blair did not try to influence his mother, Uncle Robert," she said, "if that's what you are thinking of. He didn't see her while she was sick. He has never seen her since—since—" "There are other ways of influencing people than by seeing them. He wrote to Nannie, didn't he?"

"If I thought," Elizabeth said in a low voice, "that Blair had induced Nannie to influence Mrs. Maitland, I would—" But she did not finish her sentence. "Good-by, Uncle Robert. I'm going to see Nannie."

As she hurried down toward Shantytown through the Sunday emptiness of the hot streets, she said to herself that if Nannie had made her stepmother give the money to Blair, she, Elizabeth, would do something about it! "I won't have it!" she said, passionately.

It had been a long time since Elizabeth's face had been so vivid. The old sheet-lightning of anger began to flash faintly across it. She did not know what she would do to Nannie if Nannie had induced Mrs. Maitland to rob David, but she would do something! Yet when she reached the house, her purpose waited for a minute; Nannie's tremor of loneliness and perplexity was so pitifully in evidence that she could not burst into her own perplexity.

She had been trying, poor Nannie! to make up her mind about many small, crowding affairs incident to the situation. In these weeks since Mrs. Maitland's death, Nannie, for the first time in her life, found herself obliged to answer questions. Harris asked them: "You ain't a-goin' to be livin' here, Miss Nannie; 'tain't no use to fill the coal-cellar, is it?" Miss White asked them: "Your Mamma's clothes ought to be put in camphor, dear child, or else given away; which do you mean to do?" Blair asked them: "When will you move out of this terrible house, Nancy dear?" A dozen times a day she was asked to make up her mind, she whose mind had always been made up for her!

That hot Sunday morning when Elizabeth was hurrying down to Shantytown with the lightning flickering in her clouded eyes, Nannie, owing to Miss White's persistence about camphor, had gone into Mrs. Maitland's room to look over her things.

Oh, these "things"! These pitiful possessions that the helpless dead must needs leave to the shrinking disposal of those who are left! How well every mourner knows them, knows the ache of perplexity and dismay that comes with the very touch of them. It is not the valuables that make grief shrink,—they settle themselves; such-and-such books or jewels or pieces of silver belong obviously to this or that side of the family. But what about the dear, valueless, personal things that neither side of the family wants? Things treasured by the silent dead because of some association unknown, perhaps, to those who mourn. What about these precious, worthless things? Mrs. Maitland had no personal possessions of intrinsic value, but she had her treasures. There was a little calendar on her bureau; it was so old that Nannie could not remember when it had not been there hanging from the slender neck of a bottle of German cologne. She took it up now, and looked at the faded red crescents of the new moon; how long ago that moon had waxed and waned! "She loved it," Nannie said to herself, "because Blair gave it to her." Standing on the bureau was the row of his photographs; on each one his mother had written his age and the date when the picture had been taken. In the disorder of the top drawer, tumbled about among her coarse handkerchiefs, her collars, her Sunday black kid gloves, were relics of her son's babyhood: a little green morocco slipper, with a white china button on the ankle-band; a rubber rattle, cracked and crumbling.... What is one to do with things like these? Burn them, of course. There is nothing else that can be done. Yet the mourner shivers when the flame touches them, as though the cool fingers of the dead might feel the scorch! Poor, frightened Nannie was the last person who could light such a holy fire; she took them up—the slipper or the calendar, and put them down again. "Poor Mamma!" she said over and over. Then she saw a bunch of splinters tied together with one of Blair's old neckties; she held it in her hand for a minute before she realized that it was part of a broken cane. She did not know when or why it had been broken, but she knew it was Blair's, and her eyes smarted with tears. "Oh, how she loved him!" she thought, and drew a breath of satisfaction remembering how she had helped that speechless, dying love to express itself.

She was standing there before the open drawer, lifting things up, then putting them back again, unable to decide what to do with any of them, when Elizabeth suddenly burst in:

"Nannie!"

"Oh, I am so glad you've come!" Nannie said. She made a helpless gesture. "Elizabeth, what *shall* I do with everything?"

Elizabeth shook her head; the question which she had hurried down here to ask paused before such forlorn preoccupation.

"Of course her dresses Harris will give away—"

"Oh no!" Elizabeth interrupted, shrinking. "Don't give them to a servant."

"But," poor Nannie protested, "they are so dreadful, Elizabeth. Nobody can possibly wear them, except people like some of Harris's friends. But things like these—what would you do with these?" She held out a discolored pasteboard box broken at the corners and with no lid; a pair of onyx earrings lay in the faded blue cotton. "I never saw her wear them but once, and they are *so* ugly," Nannie mourned.

"Nannie," Elizabeth said, "I want to ask you something. That certificate Mrs. Maitland gave Blair: what made her give it to him?"

Nannie put the pasteboard box back in the drawer and turned sharply to face her sister-in-law, who was sitting on the edge of Mrs. Maitland's narrow iron bed; the scared attention of her eyes banished their vagueness. "What made her give it to him? Why, love, of course! Don't you suppose Mamma loved Blair better than anybody in the world, even if he did—displease her?"

"Uncle thinks you may have influenced her to give it to him."

"I did not!"

"Did you suggest it to her, Nannie?"

"I asked her once, while she was ill, wouldn't she please be nice to
Blair,—if you call that suggesting! As for the certificate, that last morning she sort of woke up, and told me to bring it to her to sign. And I did."

She turned back to the bureau, and put an unsteady hand down into the drawer. The color was rising in her face, and a muscle in her cheek twitched painfully.

"But Nannie," Elizabeth said, and paused; the dining-room door had opened, and Robert Ferguson was standing on the threshold of Mrs. Maitland's room looking in at the two girls. The astonishment he had felt in his talk with his niece had deepened into perplexity. "I guess I'll thresh this thing out now," he said to himself, and picked up his hat. He was hardly ten minutes behind Elizabeth in her walk down to the Maitland house.

"Nannie," he said, kindly,—he never barked at Nannie; "can you spare time, my dear, to tell me one or two things I want to know?" He had come in, and found a dusty wooden chair. "Go ahead with your sorting things out. You can answer my question in a minute; it's about that certificate your mother gave Blair."

Nannie had turned, and was standing with her hands behind her gripping the edge of the bureau; she gasped once or twice, and glanced first at one inquisitor and then at the other; her face whitened slowly. She was like some frightened creature at bay; indeed her agitation was so marked that Robert Ferguson's perplexity hardened into something like suspicion. "Can there be anything wrong?" he asked himself in consternation. "You see, Nannie," he explained, gently, "I happen to know that your mother meant it for David Richie, not Blair."

"If she did," said Nannie, "she changed her mind." "When did she change her mind?"

"I don't know. She just told me to bring the check to her to sign, that—that last morning."

"Was she perfectly clear mentally?"

"Yes. Yes. Of course she was! Perfectly clear."

"Did she say why she had changed her mind?"

"No," Nannie said, and suddenly fright and anger together made her fluent; "but why shouldn't she change her mind, Mr. Ferguson? Isn't Blair her son? Her only son! What was David to Mamma? Would you have her give all that money to an outsider, and leave her only son penniless? Perhaps she changed her mind that morning. I don't know anything about it. I don't see what difference it makes when she changed it, so long as she changed it. All I can tell you is that she told me to bring her the check, or certificate, or whatever you call it, out of the little safe. And I did, and she made it out to Blair. I didn't ask her to. I didn't even know she had it; but I am thankful she did it!"

Her eyes were dilating; she put her shaking hand up to her throat, as if she were struggling for breath. Her statement was perfectly reasonable and probable, yet it left no doubt in Robert Ferguson's mind that there was something wrong,—very wrong! Even Elizabeth could see it. They both had the same thought: Blair had in some way influenced, perhaps even coerced his mother. How, they could not imagine, but Nannie evidently knew. They looked at each other in dismay. Then Elizabeth sprang up and put her arms around her sister-in-law. "Oh, Uncle," she said, "don't ask her anything more now!" She felt the quiver through all the terrified little figure.

"Mamma wanted Blair to have the money; it's his! No one can take it from him!"

"Nobody wants to, Nannie, if it is his honestly," Robert Ferguson said, gravely.

"*Honestly*?" Nannie whispered, with dry lips.

"Nannie dear, tell us the truth," Elizabeth implored her; "Uncle won't be hard on Blair, if—if he has done wrong. I know he won't."

"Wrong?" said Nannie; "Blair done wrong?" She pushed

Elizabeth's arms away; "Blair has never done wrong in his life!" She stood there, with her back against the bureau, and dared them. "I won't have you suspect my brother! Elizabeth! How can you let Mr. Ferguson suspect Blair?"

"Nannie," said Robert Ferguson, "was Blair with his mother when she signed that certificate?"

"No."

"Were you alone with her?"

Silence.

"Answer me, Nannie."

She looked at him with wild eyes, but she said nothing. Mr. Ferguson put his hand on her shoulder. "Nannie," he said, quietly, "Blair signed it; Blair wrote his mother's name."

"No! No! No! He did not! He did not." There was something in her voice—a sort of relief, a sort of triumph, even, that the other two could not understand, but which made them know that she was speaking the truth. "He did not," Nannie said, in a whisper; "if you accuse him of that, I'll have to tell you; though very likely you won't understand. I did it. For Mamma."

"Did *what*?" Robert Ferguson gasped; "not—? You don't mean—? Nannie! you don't mean that you—" he stopped; his lips formed a word which he would not utter.

"Mamma wanted him to have the money. The day before she died she told me she was going to give him a present. That day, that last day, she told me to get the check. And she wrote his name on it. No one asked her to. Not Blair. Not I. I never thought of such a thing! I didn't even know there was a check. She wanted to do it. She wrote his name. And then—she got weak; she couldn't go on. She couldn't sign it. So I signed it for her…later. It was not wrong. It was right. It carried out her wish. I am glad I did it."

Chapter 31

It was not a confession; it was a statement. In the next distressing hour, during which Robert Ferguson succeeded in drawing the facts from Blair's sister, there was not the slightest consciousness of wrong-doing. Over and over, with soft stubbornness, she asserted her conviction: "It was right to do it. Mamma wanted to give the money to Blair. But she couldn't write her name. So I wrote it for her. It was right to do it."

"Nannie," her old friend said, in despair, "don't you know what the law calls it, when one person imitates another person's handwriting for such a purpose."

"You can call it anything you want to," she said, passionately. "*I* call it carrying out Mamma's wishes. And I would do it over again this minute."

Robert Ferguson was speechless with dismay. To find rigidity in this meek mind, was as if, through layers of velvet, through fold on fold of yielding dullness that gave at the slightest touch, he had suddenly, at some deeper pressure, felt, under the velvet, granite!

"It was right," Nannie said, fiercely, trembling all over, "it was right, because it was necessary. Oh, what do your laws amount to, when it comes to dying? When it comes to a time like that! She was *dying*—you don't seem to understand—Mamma was dying! And she wanted Blair to have that money; and just because she hadn't the strength to write her name, you would let her wish fail. Of course I wrote it for her! Yes; I know what you call it. But what do I care what it is called, if I carried out her wish and gave Blair the money she wanted him to have? Now he has got it, and nobody can take it away from him."

"My dear child, if he kept it, it would be stealing."

"You can't steal from your mother," Nannie said; "Mamma would be the first one to say so!"

Mr. Ferguson looked over at his niece and shook his head; how were they to make her understand? "He can't keep it, Nannie. When he understands that it isn't his, he will simply give it back to the estate, and then it will come to you."

"To me?" she said, astounded. And he explained that she was her stepmother's residuary legatee. She looked blank, and he told her the meaning of the term.

"The estate is going to meet the bequests with a fair balance; and as that balance will come to you, this money you gave to Blair will be yours, too."

She had been standing, with Elizabeth's pitying arms about her; but at the shock of his explanation she seemed to collapse. She sank down in a chair, panting. "It wasn't necessary! I could have just given it to him."

Later, when Robert Ferguson was walking home with his niece, he, too, said, grimly: "No; it 'wasn't necessary,' as she says, poor child! She could have given it to him; just as she will give it to him, now. Well, well, to think of that mouse, Nannie, upsetting the lion's plans!"

Elizabeth was silent.

"What I can't understand," he ruminated, "is how that signature could pass at the bank; a girl like Nannie able to copy a signature so that a bank wouldn't detect it!"

"She has always copied Mrs. Maitland's writing," Elizabeth said; "that last week Mrs. Maitland said she could not tell the difference herself."

Robert Ferguson looked perfectly incredulous. "It's astounding!" he said; "and it would be impossible,—if it hadn't happened. Well, come along home with me, Elizabeth. I think I'd better tell you just how the matter stands, so that you can explain it to Blair. I don't care to see him myself—if I can help it. But in the matter of transferring the money to the estate, we must keep Nannie's name out of it, and I want you to tell him how he and I must patch it up."

"When he returns it, I suppose the executors will give it at once to

David?" she said.

"Of course not. It will belong to the estate. Women have no financial moral sense!"

"Oh!" Elizabeth said; and pondered.

Just as he was pulling out his latch-key to open his front door, she spoke again: "If Nannie gives it back to him, Blair will have to send it to David, won't he?"

"I can't go into Mr. Blair Maitland's ideals of honor," her uncle said, dryly. "Legally, if Nannie chooses to make him a gift, he has a right to keep it."

She made no reply. She sat down at the library table opposite him, and listened without comment to the information which he desired her to convey to Blair. But long before she got back to the hotel, Blair had had the information.

Nannie, left to herself after that distressing interview, sat in the dusty desolation of Mrs. Maitland's room, her face hidden in her hands. *She needn't have done it.* That was her first clear thought. The strain of that dreadful hour alone in the dining-room, with Death behind the locked door, had been unnecessary! As she realized how unnecessary, she felt a resentment that was almost anger at such a waste of pain. Then into the resentment crept a little fright. Mr. Ferguson's words about wrong-doing began to have meaning. "Of course it was against the law," she told herself, "but it was not wrong, —there is a difference." It was incredible to her that Mr. Ferguson did not see the difference. "Mamma wouldn't have let him speak so to me, if she'd been here," she thought, and her lip trembled; "oh, I wish she hadn't died," she said; and cried softly for a minute or two. Then it occurred to her that she had better go to the River House and tell her brother the whole story. "If Mr. Ferguson is angry about it perhaps Blair had better pay the money back right off; of course I'll give it to him the minute it comes to me; but he will know what to do now."

She ran up-stairs to her own room, and began to dress to go out, but she was so nervous that her fingers were all thumbs; "I don't want Elizabeth to tell him," she said to herself; and tried to hurry, dropping her hat-pin and mislaying her gloves; "oh, where is my veil!" she said, frantically.

She was just leaving her room when she heard Blair's voice in the lower hall: "Nancy! Where are you?"

"I'm coming," she called back; and came running down-stairs. "Oh, Blair dear," she said, "I want to see you so much!" By that time she was on the verge of tears, and the flush of worry in her cheeks made her so pretty that her brother looked at her appreciatively.

"Black is mighty becoming to you, Nancy. Nannie dear, I have something to tell you. Come into the parlor!" His voice, as he put his arm around her and drew her into the room, had a ring in it which, in spite of her preoccupation, caught her attention. "Sit down!" he commanded; and then, standing in front of her, his handsome face alert, he told her that he was not going to contest his mother's will. "I pitched up a penny," he said, gaily; "I was sick and tired of the uncertainty. 'Heads, I fight; tails, I cave.' It came down tails," he said, with a half-sheepish laugh. "Well, it will please Elizabeth if I don't fight. I'll go into business. I can get a partnership in Haines's office. He is a stockbroker, you know."

Nannie's attention flagged; in the nature of things she could not understand how important this decision was, so she was not disturbed that it should have been made by the flip of a penny. Blair was apt to rely upon chance to make up his mind for him, and in regard to the will, heads or tails was as good a chance as any. In her own preoccupation, she had not realized that he had reached the reluctant conviction that in any effort to break the will, the legal odds would be against him. But if she had realized it she would have known that the probable hopelessness of litigation would not have helped him much in reaching a decision, so the penny judgment would not have surprised her. Blair, as he told her about it, was in great spirits. He had been entirely sincere in his reluctance to take any step which might indicate contempt for his mother's late (if adequate) repentance; so now, though a little rueful about the money, he was distinctly relieved that his taste was not going to be sentimentally offended. He meant to live on what his mother had given him until he made a fortune for himself. For he was going to make a fortune! He was going to stand on his own legs. He was going to buy Elizabeth's interest in him and his affairs, buy even her admiration by making this sacrifice of not fighting for his rights! He was full of the fervor of it all as he stood there telling his sister of his decision. When he had finished, he waited for her outburst of approval.

But she only nodded nervously; "Blair, Mr. Ferguson says you've got to give back that money; Mamma's check, you know?"

"*What?*" Blair said; he was standing by the piano, and as he spoke he struck a crashing octave; "what on earth do you mean?"

"Well, he—I—" It had not occurred to Nannie that it would be difficult to tell Blair, but suddenly it seemed impossible. "You see, Mamma didn't exactly—sign the check."

"What are you talking about?" Blair said, suddenly attentive.

"She wanted you to have the money," Nannie began, faintly.

"Of course she did; but what do you mean about not signing the check 'exactly'?" In his bewilderment, which was not yet alarm, he put his arm around her, laughing: "Nancy, what is all this stuff?"

"I did for her," Nannie said.

"Did what?"

"Signed it."

"Nannie, I don't understand you; do you mean that mother made you indorse that certificate? Nancy, do try to be clear!" He was uneasy now; perhaps some ridiculous legal complication had arisen. "Some of their everlasting red tape! Fortunately, I've got the money all right," he said to himself, dryly.

"She wrote the first part of it," Nannie began, stammering with the difficulty of explaining what had seemed so simple; "but she hadn't the strength to sign her name, so I—did it for her."

Her brother looked at her aghast. "Did she tell you to?"

"No; she ... was dead."

"Good God!" he said. The shock of it made him feel faint. He sat down, too dumfounded for speech.

"I had to, you see," Nannie explained, breathlessly; she was very much frightened, far more frightened than when she had told Mr. Ferguson. "I had to, because—because Mamma couldn't. She was ... not alive."

Blair suddenly put his hands over his face. "You forged mother's name!"

His consternation was like a blow; she cringed away from it: "No; I—just wrote it."

"*Nannie!*"

"Somebody had to," she insisted, faintly.

Blair sprang to his feet and began to pace up and down the room. "This is awful. I haven't a cent!"

"Oh," she said, with a gasp, "as far as that goes it doesn't make any difference, except about time. Mr. Ferguson said it didn't make any difference. I'll give it all back to you as soon as I get it. Only you'll have to give it back first."

"Nannie," he said, "for Heaven's sake, tell me *straight*, the whole thing."

She told him as well as she could; speaking with that minute elaboration of the unimportant so characteristic of minds like hers and so maddening to the listener. Blair, in a fury of anxiety, tried not to interrupt, but when she reached Mr. Ferguson's assertion that the certificate had been meant for David Richie, the worried color suddenly dropped out of his face.

"For—*him?* Nannie!"

"No, oh no! It wasn't for David, except just at first—before— not when—" She was perfectly incoherent, "Let me tell you," she besought him.

"If I thought she had meant it for him, I would send it to him before night! Tell me everything," he said, passionately.

"I'm trying to," Nannie stammered, "but you—you keep interrupting me. I'll tell you how it was, if you'll just let me, and not keep interrupting. Perhaps she did plan to give it to David. Mr. Ferguson said she planned to more than two years ago. And even when she was sick Mr. Ferguson thinks she still meant to."

"I'll fight that damned will to my last breath!" he burst out. Following the recoil of disgust at the idea of taking anything —"anything *else*"—that belonged to David Richie, came the shock of feeling that he had been tricked into the sentimentality of forgiveness. "I'll break that will if I take it through every court in the land!"

"But Blair! Mamma *didn't* mean it for him at the last. Don't you see? Oh, Blair, listen! Don't be so—terrible; you frighten me," Nannie said, squeezing her hands hard together in the effort to keep from crying. "Listen: she told me on Wednesday, the day before she died, that she wanted to give you a present. She said, 'I must give him a check.' You see, she was beginning to realize how wrong her will was; but of course she didn't know she was going to die or she would have changed it."

"That doesn't follow," Blair said.

"Then came the last day"—Nannie could not keep the tears back any longer; "the last day; but it was too late to do anything about the will. Why, she could hardly speak, it was so near the—the end. And then all of a sudden she remembered that certificate. And she opened her eyes and looked at me with such relief, as if she said to herself, 'I can give him that!' And she told me to bring it to her. And she kept saying, 'Blair—Blair—Blair.' And oh, it was pitiful to see her *hurry* so to write your name! And then she wrote it; but before she could sign her name, her hand sort of—fell. And she tried so hard to raise it so she could sign it; but she couldn't. And she kept muttering that she *had* written it 'many times, many times'; I couldn't just hear what she said; she sort of—mumbled, you know. Oh, it was dreadful!"

"And then?" Blair said, breathlessly. Nannie was speechless.

"Then?" he insisted, trembling.

"Then … she died," Nannie whispered.

"But the signature! The signature! How—"

"In the night, I—" She stopped; terror spread over her face as wind spreads over a pool. "In the night, at three o'clock, I came down-stairs and—" She stopped, panting for breath. He put his arm around her soothingly.

"Try and tell me, dear. I didn't mean to be savage." His face had relaxed. Of course it was dreadful, this thing Nannie had done; but it was not so dreadful as the thought that he had taken money intended for David Richie. When he had quieted her, and she was able to speak again, she told him just what she had done there in the dining-room at three o'clock in the morning.

"But didn't you know it was wrong?" he said; "that it was a criminal offense!" He could not keep the dismay out of his voice.

"I did it for Mamma's sake and yours," she said, quailing.

"Well," he said, and in his relief at knowing that he need not think of David Richie, he was almost gay—"well, you mustn't tell any one else your motive for committing a—" Nannie suddenly burst out crying. "Mamma wouldn't say that to me," she said, "Mamma was never cross to me in her whole life! But you and Mr. Ferguson —" she could not go on, for tears. He was instantly contrite and tender; but even as he tried to comfort her, he frowned; of course in the end he would suffer no loss, but the immediate situation was delicate and troublesome. "I'll have to go and see Mr. Ferguson, I suppose," he said. "You mustn't speak of it to any one, dear; things really might get serious, if anybody but Mr. Ferguson knew about it. Don't tell a soul; promise me?"

She promised, and Blair left her very soberly. The matter of the money was comparatively unimportant; it was his, subject only to the formality of its transfer to the estate. But that David Richie should have been connected even indirectly with his personal affairs was exquisitely offensive to him—and Elizabeth knew about it! "She's probably sitting there by the window, looking like that robin, and thinking about him," he said to himself angrily, as he hurried back to the River House. There seemed to be no escape from David Richie. "I feel like a dog with a dead hen hanging round his neck," he said to himself, in grimly humorous disgust; "I can't get away from him!"

He found his wife in their parlor at the hotel, but she was not in that listless attitude that he had grown to expect,—huddled in a chair, her chin in her hand, her eyes watching the slow roll of the river. Instead she was alert.

"Blair!" she said, almost before he had closed the door behind him; "I have something to tell you."

"I know about it," he said, gravely; "I have seen Nannie."

Elizabeth looked at him in silence.

"Would you have supposed that Nannie, *Nannie*, of all people! would have had the courage to do such a thing?" he said, nervously; it occurred to him that if he could keep the conversation on Nannie's act, perhaps that—that name could be avoided. "Think of the mere courage of it, to say nothing of its criminality."

"She didn't know she was doing wrong."

"No; of course not. But it's a mighty unpleasant matter."

"Uncle says it can be arranged so that her name needn't come into it."

"Of course," he agreed.

Elizabeth did not speak, but the look in her eyes was a demand.

"It's going to be rather tough for us, to wait until she hands it over to me," Blair said.

"To *you*?"

The moment had come! He came and knelt beside her, and kissed her; she did not repulse him. She continued to look at him steadily. Then very gently, she said, "And when Nannie gives it to you, what will you do with it?"

Blair drew in his breath as if bracing himself for a struggle. Then he got on his feet, pulled up one of the big, plush-covered arm-chairs, took out his cigarette-case, and struck a match. His hand shook. "Do with it? Why, invest it. I am going into business, Elizabeth. I decided to this morning. If you would care to know why I have given up the idea of contesting the will, I'll tell you. I don't want to bore you," he ended, wistfully. Apparently she did not hear him.

"Did Nannie tell you that that money was meant for a hospital?"

Blair sat up straight, and the match, burning slowly, scorched his fingers. He threw it down with an exclamation; his face was red with his effort to speak quietly. "She told me of your uncle's misunderstanding of the situation. There is no possible doubt that my mother meant the money for me. If I thought otherwise—"

"If you will talk to Uncle Robert, you will think otherwise."

"Of course I'll go and see Mr. Ferguson; I shall have to, to arrange about the transfer of the money to the estate, so that it can come back to me through the legitimate channel of a gift from Nannie; in other words, she will carry out my mother's purpose legally, instead—poor old Nannie! of carrying it out criminally, as she tried to do. But I won't go to your uncle to discuss my mother's purpose, Elizabeth. I am perfectly satisfied that she meant to give me that money."

She was silent.

"Of course," he went on, "I will hear what Mr. Ferguson has to say about this idea of his—and yours, too, apparently," he ended, bitterly.

"Yes," she said, "and mine." The words seemed to tingle as she spoke them.

"Oh, Elizabeth!" he cried, "aren't you ever going to care for me? You actually think me capable of keeping money intended for— some one else!"

His indignation was too honest to be ignored. "I suppose that you believe it is yours," she said with an effort; "but you believe it because you don't know the facts. When you see Uncle Robert, you will not believe it." And with that meager acknowledgment of his honesty he had to be content.

They did not speak of it again during that long dull Sunday

afternoon, but each knew that the other thought of nothing else. The red September sun was sinking into a smoky haze on the other side of the river, when Blair suddenly took up his hat and went out. It had occurred to him that if he could correct Robert Ferguson's misapprehension, Elizabeth would correct hers. He would not wait for business hours to clear himself in her eyes; he would go and see her uncle at once. It was dusk when he pushed into Mr. Ferguson's library, almost in advance of the servant who announced him: "Mr. Ferguson!" he said peremptorily; "Nannie has told me. And Elizabeth gave me your message. I have come to say that the transfer shall be made at once. My one wish is that Nannie's name may not be connected with it in any possible way—of course she is as innocent as a child."

"It can be arranged easily enough," the older man said; he did not rise from his desk, or offer his hand.

"But," Blair burst out, "what I came especially to say was that I hear you are under the impression that my mother did not, at the end, mean me to have that money?"

"I am under that impression. But," Robert Ferguson added, contemptuously, "you need not be too upset. Nannie will give it back to you."

"I am not in the least upset!" Blair retorted; "but whether I'm upset or not, is not the question. The question is, did my mother change her mind about her will, and try to make up for it in this way? I believe, from all that I know now, that she did. But I have come to ask you whether there is anything that I don't know; anything Nannie hasn't told me, or that she doesn't understand, which leads you to feel as you do?"

"You had better sit down."

"If it was just Nannie's idea, I will break the will!"

"You had better sit down," Mr. Ferguson repeated, coldly,

"and I'll tell you the whole business."

Blair sat down; his hat, which he had forgotten to take off, was on the back of his head; he leaned forward, his fingers white on a cane swinging between his knees; he did not look at Elizabeth's uncle, but his eyes showed that he did not lose a word he said. At the end of the statement—brief, fair, spoken without passion or apparent prejudice—the tension relaxed and his face cleared; he drew a great breath of relief.

"It seems to me," Robert Ferguson ended, "that there can be no doubt of your mother's intention."

"I agree with you," Blair said, triumphantly, "there is no possible doubt! She called for the certificate and wrote my name on it. What more do you want than that to prove her intention?"

"You have a right to your opinion," Mr. Ferguson said, "and I have a right to mine. I cannot see that either opinion affects the situation. You will, as a matter of common honesty, return this money to the estate. What Nannie will ultimately do with it, is not my affair. It is between you and her. I can't see that we need discuss the matter further." He took up his pen with a gesture of dismissal.

Blair's face reddened as if it had been slapped, but he did not rise. "I want you to know, sir, that while my sister's act is, of course, entirely indefensible, and I shall immediately return the money which she tried to secure for me, I shall, nevertheless, allow her to give it back to me, because it is my conviction that, by my dying mother's wish, it belongs to me; not to—to any one else."

"Your convictions have always served your wishes. I will bid you good-evening." For an instant Blair hesitated; then, still scarlet with anger, took his departure. Mr. Ferguson's belief that he was capable of keeping money intended for—for any one else, was an insult; "an abominable insult!" he told himself. And it was Elizabeth's belief, too! He drew in his breath in a groan. "She thinks

I am dishonorable," he said. Well, certainly that sneak, Richie, would feel he was avenged if he could know how cruel she was; "damn him," Blair said, softly.

He thought to himself that he could not go back and tell Elizabeth what her uncle had said; he could not repeat the insult! Some time, when he was calmer, he would tell her quietly that he had been wronged, that she herself had wronged him. But just now he could not talk to her; he was too angry and too miserable.

So, walking slowly in the foggy dusk that was pungent with the smoke of bonfires on the flats, he suddenly wheeled about and went in the other direction. "I'll go and have supper with Nannie," he thought; "I'm afraid she is dreadfully worried and unhappy,—and all on my account, dear old Nancy!"

Chapter 32

"Do you think," Robert Ferguson wrote Mrs. Richie about the middle of September—"do you think you could come to Mercer for a little while and look after Nannie? The poor child is so unhappy and so incapable of making up her mind about herself that I am uneasy about her."

"Of course I will go," Mrs. Richie told her son.

David had come down to the little house on the seashore to spend Sunday with her, and in the late afternoon they were sitting out on the sand in a sunny, sheltered spot watching the slow, smooth heave of the quiet sea. David's shoulder was against her knee, his pipe had gone out, and he was looking with lazy eyes at the slipping sparkle of sunshine on the scarcely perceptible waves; sometimes he lifted his marine glasses to follow a sail gleaming like a white wing against the opalescent east.

"I wonder why Nannie is unhappy," he ruminated; "she was never, poor little Nannie! capable of appreciating Mrs. Maitland; so I don't suppose she loved her?"

"She loved her as much as she could," Mrs. Richie said; "and that is all any of us can do, David. But she misses her. If a mountain went out of your landscape, wouldn't you feel rather blank? Well, Nannie's mountain has gone. Yes; I'll go and stay with her, poor child, for a while, and perhaps bring her back for a fortnight with us —if you wouldn't mind?"

"Of course I wouldn't mind. Bring her along."

"I wonder if you could close this house for me?" she said; "I don't like to shut it up now and leave you without a roof over your head in case you had a chance to take a day off."

"Of course I can close it," he said; and added that if he

couldn't shut up a bandbox of a summer cottage he would be a pretty useless member of society. "I'll come down the first chance I get in the next fortnight.... Mother, I suppose you will see—*her?*"

Mrs. Richie gave him a startled look. "I suppose I shall."

He was silent for several minutes. She did not dare to help him by a word. Then, as if he had wrenched the question up by the roots, torn it out of his sealed heart, he said, "Do you suppose she cares for him?"

It was the first time in these later speechless months that he had turned to her. Steadying herself on that advice of Robert Ferguson's: 'when he does blurt it out don't get excited,' she answered, calmly enough, "I don't know."

He struck his heel down into the sand, then pulled out his knife and began to clean the bowl of his pipe. The blade trembled in his hand.

"Until I saw her in May," he said, "I suppose I really thought —I didn't formulate it, but I suppose I thought ... "

"What?"

"That somehow I would get her yet."

"Oh, David!" she breathed.

He glanced at her cynically. "Don't get agitated, Materna. That May visit cured me. I know I won't. I know she doesn't care for me. But I can't tell whether she cares for him."

"I hope she does," she said.

At which he laughed: "Do you expect me to agree to that?"

"David, think what you are saying!"

"My dear mother, have you been under the impression that I am a saint?" he said, dryly. "If so let me correct you. I am not. Yes, until I went out there in May I always had the feeling that I would get her, somehow, some time." He paused; his knife scraped the bowl of his pipe until the fresh wood showed under the blade. "I don't know that I ever exactly admitted it to myself; but I realize now that the feeling was there."

"You shock me very much," she said; and leaning against her knee he felt the quiver that ran through her.

"I have shocked myself several times in the last few years," he said, briefly.

His mother was silent. Suddenly he began to talk:

"At first—I mean when it happened; I thought she would send for me, and I would take her away from him, and then kill him." Her broken exclamation made him laugh. "Don't worry; I was terribly young in those days. I got over all that. It was only just at first; it was the everlasting human impulse. The cave-dweller had it, I suppose, when somebody stole his woman. But it's only the body that wants to kill. The mind knows better. The mind knows that life can be a lot better punishment than death. I knew he'd get his punishment and I was willing to wait for it. I thought that when she left him, his hell would be as hot as mine. I took it for granted that she would leave him. I thought there would be a divorce, and then"—his voice was smothered to the breaking-point; "then I would get her. Or I would get her without a divorce."

"David!"

He did not seem to hear her; his elbows were on his knees, his chin on his two fists; he spoke as if to himself; "Well; she didn't leave him. I suppose she couldn't forgive me. Curious, isn't it? how the mind can believe two entirely contradictory things at the same time: I realized she couldn't forgive me,—yet I still thought I would get her, somehow. Meantime, I consoled myself with the reflection that even if she hated me for having pushed her into his arms, she hated him worse. I thought that where I had been stabbed once, he would be stabbed a thousand times." David spoke with that look of primitive joy which must have been on the face of the cave-dweller when he felt the blood of his enemy spurt warm between his fingers.

Helena Richie gave a little cry and shrank back. These were the thoughts that her boy had built up between them in these silent years! He gave her a faintly amused glance.

"Yes, I had my dreams. Bad dreams you would call them, Materna. Now I don't dream any more. After I saw her in May, I got all over such nonsense. I realized that perhaps she ... loved him."

His mother was trembling. "It frightens me that you should have had such thoughts," she said. She actually looked frightened; her leaf-brown eyes were wide with terror.

Her son nuzzled his cheek against her hand; "Bless your dear heart! it frightens you, because you can't understand. Materna, there are several things you can't understand—and I shouldn't like it if you could!" he said, his face sobering with that reverent look which a man gives only to his mother; "There is the old human instinct, that existed before laws or morals or anything else, the man's instinct to keep his woman. And next to that, there is the realization that when it comes to what you call morals, there is a morality higher than the respectability you good people care so much about—the morality of nature. But of course you don't understand," he said again, with a short laugh.

"I understand a good many things, David."

"Oh, well, I didn't mean to talk about it," he said, sighing; "I don't know what started me; and—and I'm not howling, you know. I was only wondering whether *you* thought she had come to care for him?"

"I don't know," she said, faintly.

He snapped his knife shut. "Neither do I. But I guess she does. Nature is a big thing, Materna. When a girl's loyalty comes up against that, it hasn't much show; especially when nature is assisted by behavior like mine. Yes, I guess by this time she loves him. I'll never get her."

"Oh, David," his mother said, tremulously, "if you could only meet some nice, sweet girl, and — "

"Nice girl?" he said, smiling. "They're scarce, Materna, they're scarce. But I mean to get married one of these days. A man in my trade ought to be married. I sha'n't bother to look for one of those 'sweet girls,' however. I've got over my fondness for sugar. No more sentimentalities for me, thank you. I shall marry on strictly common-sense principles: a good housekeeper, who has good sense, and good looks — "

"And a good temper, I hope," Mrs. Richie said, almost with temper herself; and who can blame her? — he had been so cruelly injured! The sweetness, the silent, sunny honesty of the boy, the simple belief in the goodness of his fellow-creatures, had been changed to this! Oh, she could almost hate the girl who had done it! "A good temper is more important than anything else," she said, hotly.

Instantly the dull cynicism of his face flashed into anger. "Elizabeth's temper, — I suppose that is what you are referring to; her temper was not responsible for what happened. It was my assinine conceit."

She winced. "I didn't mean to hurt you," she said. He was silent. "But it is terrible to have you so hard, David."

"Hard? I? I am a mush of amiability. Come now! I oughtn't to have made you low-spirited. It's all an old story. I was only telling you how I felt at first. As for bad thoughts, — I haven't any thoughts now, good or bad! I am a most exemplary person. I don't know why I slopped over to you, anyhow. So don't think of it again. Materna! Can you see that sail?" He was looking through his glasses; "it's the eleventh since we came out here."

"But David, that you should think — "

"Oh, but I don't think any more," he declared, watching the flitting white gleam on the horizon; "I always avoid thinking, nowadays. That's why I am such a promising young medical man. I'm all right and perfectly happy. I'll hold my base, I promise you! That's a brig, Materna. Do you know the difference between a brig and a schooner? I bet you don't."

Apparently the moment of confidence was over; he had opened his heart and let her see the blackness and bleakness; and now he was closing it again. She was silent. David thrust his pipe into his pocket and turned to help her to rise; but she had hidden her face in her hands. "It is my fault," she said, with a gasp; "it must be my fault! Oh, David, have I made you wicked? If you had had a different mother—" Instantly he was ashamed of himself.

"Materna! I am a brute to you," he said. He flung his arm around her, and pressed his face against hers; "I wish somebody would kick me. You made me wicked? You are the only thing that has kept me anyways straight! Mother—I've been decent; your goodness has saved me from—several things. I want you to know that. I would have gone right straight to the devil if it hadn't been for your goodness. As for how I felt about Elizabeth, it was just a mood; don't think of it again."

"But you said," she whispered; "*without* a divorce."

"Well, I—I didn't mean it, I guess," he comforted her; "anyhow, the jig is up, dear. Even if I had a bad moment now and then in the first year, nothing came of it. Oh, mother, what a beast I am!" He was pressing his handkerchief against her tragic eyes. "Your fault? Your only fault is being so perfect that you can't understand a poor critter like me!"

"I do understand. I do understand."

In spite of himself, David laughed. "You! That's rich." He looked at her with his old, good smile, tender and inarticulate. "What would I have done without you? You've stood by and put up with my cussedness through these three devilish years. It's almost three years, you know, and yet I—I don't seem to get over it—Oh, I'm a perfect *girl*! How can you put up with me?" He laughed again, and hugged her. "Mother, sometimes I almost wish you weren't so good."

"David," she burst out passionately, "I am—" She stopped, trembling.

"I take it back," he apologized, smiling; "I seem bent on shocking you to-day. You can be as good as you want. Only, once in a while you do seem a little remote. Elizabeth used to say she was afraid of you."

"Of *me!*"

"Well, an angel like you never could quite understand her," he said, soberly.

His mother was silent; then she said in a low voice:

"I am not an angel; but perhaps I haven't understood her. I can understand love, but not hate. Elizabeth never loved you; she doesn't know the meaning of love."

"You are mistaken, dear," he said, gently.

They went back to the house very silently; David's confidences were over, but they left their mark on his mother's face. She showed the strain of that talk even a week later when she started on her kindly mission to cheer poor Nannie. On the hazy September morning, when Robert Ferguson met her in the big, smoky station at Mercer, there were new lines of care in her face. Her landlord, as he persisted in calling himself, noticed them, and was instantly cross; crossness being his way of expressing anxiety.

"You look tired," he scolded, as he opened the carriage door for her, "you've got to rest at my house and have something to eat before you go to Nannie's; besides, you don't suppose I got you on here just to cheer her? You've got to cheer me, too! It's enough to give a man melancholia to live next to that empty house of yours, and you owe it to me to be pleasant—if you can be pleasant," he barked.

But his barking was strangely mild. His words were as rough as ever, but he spoke with a sort of eager gentleness, as if he were trying to make his voice soft enough for some unuttered pitifulness. She was so pleased to see him, and to hear the kind, gruff voice, that for a minute she forgot her anxiety about David, and laughed. And when her eyes crinkled in that old, gay way, it seemed to Robert Ferguson, looking at her with yearning, as if Mercer, and the September haze, and the grimy old depot hack were suddenly illuminated.

"Oh, these children!" he said; "they are worrying me to death. Nannie won't budge out of that old house; it will have to be sold over her head, to get her into a decent locality. Elizabeth isn't well, but the Lord only knows what's the matter with her. The doctor says she's all right, but she's as grumpy a—her uncle; you can't get a word out of her. And Blair has been speculating,"—he was so cross that, when at his own door he put out his hand to help her from the carriage, she patted his arm, and said, "Come; cheer up!"

At which, smiling all over his face, he growled at her that it was a pretty thing to expect a man to cheer up, with an empty house on his hands. "You seem to think I'm made of money! You take the house *now*; don't wait till that callow doctor is ready to settle down here. If you'll move in now, I'll cheer up—and give Elizabeth the rent for pin-money." He was really cheerful by this time just because he was able to scold her, but behind his scolding there was always this new gentleness. Later, when he spoke again of the house, her face fell.

"I am doubtful about our coming to Mercer."

"Doubtful?" he said; "what's all this? There never was a woman yet who knew her own mind for a day at a time—except Mrs. Maitland. You told me that David was coming here next spring, and

I've been keeping this house for you; I've lost five months' rent" — there was a worried note in his voice; "what in thunder?" he demanded.

Mrs. Richie sighed. "I don't suppose I ought to tell you, but I can't seem to help it. I discovered the other day that David is not heart-whole, yet. He is dreadfully bitter; dreadfully! I don't believe it's prudent for him to live in Mercer. Do you? He would be constantly seeing Elizabeth."

She had had her breakfast, and they had gone into Mr. Ferguson's garden so that he might throw some crumbs to the pigeons and smoke his morning cigar before taking her to the Maitland house. They were sitting now in the long arbor, where the Isabella grapes were ripening sootily in the sparse September sunshine which sifted down between the yellowing leaves, and touched Mrs. Richie's brown hair; Robert Ferguson saw, with a pang, that there were some white threads in the soft locks. His eyes stung, so he barked as gruffly as he could.

"Well, suppose he does see her? You can't wrap him up in cotton batting for the rest of his life. That's what you've always tried to do, you hen with one chicken! For the Lord's sake, let him alone. Let him take his medicine like any other man. After he gets over the nasty taste of it, he'll find there's sugar in the world yet; just as I did. Only I hope he won't be so long about it as I was."

She sighed, and her soft eyes filled. "But you don't know how he talked. Oh, I can't help thinking it must be my fault! If he had had another kind of a mother, if his own mother had lived — "

"Own grandmother!" said Robert Ferguson, disgustedly; "the only trouble with you as a mother, is that you've been too good to the cub. If you'd knocked his head against the wall once or twice, you'd have made a man of him. My dear, you really must not be a goose, you know. It's the one thing I can't stand. Helena," he interrupted himself, chuckling, "you will be pleased to know that Cherry-pie (begging her pardon!) thinks that David will ultimately console himself by falling in love with Nannie! 'It would be very nice,' she says."

They both laughed, then David's mother sighed: "But just think how delightful to feel that life is as simple as that," she said.

Robert Ferguson picked a grape, and took careful aim at a pigeon; "Helena," he said, in a low voice, "before you see Nannie, perhaps I ought to tell you something. I wouldn't, only I know she will, and you ought to understand it. Can you keep a secret?"

"I can," Mrs. Richie said briefly.

"I believe it," he said, with a sudden dryness. Then he told her the story of the certificate.

"What! Nannie forged? *Nannie!*"

"We don't use that word; it isn't pretty. But that's what it amounts to, of course. And that's where David's money went."

"I suppose Mrs. Maitland changed her mind at the last," Mrs. Richie said; "well, I'm glad she did. It would have been too cruel if she hadn't given something to Blair."

"I don't think she did," he declared; "changing her mind wasn't her style; she wasn't one of your weak womanish creatures. *She* wouldn't have said she was coming to live in Mercer, and then tried to back out of it! No, she simply wrote Blair's name by mistake. Her mind wandered constantly in those last days. And seeing what she had done, she didn't indorse it."

Mrs. Richie looked doubtful. "I think she meant it for him."

Robert Ferguson laughed grimly. "*I* think she didn't; but you'll be a great comfort to Nannie. Poor Nannie! She is unhappy, but not in the least repentant. She insists that she did right! Would you have supposed that a girl of her age could be so undeveloped, morally?"

"She's only undeveloped legally," she amended; "and what can you expect? What chance has she had to develop in any way?"

"She had the chance of living with one of the finest women I ever knew," he said, stiffly, and paused for their usual wrangle about Mrs. Maitland. As they rose to go indoors, he looked at his guest, and shook his head. "Oh, Helena, how conceited you are!"

"I? Conceited?" she said, blankly.

"You think you are a better judge than I am," he complained.

"Nonsense!" she said, blushing charmingly; but she insisted on walking down to Nannie's, instead of letting him take her in the carriage; a carriage is not a good place to ward off a proposal.

At the Maitland house she found poor Nannie wandering vaguely about in the garret. "I am putting away Mamma's clothes," she said, helplessly. But a minute later she yielded, with tears of relief, to Mrs. Richie's placid assumption of authority;

"I am going to stay a week with you, and to-morrow I'll tell you what to do with things. Just now you must sit down and talk to me."

And Nannie sat down, with a sigh of comfort. There were so many things she wanted to say to some one who would understand! "And you do understand," she said, sobbing a little. "Oh, I am so lonely without Mamma! She and I always understood each other. You know she meant the money for Blair, don't you, Mrs. Richie? Mr. Ferguson won't believe me!"

"Yes; I am sure she did," Mrs. Richie said, heartily; "but dear, you ought not to have—"

Nannie, comforted, said: "Well, perhaps not; considering that I can give it to him. But I didn't know that, you know, when I did it." Pretty much all that day, poor Nannie poured out her full little heart to her kind listener; they sat down together at the office-dining-room table—at the head of which stood a chair that no one ever dreamed of occupying; and Harris shuffled about as he had for nearly thirty years, serving coarse food on coarse china, and taking a personal interest in the conversation. After dinner they went into Nannie's parlor that smelt of soot, where the little immortal canvas still hung in its gleaming gold frame near the door, and the cut glass of the great chandeliers sparkled faintly through slits in the old brown paper-muslin covers. Sometimes, as they talked, the house would shake, and Nannie's light voice be drowned in the roar of a passing train whose trail of smoke brushed against the windows like feathers of darkness. But Nannie gave no hint that she would ever go away and leave the smoke and noise, and just at first Mrs. Richie made no such suggestion. She did nothing but infold the vague, frightened, unhappy girl in her own tranquillity. Sometimes she lured her out to walk or drive, and once she urged her to ask Elizabeth and Blair to come to supper.

"Oh, Blair won't come while you are here!" Nannie said, simply; and the color came into David's mother's face. "I know," Nannie went on, "that Elizabeth thinks Mamma meant that money for David. And she is not pleased because Mr. Ferguson won't make the executors give it to him."

Mrs. Richie laughed. "Well, that is very foolish in Elizabeth; nobody could give your mother's money to David. I must straighten that out with Elizabeth."

But she did not have a chance to do so; Elizabeth as well as Blair preferred not to come to the old house while David's mother was there. And Mrs. Richie, unable to persuade Nannie to go back to Philadelphia with her, stayed on, in the kindness of her heart, for still another week. When she finally fixed a day for her return, she said to herself that at least Blair and Elizabeth would not be prevented by her presence from doing what they could to cheer Nannie.

"But is she going to live on in that doleful house forever?"

Robert
Ferguson protested.

"She's like a poor little frightened snail," Helena Richie said. "You don't realize the shock to her of that night when she—she tried to do what she thought Mrs. Maitland wanted to have done. She is scared still. She just creeps in and out of that dingy front door, or about those awful, silent rooms. It will take time to bring her into the sunshine."

"Helena," he said, abruptly—she and Nannie had had supper with him and were just going home; Nannie had gone up-stairs to put on her hat. "Helena, I've been thinking a good deal about your cruelty to me."

She laughed: "Oh, you are impossible!"

"No, I'm only permanent. Don't laugh; just listen to me." He was evidently nervous; the old friendly bullying had been put aside; he was very grave, and was plainly finding it difficult to say what he wanted to say: "I don't know what your reason is for refusing me, but I know it isn't a good reason. You are fond of me, and yet you keep on saying 'no' in this exasperating way;—upon my word," he interrupted himself, despairingly, "I could shake you, sometimes, it is so exasperating! You like me, well enough; but you won't marry me."

"No, I won't," she assured him, gently.

"It is so unreasonable of you," he said, simply, "that it makes me think you've got some bee in your bonnet: some silly woman-notion. You think—Heaven knows what you think! perhaps that—that you ought not to marry because of something—anything—" he stammered with earnestness; "but I want you to know this: that I don't *care* what your reason is! You may have committed murder, for all the difference it makes to me." The clumsy and elaborate lightness of his words trembled with the seriousness of his voice. "You may have broken every one of the Ten Commandments;*I* don't care!

Helena, do you understand? It's nothing to me! You may have broken—*all of them.*" He spoke with solemn passion, holding out his hands toward her; his voice shook, but his melancholy face was serene with knowledge and understanding. "Oh, my dear," he said, "I love you and you are fond of me. That's all I care about! Nothing else, nothing else."

Her start of attention, her dilating eyes, made the tears spring to his own eyes. "Helena, you do believe me, don't you?"

She could not answer him; she had grown pale and then red, then pale again. "Oh," she said in a whisper, "you are a good man! What have I done to deserve such a friend? But no, dear friend, no."

He struck her shoulder heavily, as if she had been another man. "Well, anyway," he said, "you'll remember that when you are willing, I am waiting?"

She nodded. "I shall never forget your goodness," she said, brokenly.

He did not try to detain her with arguments or entreaties, but as she turned toward the library door he suddenly pushed it shut, and quietly took her in his arms and kissed her.

She went away quite speechless. She did not even remember to say good-night and good-by to Miss White, although she was to leave Mercer the next morning. When Blair heard that Mrs. Richie was coming to stay with Nannie he said, briefly, "I won't come in while she is here." He wrote to his sister during those three weeks and sent her flowers—kindness to Nannie was a habit with Blair; and indeed he really missed seeing her, and was glad for other reasons than his own embarrassment when he heard that her visitor was going away. "I understand Mrs. Richie takes the 7.30 to-night," he said to his wife. Elizabeth was silent; it did not occur to her to mention that she had seen Nannie and heard that Mrs. Richie had decided to stay over another night. She rarely volunteered any information to Blair.

"Elizabeth," he said, "what do you say to going down to Willis's for supper, and rowing home in the moonlight? We can drop in and see Nannie on the way back to the hotel—after Mrs. Richie has gone." He saw some listless excuse trembling on her lips, and interrupted her: "Do say 'yes'! It is months since we have been on the river."

She hesitated, then seemed to reach some sudden decision. "Yes," she said, "I'll go."

Blair's face lighted with pleasure. Perhaps the silence which had hardened between them since the day the question of his money had been discussed would break now.

The late afternoon was warm with the yellow haze of October sunshine when they walked out over the bridge to the toll-house wharf, where Blair hired a boat. He made her as comfortable as he could in the stern, and when he gave her the tiller-ropes she took them in a business-like way, as if really entering into the spirit of his little expedition. A moment later they were floating down the river; there was nearly half a mile of furnaces and slag-banked shore before they left Mercer's smoke and grime behind them and began to drift between low-lying fields or through narrow reaches where the vineyard-covered hills came down close to the water.

"Elizabeth, what do you say to going East next month?" Blair said; "perhaps we can persuade Nannie to go, too."

She was leaning back against the cushions he had arranged for her, holding her white parasol so that it hid her face. "I don't see," she said, "how you can afford to travel much; where will you get the money?"

"Oh, it has all been very easily arranged; Nannie can draw pretty freely against the estate now, and she makes me an 'allowance,' so to speak, until things are settled; then she'll hand my principal over to me. It's a nuisance not to have it now; but we can get along well enough."

Then Elizabeth asked her question: "And when you get the principal, what will you do with it?"

"Invest it; pretty tough, isn't it, when you think what I ought to have had?"

"And when," said Elizabeth, very softly, "will you build the hospital?" She lifted her parasol slightly, and gave him a look that was like a knife; then lowered it again.

"Build the hospital! What hospital?"

"The hospital near the Works, that your mother put that money aside for."

Blair's hands tightened on his oars. Instinctively he knew that a critical moment was confronting him. He did not know just what the danger in it was, but he knew there was danger. "My mother changed her mind about that, Elizabeth."

She lifted the parasol again, and looked full at him; the white shadow of the silk made the dark amber of her unsmiling eyes singularly luminous. "No," she said; "your mother did not change her mind. Nannie thought she did, but it was not so." She spoke with stern certainty. "Your mother didn't mean you to have that money. She meant it for—a hospital."

Blair stopped rowing and leaned on his oars. "Why don't you speak his name?" he said, between his teeth.

The parasol fell back on her shoulder; she grew very white; the hard line that used to be a dimple was like a gash in her cheek; she looked suddenly old. "I will certainly speak his name: *David Richie*. Your mother meant the money for David Richie."

"That," said Blair, "is a matter of opinion. You think she did. I think she didn't. I think she meant it for the person whose name she wrote on the certificate. That person will keep it."

Elizabeth was silent. Blair began to row again, softly. The anger in his face died out and left misery behind it. Oh, how she hated him; and how she loved—*him*. At that moment Blair hated David as one only hates the human creature one has injured. They did not speak again for the rest of the slow drift down to Willis's. Once Blair opened his lips to bid her notice that the overhanging willows and chestnuts mirrored themselves so clearly in the water that the skiff seemed to cut through autumnal foliage, and the sound of the ripple at the prow was like the rustle of leaves; but the preoccupation in her face silenced him. It was after four when, brushing past a fringe of willows, the skiff bumped softly against a float half hidden in the yellowing sedge and grass at Willis's landing. Blair got out, and drawing the boat alongside, held up his hand to his wife, but she ignored his assistance. As she sprang lightly out, the float rocked a little and the water splashed over the planks. There was a dank smell of wet wood and rankly growing water-weeds. A ray of sunshine, piercing the roof of willow leaves, struck the single blossom of a monkey-flower, that sparkled suddenly in the green darkness like a topaz.

"Elizabeth," Blair said in a low voice—he was holding the gunwale of the boat and he did not look at her; "Elizabeth, all I want money for is to give you everything you want." She was silent. He made the skiff fast and followed her up the path to the little inn on the bank. There were some tables out under the locust-trees, and a welcoming landlord came hurrying to meet them with suggestions of refreshments.

"What will you have?" Blair asked.

"Anything—nothing; I don't care," Elizabeth said; and Blair gave an order he thought would please her.

Below them the river, catching the sunset light, blossomed with a thousand stars. Elizabeth watched the dancing glitter absently;

when Blair, forgetting for a moment the depression of the last half-hour, said impulsively, "Oh, how beautiful that is!" she nodded, and came out of her abstraction to call his attention to the reflected gold of a great chestnut on the other side of the stream.

"Are you warm enough?" he asked. He said to himself, with a sigh of relief, that evidently she had dropped the dangerous subject of the hospital. "There is a chill in these October evenings as the sun goes down," he reminded her.

"Yes."

"Elizabeth," he burst out, "why can't we talk sometimes? Haven't we anything in common? Can't we ever talk, like ordinary husbands and wives? You would show more civility to a beggar!" But as he spoke the waiter pushed his tray between them, and she did not answer. When Blair poured out a glass of wine for her she shook her head.

"I don't want anything."

He looked at her in despair: "I love you. I suppose you wouldn't believe me if I should try to tell you how I love you—and yet you don't give me a decent word once a month!"

"Blair," she said, quietly, "that is final, is it—about the money? You are going to keep it?"

"I am certainly going to keep it."

Elizabeth's eyes narrowed. "It is final," she repeated, slowly.

"You are angry," he cried, "because I won't give the money my mother gave me, all the money I have in the world, to the man whom you threw off like an old glove!"

"No," she said, slowly, "I don't *think* I am angry. But it seems somehow to be more than I can bear; a sort of last straw, I suppose," she said, smiling faintly. "But I'm not angry, I think. Still, perhaps I am. I don't really know."

Blair struck a match under the table. His hand holding his

cigarette trembled. "To the best of my knowledge and belief, Elizabeth, I am honest. I believe my mother meant me to have that money. She did not mean to have it go to—to a hospital."

Elizabeth dug the ferrule of her parasol into the gravel at her feet. "It is David's money. You took his wife. Now you are taking his money.... You can't keep both of them." She said this very gently, so gently that for a moment he did not grasp the sense of her words. When he did it seemed to him that she did not herself realize what she had said, for immediately, in the same calmly matter-of-fact way, she began to speak of unimportant things: the river was very low, wasn't it? What a pity they were cutting the trees on the opposite hill. "They are burning the brush," she said; "do you smell the smoke? I love the smell of burning brush in October." She was simpler and pleasanter than she had been for a long time. But he could not know that it was because she felt, inarticulately, that her burden had been lifted; she herself could not have said why, but she was almost happy. Blair was confused to the point of silence by her abrupt return to the commonplace. He glanced at her with furtive anxiety. "Oh, see the moon!" Elizabeth said, and for a moment they watched the great disk of the Hunter's moon rising in the translucent dusk behind the hills.

"That purple haze in the east is like the bloom on a plum," Blair said.

"I think we had better go now," Elizabeth said, rising. But though she had seemed so friendly, she did not even turn her head to see if he were following her, and he had to hurry to overtake her as she went down the path to the half-sunken float that was rocking slightly in the grassy shallows. As he knelt, steadying the boat with one hand, he held the other up to her, and this time she did not repulse him; but when she put her hand into his, he kissed it with abrupt, unhappy passion,—and she drew it from him sharply. When she took her place in the stern and lifted the tiller-ropes she looked at him, gathering up his oars, with curious gentleness.... .

She was sorry for him, for he seemed to care so much;—and this was the end! She had tried to bear her life. Nobody could imagine how hard she had tried; life had been her punishment, so with all her soul and all her body, she had tried to bear it! But this was the end. It was not possible to try any more. "I have borne it as long as I can," she thought. Yet as she had said, she was not angry. She wondered, vaguely, listening to the dip of the oars, at this absence of anger. She had been able to talk about the bonfires, and she had thought the moon beautiful. No; she was not angry. Or if she were, then her anger was unlike all the other angers that had scourged and torn the surface of her life; they had been storms, all clamor and confusion and blinding flashes, with more or less indifference to resulting ruin. But this anger, which could not be recognized as anger, was a noiseless cataclysm in the very center of her being; a tidal wave, that was lifting and lifting, moving slowly, too full for sound, in the resistless advance of an absorbing purpose of ruin. "I am not angry," she said to herself; "but I think I am dying."

The pallor of her face frightened Blair, who was straining at his oars against the current: "Elizabeth! What is the matter? Shall I stop? Shall we go ashore? You are ill!"

"No; I'm not. Go on, please."

"But there is something the matter!"

She shook her head. "Don't stop. We've gone ever so far down-stream, just in this minute."

Blair looked at her anxiously. A little later he tried to make her talk; asked her how she felt, and called her attention to the bank of clouds that was slowly climbing up the sky. But she was silent. As usual, she seemed to have nothing to say to him. He rowed steadily, in long, beautiful strokes, and she sat watching the dark water lap and glimmer past the side of the skiff. As they worked up-stream, the sheen of oil began to show again in faint and rocking iridescence; once she leaned over and touched the water with her fingers; then looked at them with a frown.

"Look out!" Blair said; "trim a little, will you?"

She sat up quickly: "I wonder if it is easy to drown?"

"Mighty easy—if you lean too hard on the gunwale," he said, good-naturedly.

"Does it take very long?"

"To drown? I never tried it, but I believe not; though I understand that it's unpleasant while it lasts." He watched her wistfully; if he could only make her smile!

"I suppose dying is generally unpleasant," she said, and glanced down into the black oily water with a shiver.

It was quite dark by this time, and Blair was keeping close to the shore to avoid the current narrowing between the piers of the old bridge. When they reached Mrs. Todd's wharf Elizabeth was still staring into the water.

"It is so black here, so dirty! I wouldn't like to have it touch me. It's cleaner down at Willis's," she said, thoughtfully. Blair, making fast at the landing, agreed: "Yes, if I wanted a watery grave I'd prefer the river at Willis's to this." Then he offered her a pleading hand; but she sat looking at the water. "How clean the ocean is, compared to a river," she said; then noticed his hand. She took it calmly enough, and stepped out of the boat. She had forgotten, he thought, her displeasure about the money; there was only the usual detachment. When he said it was too early to go to Nannie's,—"it isn't seven yet, and Mrs. Richie won't leave the house until a quarter past;" she agreed that they had better go to the hotel.

"What do you say to the theater to-night?" he asked. But she shook her head.

"You go; I would rather be alone."

"I hear there's a good play in town?"

She was silent.

Blair said something under his breath with angry hopelessness. This was always the way so far as any personal relation between them went; she did not seem to see him; she did not even hear what he was saying. "You always want to be alone, so far as I am concerned," he said. She made no answer. After dinner he took himself off. "She doesn't want me round, so I'll clear out," he said, sullenly; he had not the heart even to go to Nannie's. "I'll drop into the theater, or perhaps I'll just walk," he thought, drearily. He wandered out into the street, but the sky had clouded over and there was a soft drizzle of rain, so he turned into the first glaring entrance that yawned at him from the pavement.

Chapter 33

When Blair came home, a little after eleven, she had gone.

At first he did not grasp the significance of her absence. He called to her from their parlor: "I want to tell you about the play; perfect trash!" No answer. He glanced through the open door of her bedroom; not there. He hurried to his own room, crying: "Elizabeth! Where are you?" Then stood blankly waiting. Had she gone downstairs? He went out into the hall and, leaning over the banisters, listened to the stillness—that unhuman stillness of a hotel corridor; but there was no bang of an iron door, no clanking rumble of an ascending elevator. Had she gone out? He looked at his watch, and his heart came up into his throat; out—at this hour! But perhaps after he had left her, she had suddenly decided to spend the night at her uncle's or Nannie's. In that case she would have left word in the office. He was thrusting his arms into his overcoat and settling his hat on his head, even while he was dashing downstairs to inquire:

"Has Mrs. Maitland left any message for me?"

The clerk looked vague: "We didn't see her go out, sir. But I suppose she went by the ladies' entrance. No; she didn't leave any message, sir."

Blair suddenly knew that he was frightened. He could not have said why. Certainly he was not conscious of any reason for fright; but some blind instinct sent a wave of alarm all through him. His knees felt cold; there was a sinking sensation just below his breast-bone.

"What an ass I am!" he said to himself; "she has gone to her uncle's, of course." He said something of the kind, with elaborate carelessness, to the clerk; "if she comes back before I do, just say I have gone out on an errand." He was frightened, but not to the extent of letting that inquisitive idiot behind the counter know it. "If he had been attending to his business," he thought, angrily, "he would have seen her go, and he could have told me when it was. I'll go to Mr. Ferguson's. Of course she's there."

He stood on the curb-stone for a minute, looking for a carriage; but the street was deserted. He could not take the time to go to the livery-stable. He started hurriedly; once he broke into a run, then checked himself with the reminder that he was a fool. As he drew near her uncle's house, he began to defend himself against disappointment: "She's at Nannie's. Why did I waste time coming here? I know she is at Nannie's!"

Robert Ferguson's house was dark, except for streaks of light under the blinds of the library windows. Blair, springing up the front steps, rang; then held his breath to listen for some one coming through the hall; his heart seemed smothering in his throat. "I *know* she isn't here; she's at Nannie's," he told himself. He was acutely conscious of the dank smell of the frosted honeysuckle clinging limply to the old iron trellis that inclosed the veranda; but when the door opened he was casual enough—except for a slight breathlessness.

"Mr. Ferguson! is Elizabeth here?"

"No," Robert Ferguson said, surprised, "was she coming here?"

"She was to be here, or—or at Nannie's," Blair said, carelessly, "I didn't know which. I'll go and get her there." His own words reassured him, and he apologized lightly. "Sorry to have disturbed you, sir. Good-night!" And he was gone before another question could be asked. But out in the street he found himself running. "Of course she's at Nannie's!" he said, panting. He even had a twinge of anger at Elizabeth for giving him all this trouble. "She ought to have left word," he thought, crossly. It was a relief to be cross; nothing very serious can have happened to a person who merely makes you cross. The faint drizzle of the early evening had turned to rain, which added to his irritation. "She's all right; and it's confoundedly unpleasant to get soaking wet," he reflected. Yes; he was honestly cross. Yet in spite of the reassurances of his mind and his temper, his body was still frightened; he was hurrying; his breath came quickly. He dashed on, so absorbed in denying his alarm that on one of the crossings only a quick leap kept him from being knocked down by a carriage full of revelers. "Here, you! Look out! What's the matter with you?" the cab-driver yelled, pulling his horses back and sidewise, but not before the pole of the hack had grazed Blair's shoulder. There was a screech of laughter, a woman's vociferating fright, a whiff of cigar smoke, and a good-natured curse: "Say, darn you, you're too happy to be out alone, sonny!" Blair did not hear them. Shantytown, black and silent and wet, huddled before him; from the smokestacks of the Works banners of flame flared out into the rain, and against them his mother's house loomed up, dark in the darkness. At the sight of it all his panic returned, and again he tried to discount his disappointment: "She isn't here, of course; she has gone to the hotel. Why didn't I wait for her there? What a fool I am!" But back in his mind, as he banged the iron gate and rushed up the steps, he was saying: "If she *isn't* here—?"

The house was absolutely dark; the fan-light over the great door was black; there was no faintest glimmer of light anywhere. Everybody was asleep. Blair rang violently, and pounded on the panels of the door with both hands. "Nannie! Elizabeth! Harris!— confound the old idiot! why doesn't he answer the bell? Nannie—"

A window opened on the floor above. "What is it?" demanded a quavering feminine voice. "Who's there?"

"Nannie! Darn it, why doesn't somebody answer the bell in this house?

Is Elizabeth—" His voice died in his throat.

"Oh, Blair! Is that you? You scared me to death," Nannie called down.

"What on earth is the matter?"

"Is—is Elizabeth here?"

"Elizabeth? No; of course not! Where is she?"

"If I knew, would I be asking you?" Blair called back furiously; "she must be here!"

"Wait. I'll come down and let you in," Nannie said; he heard a muffled colloquy back in the room, and then the window closed sharply. Far off, a church clock struck one. Blair stood with a hand on the doorknob; through the leaded side-windows he saw a light wavering down through the house; a moment later Nannie, lamp in hand, shivering in her thin dressing-gown, opened the door.

"Has she been here this evening?"

"Blair! You scare me to death! No; she hasn't been here. What is the matter? Your coat is all wet! Is it raining?"

"She isn't at the hotel, and I don't know where she is."

"Why, she's at Mr. Ferguson's, of course!"

"No, she isn't. I've been there."

"She may be at home by this time," Nannie faltered, and Blair, assenting, was just turning to rush away, when another voice said, with calm peremptoriness:

"What is the matter?"

Blair turned to see Mrs. Richie. She had come quietly downstairs, and was standing beside Nannie. Even in his scared preoccupation, the sight of David's mother shook him. "I—I thought," he stammered, "that you had gone home, Mrs. Richie."

"She had a little cold, and I would not let her go until to-morrow morning," Nannie said; "you always take more cold on those horrid sleeping-cars." Nannie had no consciousness of the situation; she was far too alarmed to be embarrassed. Blair cringed; he was scarlet to his temples; yet under his shame, he had the feeling that he had when, a little boy, he clung to David's pretty mother for protection.

"Oh, Mrs. Richie," he said, "I am so worried about Elizabeth!"

"What about her?"

"She said something this afternoon that frightened me."

"What?"

But he would not tell her. "It was nothing. Only she was very angry; and—she will do anything when she is angry." Mrs. Richie gave him a look, but he was too absorbed to feel its significance. "It was something about—well, a sort of silly threat. I didn't take it in at the time; but afterward I thought perhaps she meant something. Really, it was nothing at all. But—" his voice died in his throat and his eyes were terrified. There was such pain in his face that before she knew it David's mother was sorry for him; she even put her hand on his shoulder.

"It was just a mood," she comforted him. And Blair, taking the white, maternal hand in both of his, looked at her speechlessly; his chin trembled. Instantly, without words of shame on one side or of forgiveness on the other, they were back again, these two, in the old friendship of youth and middle age. "It was a freak," said Mrs. Richie, soothingly. "She is probably at the hotel by this time. Don't be troubled, Blair. Go and see. If she isn't at the hotel let me know at once."

"Yes, yes; I will," Blair said. "She must be there now, of course. I know there's nothing the matter, but I don't like to have her out so late by herself." He turned to open the front door, fumbling with haste over the latch; Nannie called to him to wait and she would get him an umbrella. But he did not hear her. He was saying to himself that of course she was at the hotel; and he was off again into the darkness!

As the door banged behind him the two women looked at each other in dismay. "Oh, Mrs. Richie, what can be the matter?" Nannie said.

"Just one of Elizabeth's moods. She has gone out to walk."

"At this time of night? It's after one o'clock!"

"She is probably safe and sound at the River House now."

"I wish we had one of those new telephone things," Nannie said. "Mamma was always talking about getting one. Then Blair could let us know as soon as he gets to the hotel." Nannie was plainly scared; Mrs. Richie grave and a little cold. She had had, to her amazement, a wave of tenderness for Blair; the reaction from it came in anger at Elizabeth. Elizabeth was always making trouble! "Poor Blair," she said, involuntarily. At the moment she was keenly sorry for him; after all, abominable as his conduct had been, love, of a kind, had been at the root of it. "I can forgive love," Helena Richie said to herself, "but not hate. Elizabeth never loved David or she couldn't have done what she did.... Nothing will happen to her," she said aloud. It occurred to this gentle woman that nothing ever did happen to the people one felt could be spared from this world; which wicked thought made her so shocked at herself that she hardly heard Nannie's nervous chatter: "If she hasn't come home, Blair will be back here in half an hour; it takes fifteen minutes to go to the hotel and fifteen minutes to come back. If he isn't here at a quarter to two, everything is all right."

They went into the parlor and lit the gas; Nannie suggested a fire, but Mrs. Richie said it wasn't worth while. "We'll be going up-stairs in a few minutes," she said. She was not really worried about Elizabeth; partly because of that faintly cynical belief that nothing could happen to the poor young creature who had made so much trouble for everybody; but also because she was singularly self-absorbed. Those words of Robert Ferguson's, when he kissed her in his library, had never left her mind. She thought of them now when she and Nannie sat down in that silence of waiting which seems to tingle with speech. The dim light from the gas-jet by the mantelpiece did not penetrate beyond the dividing arch of the great room; behind the grand piano sprawling sidewise between the black marble columns, all was dark. The shadow of the chandelier, muffled in its balloon of brown paper muslin, made an island of darkness on the ceiling, and the four big canvases were four black oblongs outlined in faintly glimmering gilt.

"I remember sitting here with your mother, the night you children were lost," Mrs. Richie said. "Oh, Nannie dear, you must move out of this house; it is too gloomy!" But Nannie was not thinking of the house.

"Where *can* she have gone?" she said.

Mrs. Richie could offer no suggestion. Her explanation to herself was that Blair and Elizabeth had quarreled, and Elizabeth, in a paroxysm of temper, had rushed off to spend the night in some hotel by herself. But she did not want to say this to Nannie. To herself she said that things did sometimes turn out for the best in this world, after all—if only David could realize it! "She would have made him dreadfully unhappy," Helena Richie thought; "she doesn't know what love means." But alas! David did not know that he had had an escape. She sighed, remembering that talk on the beach, and those wicked things he had said,—things for which she must be in some way to blame. "If he had had a different mother," she thought, heavily, "he might not have—" A sudden shock of terror jarred all through her—*could Elizabeth have gone to David?* The very thought turned her cold; it was as if some slimy, poisonous thing had touched her. Then common sense came in a wave of relief: "Of course not!

Why should she do such an absurd thing?" But in spite of common sense, Helena Richie's lips went dry.

"It's a quarter to two," Nannie said. "He hasn't come; she must be at the hotel."

"I'm sure she is," Mrs. Richie agreed.

"Let's wait five minutes," Nannie said; "but I'm certain it's all right."

"Of course it's all right," Mrs. Richie said again, and got on her feet with a shiver of relief.

"It gave me a terrible scare," Nannie confessed, and turned out the gas. "I had a perfectly awful thought, Mrs. Richie; a wicked thought. I was afraid she had—had done something to herself. You know she is so crazy when she is angry, and—"

The front gate banged. Nannie gave a faint scream. "Oh, Mrs. Richie!
Oh—"

It was Helena Richie who opened the door before Blair had even reached it. "Well? Well?"

"Not there... ."

Chapter 34

All night long Elizabeth watched a phantom landscape flit past the window of the sleeping-car. Sometimes a cloud of smoke, shot through with sparks, brushed the glass like a billowing curtain, and sometimes the thunderous darkness of a tunnel swept between her and spectral trees or looming hilltops. She lay there on her pillows, looking at the flying glimmer of the night and drawing long breaths of peace. The steady, rhythmical pounding of the wheels, the dull, rushing roar of the rails, the black, spinning country outside her window, shut away her old world of miseries and shames. Behind the stiff green curtains, that swung in and out, in and out, to the long roll of the car, there were no distractions, no fears of interruption, no listening apprehensions; she could relax into the wordless and exultant certainty of her purpose.

For at last, after these long months of mere endurance, she had a purpose.

And how calmly she was fulfilling it! "For I am not angry," she said to herself, with the same surprise she had felt when, at Willis's that afternoon, she had denied Blair's charge of anger. Outside in the darkness, all the world was asleep. The level stretches of vanishing fields, the faint glisten of roads, were empty. When the train swept thundering through little towns, the flying station lights, the twinkle of street lamps, even the solitary lanterns of switchmen running along the tracks, made the sleep seem only more profound. But Elizabeth was awake in every fiber; once or twice, for the peace of it, she closed her eyes; but she did not mean to sleep. She meant to think out every step that she must take; but just at first, in the content of decision, she did not even want to think. She only wanted to feel that the end had come.

It was during the row up the river that her purpose had cleared before her eyes; for an instant the sight of it had startled her into that pallor which had frightened Blair; then she accepted it with a passionate satisfaction. It needed no argument; she knew without reasoning about it what she must do. But the way to do it was not plain; it was while she and Blair sat at dinner, and he read his paper and she played with her food, that a plan grew slowly in her mind. The carrying it out—at least to this point; the alert and trembling fear of some obstacle, had greatly exhausted her. It had also blotted out everything but itself. She forgot her uncle and Miss White; that she was going to give them pain did not occur to her until safe from their possible interference, in the dark, behind the slowly swaying curtains of her section, her fatigue began to lessen. Then, vaguely, she thought of them.... they would be sorry. She frowned, faintly troubled by their sorrow. It was midnight before she remembered Blair: poor Blair! he cared so much about her. How could he,—when she did not care for him? Still, it did not follow that not being loved prevented you from loving. David had ceased to love her, but that had not made her love cease. Yes; she was afraid they would all be unhappy; but it would be only for a while. She sighed; it was a peaceful sigh. Her regret for the sorrow that she would cause was the regret of one far off, helpless to avert the pain, who has no relation to it except that of an observer. She said to herself, calmly, "Poor Uncle Robert."

As she grew more rested, the vagueness of her regret sharpened a little. She realized with a pang how worried they would be—before they began to be sorry; and worry is so hard to bear! "I wish I could have spared Uncle Robert and Cherry-pie," she said, in real distress. It occurred to her that she had given them many unhappy moments. "I was always a trouble; what a pity I was ever born." She thought suddenly of her mother, remembering how she used to excuse her temper on the ground that her mother had had no

420

self-control. She smiled faintly in the darkness at the childishness of such an excuse. "She wasn't to blame. I could have conquered it, but I didn't. I did nothing all my life but make trouble." She thought of her life as a thing of the past. "I was a great trial to them; it will be better for everybody this way," she said; and nestled down into the thought of the "way," with a satisfaction which was absolute comfort. Better; but still better if she had never lived. Then Blair would not have been disinherited, and by being disinherited driven into the dishonor of keeping money not intended for him. "It's really all my fault," she reflected, and looked out of the window with unseeing eyes. Yes; all that had happened was her fault. Oh, how many things she had hurt and spoiled! She had injured Blair; his mother had said so. And poor Nannie! for Nannie's offense grew out of Elizabeth's conduct. As for David—David, who had stopped loving her.... .

Well, she wouldn't hurt people any more, now. Never any more.

Just then the train jarred slowly to a standstill in a vast train-shed; up under its glass and girders, arc-lamps sent lurching shadows through the smoke and touched the clouds of steam with violet gleams. Elizabeth could see dark, gnome-like creatures, each with a hammer, and with a lantern swinging from a bent elbow, crouching along by the cars and tapping every wheel. She counted the blows that tested the trucks for the climb up the mountains: click-click; click-click. She was glad they were testing them; she must get across the mountains safely; there must be no interference or delay; she had so little time! For by morning they would guess, those three worried people—who had not yet begun to be sorry—they would guess what she had done, and they would follow her. She saw the gnomes slouching back past the cars, upright this time; then she felt the enormous tug of the engine beginning the up-grade. It grew colder, and she was glad of the blankets which she had not liked to touch when she first lay down in her berth. Outside there was a faint whitening along the horizon; but it dimmed, and the black outlines of the mountains were lost, as if the retreating night hesitated and returned; then she saw that her window was touched here and there by slender javelins of rain. They came faster and faster, striking on and over one another; now they turned to drops; she stopped thinking, absorbed in watching a drop roll down the glass—pause, lurch forward, touch another drop; then a third; then zigzag rapidly down the pane. She found herself following the racing drops with fascinated eyes; she even speculated as to which would reach the bottom first; she had a sense of luxury in being able, in the fortress of her berth, to think of such things as racing raindrops. By the time it was light enough to distinguish the stretching fields again, it was raining hard. Once in a while the train rushed past a farm-house, where the smoke from the chimney sagged in the gray air until it lay like a rope of mist along the roof. It was so light now that she could see the sodden carpet of yellow leaves under the maples, and she noticed that the crimson pennons of the sumacs drooped and dripped and clung together. The monotonous clatter of the wheels had fallen into a rhythm, which pounded out steadily and endlessly certain words which were the refrain of her purpose: "*Afterward, they will say I had the right to see him.*" Sometimes she reminded herself, meekly, that he no longer loved her. But there was no trace of resentment in her mind; how could he love her? Nor did the fact that his love had ceased make any difference in her purpose: "Afterward, they will say I had the right to see him."

When the day broke—a bleary, gray day, cold, and with sweeping showers of rain, she slept for a little while; but wakened with a start, for the train was still. Had they arrived? Had she lost a moment? Then she recognized the locality, and knew that there was an hour yet before she could be in the same city with him; and again the wheels began their clamorous assertion: "the right to see him; the right to see him."

Her plan was simple enough; she would go at once to Mrs. Richie's house and ask for the doctor. "I won't detain him very long; it will only take a little while to tell him," she said to herself. It came over her with the shivering sense of danger escaped, that in another day she would have been too late, his mother would be at home! "She wouldn't let him see me," she thought, fearfully. Afterward, after she had seen him, she would take a train to New York and cross the ferry…. "The water is pretty clean there," she thought.

She was dressed and ready to leave the train long before the station was reached. When the unkempt, haggard crowd swarmed off the cars and poured its jostling, hurrying length through the train-shed dim with puffing clouds of steam and clamorous with engines, Elizabeth was as fresh as if she had just come from her own house. She looked at herself in one of the big mirrors of the station dressing-room with entire satisfaction. "I am a little pretty even yet," she told herself, candidly. She wanted very much to be pretty now. When she went out to the street and found it raining in a steady, gray downpour, her heart sank,—oh, she must not get wet and draggled, now! Just for this hour she must be the old Elizabeth, the Elizabeth that he used to love, fresh, with starry eyes and a shell-like color in her cheeks!—and indeed the cold rain was making her face glow like a rose; but her eyes were solemn, not starry. As her cab jolted along the rainy streets, past the red-brick houses with their white shutters and scoured door-steps—houses were people were eating their breakfasts and reading their morning papers—Elizabeth, sitting on the frayed seat of the old hack, looked out of the window and thought how strange it all was! It would be just like this to-morrow morning, and she would not know it. "How queer!" she said to herself. But she was not frightened. "I suppose at the last minute I shall be frightened," she reflected. Then, for a moment, she forgot David and tried to realize the unrealizable: "everything will be going on just the same, and *I*—" She could not realize it, but she did not doubt it. When the cab drew up at Mrs. Richie's door, she was careful to pay the man before she got out so that her hat should not be spoiled by the rain when David saw it.

"He isn't in, miss," the maid told her in answer to her ring.

Elizabeth gasped. "What! Not here? Where is he?"

"He went down to the beach, 'm, yesterday, to see to the closing-up of the cottage, 'm."

"When is he coming back?" she said, faintly; and the woman said, smiling, "To-morrow, 'm."

Elizabeth stood blankly on the door-step. To-morrow? There was not going to be any to-morrow! What should she do? Her plan had been so definite and detailed that this interruption of his absence —a possibility which had not entered into her calculations—threw her into absolute confusion. He was away from home! What could she do?

Entirely forgetting the rain, she turned away and walked aimlessly down the street. "They'll know I've come here, and they'll find me before I can see him!" she said to herself, in terror. "I must go somewhere and decide what to do." She went into the nearest hotel and took a room. "I must plan; if I wait until he comes back, they'll find me!" But it was an hour before her plan was made; when it was, she sprang up with the old, tumultuous joyousness. Why, of course! How stupid not to have thought of it at once! She was so entirely oblivious of everything but her own purpose that she would have gone out of the hotel on the moment, had not the clerk checked her with some murmur about "a little charge." Elizabeth blushed to her temples. "Oh, I *beg* your pardon!" she said. In her mortification she wished that the bill had been twice as large. But when she was out in the rain, hurrying to the station, again she forgot everything except her consuming purpose. In the waiting-room—there were four hours before the train started—the panic thought took possession of her that she might miss him if she went down to the beach. "It's raining, and he may not stay over until to-morrow; he may be coming up this afternoon. But if I stay here they'll come and find me!" She could not face this last alternative. "They'll find me, and I won't be able to tell him; they'll take me home, and he will not have been told!" Sitting on the wooden settee in the ladies' waiting-room, she watched the clock until its gaunt white face blurred before her eyes. How the long hand crawled! Once, in a spasm of fright, she thought that it had stopped, and perhaps she had lost her train!

But at last the moment came; she started,—and as she drew nearer and nearer her goal, her whole body strained forward, as a man dying of thirst strains toward a spring gleaming in the desert distance; once she sighed with that anticipation of relief that is a shiver. Again the monotonous clatter of the wheels beat out the words that all night long over the mountains had grooved themselves into her brain: "Afterward, they will say I had the right to see him." Love, which that one mad hour, nearly three years before, had numbed and paralyzed, was awakening. It was as if a slowly rising torrent, dammed by some immovable barrier, had at last reached the brim,—trembled, hesitated: then leaped in foaming overflow into its old course! She thought of all the things she was going to tell him (but oh, they were so many, so many; how could she say them all?). "'I never was so true as when I was false. I never loved you so much as when I hated you. I never longed for your arms as I did when—' O God, give me time to tell him that! Don't let them find me before I can tell him that. *Don't* let him have gone back. God, please, *please* let me find him at the cottage so I can tell him." She was sitting on the plush cushion of the jolting, swaying old car, her hand on the back of the seat in front of her, every muscle tense with readiness to spring to her feet the moment the train stopped.

It was still raining when she got off at the little station which had sprung up out of the sand to accommodate a summer population. It was deserted now, and the windows were boarded over. A passer-by, under a dripping umbrella, lounged along the platform and stopped to look at her. "Come down to see cottages?" he inquired. She said no; but could she get a carriage to take her over to Little Beach?

He shook his head sympathetically. "A hack? *Here?* Lord, no! There isn't no depot carriage running at this time of year. You'd ought to have got off at Normans, the station above this, and then you could have drove over; fourteen miles, though. Something of a drive on an evening like this! But Normans is quite a place. They run two depot carriages there all winter and a dozen in summer."

"I'll walk," she told him, briefly.

"It's more 'an three miles," he warned her; "and it's sheeting down! If
I had such a thing as an umbrella, except this one, I'd—"

But she had gone. She knew the way; she remembered the summer—oh, so long ago!—when she and Nannie had driven over that sandy road along the beach on their way to Mrs. Richie's house. It was so deep with mud now that sometimes she had to walk outside the wheel-ruts into the wiry beach-grass. The road toiled among the dunes; on the shore on her right she could hear the creaming lap of the waves; but rain was driving in from the sea in an impenetrable curtain, and only when in some turn of the wind it lifted and shifted could she catch a glimpse of the scarf of foam lying on the sands, or see the gray heave of an endless expanse that might be water or might be sky folded down into the water. It was growing dark; sometimes she blundered from the road to one side or the other; sometimes she thought she saw approaching figures—a man, perhaps, or a vehicle; but as she neared them they were only bushes or leaning, wind-beaten pines. She was drenched and her clothes seemed intolerably heavy. Oh, how David would laugh at her hat! She put up her hand, in its soaked and slippery glove, and touched the roses about the crown and laughed herself. "He won't mind," she said, contentedly. She had forgotten that he had stopped loving her. She began to sing under her breath the old tune of her gay, inconsequent girlhood—

"Oh, won't it be joyful, joyful, joyful,
Oh, won't it be joyful, to meet..."

She stopped; something warm was on her face; she had not known that she was weeping. Suddenly, far off, she saw a glimmer of light.... Mrs. Richie's house! Her heart rose in her throat. "David," she said aloud, weakly, "David, I'm coming just as fast as I can."

But when she opened the door of the living-room in the little house that sat so close to the crumpling lap and crash of the tide, and saw him, his pipe in his hand, half rising from his chair by the fire and turning around to see who had entered, she could hardly speak his name—"*David*."

Chapter 35

"... And that was Thursday; your letter had come in the first mail; and—oh, hush, hush; it was not a wicked letter, David. Don't you suppose I know that, now? I knew it—the next day. And I read it. I don't know just what happened then. I can't remember very clearly. I think I felt 'insulted.' ... It sounds so foolish to say that, doesn't it? But I was just a girl then, and you know what girls are like.... David, I am not making any excuse. There isn't any excuse. I am just—telling you. I have to talk slowly; I am tired. You won't mind if I talk slowly? ... I suppose I thought I had been 'insulted'; and I remember something seemed to flame up. You know how it always was with me? David, I have never been able to be angry since that day. Isn't that strange? I've never been angry since. Well, then, I went out to walk. I remember Cherry-pie called down-stairs to know if I had a clean pocket-handkerchief. I remember that; and yet I can't seem to remember why I went out to walk. ... And he came up and spoke to me. Oh, I forgot to tell you: he'd been in love with me. I meant to tell you about that as soon as we were married.... Where was I?—Oh, yes; he spoke to me...."

Her voice broke with exhaustion; she closed her eyes and lay back in the big chair. David put her hand against his face, and held it there until she opened her eyes. She looked at him dumbly for a little while; then the slow, monotonous outpouring of all the silent months began again: "And I said I hated you. And he said if I married him, it would show you that I hated you. David, he was fond of me. I have to remember that. It wouldn't be fair not to remember that, would it? I was really the one to blame. Oh, I must be fair to him; he was fond of me.... And all that afternoon, after he married me, I was so glad to think how wicked I was. I knew how you would suffer. And that made me glad to be wicked...."

There was a long pause; he pulled a little shawl across her feet, and laid her hand over his eyes; but he was silent.

"Then," she said, in a whisper, "I died, I think. I suppose that is why I have never been angry since. Something was killed in me.... I've wondered a good deal about that. David, isn't it strange how part of you can die, and yet you can go on living? Of course I expected to die. I prayed all the time that I might. But I went on living;—you are glad I lived?" she said, incredulously, catching some broken murmur from behind his hands in which his face was hidden; "glad? Why, I should have thought—Well, that was the most awful time of all. The only peace I had, just single minutes of peace, was when I remembered that you hated me."

He laid his face against her knee, and she felt the fierce intake of his breath.

"You *didn't* hate me? Oh, don't say you didn't, David. Don't! It was the only comfort I had, to have you despise me. Although that was just at first. Afterward, last May, when you walked down to Nannie's with me that afternoon, and I thought you had got all over it, I...something seemed to be eating my heart away. That seems like a contradiction, doesn't it? I don't understand how I could feel two ways. But just at first I wanted you to hate me. I thought you would be less unhappy if you hated me; and besides, I wanted to feel the whips. I felt them—oh, I felt them!...And all the time I thought that soon I would die. But death would have been too easy. I had to go on living." There was another long silence; he kissed her hand once; but he did not speak.... "And the days went on, and went on, and went on. Sometimes I didn't feel anything; but sometimes it was like stringing sharp beads on a red-hot wire. I suppose that sounds foolish? But when his mother disinherited him, I knew I would have to go on—stringing beads. Because it would have been mean, then, to leave him. You see that, David? Besides, I was a spoiled thing, a worthless thing. If staying with him would make up for the harm I had done him,—Mrs. Maitland told me I had injured him; why of course, there was nothing else to do. I knew you would understand. So I stayed. 'Unkind to me?'" She bent forward a little to hear his smothered question. "Oh no; never. I used to wish he would be. But he—loved me"—she shuddered. "Oh, David, how I have dreamed of your arms. David … David … "

They had forgotten that each had believed love had ceased in the other; they did not even assert that it was unchanged. Nor was there any plea for forgiveness on either side. The moment was too great for that.

She sank back in her chair with a long breath. He rose, and kneeling beside her, drew her against his breast. She sighed with comfort. "*Here*! At last to be here. I never thought it would be. It is heaven. Yes; I shall remember that I have been in heaven. But I don't think I shall be sent to hell. No; God won't punish me any more. It will be just sleep."

He had to bend his ear almost to her white lips to catch her whisper. "What did I say? I don't remember exactly; I am so happy… . Let me be quiet a little while. I'm pretty tired. May I stay until morning? It is raining, and if I may stay … I will go away very early in the morning." The long, rambling, half-whispered story had followed the fierce statement, flung at him when she burst in out of the storm, and stood, sodden with rain, trembling with fatigue and cold, and pushing from her his alarmed and outstretched hands,—the statement that she had left Blair! There were only a few words in the outburst of terrible anger which had been dormant in her for all these years: "He stole your wife. Now he is stealing your money. I told him he couldn't keep them both. Your wife has come back to you. I have left him— "

Even while she was stammering, shrilly, the furious finality, he caught her, swaying, in his arms. It was an hour before she could speak coherently of the happenings of the last twenty-four hours; she had to be warmed and fed and calmed. And it was curious how the lover in him and the physician in him alternated in that hour; he had been instant with the soothing commonplace of help,—her wet clothes, her chilled body, her hunger, were his first concern. "I know you are hungry," he said, cheerfully; but his hands shook as he put food before her. When he drew her chair up to the fire, and kneeling down, took off her wet shoes, he held her slender, tired feet in his hands and chafed them gently; but suddenly laid them against his breast, warming them, murmuring over them with a sobbing breath, as though he felt the weariness of the little feet, plodding, plodding, plodding through the rain to find him. The next minute he was the doctor, ordering her with smiling words to lie back in her chair and rest; then looking at her with a groan.

When at last she was coherent again, she began that pitiful confession, and he listened; at first walking up and down; then coming nearer; sitting beside her; then kneeling; then lifting her and holding her against his breast. When, relaxing in his arms like a tired child, she ended, almost in a whisper, with her timid plea to be allowed to stay until morning, the tears dropped down his face.

"Until morning?" he said, with a laugh that broke into a sob —"until death!"

Long before this his first uneasiness, at the situation—for her sake,—had disappeared. The acquired uneasinesses of convention vanish before the primal realities. The long-banked fire had glowed, then broken into flames that consumed such chaff as "propriety." As he held her in his arms after that whispered and rambling story of despair, he trembled all over. For Elizabeth there had never been a single moment of conventional consciousness; she was solemnly unaware of everything but the fact that they were together for this last moment. When he said "until death," she lifted her head and looked at him.

"Yes," she said, "*until death.*"

Something in her broken whisper touched him like ice. He was suddenly rigid. "Elizabeth, where did you mean to go to-morrow morning?" She made no answer, but he felt that she was alert. "Elizabeth! Tell me! what do you mean?" His loud and terrified command made her quiver; she was bewildered by the unexpectedness of his suspicion, but too dulled and stunned to evade it. David, with his ear close to her lips, raised his head. "Elizabeth, don't you understand? Dear, this is life, not death, for us both."

She drew away from him with a long sigh, struggling up feebly out of his arms and groping for her chair; she shook her head, smiling faintly. "I'm sorry you guessed. No, I can't go on living. There's no use talking about it, David. I can't."

He stood looking down at her, pale from the shock of his discovery. "Listen to me, Elizabeth: you belong to me. Don't you understand, dear? You always have belonged to me. He knew it when he stole you from yourself, as well as from me. You have always been mine. You have come back to me. Do you think I will let Blair Maitland or death or God Almighty, steal you now? Never. You belong to me! to me!"

"But—" she began.

"Oh, Elizabeth, what do we care for what they call right and wrong?
'Right' is being together!"

She frowned in a puzzled way. She had not been thinking of "right and wrong"; her mind had been absorbed by the large and simple necessity of death. But his inevitable reasonableness, ignoring her organic impulse, was already splitting hairs to justify an organic impulse of his own.

"God gave you to me," he said, "and by God I'll keep you! That's what is right; if we parted now it would be wrong."

It seemed as if the gale of passion which had been slowly rising in him in these hours they had been together blew away the mists in which her mind had been groping, blew away the soothing fogs of death which had been closing in about her, and left her, shrinking, in sudden, confusing light.

"Wrong?" she said, dazed; "I hadn't thought about that. David, I wouldn't have come to you except—except because it was the end. Anything else is impossible, you know."

"Why?" he demanded.

"I am married," she said, bewildered.

He laughed under his breath. "Blair Maitland will take his own medicine, now," he said;—"you are married to *me!*"

The triumph in his voice, while it vaguely alarmed her, struck some answering chord in her mind, for while mechanically she contradicted him, some deeper self was saying, "yes; yes."

But aloud she said, "It can't be, David; don't you see it can't be?"

"But it *is* already; I will never let you go. I've got you—at last. Elizabeth, listen to me; while you've been talking, I've thought it all out: as things are, I don't think you can possibly get a divorce from Blair and marry me. He's 'kind' to you, you say; and he's 'decent,' and he doesn't drink—and so forth and so forth. I know the formula to keep a woman with a man she hates and call it being respectable. No, you can't get a divorce from him; but he can get a divorce from you ... if you give him the excuse to do so."

Elizabeth looked at him with perfectly uncomprehending eyes. The innocence of them did not touch him. For the second time in her life she was at the mercy of Love. "Blair is fond of me," she said; "he never would give me a divorce. He has told me so a hundred times. Do you suppose I haven't begged him to let me go? On my knees I begged him. No, David, there is no way out except—"

"There is a way out if you love me enough to—come to me. Then," he said in a whisper, "he will divorce you and we can be married. Oh, Elizabeth, death is not the way out; it is *life*, dear, life! Will you live? Will you give me life?" He was breathing as if he had been running; he held her fingers against his lips until he bruised them.

She understood. After a minute of silence she said, faintly: "As for me, nothing matters. Even if it is wicked—"

"It is not wicked!"

"Well, if it were, if you wanted me I would come. I don't seem to care. Nothing seems to me wrong in the whole world. And nothing right. Do you understand, David? I am—done. My life is worthless, anyhow. Use it—and throw it away. But it would ruin you. No, I won't do it."

"Ruin me? It would make me! I have shriveled, I have starved, I have frozen without you. Ask my mother if what I tell you isn't true." She caught her breath and drew away from him. "Your mother!" she said, faintly. But he did not notice the recoil.

"It would end your career," she said. She was confused by the mere tumult of his words.

"Career! The only career I want is *you*. Medicine isn't the only thing in the world, nor Philadelphia the only place to practise it. And if I can't be a doctor, I can break stones for my wife. Elizabeth, to love you is the only career I want. But you—can you? Am I asking more than you can give? Do you care what people say? We may not be able to be married for a year. Longer, perhaps; the law takes time. They will call it disgrace, you know, the people who don't know what love means. Could you bear that—for me? Do you love me enough for that, Elizabeth?"

His voice was hoarse with passion. He was on his knees beside her, his face hot against hers, his arms around her. Not only his bitterly thought-out theories of individualism, but all his years of decent living, contributed to his overthrow at that moment. He was a man; and here was his woman, who had been torn from him by a thief: she had come back to him, she had toiled back through the storm, she had fought back through cruel and imprisoning ties that had held her for nearly three years; should he not keep her, now that she had come? The cave-dweller in him cried out "*Yes!*" To let her go now, would be to loosen his fingers just as they gripped the neck of the thief who had robbed him! In the madness of that moment of hate and love, his face on hers, his arms around her, David did not know that his tears were wet on her lips.

"Mine," he said, panting; "*mine*! my own has come back to me. Say so; tell me so yourself. Say it! I want to hear you say it."

"Why David, I have always been yours. But I am not worth taking. I am not—"

[Illustration: "WILL YOU LIVE? WILL YOU GIVE ME LIFE?"]

"Hush! You are mine. They shall never part us again. Elizabeth—to-morrow we will go away." She sank against him in silence; for a while he was silent, too. Then, in a low voice, he told her how they must carry out a plan which had sprung, full-winged, from his mind; "when he knows you have been here to-night," David said,—and trembled from head to foot; "he will divorce you."

She listened, assenting, but bewildered. "I was going to die," she said, faintly; "I don't know how to live. Oh, I think the other way would be better."

But he did not stop to discuss it; he had put her back into the reclining chair—once in a while the physician remembered her fatigue, though for the most part the lover thought only of himself; he saw how white she was, and put her in the big chair; then, drawing up a footstool, he sat down, keeping her hand in his; sometimes he kissed it, but all the time he talked violently of right and wrong. Elizabeth was singularly indifferent to his distinctions; perhaps the deep and primitive experience of looking into the face of Death made her so. At any rate, her question was not "Is it right?" it was only "Is it best?" Was it best for him to do this thing? Would it not injure him? David, brushing away her objections with an exultant belief in himself, was far less elemental. Right? What made right and wrong? Law? Elizabeth knew better! Unless she meant God's law. As far as that went, she was breaking it if she went on living with Blair. As for dying, she had no right to die! She was his. Would she rob him again?

It was all the everlasting, perfectly sincere sophistry of the man who has been swept past honor and prudence and even pity, that poured from David's lips; and with it, love! love! love! Elizabeth, listening to it, carried along by it, had, in the extraordinary confusion of the moment, nothing to oppose to it but her own unworth. To this he refused to listen, closing her lips with his own, and then going on with his quite logical reasoning. His mind was alert to meet and arrange every difficulty and every detail; once, half laughing, he stopped to say, "We'll have to live on your money, Elizabeth. See what I've come to!" The old scruples seemed, beside this new reality, merely ridiculous—although there was a certain satisfaction in throwing overboard that hideous egotism of his, which had made all the trouble that had come to them. "You see," he explained, "we shall go away for a while, until you get your divorce. And it will take time to pick up a practice, especially, in a new place. So you will probably have to support me," he ended, smiling. But she was too much at peace in the haven of his clasping arms even to smile. Once, when he confessed his shame at having doubted her—"for I did," he said; "I actually thought you cared for him!" she roused herself: "It was my fault. I won't let you blame yourself; it was all my fault!" she said; then sank again into dreaming quiet.

It was midnight; the fire had died down; a stick of drift-wood on the iron dogs, gnawed through by shimmering blue and copper flames, broke apart, and a shower of sparks flew up, caught in the soot, and smoldered in spreading rosettes on the chimney-back. The night, pressing black against the windows, was full of the murmurous silence of the rain and the soft advancing crash of the incoming tide; the man and woman were silent, too. Sometimes he would kiss the little scar on her wrist; sometimes press his lips into the soft cup of her palm; there seemed no need of words. It was in one of these silences that David suddenly raised his head and frowned.

"Listen!" he said; then a moment later: "wheels! *here?* at this time of night!"

Elizabeth crouched back in her chair. "It is Blair. He has followed me—"

"No, no; it is somebody who has lost his way in the rain. Yes, I hear him; he is coming in to ask the road."

There were hurried steps on the porch, and Elizabeth grew so deadly white that David said again, reassuringly: "It's some passer-by. I'll send him about his business."

Loud, vehement knocking interrupted him, and he said, cheerfully: "Confound them, making such a noise! Don't be frightened; it is only some farmer—"

He took up a lamp and, closing the door of the living-room behind him, went out into the hall; some one, whoever it was, was fumbling with the knob of the front door as if in terrible haste. David slipped the bolt and would have opened the door, but it seemed to burst in, and against it, clinging to the knob, panting and terrified, stood his mother.

"David! Is she—Am I too late? David! Where is Elizabeth? *Am I too late?*"

Chapter 36

The rainy dawn which Elizabeth had seen glimmering in the steam and smoke of the railroad station filtered wanly through Mercer's yellow fog. In Mrs. Maitland's office-dining-room the gas, burning in an orange halo, threw a livid light on the haggard faces of four people who had not slept that night.

When Blair had come frantically back from his fruitless quest at the hotel to say, "Is she here, *now?*" Mrs. Richie had sent him at once to Mr. Ferguson, who, roused from his bed, instantly took command.

"Tell me just what has happened, please?" he said.

Blair, almost in collapse, told the story of the afternoon. He held nothing back. In the terror that consumed him, he spared himself nothing; he had made Elizabeth angry; frightfully angry. But she didn't show it; she had even said she was not angry. But she said —and he repeated that sword-like sentence about "David's money and David's wife." Then, almost in a whisper, he added her question about—drowning. "She has—" he said; he did not finish the sentence.

Robert Ferguson made no comment, but his face quivered. "Have you a carriage?" he asked, shrugging into his overcoat. Blair nodded, and they set out.

It was after five when they came back to Mrs. Maitland's dining-room, where the gaslight struggled ineffectually with the fog. They had done everything which, at that hour, could be done.

"Oh, when will it ever get light!" Blair said, despairingly. He pushed aside the food Nannie had placed on the table for them, and dropped his face on his arms. He had a sudden passionate longing for his mother; she would have *done* something! She would have told these people, these dazed, terrified people! what to do. She always knew what to do. For the first time in his life he needed his mother.

Robert Ferguson, standing at the window, was staring out at the blind, yellow mist. "As soon as it's light enough, we'll get a boat and go down the river," he said, with heavy significance.

"But it is absurd to jump at such a conclusion," Mrs. Richie protested.

"You don't know her," Elizabeth's uncle said, briefly.

Blair echoed the words. "No; you don't know her."

"All the same, I don't believe it!" Mrs. Richie said, emphatically. "For one thing, Blair says that her comb and brush are not on her bureau. A girl doesn't take her toilet things with her when she goes out to—"

"Elizabeth might," Mr. Ferguson said.

Blair, looking up, broke out: "Oh, that money! It's that that has made all the trouble. Why did I say I wouldn't give it up? I'd throw it into the fire, if it would bring her back to me!"

Mrs. Richie was silent. Her face was tense with anxiety, but it was not the same anxiety that plowed the other faces. "Did you go to the depot?" she said. "Perhaps she took the night train. The ticket-agent might have seen her."

"But why should she take a night train?" Blair said; "where would she go?"

"Why should she do a great many things she has done?" Mrs. Richie parried; and added, softly, "I want to speak to you, Blair; come into the parlor for a minute." When they were alone, she said, —her eyes avoiding his; "I have an idea that she has gone to Philadelphia. To see me."

"You? But you are here!"

"Yes; but perhaps she thought I went home yesterday; you thought so."

Blair grasped at a straw of hope. "I will telegraph—" "No;

that would be of no use. The servants couldn't answer it; and—and there is no one else there. I will take the morning express, and telegraph you as soon as I get home."

"But I can't wait all day!" he said; "I will wire—" he paused; it struck him like a blow that there was only one person to whom to wire. The blood rushed to his face. "You think that she has gone to him?"

"I think she has gone to me," she told him, coldly. "What more natural?
I am an old friend, and she was angry with you."

"Yes; she was, but—"

"As for my son," said Mrs. Richie, "he is not at home; but I assure you,"—she stumbled a little over this; "I assure you that if he were he would have no desire to see your wife."

Blair was silent. Then he said, in a smothered voice: "If she is at your house, tell her I won't keep the money. I'll make Nannie build a hospital with it; or I'll ... tell her, if she will only just come back to me, I'll—" He could not go on.

"Blair," Robert Ferguson said, from the doorway, "it is light enough now to get a boat."

Blair nodded. "If she has gone to you, if she is alive," he said, "tell her I'll give him the money."

Helena Richie lifted her head with involuntary hauteur. "My son has no interest in your money!"

"Oh," he said, brokenly, "you can't seem to think of anything but his quarrel with me. Somehow, all that seems so unimportant now! Why, I'd ask David to help me, if I could reach him." He did not see her relenting, outstretched hand; for the first time in a life starved for want of the actualities of pain, Blair was suffering; he forgot embarrassment, he even forgot hatred; he touched fundamentals: the need of help and the instinctive reliance upon friendship. "David would help me!" he said, passionately; "or my mother would know what to do; but you people—" He dashed after Mr. Ferguson, and a moment later Mrs. Richie heard the carriage rattling down the street; the two men were going to the river to begin their heart-sickening search.

It was then that she started upon a search of her own. She made a somewhat lame excuse to Nannie—Nannie was the last person to be intrusted with Helena Richie's fears! Then she took the morning express across the mountains. She sat all day in fierce alternations of hope and angry concern: Surely Elizabeth was alive; but suppose she was alive—with David! David's mother, remembering what he had said to her that Sunday afternoon on the beach, knew, in the bottom of her heart, that she would rather have Elizabeth dead than alive under such conditions. Her old misgivings began to press upon her: the conditions might have held no danger for him if he had had a different mother! She found herself remembering, with anguish, a question that had been asked her very long ago, when David was a little boy: Can *you* make him brave; can *you* make him honorable; can *you*— "I've tried, oh, I have tried," she said; "but perhaps Dr. Lavendar ought not to have given him to me!" It was an unendurable idea; she drove it out of her mind, and sat looking at the mist-enfolded mountains, struggling to decide between a hope that implied a fear and a fear that destroyed a hope;—but every now and then, under both the hope and the fear, came a pang of memory that sent the color into her face: Robert Ferguson's library; his words; his kiss....

As the afternoon darkened into dusk, through sheer fatigue she relaxed into certainty that both the hope and the fear were baseless: Elizabeth had not gone to David; she couldn't have done such an insane thing! David's mother began to be sorry she had suggested to Blair that his wife might be in Philadelphia. She began to wish she had stayed in Mercer, and not left them all to their cruel anxiety. "If she has done what they think, I'll go back to-morrow. Robert will need me, and David would want me to go back." It occurred to her, with a lift of joy, that she might possibly find David at home. Owing to the bad weather, he might not have gone down to the beach to close the cottage as he had written her he meant to do. She wondered how he would take this news about Elizabeth. For a moment she almost hoped he would not be at home, so that she need not tell him. "Oh," she said to herself, "when will he get over her cruelty to him?" As she gathered up her wraps to leave the car, she wondered whether human creatures ever did quite "get over" the catastrophes of life. "Have I? And I am fifty,—and it was twenty years ago!"

When with a lurch the cab drew up against the curb, her glance at the unlighted windows of her parlor made her sigh with relief; there was nobody there! Yes; she had certainly been foolish to rush off across the mountains, and leave those poor, distressed people in Mercer.

"The doctor is at Little Beach, I suppose?" she said to the woman who answered her ring; "By-the-way, Mary, no one has been here to-day? No lady to see me?"

"There was a lady to see the doctor; she was just possessed to see him. I told her he was down at the beach, and she was that upset," Mary said, smiling, "you'd 'a' thought there wasn't another doctor in Philadelphia!" Patients were still enough of a rarity to interest the whole friendly household.

"Who was she? What was she like? Did she give her name?" Mrs. Richie was breathless; the servant was startled at the change in her; fear, like a tangible thing, leaped upon her and shook her.

"Who was she?" Mrs. Richie said, fiercely.

The surprised woman, giving the details of that early call, was, of course, ignorant of the lady's name; but after the first word or two David's mother knew it. "Bring me a time-table. Never mind my supper! I must see the lady. I think I know who she was. She wanted to see me, and I must find her. I know where she has gone. Hurry! Where is the new time-table?"

"She didn't ask for you, 'm," the bewildered maid assured her.

Mrs. Richie was not listening; she was turning the leaves of the *Pathfinder* with trembling fingers; the trains had been changed on the little branch road, but somehow she must get there,— "*to-night!*" she said to herself. To find a train to Normans was an immense relief, though it involved a fourteen-mile drive to Little Beach. She could not reach them ("them!" she was sure of it now), she could not reach them until nearly twelve, but she would be able to say that Elizabeth had spent the night with her.

The hour before the train started for Normans seemed endless to Helena
Richie. She sent a despatch to Blair to say:

"*I have found her. Do not come for her yet. This is imperative. Will telegraph you to-morrow.*"

After that she walked about, up and down, sometimes stopping to look out of the window into the rainswept street, sometimes pausing to pick up a book but though she turned over the pages, she did not know what she read. She debated constantly whether she had done well to telegraph Blair. Suppose, in spite of her command, he should rush right on to Philadelphia, "then what!" she said to herself, frantically. If he found that Elizabeth had followed David down to the cottage, what would he do? There would be a scandal! And it was not David's fault—she had followed him; how like her to follow him, careless of everything but her own whim of the moment! She would have recalled the despatch if she could have done so. "If Robert were only here to tell me what to do!" she thought, realizing, even in her cruel alarm, how greatly she depended on him. Suddenly she must have realized something else, for a startled look came into her eyes. "No! of course I'm not," she said; but the color rose in her face. The revelation was only for an instant; the next moment she was tense with anxiety and counting the minutes before she could start for the station.

It was a great relief when she found herself at last on the little local train, rattling out into the rainy night. When she reached Normans it was not easy to get a carriage to go to Little Beach. No depot hack-driver would consider such a drive on such a night. She found her way through the rainy streets to a livery-stable, and standing in the doorway of a little office that smelled of harnesses and horses, she bargained with a reluctant man, who, though polite enough to take his feet from his desk and stand up before a lady, told her point-blank that there wasn't no money, no, nor no woman, that he'd drive twenty-eight miles for—down to the beach and back; on no such night as this; "but maybe one of my men might, if you'd make it worth his while," he said, doubtfully.

"I will make it worth his while," Mrs. Richie said.

"There's a sort of inlet between us and the beach, kind of a river, like; you'll have to ferry over," the man warned her.

"Please get the carriage at once," she said.

So the long drive began. It was very dark. At times the rain sheeted down so that little streams of water dripped upon her from the top of the carryall, and the side curtains flapped so furiously that she could scarcely hear the driver grumbling that if he'd 'a' knowed what kind of a night it was he wouldn't have undertook the job.

"I'll pay you double your price," she said in a lull of the storm; and after that there was only the sheeting rain and the tugging splash of mud-loaded fetlocks. At the ferry there was a long delay. "The ferry-man's asleep, I guess," the driver told her; certainly there was no light in the little weather-beaten house on the riverbank. The man clambered out from under the streaming rubber apron of the carryall, and handing the wet reins back to her to hold — "that horse takes a notion to run sometimes," he said, casually; made his way to the ferry-house. "Come out!" he said, pounding on the door; "tend to your business! there's a lady wants to cross!"

The ferry-man had his opinion of ladies who wanted to do such things in such weather; but he came, after what seemed to the shivering passenger an interminable time, and the carryall was driven onto the flat-bottomed boat. A minute later the creak of the cable and the slow rock of the carriage told her they had started. It was too dark to see anything, but she could hear the sibilant slap of the water against the side of the scow and the brush of rain on the river. Once the dripping horse shook himself, and the harness rattled and the old hack quivered on its sagging springs. She realized that she was cold; she could hear the driver and the ferryman talking; there was the blue spurt of a match, and a whiff of very bad tobacco from a pipe. Then a dash of rain blew in her face, and the smell of the pipe was washed out of the air.

It was after twelve when, stumbling up the path to her own house, she leaned against the door awaiting David's answer to her knock; when he opened it to the gust of wet wind and her drawn, white face, he was stunned with astonishment. He never knew what answer he made to those first broken, frantic words; as for her, she did not wait to hear his answer. She ran past him and burst into the fire-lit silence that was still tingling with emotion. She saw Elizabeth rising, panic-stricken, from her chair. Clutching her shoulder, she looked hard into the younger woman's face; then, with a great sigh, she sank down into a chair.

"Thank God!" she said, faintly.

David, following her, stammered out, "How did you get

here?" The full, hot torrent of passion of only a moment before had come to a crashing standstill. He could hardly breathe with the suddenness of it. His thoughts galloped. He heard his own voice as if it had been somebody else's, and he was conscious of his foolishness in asking his question; what difference did it make how she got here! Besides, he knew how: she had come over the mountains that day, taken the evening train for Normans, and driven down here, fourteen miles—in this storm! "You must be worn out," he said, involuntarily.

"I am in time; nothing else matters. David, go and pay the man. Here is my purse."

He glanced at Elizabeth, hesitated, and went. The two women, alone, looked at each other for a speechless instant.

Chapter 37

"You ought not to be here, you know," Helena Richie said, in a low voice.

Elizabeth was silent.

"They are all very much frightened about you at home."

"I am sorry they are frightened."

"Your coming might be misunderstood," David's mother said; her voice was very harsh; the gentle loveliness of her face had changed to an incredible harshness. "I shall say I was here with you, of course; but you are insane, Elizabeth! you are insane to be here!"

"Mother," David said, quietly, "you mustn't find fault with Elizabeth." He had come back, and even as he spoke retreating wheels were heard. They were alone, these three; there was no world to any of them outside that fire-lit room, encompassed by night, the ocean, and the storm. "Elizabeth did exactly right to come down here to—to consult me," David said; "but we won't talk about it now; it's too late, and you are too tired."

Then turning to Elizabeth, he took her hand. "Won't you go up-stairs now? You are as tired as Materna! But she must have something to eat before she goes to bed." Still holding her hand, he opened the door for her. "You know the spare room? I'm afraid it's rather in disorder, but you will find some blankets and things in the closet."

Elizabeth hesitated; then obeyed him.

David was entirely self-possessed by this time; in that moment while he stood in the rain, counting out the money from his mother's purse for the driver, and telling the man of a short cut across the dunes, the emotion of a moment before cooled into grim alertness to meet the emergency: *there must be no scene.* To avoid the possibility of such a thing, he must get Elizabeth out of the room at once. As he slipped the bolt on the front door and hurried back to the living room, he said a single short word between his teeth. But he was not angry; he was only irritated—as one might be irritated at a good child whose ignorant innocence led it into meddling with matters beyond its comprehension. And he was not apprehensive; his mother's coming could not alter anything; it was merely an embarrassment and distress. What on earth should he do with her the next morning! "I'll have to lie to her," he thought, in consternation. David had never lied to his mother, and even in this self-absorbed moment he shrank from doing so. He was keenly disturbed, but as the door closed upon Elizabeth he spoke quietly enough: "You are very tired, Materna; don't let's get to discussing things tonight. I'll bring you something to eat, and then you must go up to your room."

"There is nothing to discuss, David," she said; "of course Elizabeth ought not to have come down here to you. But I am here. To-morrow she will go home with me."

She had taken off her bonnet, and with one unsteady hand she brushed back the tendrils of her soft hair that the rain had tightened into curls all about her temples; the glow in her cheeks from the cold air was beginning to die out, and he saw, suddenly, the suffering in her eyes. But for the first time in his life David Richie was indifferent to pain in his mother's face; that calm declaration that Elizabeth would go home with her, brushed the habit of tenderness aside and stung him into argument—which a moment later he regretted. "You say she'll 'go home.' Do you mean that you will take her back to Blair Maitland?"

"I hope she will go to her husband."

"Why?" He was standing before her, his shoulder against the mantelpiece, his hands in his pockets; his attitude was careless, but his face was alert and hard; she no longer seemed a meddlesome good child; she was his mother, interfering in what was not her business. "Why?" he repeated.

"Because he is her husband," Helena Richie said.

"You know how he became her husband; he took advantage of an insane moment. The marriage has ended."

"Marriage can't end, David. Living together may end; but Blair is not unkind to Elizabeth; he is not unfaithful; he is not unloving—"

"No, my God! he is not. My poor Elizabeth!"

His mother, looking at the suddenly convulsed face before her, knew that it was useless to pretend that this was only a matter of preserving appearances by her presence. "David," she said, "what do you mean by that?"

"I mean that she has done with that thief." As he spoke it flashed into his mind that perhaps it was best to have things out with her now; then in the morning he would arrange it, somehow, so that she and Elizabeth should not meet;—for Elizabeth must not hear talk like this. Not that he was afraid of its effect; certainly this soft, sweet mother of his could not do what he had declared neither Blair Maitland, nor death, nor God himself could accomplish! But her words would make Elizabeth uncomfortable; so he had better tell her now, and get it over. In the midst of his own discomfort, he realized that this would spare him the necessity of a lie the next morning; and he was conscious of relief at that. "Mother," he said, gently, "I was going to write to you about it, but perhaps I had better tell you now…. She is coming to me."

"Coming to you!"

He sat down beside her, and took her hand in his; the terror in her face made him wince. For a moment he wished he had not undertaken to tell her; a letter would have been better. On paper, he could have reasoned it out calmly; now, her quivering face distressed him so that he hardly knew what he said.

"Materna, I am awfully sorry to pain you! I do wish you would realize that things *have* to be this way."

"What way?"

"She and I have to be together," he said, simply. "She belongs to me. When I keep her from going back to Blair I merely keep my own. Mother, can't you understand? there is something higher than man's law, which ties a woman to a man she hates; there is God's law, which gives her to the man she loves! Oh, I am sorry you came to-night! To-morrow I would have written to you. You don't know how distressed I am to pain you, but—poor mother!"

She had sunk back in her chair with a blanched face. She said, faintly, "*David!*"

"Don't let's talk about it, Materna," he said, pitifully. He could not bear to look at her; it seemed as if she had grown suddenly old; she was broken, haggard, with appalled eyes and trembling lips. "You don't understand," David said, greatly distressed.

Helena Richie put her hands over her face. "Don't I?" she said. There was a long pause; he took her hand and stroked it gently; but in spite of tenderness for her he was thinking of that other hand, young and thrilling to his own, which he had held an hour before; his lips stung at the memory of it; he almost forgot his mother, cowering in her chair. Suddenly she spoke:

"Well, David, what do you propose to do? After you have seduced another man's wife and branded Elizabeth with a—a dreadful name—"

His pity broke like a bubble; he struck the arm of his chair with a clenched hand. "You must not use such words to me! I will not listen to words that soil your lips and my ears! Will you leave this room or shall I?"

"Answer my question first: what do you mean to do after you

have taken
Elizabeth?"

"I shall marry her, of course. He will divorce her, and we shall be married." He was trembling with indignation: "I will not submit to this questioning," he said. He got up and opened the door. "Will you leave me, please?" he said, frigidly.

But she did not rise. She was bending forward, her hands gripped between her knees. Then, slowly, she raised her bowed head and there was authority in her face. "Wait. You must listen. You owe it to me to listen."

He hesitated. "I owe it to myself not to listen to such words as you used a moment ago." He was standing before her, his arms folded across his breast; there was no son's hand put out now to touch hers.

"I won't repeat them," she said, "although I don't know any others that can be used when a man takes another man's wife, or when a married woman goes away with a man who is not her husband."

"You drag me into an abominable position in making me even defend myself. But I will defend myself. I will explain to you that, as things are, Elizabeth cannot get a divorce from Blair Maitland. But if she leaves him for me, he will divorce her; and we can marry."

"Perhaps he will not divorce her."

"You mean out of revenge? I doubt if even he could be such a brute as that."

"There have been such brutes."

"Very well; then we will do without his divorce! We will do without the respectability that you think so much of."

"Nobody can do without it very long," she said, mildly. "But we won't argue about respectability; and I won't even ask you whether you will marry her, if she gets her divorce."

His indignation paused in sheer amazement. "No," he said. "I should hardly think that even you would venture to ask me such a question!"

"I will only ask you, my son, if you have thought how you would smirch her name by such a process of getting possession of her?"

"Oh," he said, despairingly, "what is the use of talking about it? I can't make you understand!"

"Have you considered that you will ruin Elizabeth?" she insisted.

"You may call happiness 'ruin,' if you want to, mother. We don't—she and I."

"I suppose you wouldn't believe me if I told you it wouldn't be happiness?"

Her question was too absurd to answer. Besides, he was determined not to argue with her; argument would only prolong this futile and distressing interview. So, holding in the leash of respect for her, contempt for her opinions, he listened with strained and silent patience to what she had to say of duty and endurance. It all belonged, he thought, to her generation and to her austere goodness; but from his point of view it was childish. When at last he spoke, in answer to an insistent question as to whether Elizabeth realized how society would regard her course, his voice as well as his words showed his entire indifference to her whole argument. "Yes," he said; "I have pointed out to Elizabeth the fact that though our course will be in accordance with a Law that is infinitely higher than the laws that you think so much of, there will be, as you say, people to throw mud at her."

"A 'higher law,'" she said, slowly. "I have heard of the 'higher law,'
David."

"That Elizabeth will obey it for me, that she is willing to expose herself to the contempt of little minds, makes me adore her! And I am willing, I love her enough, to accept her sacrifice—"

"Though you did not love her enough to accept the trifling matter of her money?" his mother broke in.

Sarcasm from her was so totally unexpected that for a moment he did not realize that his armor had been pierced. "God knows I believe it is for her happiness," he said; then, suddenly, his face began to burn, and in an instant he was deeply angry.

"David," she said, "you seem very sure of God; you speak His name very often. Have you really considered Him in your plan?"

He smothered an impatient exclamation; "Mother, that sort of talk means nothing to me; and apparently my reason for my course means nothing to you. I can't make you understand—"

"I don't need you to make me understand," she interrupted him; "and your reason is older than you are; I guess it is as old as human nature: You want to be happy. That is your reason, David; nothing else."

"Well, it satisfies us," he said, coldly; "I wish you wouldn't insist upon discussing it, mother, you are tired, and—"

"Yes, I am tired," she said, with a gasp. "David, if you will promise me not to speak to Elizabeth of this until you and I can talk it over quietly—"

"Elizabeth and I are going away together, to-morrow."

"You shall not do it!" she cried.

His eyes narrowed. "I must remind you," he said, "that I am not a boy. I will do what seems to me right,—right?" he interrupted himself, "why is it you can't see that it is right? Can't you realize that Elizabeth is *mine*? It is amazing to me that you can't see that Nature gives her to me, by a Law that is greater than any human law that was ever made!"

"The animals know that law," she said. He would not hear her: "That unspeakable scoundrel stole her; he stole her just as much as if he had drugged her and kidnapped her. Yes; I take my own!"

His voice rang through the house; Elizabeth, in her room, shivering with excitement, wondering what they were saying, those two—heard the jar of furious sound, and crept, trembling, halfway down-stairs.

"I take my own," he repeated, "and I will make her happy; she belongs in my arms, if, my God! we die the next day!"

"Oh," said Helena Richie, suddenly sobbing, "what *am* I to do? what am I to do?" As she spoke Elizabeth entered. David's start of dismay, his quick protest, "Go back, dear; don't, don't get into this!" was dominated by his mother's cry of relief; she rose from her chair and ran to Elizabeth, holding out entreating hands. "You will not let him be so mad, Elizabeth? You will not let him be so bad?"

"Mother, for Heaven's sake, stop!" David implored her; "this is awful!"

"He is not bad," Elizabeth said, in a low voice, passing those outstretched hands without a look. All her old antagonism to an untempted nature seemed to leap into her face. "I heard you talking, and I came down. I could not let you reproach David."

"Haven't I the right to reproach him?—to save him from dishonoring himself as well as you?"

"You must not use that word!" Elizabeth cried out, trembling all over.
"David is not dishonorable."

"Not dishonorable! Do you say there is nothing dishonorable in taking the wife of another man?"

"Elizabeth," David said, quietly, putting his arm around her, "my mother is very excited. We are not going to talk any more to-night. Do go up-stairs, dear." His one thought was to get her out of the room; it had been dreadful enough to struggle with his mother alone—power and passion and youth, against terror and weakness. But to struggle in Elizabeth's presence would be shocking. Not, he assured himself, that he had the slightest misgiving as to the effect upon her of the arguments to which he had been obliged to listen, but...

"Do leave us, dearest," he said, in a low voice; the misgiving which he denied had driven the color out of his face.

His mother raised her hand with abrupt command: "No, Elizabeth must hear what I have to say." She heard it unmoved; the entreaty not to wound her uncle's love, and hurt Nannie's pride, and betray old Miss White's trust, did not touch her. All she said was, "I am sorry; but I can't help it. David wants me."

Then Helena Richie turned again to her son. "How do you mean to support your mistress, David? Of course the scandal will end your career."

Instantly Elizabeth quivered; the apprehension in her eyes made his words stumble: "There—there are other things than my profession. I am not afraid that I cannot support my *wife*."

But that flicker of alarm in Elizabeth's eyes had caught Helena Richie's attention. "Why, Elizabeth," she said, in an astonished voice. "*You love him!*" Then she added, simply: "Forgive me." Her words were without meaning to the other two, but they brought a burst of hope into her entreaty: "Then you won't ruin him! I know you won't ruin my boy—if you love him."

Elizabeth flinched: "David! I told you—that is what I—"

He caught her hand and pressed it to his mouth. "Darling, she doesn't understand."

"I *do* understand!" his mother said. She paused for a breathless moment, and stood gripping the table, looking with dilating eyes and these two, who, loving each other, were yet preparing to murder Love. "I thank God," she said, and the elation in her face was almost joy; "I thank God, Elizabeth, that I understand the disgrace such wickedness will bring! No honest man will trust him; no decent woman will respect you! And listen, Elizabeth: even *you* will not really trust him; and he will never entirely respect you!"

Elizabeth slowly drew her hand from David's—and instantly he knew that she was frightened. What! Was he to lose her again? He shook with rage. When under that panic storm of words, that menace of distrust and disgrace, Elizabeth, in an agony of uncertainty, hid her face in her hands, David could have killed the robber who was trying to tear her from him. He burst into denunciation of the littleness which could regard their course in any other way than he did himself. He had no pity because his assailant was his mother. He gave no quarter because she was a woman; she was an enemy! an enemy who had stolen in out of the night to rob him of his lately won treasure. "Don't listen to her," he ended, hoarsely; "she doesn't know what she is talking about!"

"But, David, that was what I said. I said it would be bad for you; she says it will ruin you—"

"It is a lie!" he said.

It was nearly three o'clock. They were all at the breaking-point of anger and terror.

"Elizabeth," Helena Richie implored, "if you love him, are you willing to destroy him? You could not bear to have me, his mother, speak of his dishonor; how about letting the world speak of it—if you love him?"

"David," Elizabeth said again, her shaking hands on his arm; "you hear what she says? Perhaps she is right. Oh, I think she is right! What shall I do?"

The entreaty was the entreaty of a child, a frightened, bewildered child. Helena Richie caught her breath; for a single strange moment she forgot her agony of fear for her son; the woman in her was stronger than the mother in her; some obscure impulse ranged her with this girl, as if against a common enemy. "My dear, my dear!" she said, "he shall not have you. I will save you."

But Elizabeth was not listening. "David, if I should injure you" —

"You will ruin him," his mother repeated.

David gave her a deadly look. "You will kill me, Elizabeth, unless you come to me," he said, roughly. "Do you want to rob me again?—You've done it once," he reminded her; love made him brutal.

There was a moment of silence. The eyes of the mother and son crossed like swords. Elizabeth, standing between them, shivered; then slowly she turned to David, and held out her hands, her open palms falling at her sides with a gesture of complete and pitiful surrender. "Very well, David. I won't do it again. I won't hurt you again. I will do whatever you tell me."

David caught her in his arms. His mother trembled with despair; the absolute immovability of these two was awful!

"Elizabeth, he is selfish and wicked! David, have you no manhood? Shame on you!" Contempt seemed her last resource; it did not touch him. "Wait two days," she implored him; "one day, even —"

"I told you we are going to-morrow," he said. He was urging Elizabeth gently from the room, but at his mother's voice she paused.

"Suppose," Helena Richie was saying—"suppose that Blair does not give you a divorce?"

Elizabeth looked into David's eyes silently.

"And," his mother said, "when David gets tired of you—what then?"

"Mother!"

"Men do tire of such women, Elizabeth. What then?"

"I am not afraid of that," the girl said.

The room was very still. The two looking into each other's eyes needed no words; the battling mother had apparently reached the end of effort. Yet it was not the end. As she stood there a slow illumination grew in her face—the knowledge, tragic and triumphant, that if Love would save others, itself it cannot save! ... "I'm not afraid that he will tire of me," Elizabeth had said; and David's mother, looking at him with ineffable compassion, said, very gently:

"I was not afraid of that, once, myself."

That was all. She was standing up, clinging to the table; her face gray, her chin shaking. They neither of them grasped the sense of her words; then suddenly David caught his breath:

"What did you say?"

"I said—" She stopped. "Oh, my poor David, I wouldn't tell you if I could help it; if only there was any other way! But there isn't. I have tried, oh, I have tried every other way." She put her hands over her face for an instant, then looked at him. "David, I said that *I* was not afraid, once, myself, that *my* lover would tire of me." There was absolute silence in the room. "But he did, Elizabeth. He did. He did."

Then David said, "I don't understand."

"Yes, you do; you understand that a man once talked to me just as you

are talking to Elizabeth; he said he would marry me when I got my divorce. I think he meant it—just as you mean it, now. At any rate, I believed him. Just as Elizabeth believes you."

David Richie stepped back violently; his whole face shuddered. "You?" he said, "my mother? No!—no!—no!"

And his mother, gathering up her strength, cringing like some faithful dog struck across the face, pointed at him with one shaking hand.

"Elizabeth, did you see how he looked at me? *Some day your son will look that way at you.*"

Chapter 38

No one spoke. The murmuring crash along the sands was suddenly loud in their ears, but the room was still. It was the stillness of finality; David had lost Elizabeth.

He knew it; but he could not have said why he knew it. Perhaps none of the great decisions of passion can at the moment say "why." Under the lash of some invisible whip, the mind leaps this way or that without waiting for the approval of Reason. Certainly David did not wait for it to know that all was over between him and Elizabeth. He did not reason—he only cringed back, his eyes hidden in his bent arm, and gasped out those words which, scourging his mother, arraigned himself. Nor was there any reason in Elizabeth's cry of "Oh, Mrs. Richie, I love you"; or in her run across the room to drop upon the floor beside David's mother, clasping her and pressing her face against the older woman's shaking knees. "I *do* love you—" Only in Helena Richie's mind could there have been any sort of logic. "This," her ravaged and exalted face seemed to say, "this was why he was given to me." Once he had told her that her goodness had saved him; that night her goodness had not availed. And God had used her sin! Aloud, all that she said was:

"David, don't feel so badly. It isn't as if I were your own mother, you know; you needn't be so un-happy, David." Her eyes yearned over him. "You won't do it?" she said, in a breathless whisper.

To himself he was saying: "It makes no difference! What difference can it possibly make? Not a particle; not a particle." Yet some deeper self must have known that the difference was made, for at that whispered question he seemed to shake his head. But Elizabeth, weeping, said:

"No; we won't—we won't! Dear Mrs. Richie, I love you. David! Speak to her."

He got up with a stupid look, then his eye fell on his mother's face.

"You are worn out," he said in a dazed way, "You'll come up-stairs now?

Elizabeth, make her go up-stairs."

She was worn out; she nodded, with a sort of meek obedience, and put out her hand to Elizabeth. David opened the door for them and followed them up-stairs. Would his mother have this or that? Could he do anything? Nothing, nothing. No, Elizabeth must not stay with her, please; she would rather be alone. As he turned away she called to him, "Elizabeth and I will take the noon train, David."

And he said, "Yes, I will have a carriage here."

The door closed; on one side of it was the mother, exhausted almost to unconsciousness, yet elate, remembering no more the anguish for joy of what had been born out of it. On the other side these two, still ignorant—as the new-born always are—of the future to which that travail had pledged them. They stood together in the narrow upper hall and their pitiful eyes met in silence. Then David took her in his arms and held her for a long moment. Then he kissed her. She whispered, "Good-by, David." But he was speechless. He went with her to her own door, left her without a word, and went down-stairs.

In the clamorous emptiness of the living-room he looked about him; noticed that the table-cover was still crumpled from his mother's hands and smoothed it automatically; then he sat down. He had the sensation, spiritually, that a man might have physically whose face had been violently and repeatedly slapped. The swiftness of the confounding experiences of the last nine hours made him actually dizzy. His thoughts rushed to one thing, then to another. Elizabeth? No, no; he could not think of her yet. His mother? No, he could not think of her, either. It occurred to him that he was cold, and getting up abruptly, he went to the fireplace, and kicked the charred sticks of driftwood together over a graying bed of ashes. Then he heard a chair pushed back overhead and a soft, tired step, and he wondered vaguely if his mother's room was comfortable. Reaching for the bellows, he knelt down and blew the reluctant embers into a faint glow; when a hesitant flicker of flame caught the half-burned logs he got on his feet and stood, his fingers on the mantelpiece, his forehead on the back of his hand, watching the fire catch and crackle into cheerful warmth. He stood there for a long time. Suddenly his cheek grew rigid: some man, some *beast*, had—my God! wronged Materna! It was the first really clear thought; instantly some other thought must have sprung up to meet it, for he said, under his breath, "No, because I didn't mean ... it is different with us; quite different!" The thought, whatever it was, must have persisted, for it stung him into restless movement. He began to walk about; once or twice he stumbled over a footstool, that his eyes, looking blindly at the floor, apparently did not see. Once he stood stock-still, the blood surging in his ears, his face darkly red. But his mind was ruthlessly clear. He was remembering; he was putting two and two together. She was a widow; he knew that. Her marriage had been unhappy; he knew that. There had been a man—he dimly remembered a man. He had not thought of him for twenty years! ... "Damn him," David said, and the tears stood in his eyes. Then again that thought must have come to him, for he said to himself, violently, "But I *love* Elizabeth, it is different with me!" Perhaps that persistent inner voice said, "In what way?" for he said again, "Entirely different! It is the only way to make him divorce her so we can be married." Again he stood still and stared blindly at the floor. That a man could live who would be base enough to take advantage of—*Materna!* Between rage and pity, and confusion he almost forgot Elizabeth, until suddenly the whirl of his thoughts was pierced by the poignant realization that his outcry of dismay at his mother's confession had practically told Elizabeth that he was willing to let her do what he found unthinkable in his mother. His whole body winced with mortification. It was the first prick of the sword of shame—that sword of the Lord! Even while he reddened to his forehead the sword-thrust came again in a flash of memory. It was only a single sentence; neither argument nor entreaty nor remonstrance; merely the statement of a fact: "*you did not love her enough to accept her money.*" At the time those ironical words were spoken they had scarcely any meaning to him, and what meaning they had was instantly extinguished by anger. Now abruptly they reverberated in his ears. He forgot his mother; he forgot the "beast," who was, after all, only the same kind of a beast that he was himself. "You, who could not accept a girl's money could take her good name; could urge her to a course which in your mother overwhelms you with horror; could ask her to give you that which ranks a man who accepted it from your mother as a 'beast.'" David had never felt shame before; he had known mortification, and regret, too, to a greater or less degree; and certainly he had known remorse; he had experienced the futile rage of a man who realizes that he has made a fool of himself; these things he had known, as every man nearly thirty years old must know them. Especially and cruelly he had known them when he understood the effect of the reasoning egotism of his letter upon Elizabeth. But the beneficent agony of shame he had never known until this moment.

In the next hour or two, while the flame of the lamp still burning on the table, whitened in the desolating morning light that crept into the room, David Richie did not reason things out consecutively. His thoughts came without apparent sequence;

sometimes he wondered, dully, if it were still raining; wondered how he would get a carriage in the morning; wondered if Elizabeth was asleep; wondered if she would go back to Blair Maitland? "No, no, no!" he said aloud; "not that; that can't be." Yet through all this disjointed thought his eyes, cleared by shame, saw Reason coming slowly up to explain and confirm his conviction that, whatever Elizabeth did or did not do, for the present he had lost her. And Reason, showing him his likeness to that other "beast," showing him his arrogance to his mother, his cruelty to his poor girl, his poor, pitiful Elizabeth! showed him something else: his assertions of his intrinsic right to Elizabeth—how much of their force was due to love for her, how much to hatred of Blair? David's habit of corroborating his emotions by a mental process had more than once shackled him and kept him from those divine impetuosities that add to the danger and the richness of life; but this time the logical habit led him inexorably into deeper depths of humiliation. It was dawn when he saw that he had hated Blair more than he had loved Elizabeth. This was the most intolerable revelation of all; he had actually been about to use Love to express Hate!

Up-stairs Elizabeth had had her own vision; it was not like David's. There was no sense of shame. There was only Love! Love, pitiful, heart-breaking, remorseful. When David left her she sank down on the edge of her bed and cried—not for disappointment or dread or perplexity, not for herself, not for David, but for Helena Richie. Once she crept across the hall and listened at the closed door. Silence. Then she pushed it open and listened again. Oh, to go to her, to put her arms about her, to say, "I will be good, I will do whatever you say, I love you." But all was still except for soft, scarcely heard, tranquil breathing. For David's mother slept.

When Elizabeth came down the next morning it was to the crackle of flames and the smell of coffee and the sight of David scorching his face over toasting bread. It was so unheroic that it was almost heroic, for it meant that they could keep on the surface of life. David said, simply, "Did you get any sleep, Elizabeth?" and she said: "Well, not much. Here, let me make the toast; you get something for your mother." But when she carried a little tray of food up to Mrs. Richie, and kneeling by the bedside took the soft mother-hand in hers, she went below the surface.

"I am going back to him," she said; and put Mrs. Richie's hand against her lips.

David's mother gave her a long look, but she had nothing to say.

Later, as they came down-stairs together, Elizabeth, still holding that gentle hand in hers, felt it tremble when Helena Richie met her son. Perhaps his trembled, too. Yet his tenderness and consideration for her, as he told her how he had arranged for her journey to town was almost ceremonious; it seemed as if he dared not come too near her. It was not until he was helping her into the carriage that he made any reference to the night before:

"I have given her up," he said, almost in a whisper, "but she can't go back to him, you know—that can't be! Mother, that can't be?"

But she was silent. Then Elizabeth came up behind him and got into the carriage; there were no good-bys between them.

"I shall come to town to-morrow on the noon train," he told his mother; and she looked at him as one looks at another human creature who turns his face toward the wilderness. There was nothing more that she could do for him; he must hunger and know how he might be fed; he must hear the lying whisper that if he broke the Law, angelic hands would prevent the law from breaking him; he must see the Kingdom he desired, the glory of it, and its easy price. He must save himself.

Elizabeth, groping for Mrs. Richie's hand, held it tightly in hers, and the old carriage began its slow tug along the road that wound in and out among the dunes....

The story of David and Elizabeth and Blair pauses here.

Or perhaps one might say it begins here. A decision such as was reached in the little house by the sea is not only an end, it is also a beginning. In their bleak certainty that they were parted, David and Elizabeth had none of that relief of the dismissal of effort, which marks the end of an experience. Effort was all before them; for the decision not to change conditions did not at the moment change character; and it never changed temperaments. Elizabeth was as far from self-control on the morning after that decision as she had been in the evening that preceded it. There had to be many evenings of rebellion, many mornings of taking up her burden; the story of them begins when she knew, without reasoning about it, that the hope of escape from them had ceased.

Because of those gray hours of dawn and shame and self-knowledge, love did not end in David, nor did he cease to be rational and inarticulate; there had to be weeks of silent, vehement refusal to accept the situation: something must be done! Elizabeth must get a divorce "somehow"! It would take time, a long time, perhaps; but she must get it, and then they would marry. There had to be weeks of argument: "why should I sacrifice my happiness to 'preserve the ideal of the permanence of marriage'?" There had to be weeks of imprisonment in himself before a night came when his mother woke to find him at her bedside: "Mother—mother—mother," he said. What else he said, how in his agonizing dumbness he was able to tell her that she was the mother, not, indeed, of his body, but of his soul —was only for her ears; what his face, hidden in her pillow, confessed, the quiet darkness held inviolate. This silent man's experiences of shame and courage, began that night when, in the firelit room, besieged by darkness and the storm, that other experience ended.

Blair's opportunity—the divine opportunity of sacrifice, had its beginning in that same desolate End. But there had to be angry days of refusing to recognize any opportunity—life had not trained him to such courageous recognition! There had to be days when the magnanimity of his prisoner in returning to her prison was unendurable to him. There had to be months, before, goaded by his god, he urged his hesitating manhood to abide by the decision of chance whether or not he should offer her her freedom. There even had to be days of deciding just what the chance should be!

There had to be for these three people, caught in the mesh of circumstance, time for growth and for hope, and that is why their story pauses just when the angel has troubled the water. All the impulses and the resolutions that had their beginnings in that End, are like circles on that troubled water, spreading, spreading, spreading, until they touch Eternity. At first the circles were not seen; only the turmoil in the pool when the angel touched it. And how dark the water was with the sediment of doubt and fear and loss in the days that followed that decision which was the beginning of all the circles!

Robert Ferguson and David's mother used to wonder how they could any of them get through the next few months. "But good is going to come out of it somehow," Helena Richie said once. "Oh, you mean 'character' and all that sort of thing," he said, sighing. "I tell you what it is, I'm a lot more concerned about my child's happiness than her 'character.' Elizabeth is good enough for me as she is."

David's mother had no rebuke for him; she looked at him with pitying eyes; he was so very unhappy in his child's unhappiness! She herself was doing all she could for the "child"; she was in Mercer most of that winter. "No, I won't hire the house," she told the persistent landlord; "I can't afford it; I'm only here for a few days at a time. No, you *sha'n't* lower the rent! Robert, Robert, what shall I do to keep you from being so foolish? I wouldn't live there if you gave me the house! I want to stay at the hotel and be near Elizabeth."

In her frequent visits in those next few months she grew very near to Elizabeth; it was a wonderfully tender relation, full of humility on both sides.

"I never knew how good you were, Mrs. Richie," Elizabeth said.

"I never really understood you, dear child," Helena Richie confessed. She drew near Blair, too; she knew how he had borne the story Elizabeth told him when she came back to Mercer; she knew the recoil of anger and jealousy, then the reaction of cringing acceptance of the fact; she knew his passionate efforts, as the winter passed, to buy his way into his wife's friendship by doing everything he fancied might please her. She knew why he asked Mr. Ferguson to find a place for him in the Works, and why he induced Nannie to take the money he believed to be his, and build a hospital. "He is going to use the old house for it," Mrs. Richie told Mr. Ferguson; "well! it's one way of getting Nannie out of it, though I'm afraid he'll have to turn the workmen in and rebuild over her head before he can move her."

"It's the bait in the trap," Robert Ferguson said, contemptuously.

"Well, suppose it is? Can you blame him for trying to win her?"

"He'll never succeed. If he was half-way honest he would have offered to let her go in the first place. If he expects any story-book business of 'duty creating love' he'll come out the small end of the horn."

"I suppose he hopes," she admitted. But she sighed. She knew those hopes would never be realized, and she felt the pain of that poor, selfish, passionate heart until her own ached. Yes, of course he ought to 'offer to let her go.' She knew that as well as Elizabeth's uncle himself. "And he will," she said to herself. Then her face was softly illuminated by the lambent flame of some inner serenity: "But she won't go!"

Those were the days when Blair would not recognize his opportunity. It was not because it was not pointed out to him.

"I'm certain that a divorce could be fixed up some way," Robert Ferguson said once, "and I hinted as much to him. I told him she couldn't endure the sight of him."

"Do you call that a hint?"

"Well, he didn't take it, anyway. Of course, if nothing moves him, I suppose I can shoot him?"

She smiled. "You won't have to shoot him. He is very unhappy. Wait."

"For a change of heart? It will never come! No, the marriage was a travesty from the beginning, and I ought to have pulled her out of it. I did suggest it to her, but she said she was going to stick it out like a man."

Blair was indeed unhappy. His god was tormenting him by contrasting Elizabeth's generosity with his selfishness. It was then that he saw, terror-stricken, his opportunity. He tried not to see it. He denied it, he struggled against it; yet all the while he was drawn by an agonized curiosity to consider it. Finally, with averted eyes, he held out shrinking hands to chance, to see if opportunity would fall into them. This was some six months after she had come back to him; six months on her part of clinging to Mrs. Richie's strength; of wondering if David, working hard in Philadelphia, was beginning to be happier; of wondering if Blair was really any happier for her weariness of soul. Six months on Blair's part, of futile moments of hope because Elizabeth seemed a little kinder;—"perhaps she's beginning to care!" he would say to himself; six months of agonizing jealousy when he knew she did not care; of persistent, useless endeavors to touch her heart; of endless small, pathetic sacrifices; of endless small, pathetic angers and repentances. "Blair," she used to say, with wonderful patience, after one of these glimmerings of hope had arisen in him because of some careless amiability on her part, "I am sorry to be unkind; I wish you would get over caring about me, but all I can do *ever* is just to be friends. No, I don't hate you. Why should I hate you? You didn't wrong me any more than I wronged you. We are just the same; two bad people. But I'm trying to be good, truly I am; and—and I'm sorry for you, Blair, dear. That's all I can say."

It was after one of those miserable discussions between the husband and wife that Blair had gone out of the hotel with violent words of despair. He never knew just where he spent that day— certainly not in the office at the Works; but wherever it was, it brought him face to face with his opportunity. Should he accept it? Should he refuse it? He said to himself that he could not decide. Perhaps he was right; he had shirked decisions all his life; perhaps so great a decision was impossible for him. At any rate, he thought it was. Something must decide for him. What should it be? All that afternoon he tried to make a small decision which should settle the great decision. Of course, he might pitch up a penny? no, the swiftness of such judgment seemed beyond endurance; he might say: "if it rains before noon, I'll let her go;" then he could watch the skies, and meet the decision gradually; no; it rained so often in March! If when he got back to the hotel he found her wearing this piece of jewelry or that; if the grimy pigeon, teetering up and down on the granite coping across the street, flew away before he reached the next crossing... . On and on his mind went, jibing away, terrified, from each suggestion; then returning to it again. It was dusk when he came back to the hotel. David's mother was sitting with Elizabeth, and they were talking, idly, of Nannie's new house, or Cherry-pie's bad cold, or anything but the one thing that was always on their minds, when, abruptly, Blair entered. He flung open the door with a bang,— then stood stock-still on the threshold. He was very pale, but the room was so shadowy that his pallor was not noticed.

"Why are you sitting here in the dark!" he cried out, violently. "Why don't you light the gas? Good God!" he said, almost with a sob. Elizabeth looked at him in astonishment; before she could reply that she and Mrs. Richie liked the dusk and the firelight, he saw that she was not alone, and burst into a loud laugh: "Mrs. Richie here? How appropriate!" He came forward into the circle of flickering light, but he seemed to walk unsteadily and his face was ghastly. Helena Richie gave him a startled look. Blair's gentleness had never failed David's mother before; she thought, with consternation, that he had been drinking. Perhaps her gravity checked his reckless mood, for he said more gently: "I beg your pardon; I didn't see you, Mrs. Richie. I was startled because everything was dark. Outer darkness! Please don't go,—it's so appropriate for you to be here!" he ended. Again his voice was sardonic. Mrs. Richie said, coldly, that she had been just about to return to her own room. As she left them, she said to herself, anxiously, that she was afraid there was something the matter. She would have been sure of it had she stayed in the twilight with the husband and wife.

"I'll light the gas," Elizabeth said, rising. But he caught her wrist. "No! No! there's no use lighting up now." As he spoke he pulled her down on his knee. "Elizabeth, is there no hope?" he said; "none? *none?*" She was silent. He leaned his forehead on her shoulder for a moment, and she heard that dreadful sound—a man's weeping. Then suddenly, roughly, he flung his arms about her, and kissed her violently—her lips, her eyes, her neck; the next moment he pushed her from his knee. "Why, why did you sit here in the dark to-night? I never knew you to sit in the dark!" He got on his feet, leaving her, standing amazed and offended, her hair ruffled, the lace about her throat in disorder; at the window, his back turned to her, he flung over his shoulder: "Look here—you can go. I won't hold you any longer. I suppose your uncle can fix it up; some damned legal quibble will get you out of it. I—I'll do my part."

Before she could ask him what he meant he went out. He had accepted his opportunity!

But it was not until the next day that she really understood.

"He says," Mrs. Richie told Robert Ferguson, "that he will take Nannie and go abroad definitely; she can call it desertion. Yes; on Nannie's money of course; how else could he go? Oh, my poor Blair!"

"'Poor Blair'? He deserves all he gets," Elizabeth's uncle said, after his first astonishment. Then, in spite of himself, he was sorry for Blair. "I suppose he's hard hit," he said, grudgingly, "but as for 'poor Blair,' I don't believe it goes very deep with him. You say he was out of temper because she had not lighted up, and told her she could go? Rather a casual way of getting rid of a wife."

"Robert, how can you be so unjust?" she reproached him. "Oh, perhaps he will be a man yet! How proud his mother would be."

"My dear Helena, one swallow doesn't make a summer." Then, a little ashamed of his harshness, he added, "No, he'll never be very much of a person; but he's his mother's son, so he can't be all bad; he'll just wander round Europe, with Nannie tagging on behind, enjoying himself more or less harmlessly."

"Robert," she said, softly, "I'm not sure that Elizabeth will accept his sacrifice."

"What! Not accept it? Nonsense! Of course she'll accept it. I should have doubts of her sanity if she didn't. If Blair had been half as much of a man as his mother, he'd have made the 'sacrifice,' as you call it, long ago. Helena, you're too extreme. Duty is well enough, but don't run it into the ground."

Mrs. Richie was silent.

"Helena, you *know* she ought to leave him!"

"If every woman left unpleasant conditions—mind, he isn't unkind or wicked; what would become of us, Robert?"

Elizabeth's uncle would not pursue her logic; his face suddenly softened: "Well, David will come to his own at last! I wonder how soon after the thing is fixed up (*if* it can be fixed up) they can marry?"

The color rose sharply in her face.

"You think they won't?" he exclaimed.

"I hope not. Oh, I hope not!"

"Why not?" he said, affronted.

"Because I don't want them, just for their own happiness, to do what seems to me wrong."

"Wrong! If the law permits it, you can't say 'wrong.'"

"*I* think it is," she said timidly; then tried to explain that it seemed to her that no one, for his own happiness, had a right to do a thing which would injure an ideal by which the rest of us live; "I don't express it very well," she said, flushing.

Robert Ferguson snorted. "That's high talk; well enough for angels; but no men and mighty few women are angels. I," he interrupted himself hurriedly, "I don't like angel women myself."

She smiled a little sadly. "And besides that," she said, "it seems to me we ought to take the consequences of our sins. I think they ought, all three of them, to just try and make the best of things. Robert, did it ever strike you that making the best of things was one way of entering the Kingdom of Heaven?"

He gave her a tender look, but he shook his head. "Helena," he said, gently, "do you mind telling me how you finally brought them to their senses that night? Don't if you'd rather not."

Her face quivered. "I would rather. There was only one way; I ... told them, Robert."

There was a moment of silence, then Robert Ferguson twitched his glasses off and began to polish them. "You are an angel, after all," he said. Then he lifted a ribbon falling from her waist, and kissed it.

"I sha'n't try to influence either David or Elizabeth," she said; "they will do what they think right; it may not be *my* right—"

"It won't be," he told her, dryly; "once a man is free to marry his girl, mothers take a back seat."

She smiled wisely.

"Oh, you can smile; but, my dear Helena, the apron-string won't do for a man who is thirty years old. Yes, they'll do as they choose, in spite of either you or me—and *I* know what it will be!"

"Poor Blair," she said, sighing. "Robert, if she leaves him you will be kind to him, won't you? He's never had a chance—"

But he was not thinking of Blair; he was looking into her face, and his own face moved with emotion: "Helena, don't be obstinate any longer. We have so little time left! I don't ask you to love me, but just marry me, Helena."

"Oh, my dear Robert—"

"Will you?"

"If I lived here," she said breathlessly, "my boy could not come to see me."

"Is that the reason you won't say yes?"

She was silent.

"Will you?" he said again.

Her voice was so low he could hardly hear her answer: "No."

And at that his face glowed with sudden, amazed assurance. "Why," he cried, "*you love me!*"

She looked at him beseechingly. "Robert, please—"

"Life has been good to me, after all," he said, joyously: "I've got what I don't deserve!"

Helena was silent.

Lightning Source UK Ltd.
Milton Keynes UK
UKHW021955270519
343419UK00005B/190/P